PRAISE FOR
MARY-ROSE MACCO

In Falling Snow

"An epic tale of love, heartache, and a sisterhood created by nursing in a time of war, *In Falling Snow* is one of those novels you will want to read again. If you liked *The Aviator's Wife*, you will love this book!"
—Michelle Moran, bestselling author of *Cleopatra's Daughter*

"This is a story of love, ultimately, and a woman whose life has sought to atone for a mistake she hardly knew she made. Caught between the past and her impending mortality, Iris relives her life as a nurse in World War I, when she was too young to understand what her choices would mean not only for her, but for the family she cobbled together out of the rubble. At once perceptive and sympathetic, *In Falling Snow* beguiles, a tale of selflessness and youthful indiscretion as singular and seductive as one could hope for."
—Robin Oliveira, *New York Times*
bestselling author of *My Name Is Mary Sutter*

"Well-crafted . . . easily slipping through time."
—*Publishers Weekly*

"This satisfying saga from an award-winning Australian author takes the reader across continents and time. . . . Women as healers, family secrets, medical mysteries, historical setting—call the producers of Call the Midwife."   —*Booklist*

"*In Falling Snow* is expertly researched and written with a keen eye to the complexities of wartime and the mighty role of women therein. From past to present, Australia to France, MacColl guides readers through unknown lands abroad and territories of the heart. For readers, like me, who love to see history's forgotten heroes given powerful voice, you will delight in this novel."
—Sarah McCoy, author of
the international bestseller *The Baker's Daughter*

PENGUIN BOOKS

SWIMMING HOME

Mary-Rose MacColl's first novel, *No Safe Place*, was a runner-up for the *Australian*/Vogel Literary Award, and her first non-fiction book, *The Birth Wars*, was a finalist in the 2009 Walkley Awards for journalism. Her novel *In Falling Snow* was an international bestseller. She lives is Brisbane, Australia, with her husband and son, and is an ordinary swimmer.

MARY-ROSE MacCOLL

SWIMMING HOME

A Novel

PENGUIN BOOKS

PENGUIN BOOKS

An imprint of Penguin Random House LLC
375 Hudson Street
New York, New York 10014
penguin.com

First published in Australia by Allen & Unwin, 2015
Published in Penguin Books 2017

LIBRARY OF CONGRESS CATALOGING-IN-PUBLICATION DATA

Names: MacColl, Mary-Rose, 1961– author.
Title: Swimming home : a novel / Mary-Rose MacColl.
Description: First edition. | New York : Penguin Books, 2017.
Identifiers: LCCN 2016047796 | ISBN 9780143129967 (softcover)
Subjects: LCSH: Women swimmers—Fiction. |
Teenage girls—Fiction. | Sports stories. | BISAC: FICTION / Historical. |
FICTION / Literary. | FICTION /Sports.
Classification: LCC PR9619.3.M23 S95 2017 | DDC 823/.914—dc23
LC record available at https://lccn.loc.gov/2016047796

Printed in the United States of America
1 3 5 7 9 10 8 6 4 2

Set in Bembo Std
Designed by Katy Riegel

For Andrée MacColl

SWIMMING HOME

NEW YORK DAILY NEWS

August 19, 1925

FAIRER SEX FAILS FATHOMS

AMERICAN SWIMMER Miss Gertrude Ederle has been taken unconscious from the icy waters of the English Channel, which have proven more than a match for even the strongest female swimmers of the world.

Miss Ederle, eighteen, of Amsterdam Avenue, New York, has been training for the Channel swim since her triumphant return from the Olympic Games of Paris 1924. She set out from France in the early hours of Wednesday and battled rain, fog, shifting tides and freezing temperatures. She was pulled from the water after nine hours by her coach, experienced distance swimmer Mr. Jabez Wolffe, just over halfway across from France to the English shore.

Miss Ederle swims with the Women's Swimming Association in New York, which produced the swimmers that saw America triumphant in the Olympics, winning more Olympic medals in the water than any other nation, with most won by the women swimmers.

But English swim coach Sir Michael Brossley said he'd seen no evidence in swimmers like Miss Ederle or British swimmer Mercedes Gleitze, also a Channel contender, of the kind of stamina required.

"If women think they can swim the English Channel, then let's find one who can actually do it," Sir Michael said. "I think you'll find that these two are the strongest of them and they are not up to the task, nor ever will be."

Thursday Island, Australia, June 1924

The sand was so hot it burned the soles of her feet. Catherine moved to her toes to relieve the tender middle parts of her feet, back to her heels to relieve her toes, jumped from one foot to the other, watched the sunlight on the sea until it hurt her eyes, sucked hard on her bottom lip. The heat came up toward her, making the water shimmer and wobble to her eyes. She breathed it in.

When finally Michael yelled, "Go!," she wasn't ready.

Oh, but the relief of it when her feet first hit the water. They stung with cold and it was delicious.

Michael was in front of her at first, but she was those inches taller, and she caught him up when the water got to thigh height and tackled him. They both went under. She came up to swim but he'd wormed out of her grasp and had disappeared. When he came up, he was ahead again. Bid, she muttered to herself, his Islander name. It meant dolphin.

They swam out to the reef, the farthest reef from the shore, where they'd first seen the turtles, two of them.

They dived down to the rocks together. "The big one, he'd be a hundred I reckon," Catherine said when they came back up.

"At least," Michael said. "Big fella."

"They don't harm anything," she said.

"I should tell the Walton boys," he said, grinning.

The Walton boys liked killing things. "Don't you dare," she said. "Did you notice the other one is back today, the smaller one? Did you see?"

He nodded and then whipped his bangs back off his face, the water flicking off his black curls. "You think that's his woman?" His skin shone dark, his blue eyes on fire.

"Do turtles have women?"

"They're our turtles, Waapi." Her name on the island, Waapi, for fish.

"I think it could be worse than to be a turtle, don't you?"

"Except when the fishermen are coming."

"Yes, except for that. But they look . . ."

"What?"

"Like we're meant to look. Come on, I'll race you to the shore." She dived under and started swimming.

PART I

London, August 1925

1

Louisa Quick emerged into a morning as joyous as London offered. Princes Square was wearing summer finally, this late in August, almost as if the strange wintery weather of these last few weeks had never happened. The still-wet pavement glistened in the sunlight. There were birds—Louisa had no idea where they'd been until today. Her life seemed unimportant suddenly—the waiting room full of patients, the mountain of paperwork in the office, the grumbling nursing staff—all of it gone. Louisa might skip, she thought, or dance a jig, in weather like this. Well, someone else might skip or dance a jig. Normally, Louisa wouldn't even be outside at this time of morning. She'd be inside, working. Where I would be still, she thought, if it weren't for Helen Anderson.

Louisa had been in the treatment area off the waiting room with a patient when the front desk nurse parted the curtains and told her she was wanted on the telephone.

"Can I call them back?" Louisa had said. The nurse shook her head.

"They said it was urgent, Doctor."

"From the surgery or here?" Louisa had said.

The nurse didn't know.

It was terrible to admit, but Louisa would hurry more for a patient from her surgery in Harley Street. It was a simple equation. The Harley Street patients paid, and expected more. Louisa needed their money for her work here at the clinic. She left her patient with the nurse to finish up and went to take the call.

The caller was Helen Anderson, a patient who'd come to the surgery two years before. Louisa couldn't remember what had been the matter with her, only that she was one of those patients who knew more than her doctor and wouldn't do as she was told. Louisa had seen her again just before Catherine started at the Henley School in the spring but Helen, the school's principal, didn't acknowledge their history. Sometimes patients didn't want to see their doctors in other settings, and who could blame them?

When Louisa asked on the telephone now if she was all right, Helen sounded exasperated. "Of course," she spluttered. "But you must come quickly. Write down the address." Louisa scribbled down an address as ordered. She was about to ask if anything had happened to Catherine when Helen Anderson hung up.

What the devil could be wrong? Louisa had thought. It had been a tumor, Louisa recalled, abdominal, large. Perhaps it had regrown.

Louisa hurried through the lane to the Ratcliffe Highway

and put her hand out to signal a passing taxicab. As the driver pulled over, she realized she'd forgotten her hat and coat; she must look a fright, her dark brown hair, the armory of pins it took to secure it—she really needed a cut—adding to the view she was fairly confident others experienced of her, a woman of difficult-to-determine age a little addled by life. Forty-one, she'd tell anyone who asked. I'm really only forty-one, although everyone thinks I'm a hundred. And I'm not addled, just busy. At least she'd taken off the stained pinafore she'd been wearing—she'd had to dress a nasty head wound earlier and the apron was still covered in blood.

"Why you going down there, ma'am?" the driver said, tapping the piece of paper she'd handed him.

"I'm a doctor," she said.

The driver turned around and looked at her with raised eyebrows but said no more.

Louisa rarely took taxicabs, mostly walked where she needed to go, but she didn't have time today. What the devil was the problem with Helen Anderson? she wondered.

Brusque, that was how Louisa's colleague and friend Ruth Luxton had described Louisa. "Sometimes, Louisa, you can be brusque." Ruth said Louisa needed a holiday.

She and Ruth were both working too hard, truth be told, keeping the clinic running with the money they earned from their Harley Street practices. Louisa had upset one of the nurses, Ruth said. The girl had handed Louisa a swab when she'd asked for something else. She wasn't brusque, she was busy, she told Ruth. Still, Louisa went and apologized to the girl. She wished they were a bit tougher, these nurses. And, yes, she wished she hadn't been brusque.

Princes Square still had the stateliness of the grand London dock years, but it was a tired stateliness now more than anything, visited regularly by the reek of burned sugar from the refineries combined with the rich smell of ale from the inn that now graced the opposite corner of the square. The clinic, which both Ruth and Louisa insisted was run on Nightingale principles, was spotless inside, or as spotless as the nurses and orderlies could make it, but it was, Louisa knew, in need of maintenance. And now, the health inspector of greater London was planning a visit, they'd just been informed. Louisa had read through the list of facilities all medical institutions were supposed to provide. Princes Square had hardly any of them. Of course, if they weren't there, the poor of London's east would have nothing in terms of health care. But that seemed to matter little to the new inspectorate.

The driver turned into John Street. "Ratcliffe will be faster," Louisa said, looking at her pocket watch. The line of patients had been out the clinic's front door when she left. It would be all the way down Princes Street by the time she returned, with no other doctor expected in before noon.

"No, ma'am," the driver said evenly. "They're digging the sewers, so it's closed further along today."

"Very well," she said.

The driver stopped in Narrow Street near the Ratcliffe stairs, in front of a group of tired brick buildings. Louisa could see the masts of ships at anchor on the wharf to her left. The driver turned to look at her when he handed her the change. "You want me to wait?" he said. He smiled, a gap between two of his teeth, an incisor gone; he'd miss it when he bit into an apple, she thought.

"Of course not," Louisa said.

He sighed and shook his head, then drove off.

She looked around. Most of the buildings had broken windows and looked as if no one lived in them. It was a forsaken place, she thought, such a contrast with the pleasantness of the day, the only relief a group of boys playing soccer in one of the lanes, using what looked like an unraveling cabbage for a ball, a roughly painted line on the end wall to mark one goal, a couple of dustbins to mark the other. They were dwarfed by the buildings on either side of the lane, which were in worse shape than those on the street, windows boarded over or stuffed with newspaper, laundry hanging off ledges. But the boys' faces, Louisa saw as she looked over, carried the hope of children the world over, their calls ringing out like an antidote to despair.

"Score!"

"Nah, you was offside."

"Was not."

"Was too."

"Are you lads playing hooky?" Louisa called to them.

They scattered quickly then, disappearing like rats into the maze of passageways that ran off every street. Louisa hadn't meant to frighten them. Perhaps they thought she'd come to cart them off to school or, worse, give them a needle.

In among the houses and inns were the large warehouses of the docks. It was to one of these that Helen Anderson had directed Louisa. She stood in front of the dark wooden door, which looked bolted fast, and checked the piece of paper where she'd written the address. She was in the right place, although she couldn't imagine Helen Anderson anywhere here.

Louisa heard cheering down on the bank below. She turned to see that a crowd had gathered there, perhaps a dozen or more. She looked out toward the river where someone was pointing. Halfway across was a swimmer, solid, strong, determined, an Oxford or Cambridge freshman no doubt, conquering the Thames on a dare. That must be what they were cheering about. How could you swim in that? Louisa thought. She didn't swim at all, but the thought of the filthy river made her sick.

As she watched, the sun shone on the water and it made the swimmer golden. Louisa was mesmerized by the slow, sure stroke. There were two large sailing boats beside the wharf and a steamer coming up the river, half a dozen barges and ferries.

What mad boys they were, she thought, a strange feeling building in the pit of her stomach, a nervousness she couldn't account for. Intuition, Ruth Luxton would say. Never underestimate your intuition. Something was very wrong. The taxi driver had gone. She was alone here. Where was Helen Anderson?

Just then she saw Helen herself, puffing as she climbed the bank. "Well, what do you think?" Helen Anderson said. She was flushed, breathless.

"I'm sorry?"

"I'm sorry too, Dr. Quick. We've tried to be patient, but this has gone too far." She had her hands on her hips now, trying to get more air into her lungs.

"What are you talking about?" Louisa said, beginning to wonder if Helen Anderson was in her right mind.

"That." Helen pointed toward the river, the sun disappearing behind a cloud just at that moment. And then the truth fluttered into Louisa's brain, where it landed lightly and began to work its way into her consciousness. The lone swimmer, turning over now to switch to a perfectly executed back crawl, wasn't Oxford or Cambridge, wasn't a man.

It was a woman, a girl. It was Catherine.

Of course it was Catherine.

2

atherine had jumped in feetfirst from the steps. The water was deeper than it looked. Her head went right under and she felt as if her whole body had been dunked in a bowl of ice and held there. When she reached the bottom, it was soft and squelchy, nothing like the sandy sea floor at home. She sank down into mud.

No turning back now, she'd thought to herself as she pushed up.

She began to swim, one arm up and over, the other up and over, kicking with her legs, trying to generate heat. Her head felt as if it would burst from the cold. She was aware of the outline of her skull, her jaw. Her lips wouldn't move properly. They were too cold to blow bubbles. They were too cold for the laughter that wanted to come, inexplicably. Was it water that made her want to laugh? Was it being back in water, even water so different from home? She couldn't see her hand in front of her. On the island you'd never go into such brackish water, where a log might be a crocodile. No crocs here, though, no life in the water at all as far as she could tell.

Soon she was in the rhythm of the swim, a rhythm she knew so well it was like waking in the morning. It was still cold, but after some minutes the movement of the swim was creating enough warmth to sustain her. Keep swimming. It was her father's voice she heard. Even now, it soothed her. She loved the story, the story of how he'd saved her. Keep swimming, bonny Cate, he'd sung that night, and she had kept swimming, or at least she'd held on to him, and by morning, when they reached land, Catherine could swim. That's how her father always told the story. She doubted it now, having watched other children learn. Swimming didn't come naturally, not even to the Islanders, and Catherine had only been three years old.

Her father's story of that night sounded made up, along with everything he'd told her about her mother. "What was she like?" Catherine had asked. She had no recollection of her, this mother who was the subject of the story—the sailing boat, the storm, her father saving Catherine, losing Julia.

"She shone," Catherine's father had said.

"Am I like her?"

Her father couldn't speak for a moment. "Perhaps you are," he said then. "Perhaps you are, Cate."

Her father was the only one who called her Cate. She didn't know what her mother had called her. Mothers on the island who knew the story often said how sad it was, not to Catherine but to one another when they thought she wasn't listening. If they ever said anything to Catherine, she told them matter-of-factly that you couldn't miss what you'd never had. "And anyway, I have Florence," she'd say. "And Florence is worth ten mothers." They'd look at her more sadly then, as if there were some aspect of their pity she was failing to understand.

But sometimes when they talked about her mother, the accident, how awful, Julia so young, such promise, she'd wonder what it might have been like if her mother hadn't died, what it might have been like if her mother was alive.

Catherine had only ever seen one photograph of her mother, deep in the bottom drawer of her father's dresser. She'd found her father sitting on the little stool by the bed one day. When he'd looked up, she saw there were tears running down his cheeks, which shocked her. She'd never seen her father cry before. He'd wiped the tears away quickly with one hand, while keeping his other hand, the hand that held the photograph, down by his side. Catherine pretended she didn't notice, but watched from the corner of her eye as he put the photograph in a drawer. Next time he was out at the hospital, she went back to the drawer and found it.

At first it gave her a fright. Here was a person, a person who had lived. Not the Julia of her imagination but Julia herself, or her likeness at least. This Julia was sitting on the end of a sofa Catherine had never seen in a room Catherine didn't recognize. She had an impression it was somewhere in America, where her mother and father had met, but she couldn't have said why she thought that. Julia was wearing an emerald-green dress and, high on her head, above her dark red-brown hair, a large bronze-colored hat with soft feathers hanging off the sides.

Catherine touched the photograph, touched that face, left her fingerprint on it. She couldn't see herself in this woman the way she saw herself in her father—his laugh, his feet, his way of tilting his head when he was thinking. Still, it felt as if the woman in the photograph laid some claim on her. She ran her finger over the image again, wishing, although she wouldn't have been able to say what it was she was wishing for.

She'd asked Florence about her mother, not mentioning that she'd seen the photograph. "Oh, she was a beautiful girl, your mother, a beautiful girl." Florence shook her head slowly, ran her long fingers down Catherine's cheeks, holding on to her chin for a moment, her own fingers soft and warm on Catherine's skin. "That red hair and those green eyes. But being beautiful can be a curse."

"She was cursed?" Catherine said.

Florence's eyes widened then, as if she'd caught a fright. She paused before she answered. "Being beautiful didn't make her happy. She wasn't happy like you. You're just a bucket of happiness to the brim. It's children who make women happy."

That didn't make sense. "So what about my mother? Why wasn't my mother happy then?" Catherine asked.

"Because children make us sad too." Florence tilted her head.

"Why?"

"All mothers are sad, because mothering is a giving away, always a giving away."

A bucket of happiness, Florence called Catherine. Catherine didn't feel that way now in the cold water of the Thames; more like a bucket of cold. She lifted her head out of the water and looked toward the far bank. She was veering off course. The point toward which she was swimming—A. J. Smellie Warehouses—was to her left now. It should have been directly in front. She was drifting. That was the thing. You had to account for your drift. Perhaps the tide had turned already.

Perhaps she'd miscalculated. Michael could aim for a reef a mile out and use the current to get there by the shortest route. Sometimes he'd swim in the opposite direction of his goal for a while, but always he'd come back to it effortlessly.

She swam a few more strokes and looked up, correcting again slightly, then put her head back under. She should be better at this, she thought. She'd pictured the swim in the weeks since she'd made up her mind to do it, but the reality was so different. Think about what you're trying to achieve. Her father's voice. And don't go to sleep. The first shock had been replaced now by a deeper feeling, a hankering in her bones to be free of the cold. It was almost comfortable but she suspected being comfortable might be worse. She suspected it might be how she'd give up.

"Swim," she said out loud, which felt good, to have a voice out in this dark, old water.

She could see on the bank the girls who'd come down to watch her this morning. She'd show them, she thought, especially Darcy. It was Darcy who'd dared her. On the island, swimming had been something everyone did, but here in England, Catherine thought, swimming was rare. Maybe if she swum, they would begin to like her.

3

A ferry sounded its horn. Louisa didn't know if it was a warning or a greeting, but Catherine raised an arm to wave. It seemed a hopeful gesture. Passengers waved and cheered, but the other boats and barges looked as if they might run the girl down. There was a smell like fresh meat on the turn, sweet, a little rancid. Louisa looked back at the bank where half a dozen others from the school were waiting, cheering along with the builders from the next-door site. The beauty of the day was with them all, except for Helen Anderson, who still stood there, hands on hips, awfully red in the face.

Catherine's arms were bare. They looked so slight as they came up out of the water, as if they wouldn't be strong enough to propel her along at all. Yet she moved so easily, like a creature born to the water. She seemed to drift with a tide. What if she failed? Should Louisa jump in to try to help? Louisa couldn't, she realized. She couldn't swim to save herself, let alone someone else. Oh dear, the poor girl, Louisa thought. The poor silly girl.

Catherine had asked her aunt about swimming two weeks before, Louisa thought now, although it was Louisa's housekeeper, Nellie, who first raised it. Louisa had assumed it was some harebrained scheme of Nellie's. On Catherine's birthday on the third, Nellie had cooked pancakes. "She's fifteen now," Nellie had said, as if that had anything to do with it, "and so perhaps she could swim."

So was this what Nellie meant? It must have been. And Louisa had ignored her. You can't ignore children, Louisa heard her mother say behind her, so clearly she turned and looked, as if her mother would be there. "I wasn't ignoring her," Louisa said.

Helen Anderson cocked her head. "I beg your pardon, Doctor?"

"Nothing," Louisa said. "I'm sure there's a perfectly rational explanation for this." Louisa had a hunch there was no rational explanation at all but she desperately wanted Helen Anderson to believe there might be one. "Will she be all right do you think?" Louisa began to feel queasy now. She steadied herself on the railing in front of her.

She looked again at the group cheering Catherine on, the girls, the builders, and now a few others from neighboring buildings, Louisa noticed, men in expensive suits. Among the group of builders she noticed a patient from the clinic. What was his name? "Robert!" she called when she remembered. He turned around, peering into the sun at her. "That's my niece. Should one of you lads go in and get her?" Louisa could hear the fear in her own voice.

Robert jogged up the bank, gave Helen Anderson a sideways

glance and stood just below Louisa. "Oh I wouldn't think we'll be needing to do that, Doctor," he said, breaking into a grin. "She'll be doing the rescuing, not us. She's a swimmer, that one. Your niece, you say? Why, she's just like a little fish." He laughed. "Don't you worry about her none." Louisa felt a little relieved, but still, Catherine looked so tiny in the river among the boats and barges.

A motor car pulled up and a young man holding a large camera got out, followed by another in a tan suit. They went running past Louisa and Helen Anderson and down to the group on the bank.

"I think that might be a journalist," Louisa said to Helen, "talking to your students."

"Oh goodness, stop that! Stop that this instant!" Helen Anderson called out, flapping her arms like a flightless bird as she made her way back down the bank toward the group. "Just one minute, young man."

The journalist, a compact lad with blue eyes and a mischievous grin, lifted his hat and said, "I believe she's one of your students, Miss Anderson. Is this the school's three R's, then? Readin', 'Ritin' and the River?"

They'd tried to be patient, Helen Anderson had said. What did she mean? Had there been trouble for Catherine at the school? Whenever Louisa asked her, Catherine had said it was going well, although in truth Louisa was so busy with work she hadn't really spoken to Catherine at length of late. Ruth Luxton had asked how Catherine was doing just the week before, and Louisa had said the girl was fine, but afterward it had occurred to her that she had no idea how Catherine was doing. She should know. Of course she should. She was Catherine's guardian.

Ruth had that way of looking at Louisa that made Louisa think she wasn't telling the truth even when she was.

"What?" Louisa had said.

"Are *you* all right, Louisa?" Ruth had said.

"We're not going to discuss this," Louisa had said emphatically.

Ruth had nodded, but there was a little frown on her face and Louisa knew it wasn't the last she'd hear.

Louisa had first met Ruth at the London School of Medicine for Women when Louisa's own mother, Elizabeth, was teaching there. At ten, Louisa had come along to a lecture her mother was giving because the governess hadn't turned up at home.

"Are you a doctor?" Ruth, then one of her mother's students, had asked Louisa. Ruth's hair, dark brown in those days, was middle parted and sat like a heart around her face. Her kindly dark eyes took Louisa in.

"My mother is your tutor," Louisa had said.

"So she is," Ruth said, smiling. "But are you here for the class?"

Louisa had considered her answer carefully. "I will be," she said.

"Good," Ruth said. "You have the eyes of a doctor."

Louisa never forgot. After she graduated, she and Ruth had worked together at the hospital in France. They became dear friends. Ruth had been there for Louisa through the most difficult years. She was the person Louisa was most likely to turn to for advice and support. She also knew more about Louisa than anyone alive.

Louisa had picked the Henley School for Catherine, which valued education for women, according to its prospectus, while accepting the importance of manners. The perfect school, Louisa had decided. She herself had been educated in this kind of environment. Louisa's mother, Elizabeth, one of the first women to study medicine in England, had always believed women were the equal of men, and education mattered a great deal.

Louisa shuddered momentarily as she thought of her young niece out there on the water.

Henley was the best of the past while keeping a gaze firmly on the future, Louisa had thought, perfect for Catherine, who knew so little about how to behave in the world. They'd teach her manners but remain committed to her learning. It was also a school that didn't stop for the long summer break all the other local schools had, which meant Louisa wouldn't have to find something to do with Catherine across a summer holiday.

Now, it seemed, either the school had failed. Or Catherine had.

Louisa had a notion that Helen Anderson, at least, was convinced it was Catherine.

Louisa had a picture in her mind, then, of Catherine on the island at three, running full pelt into the sea behind her father, catching him up, catching him up, Harry pretending to run as fast as he could, letting her grab him around the legs, both of them crashing over into the water, Harry coming up first, shaking the water from his sandy curls. Louisa, waiting on the beach, was afraid, for where was the child? And then, suddenly, there she was, out in the deeper water, calling, "Daddy! Come on or we'll miss the wave," just like a little fish, as Robert had suggested.

Catherine's mother had drowned, that was the thing. The water was the last place you'd expect to find her, and yet it was like a siren to the girl. Always had been, Louisa thought now.

4

Catherine could hear their cries, like gulls in the evening. "Swimmer!" they were chanting over and over. The sun was shining on her face and it made her feel she might be warm again even though it carried so little warmth. The bank didn't seem any closer. She wasn't tired. She wasn't even cold now. She was beyond cold. As the cries grew louder in her ears and she started to make out people on the bank, she had an inexplicable desire to turn around and swim back to the other side. She didn't want to return to dry land, to London. She just wanted to swim away.

Always plan success, her father used to say. Had he known? she wondered. Had he known his days were numbered? Had he been given some warning? Did he have some inkling that this might happen, that he might leave her without a home, without him, without anyone?

It had been Sister Ursula who'd told her. Sister Ursula had come to the house with Roy Macklin, the police officer, that

Sunday morning. Her father had left two days before, to travel to Cairns with the harbormaster's wife, who'd become ill during her confinement. But then Sister Ursula and Sergeant Macklin were at the front door. They were so sorry, they kept saying. Sister Ursula stayed through the morning but Catherine didn't want her there, in the house. She liked Sister Ursula, but she wanted to be small again and climb into Florence's lap and have Florence rub her shoulders and sing a song. She felt very frightened and alone.

She wondered now if she could just keep swimming, head out to the North Sea, down and across the Atlantic to the Indian Ocean, eventually the Arafura Sea, then the green of Saibai or New Guinea and from there to Thursday Island and her home. You could sleep while swimming on your back, she thought, as she turned over onto her back. You'd eventually get to the Arafura Sea, warm year-round, so different from this oily, cold river.

The Torres Strait could be treacherous, she knew. So many ships had been wrecked and so many lives lost. Many of the Islander families Catherine knew were fishermen, and every one of them had lost someone to the sea. But the sea could be kind too. Catherine and Michael had swum wherever they'd wanted to. The sea would protect them. That's what Michael always said. The sea would protect her own.

The islands in the north and west of the Torres Strait were rock, originally part of the mountain range that divided the east of Australia from the interior, her father had told her, tracing the line in the atlas from the mainland north, north, north and off the tip of Australia's most northern point. He believed there had been a land bridge between Australia and Papua New Guinea. "Boigu and Saibai—where I go for the clinics—are only a few miles from New Guinea," he said. His finger ran over the island they'd visited the day her mother drowned, but he didn't say anything about it. "If you look at the map," he said, "you can see where the bridge was. A giant might still use it." He smiled, stepping from island to island with his fingers.

On the island, she would never have worried about getting cold. They'd dry themselves in the sun after they swam. They'd sit on the sand for a while and then dive back into the sea. It only ever felt soothing. Oh, that feeling of the breeze on your skin when you first came out of the water, giving you just a hint of a chill on those hot, hot days and then, when you'd heated up, the plunge into the cool water.

Michael always swam with her, every afternoon after school. When they were older, they'd set out swimming most Sundays while Harry paddled in a canoe with Florence. They'd meet up on one of the nearby islands and cook fish for lunch. "You must put those days in the past, darling," Louisa had said. "You have to move on." Catherine had tried. She really had. But it was all so different and new.

And Michael? Catherine thought suddenly. What was Michael doing without her? She imagined his life going on, the life they'd shared, whereas her own life had completely changed.

She looked toward the bank. "I'm swimming," she said out loud. "I'm swimming the Thames."

She was wearing the woolen swimming suit she'd bought at Peter Robinson with Nellie. It had short sleeves that dragged through the water and a skirt over leggings. There were much better suits, sleeveless without a skirt, but Nellie said they were racy. Nellie had been a dear, though. When Catherine had said she thought swimming might make her feel more at home, Nellie had said they'd get her set up to swim and then tell Louisa. "If we do it that way, she's more like to agree, I think," Nellie had said.

On the island, Catherine had swum in a boy's costume, thin straps on her shoulders and bare legs. But you couldn't do that in London, Nellie said. You have to wear a woman's suit, she said, and at your age it needs to cover you. Louisa would have agreed, Catherine was sure. She was always talking about the young girls with their short hair and dresses. It wouldn't have occurred to Catherine to cover up her legs and arms before she came to London. On the island, she did as she pleased, although in the last year Florence and Sister Ursula had tried to get her to wear skirts to school instead of the dungarees she normally went around in, and she did cover up in the sun. She didn't much like the skirts but went along to keep them happy.

It took effort to get the swimming suit on, and Catherine didn't have an opportunity to swim in it before she took to the river. It weighed her down now and chafed under her arms and around her neck. She was wearing a rubber cap that made the water roar in her ears.

She'd tried to get along at school. She'd tried to get along with her aunt, Louisa. But Louisa was so very different from Catherine. She saw little reminders of her father occasionally. He was a doctor and both he and Louisa cared about their patients. But he was on Catherine's team in a way Louisa wasn't.

The mothers back on the island who felt sorry for Catherine, Catherine had never understood them, not really, not until her father was gone. And then Catherine knew what they were talking about. "Learning to swim," her father had said once, "is like learning how to breathe again. It's that simple, and that complicated."

Learning to live without him was like learning how to breathe again too.

5

Louisa was relieved when Catherine finally reached the bank. The poor girl shivered visibly as she pulled herself up the little stairs. Louisa was about to go down and find something to put around Catherine's shoulders when a building worker took off his coat and wrapped it around her. One of the others produced a blanket, which they put around the coat. Someone produced hot tea from a flask. They were cheering all the while, yelling Catherine's name over and over. The beauty of the day was with them. Louisa felt torn suddenly, wanting to go to Catherine but with no idea what she should say. She held back.

Now would come the trouble, Louisa knew. This wouldn't go unremarked. Helen Anderson looked livid. The journalist Louisa had seen earlier had gotten through the crowd and was talking to Catherine, who smiled as she replied. Her eyes, that intense green in the soft light of London, the Quick green, were on fire. She was Harry's daughter right then, Louisa thought.

He'd always been passionate about whatever he did—look at him going to the island in the first place, committed to helping a native people on the other side of the world, a commitment he devoted his life to. It was something people had said about Louisa when she was young too, passionate about her vocation. Where had that ever gotten her? And now, look at Harry's daughter. Catherine looked like those paintings of the saints just then, as if that baptism in the filthy Thames had beatified her. She still hadn't seen Louisa but her eyes scanned the bank, searching.

Suddenly, Helen Anderson stepped into Louisa's line of sight. "Now you see why I didn't want to discuss this on the telephone. We've never had a girl do something like this. There are rules at the school. The girls must not leave during school hours."

Louisa nodded. "I really don't know what to say. Catherine asked me about swimming a few weeks ago, but I didn't think she meant . . ." Louisa had a flash of memory then, Catherine with the boy, Michael, the second time Louisa visited the island, to bring Catherine home to London after Harry's death, the two of them long and lean as they ran together into the sea, his dark skin, hers dark too from the sun.

"We have a rule," Helen Anderson was saying. "If girls leave the school grounds without permission, expulsion is automatic. She took eight girls with her. Eight! It was carefully thought out, the whole thing. The girl who came to me, the only one who came to me—one of our prefects, Darcy Williams—said Catherine's been planning it for a month. Catherine told them all to come and watch. And swimming, hardly a Henley activity! I cannot put up with this, Dr. Quick."

Yes, swimming, Louisa thought, hardly a Quick activity, in her own mind. "Well, the eight on the bank were just following," Louisa said. "They shouldn't be in trouble."

"I should think that's my responsibility, not yours, Dr. Quick." Helen Anderson closed her mouth tightly before she spoke again. "I don't like to do this, but I don't want to see Catherine back at Henley."

"What am I supposed to do with her?" Louisa said. She thought of the long line of patients back at the clinic, the paperwork she still hadn't done from the week before. She thought of having to confront her niece. She didn't want to, not until she'd sorted this business out.

"It's not as if this is the only problem," Helen Anderson said.

"Well, this is the first I've heard of there being any problems at all, Miss Anderson," Louisa said, regaining her composure, finding herself trying to defend her niece. "I do wish you'd contacted me before now." It was no good blaming Helen Anderson, Louisa knew, but it was the only thing she *could* do. What a mess.

"I suggest you talk to the girl," was all Helen Anderson said.

Louisa walked toward Catherine, who was standing below them on the bank, surrounded by men. She looked up at her aunt, frowned slightly and then burst into a smile. "I did it, Louisa. I swam."

Louisa put a hand on her forehead. She was planning to be stern, to tell Catherine that what she'd done was inexcusable, that she'd been expelled from Henley and she'd caused trouble for eight other girls. These were the words forming in her head. But when she got close to her tall, lithe niece she found, almost in spite of herself, she was returning Catherine's smile.

She couldn't help it. The other girls were still chanting Catherine's name. The reporter was trying to get Catherine's attention again.

Catherine was still smiling at her aunt. And the blue of the sky was so very beautiful. Louisa was eye to eye with her niece for once, standing higher on the bank than Catherine was, her little brown boots sinking slightly into river mud. She felt tears forming in her eyes. She swallowed hard. "Yes, you did, Catherine," she said. "Yes, you did."

Catherine looked around for Darcy. She saw Ida and some of the other girls but no Darcy. She climbed the stairs. She was shivering, she realized. One of the workmen had come down and was wrapping his coat around her shoulders. "Aye, you made it, girl." She grinned. There was a man taking pictures. She could smell the fire of the camera flash. It was a warm smell, like striking matches. Someone came with a blanket and wrapped that around the jacket, another had hot tea, Nellie's cure for everything.

Suddenly she saw Louisa up on the bank with Miss Anderson. They were both frowning, looking at Catherine. How did Louisa get here? Catherine thought. And Miss Anderson. How did Miss Anderson get here?

Ida came down the bank. "You did it!" she called out, then added, more quietly, "But you're done for."

"Why? Where's Darcy?"

"That's just it. She told Miss Anderson. Miss Anderson is fuming."

"Am I in trouble?"

Ida nodded, her eyes wide. "Darcy did you in. She came over last night, said she felt it her duty to warn the authorities of your intended swim. She told me I shouldn't come. What a snake. I'm so sorry."

Catherine couldn't stop shivering. "But it was Darcy's idea," she said, her teeth chattering between the words.

"I'm sorry," Ida repeated. She was moving away now, as Louisa approached, her expression impossible to read.

"I did it, Louisa. I swam," Catherine said.

Louisa paused a moment before her face softened into a smile. "Yes, you did, Catherine," she said. "Yes, you did." She looked back toward the group on the bank. "But we're in real trouble now."

6

The girls on reception looked up as Louisa came in with Catherine, who was still wearing her swimming suit, wrapped only in the blanket that didn't cover her properly—they'd returned the coat to its owner. Louisa took Catherine into a treatment area and telephoned Nellie at home. "You'll have to come over to the clinic," Louisa told her housekeeper. "And bring some clothes for Catherine. She's been swimming on the blessed river, Nellie." Louisa felt her voice give way as she said it out loud.

"I'll be there as soon as I can," Nellie said, without asking questions. Did she know about it already? Was she in on the plan? Were they all gone mad?

Louisa had recovered from her brief euphoria on the river-bank to face the fact that Catherine really had been expelled from Henley. Not only that, the newspaper had photographed Catherine Quick in a swimming suit. Louisa didn't like the way the newspapers took an interest in women swimmers. They pretended it was because these women were breaking through some barrier. They pretended they were interested in sports. But in truth, they always photographed the women swimmers on dry land in clinging suits, all their curves and bumps on show, never in the water doing the thing that was supposed to be new and wonderful. The men were in the water, of course, but the women were always just standing there. Her niece, Catherine, was about to be one of those women. There was that one from Brighton. What was her name? She looked like a nice girl, but they made her look cheap. Lascivious. Elizabeth would turn in her grave to see her granddaughter on display like this, to think this was what she and the others fought for.

"You're the one who says women can do whatever men do," Catherine had said on the way to the clinic, which only exasperated Louisa further.

"Yes, but I didn't mean getting all their clothes off and jumping in the river."

Louisa had remained loyal to the Cause, even after the war when it seemed more hopeless than ever. Her mother was a great friend of Dr. Elizabeth Garrett Anderson's, sister of Millicent Fawcett. Their generation had believed so passionately that right would win the day, that a good letter, carefully constructed and thoughtfully argued, would get them the vote. Then the war, and afterward it seemed briefly as if women could do anything. Hah! They'd been wrong, wrong about it all. In truth, the Pankhursts were more effective. Sometimes violence had its advantages.

Louisa had attended one of the protests, against her mother's strong objections. "We achieve nothing through violence,"

Elizabeth told Louisa afterward. "You smashed windows and resisted the police." Louisa had been hurt to hear her mother speak that way. But now, Catherine! The last thing Elizabeth would have wanted was her granddaughter parading herself around in a swimming suit. A swimming suit! What had Louisa done wrong? For Louisa was responsible for Catherine, and if Catherine was acting this way, then Louisa had to take responsibility.

"It was just swimming," Catherine said in the little treatment room now. She looked less sure against the white wall, the curtains surrounding them. She looked even younger than her fifteen years, Louisa thought.

"Catherine, I just don't understand." Louisa felt queasy again. She put her fingers to her eye sockets. Catherine hadn't settled at the school. She hadn't settled in London. The only thing that seemed to make her happy was the weekly letter she received from Australia. "Just give me a moment to work this out," she said. She could tell Catherine was on the verge of tears. She left her in the treatment room and went out to the little office on her own. She breathed deeply, couldn't shake the fear, quickly escalating to dread. What was the matter with her? she thought. Catherine had swum in the river and it was Louisa who was afraid. Why was that? She couldn't think. She made herself breathe more slowly.

When she felt a little more calm, she went back to the treatment area. Nellie had arrived, thank goodness, with a skirt and blouse and underthings. Catherine went to change into the clothes in the bathroom. "Did you know about this?" Louisa said.

"Of course not," Nellie said, shaking her head, her dark curls wobbling. "But I'm less surprised than you," she said. "Poor girl's totally out of her element. Anyone can see that."

Nellie had come to Louisa through the clinic three years before. It was a bitter February morning and she'd waited on the stoop through the night, the nurse told Louisa quietly. Just a street girl, the nurse said, sniffing loudly. Louisa came into the waiting room to see a child, no more, with light blue eyes and that black curly hair, greasy but tied neatly, a skirt caked with mud at the hem, ancient shoes and a dirty blouse. Her fever was high, and she had a nasty cough on her chest. She was just turned eighteen, she told Louisa in a tiny voice. By then she'd been living on the street for over a year. Although she didn't know it, she was in the early stages of pregnancy.

Nellie's parents and brother had been taken by the influenza after the war and Nellie alone had survived. There was nothing put aside, so the family doctor arranged a position in a house in London. After two years the young master came home from school. Nellie wouldn't say what had happened but Louisa surmised that the young man had taken advantage of Nellie. She left the house and was living under the Hackney bridge for a time. She was working the docks area now.

Louisa was struck by the heart of the girl, which was intact, you could see. What chance did she have? Louisa had thought. She'd admitted her to the hospital to clear the cough from her chest, but what would happen after that? A girl alone, no money, no education, living on the streets. The veneer of propriety was thin. You could tear through it and then have nothing of the civilized world left. The vile creatures who would take advantage of a child like Nellie were there always, ready to rise up from their slime when they saw an opportunity.

The next day, Louisa asked Nellie if she'd be interested in another housekeeping position. There would be a small weekly wage, and room and board. Nellie was hesitant. "Where would it be, miss?"

"It would be at my house," Louisa said, "and there are no masters there but me, Nellie—and the two Scotties, of course, the real masters."

Louisa had thought long and hard about the matter of Nellie's pregnancy. Her responsibility was to tell the girl the truth, but she also knew that Nellie would be faced with a decision she shouldn't have to face at her age.

"She might want the child," Ruth Luxton said when Louisa asked her.

"She won't want the child," Louisa responded, feeling annoyed with Ruth, a rare experience. They were generally of one mind on clinical issues.

"She might," Ruth argued. "Or she might want to give the baby away; these girls often do."

"Are you against abortion?" Louisa had said, intending to wound.

"It's never a simple decision," Ruth said. "And it's hers, not yours."

"I disagree," Louisa said, although Ruth's objections rattled her—abortion divided her colleagues, she knew. Some doctors used the law as a way to shirk their responsibilities to their patients, as far as Louisa was concerned. Abortion could be performed if the mother's life was at stake. It often was, in one way or another. Other doctors would fail to act or pass the decision on to the woman, in this case, barely more than a child herself. For goodness' sake, what was the girl supposed to do? She couldn't even look after herself. If she had a baby, it would end any chance she'd have of amounting to anything.

Louisa told Nellie she had an infection, which was why her period had stopped. Nellie would need to undergo a minor procedure to fix it. The girl readily agreed.

When she was well enough to leave the hospital, Nellie moved into Louisa's house at Wellclose Square. She was fine company, with a good brain and a sharp, practical wit that appealed to Louisa. It was soon clear she was not the meek, quiet girl frightened to say her own name who'd come to the clinic that first day. It enlivened Louisa's evenings knowing she was going home not just to the two old dogs and cold meat for dinner but to someone who would challenge her and, more often than not, provide a hot meal. Nellie had a finer moral compass than Louisa, Louisa often thought, a better understanding of right and wrong and of people. Louisa generally relied on her to tell the truth.

She could see what Nellie was saying now, that Catherine wasn't fitting in, but it didn't make the girl's behavior any less difficult. "I have the clinic, Nellie," Louisa said. "So you'll have to take her home. We'll talk tonight."

"Louisa, she just wants . . ." Nellie hesitated, the sharp look on Louisa's face.

"Wants what?" Louisa said.

"Nothing. You're right. We'll talk tonight. I'll look after Catherine from here."

~

Louisa went into her office to compose herself before going back to the patients. Suddenly, she remembered the newspapermen on the river. There would be a story that evening or the next day about Catherine. Louisa's older brother, Alexander, would see it. She must get in first.

She looked at the clock. It was past eleven now. She telephoned Alexander's office at the docks. He answered straightaway, as always. Louisa had hardly finished telling him the story, half implying she'd known about the swim in advance and had approved, before he was lecturing her. "I tried to tell you, Louie. She ran around the island like a savage," Alexander said. "Her feet were like little hoofs. She showed off to me about it, was proud of it. And she'd wear nothing but a pair of old shorts with a pin in the front to hold them up and a big old shirt. That's no way for a girl to be dressed."

"It's that kind of place, Alex," Louisa said. "And there *is* a school on the island. She wasn't totally uneducated." In fact, if she were truthful Louisa had rather liked the school. The nuns were kindly and whip-smart. Catherine could do worse, it had occurred to Louisa. And let's face it, at Henley she was doing much worse, although that had only become clear now.

"Oh the island school," Alexander said. "I would think that would be of high quality, wouldn't you? There must be twenty students. I tell you, Harry just didn't bother with her."

"Harry adored her," Louisa said. "You're not being fair."

Louisa could hear shouting behind Alexander but he seemed unperturbed. It was probably just the workers down on the dock. They always sounded furious with one another even when they were just tossing sacks of grain.

"Possibly. But he hasn't given her even the most basic training in manners."

"Manners are always a little overemphasized," Louisa said, flicking through the morning's hospital reports from the nurses, pulling one out for later reading. "And are notoriously harder on women than men. I look forward to the day when women won't be trussed up in corsets and stays their whole lives, when they're free." She surprised herself, defending Catherine so vehemently. The things Alexander was saying were the very things Louisa herself had thought when she'd gone to the island to bring Catherine home to London. But she didn't like hearing her older brother say it. He was always so self-righteous.

"Louie, you could hardly argue that you've been trussed up in anything. Mama and Papa always encouraged you, more than me, if truth be known. But Catherine's not a Quick," Alexander said. "Perhaps they were wild on her mother's side."

Louisa threw the files back onto the desk and stood. "What's that supposed to mean?" she said. She should have known Alexander would be no help. He'd never liked Harry, and he saw Catherine as Harry's problem, left to Louisa now to sort out. He'd not think twice about blaming his sister. Louisa hoped the newspapermen hadn't caught the fact that Catherine had been expelled so at least she'd be spared more gloating by her older brother.

Louisa's young life had been filled with duty, to her parents, especially to her mother, to her sex, to the profession. Louisa knew she'd pursued a course that few before her had been able to. She'd become a medical doctor. It was a great privilege. When she started medicine, the women who'd already graduated, her teachers, impressed on Louisa and her colleagues the need for them to be cooler-headed than their male colleagues, for fear a man would brand them hysterical. Louisa always needed to guard herself, to be above reproach. She had to be a better doctor than any man.

And things had happened, things Louisa never spoke about, that she knew had affected her. She wasn't normal anymore. That's what she'd decided. She was . . . she was marked. Oh, she focused on doing her work well, being the best surgeon she could be. But in truth she was a little bit afraid almost all the time. And then Catherine. These six months had been unsettling. It was like watching herself as a young woman, watching herself embrace the world the way Catherine did. Herself if . . .

"Just that we'd know not to do something so garish," Alexander said on the telephone now, attempting appeasement in response to Louisa's sharp tone.

He really was no help, Louisa thought, although she wasn't sure she knew quite what she'd hoped for.

It had been one thing after another with Catherine. She'd cut off her hair in the week after her birthday, without first asking Louisa, who came home from work to find Nellie in tears in the kitchen, thinking she'd be blamed. When finally Nellie could speak to tell Louisa what had happened, it made even less sense. The girl had taken herself off to a barber and had her hair cut off, Nellie said. "She looks like a monster."

"Good God, Nellie," Louisa had replied. "You mean she's

had her plaits taken off and you think it's your fault?" Nellie was sobbing. "Look at me," Louisa said. But Nellie wouldn't. "I said look at me!" She sneaked a glance. "My hair is short. It hasn't killed me."

"But she's just a child," Nellie wailed. "And yours is normal."

Louisa softened when she remembered suddenly that Nellie had been a child too, when she'd had her hair cut off. She'd sold whatever she still had, including her hair.

"It's all right, Nellie. It really is."

Louisa was smiling to herself on the way up the stairs. She stopped smiling before knocking on the bedroom door. "Go away," Catherine called out.

"I will not be spoken to like that in my own house," Louisa had said, opening the door, regretting immediately the sharp tone she could hear in her own voice. Sometimes it was as if another creature moved in and took over when it came to Catherine. More gently, she said, "Catherine . . ." and then saw.

Oh, good Lord, Nellie was right. The haircut lacked any style at all. It looked as if it had been done by a butcher. The plaits had been hacked off on each side, leaving the remaining hair uneven at about collar length. There were no bangs, and Catherine had swept her hair to one side like a boy might. It was as bad as Nellie said.

But for all that, Louisa saw that the bigger surprise was the way the haircut transformed Catherine's face. She looked older and younger at the same time. She'd been crying, Louisa could see. "Well," Louisa said, recovering herself. "You've managed to upset Nellie, which I don't much like, Catherine. What did you go and do this for?"

"I'm sorry, Aunt Louisa," Catherine mumbled. She didn't

look sorry, Louisa thought. Her eyes looked angry. The girl was perpetually angry, as far as Louisa could see, for no reason Louisa understood.

"You say sorry awfully more than most people, Catherine. You have to think about the things you do." Catherine only nodded. Louisa wanted to say something that might help Catherine but she couldn't think of anything. "Why?"

"I just wanted to," Catherine said.

What Nellie told Louisa now back in the kitchen the night after the swim was that Catherine had used the money from the hair she'd sold to purchase her swimming costume and pay the ferryman to take her to the far bank, where she began her swim. Nellie knew about the swimming costume—she'd thought it would help Catherine—but not about the planned river swim. "She wanted to swim, Louisa. I thought if she and I set it all up, you'd be more amenable. At least she's resourceful."

"Quite," Louisa said. She was at a loss as to what to do. She'd never had children. It was what everyone always said to Louisa. Don't you wish you'd married and had children? Even the ones who didn't say it thought it. No! she wanted to scream. It was a question they never asked bachelors. Even the word *spinster* was nasty sounding. Don't you wish, Louisa, you'd had an opportunity to experience that higher calling? Hah. Louisa had seen their higher calling. Their lives wasted, wasted. Even Ruth, who was her best friend and made a huge contribution to the clinic, had to put her children first. It was always Louisa who ended up having to fill in when something was wrong at home. Louisa, who had no one to worry about but herself, they all thought.

And now, saddled with her brother's child, who was in real

trouble. Everyone said how lucky she was, how it would change her, soften her. But Catherine was almost fully formed. She was so quietly difficult, that was the thing. She didn't outwardly rebel. She didn't even storm. She just quietly went about her business. And now, she'd swum the Thames. What were they to do now but go on? Louisa thought.

She went out to the waiting area, took a stack of patient files and looked at the sea of faces, all looking up at her expectantly. "Annie Johnson," she called out. A little bustle of a woman in an old wool skirt popped up. Louisa smiled. "Sorry to keep you, dear," Louisa said. "Let's get along now."

7

Louisa had always liked coming home to her little house in Wellclose Square. She could walk to and from the clinic with ease, even in the most inclement weather, and whatever might be happening in the world outside, she always felt safe here. Even though she knew Catherine and conflict were within on this particular evening, the house was still home. After she'd finished up in the clinic, she'd popped in at the hospital to visit her patients there and had spent the remainder of the day in her surgery seeing new patients.

She unlocked the door and went inside, hung her coat and hat on the stand in the entry and put her bag on the little table. There was a narrow central hallway with rooms on either side. She passed the formal sitting room—or parlor, as Nellie called it—such as it was: a sofa and two large chairs, velvet drapes, a fireplace, flowers on a little table that were looking tired by the end of the week, a rug on the floor, a tiger skin, the tiger having been shot many years ago by one of the shooting Quicks of her grandfather's generation. Louisa wasn't quite clear why she'd allowed the tiger to come to rest in Wellclose Square, but that was where he now lay.

The parlor wasn't a room that welcomed the visitor, Louisa had often thought, although she never understood quite why, the tiger notwithstanding. She herself would become gloomy if she sat too long there, although the dogs liked it well enough, or at least Sooty did. He spent his days in front of the grate hoping for a fire, lying on the tiger's backside. Marble was always more particular, preferring the kitchen where Nellie spent much of her day and scraps could be had.

Louisa had inherited the dogs from Elizabeth when Elizabeth was no longer able to care for them. Louisa's mother had lost her memory first. She'd always been particular about writing well. But when Louisa was in Baltimore, doing a term at Johns Hopkins, she received a letter from her mother, written entirely in French. At first, Louisa had thought her mother must be trying to encourage Louisa to go back to learning the language, or making a joke, but when Louisa arrived home, she realized Elizabeth was confused about other things. She was forgetting people's names, words, places she'd been. Soon it was too much for her. Louisa arranged for a nurse at home. They had to tell Elizabeth the nurse was one of Louisa's friends who needed a place to stay. Quietly, Louisa withdrew her mother from the boards she was still involved with. If Elizabeth asked, the nurse would tell her the meeting was next month. She eventually stopped asking. It took longer than you'd think.

The dogs met Louisa at the door. She'd been so glad of them after Elizabeth died. They were a link to her mother, and until Nellie arrived they were the only creatures there to talk to in the evenings; unlike everyone else in her life, they didn't talk back. Sooty did as he pleased but was mostly happy. Marble was more cantankerous, withdrew affection unless treats were forthcoming, barked at flies or the moon or rocks.

On the right, farther along the hallway, was the dining room. It was so far from the kitchen Louisa didn't bother eating in there unless there were visitors, and the dining table was spread now with her papers, along with Catherine's school books. Catherine wouldn't be needing those for a while, Louisa thought bitterly.

At the back of the house, Louisa had hired a carpenter to add a small room with a bath, which was glorious and by far Louisa's favorite room. There was a family story about baths, Elizabeth's father demanding that when his three daughters went off to boarding school they be allowed to have a weekly bath. It was unheard of, but the school acquiesced. "So you see, hot baths run in the family," Louisa had told the carpenter who'd come to install her bathroom, but he was less interested in the story that she thought he ought to be.

Upstairs were two bedrooms. Nellie and Catherine shared. Nellie had offered to move to the back of the kitchen after Catherine arrived but Catherine insisted she stay in the room. "To be honest, I'd like some company," she told Nellie. "It will make me less lonely."

Louisa found Nellie at the back of the house in the kitchen now stirring something on the stove. The night had turned chilly and the fire was burning. Catherine wasn't about. Louisa raised her eyebrows. "In bed," Nellie said quietly. "I think she's sleeping." There was beef and boiled potatoes, Nellie said, taking down a plate for Louisa.

"I'm not hungry," Louisa said. "I'll take it for lunch tomorrow."

"You must eat," Nellie said, her eyes shining in the firelight.

"Just not tonight." She sighed. "God, Nellie, what are we to do with her?" Louisa took a bottle of scotch from the pantry and sat down at the table against the wall. She poured herself a dram and drank it down. She took a big breath into her lungs and exhaled.

"It's not been easy for her," Nellie said.

"No, I suppose it hasn't. But if I compare her to you—look at what you've done with your life. Catherine's had so many opportunities."

"Well, that's the thing, Louisa. You're just so busy, and she's of an age where a girl most needs her mother."

"Well, she doesn't have a mother," Louisa said sharply, although Nellie had a point, Louisa knew.

"I know, but you're in that role, if you don't mind my saying. You're her guardian."

"Are you saying I haven't done enough?"

"No, of course not," Nellie said—carefully, it occurred to Louisa. Nellie was not normally careful with her words. "But, Louisa, you're easier with me than with Catherine. She's your blood."

"But she's just so very different from me, Nellie. How can she be so . . ."

"So what?" Catherine said then. Louisa turned around to find her niece standing in the doorway. She was dressed in a baggy flannel nightdress, but Louisa could make out the powerful frame beneath. And if you didn't notice the outline of muscle and sinew in her frame, the fire in those eyes told a story.

The dark skin might have paled to a gray in the London winter, but those blazing green eyes demanded attention.

"Ungrateful," Louisa said flatly. It wasn't what she meant, but it would have to do at short notice. She looked away and then back at the girl. She tried to be more reasonable. "Catherine, I just can't imagine doing something like that—swimming the river. Something I'm very sure you knew you shouldn't do." This wasn't what she meant either.

Catherine didn't respond, just stood with her arms folded, that fierce look in her eyes.

Nellie sat down across from Louisa. "I do think she's been very unhappy at the school." She was frowning hard, trying to make Louisa understand.

Louisa felt a flash of anger. She had so much on her plate already, and Catherine had done something entirely stupid. "Unhappiness doesn't lead the rest of us to jump in the river," she said to Nellie. She looked up and saw Catherine's face. She looked so young, Louisa thought, and the fierceness in her eyes looked more like fear now. "You knew you shouldn't," Louisa said more gently.

The girl gave a small nod. "I wanted . . ." She sobbed suddenly, an awful noise.

"What?" Louisa said, standing up, moving toward Catherine without thinking, putting her hand up near the girl's bowed head, not quite making contact. She held her hand there for a moment and then put it back by her side. "What did you want, Catherine?" she said softly.

Catherine looked up, her face distraught, but didn't respond.

"Very well," Louisa said. "Back to bed and we'll talk more

tomorrow. Perhaps Helen Anderson will have calmed down by then. We can but hope, my dear." Louisa tried to smile encouragingly, but the look on Catherine's face when she raised her head, the anguish there, was awful.

"I don't ever want to go back there," Catherine said then, her voice shaky. "I just want to go home, Aunt Louisa. I hate it here. I hate school. I hate everything."

Louisa felt at a loss. It was Nellie who spoke. "Come, child, let's go to bed. We won't sort this out tonight." Nellie always knew exactly the tone to take with Catherine. Where did she learn that? It must have come from having younger siblings, although Louisa had Harry. Perhaps Nellie was just better at it. At any rate, it was clear that everything Louisa did when it came to Catherine was wrong.

Nellie had tried to warn Louisa about this, Louisa recalled, about the swimming but also about this unhappiness. It had been over breakfast in the kitchen a week ago. Louisa was reading the letter from the new health inspector. They were sending an official to inspect the clinic and Louisa had just read their list of requirements. She would have laughed if it hadn't been so serious. Sooty waddled up—they were getting so fat; she wished Catherine would walk them—and she threw him a biscuit. "Who's a good boy?" she said distractedly, and gave him a little pat.

"She's unhappy," Nellie said.

"What about?" Louisa said, still reading the letter.

"The school."

"What's wrong with the school?"

"Ask her."

So when Catherine came downstairs in her uniform a few minutes later, Louisa said, "School's going well?"

"Oh yes," Catherine said, nodding furiously.

Louisa looked at Nellie, who said to Catherine, "Go on, ask her."

Catherine shook her head.

"Ask her what?" Louisa said. She took off her spectacles and looked at Catherine.

"I . . . ," Catherine said, then stopped.

"What?"

"Just, I was wondering if I might swim now that it's coming into summer."

"Swim," Louisa said, putting down the letter. "What for?"

"I just . . . I've always been able to swim."

"Oh," Louisa said. "I suppose you have. The boys swim up at Hampstead Ponds, don't they, Nellie?" Nellie had mentioned the ponds a week prior to that, on Catherine's birthday. This must have been why.

Nellie nodded enthusiastically.

Swimming. What next? Louisa had wanted to say. She knew some of the nurses went in for that sort of thing. They had their hair cut short, wore men's swimming suits and strutted around like nobody's business. Asking for trouble, Elizabeth would have said, and with no brains at all.

"I don't see how, dear," Louisa had said to Catherine. "Can't you run in the park?"

She should have paid more attention, she thought now. She should have seen this coming.

What Louisa loved most about surgery, what she'd loved from the beginning, was its clarity. You cut or you didn't. And when you cut, you cut in a particular place and not in another. It was neat. You made mistakes, rarely, and you moved on from those, but for the most part you transformed. You cut.

It was why Louisa would never have specialized in medicine rather than surgery. Ruth Luxton was entirely suited to medicine. In medicine, you tried a treatment. You waited. A few weeks later, you saw the treatment hadn't quite done what you'd intended, or the patient had changed, or the environment had changed, and so you changed the treatment. You waited again. And it was months and months before you finished. That's what Catherine was like, a constant recalibration of decisions that turned out to be wrong, through no fault of your own, with insufficient information to make the right decision.

What would they do now? Louisa wondered, sitting alone in the quiet kitchen. Find another school, start again? If she'd known Catherine would be so unhappy, would she have acted differently? Should she have left the girl in Australia? Of course not. Should she have picked a different school? Was the change just too severe? Would it have helped if Catherine had been able to swim a few weeks ago when Nellie suggested it? Should Louisa know all this?

She poured a second dram of scotch and took herself off to her study to go over the day's reports. As she took them out of her briefcase, the morning's mail, which she'd picked up on her way to the clinic, fell out onto the floor. There was an account from the carpenter, hand-delivered, Louisa must pay—she threw it on the bills-to-be-paid file—and there was a letter, for Catherine. Louisa had seen it this morning. The letters from Australia—they came each week—were a problem. They unsettled Catherine. She had fully intended to give the letter to Catherine, but instead she'd tossed it into her briefcase and had forgotten about it.

Louisa turned the letter over in her hand now. She had the strangest urge to open it. Of course she mustn't, she thought. It was a letter addressed to Catherine. She looked at the writing. Florence had lovely handwriting, with a flourish on the C of Catherine and the Q of Quick. She mustn't open it. She mustn't.

But Louisa didn't put the letter away. Perhaps, after all, she should open it. Perhaps if she was careful she could open the envelope and then reseal it so that Catherine would be none the wiser. For when she thought about it, the letters from Australia, one every week, had always unsettled Catherine. Perhaps Florence was putting pressure on the girl to return to the island. Perhaps she was voicing opinions about Catherine's new life. By the time she'd finished the second scotch, Louisa had convinced herself that opening the letter was not only an acceptable thing to do, it was imperative.

She set her glass down on the table and focused on the task. The envelope was difficult, glued seemingly by the number of miles it had traveled. She coaxed with her nail. She picked with her thumb. After a few minutes, she tore the envelope open in frustration. She felt the shock of what she'd done then, didn't immediately unfold the page inside. She could remedy this, she thought; she could tell Catherine she'd opened the envelope in error and that she hadn't read the letter.

But Louisa would read the letter. She knew she would.

It was from the boy, Michael, whom they called Bid, not his mother, which surprised Louisa. She hadn't known they were writing to one another; Catherine had certainly never mentioned it. Catherine always took the letters from Australia straight up to her room and read them there. Catherine had only ever mentioned letters from Florence, never from her son Michael.

Waapi, he wrote. This was what they called Catherine.

I'm sorry I didn't reply to your last letter. I have not forgotten you and I'm sorry that my last words were angry ones. I see you in every place on the island we've been, which is everywhere.

I am hating school and hating home and hating swimming, all because of missing you. I was so glad to have another letter from you, and I won't stop writing again, I promise. Mum says I'm a bad friend and it's a wonder you even bother with me. But you know I will never let you down, Waapi. We are promised, joined in body.

I worry what will happen. Come home. I love you.

> *From,*
> *Bid*

Louisa looked at the letter again. "We are promised, joined in body." Louisa thought of them running down to the sea together. How dare he? Louisa thought. How dare he take advantage of the girl? Had they been lovers, her poor young niece and this boy?

Oh, poor dear Catherine. And then another thought crossed Louisa's mind. Had the housekeeper, Florence, known? Had she let it happen? Oh, what a mess Harry had left.

Louisa felt a shiver, although there was no draft. What was she to do?

She must give her niece the letter. That was the correct thing.

But was it? Perhaps she should hold on to the letter, at least for now. Catherine was a girl. If he *was* taking advantage of her, all communication must stop.

Louisa took the letter upstairs to her room, opened the drawer where she kept her private papers, and slipped it under the pile. At least for now, she thought. Closing the drawer, she sat down heavily on her bed. At least for now.

PART II

Thursday Island, Australia,
February 1914

8

It was eight months since Harry's wife, Julia, had died and Louisa knew she must go to him. She'd put off the trip—selfish, really, but she'd been setting up her surgery in Harley Street—and before she knew it, the time had passed. She had fears about seeing Harry again, about seeing a child, any child, if she was honest with herself. Elizabeth had counseled against her going for this very reason. "If Harry wants to come home, he will," their mother said. But Elizabeth was already confused by then, good days and bad. Louisa felt it was her duty to go to her brother and do her best to convince him to come home, no matter how she herself might feel. Perhaps, too, she wanted him back in her life. At any rate, she set out, hopeful.

She'd left London on the *Osterley* in the middle of a cold winter, reaching Sydney nearly two months later in high summer. Australia was delightful for the first days, but then, as Louisa moved steadily north—Brisbane, Townsville, Cairns—the weather became hot then unbearable, relieved only by the sea. It was late on a Sunday when the ferry from the mainland at Bamaga pulled in beside the long pier that jutted out into the little bay on Thursday Island.

On the ferry, Louisa had sat outside with the Islanders, hoping to find a breeze. Their skin was beautiful, with such a depth to the color. Strangely, they reminded Louisa of the women of the East End, who were generous with their time and inexhaustibly—and, given the cruelty of their lives, inexplicably—happy. One shy young woman offered Louisa a white fruit with a brown hairy skin. Coconut, Louisa thought. She shook her head no, although it smelled delicious. There was something about these women with their full smiling faces, the easy way they had with one another and with their children. Louisa couldn't stop staring at them.

Louisa stepped down the gangplank and onto the jetty. To one side was a muddy bank and to the other the long, curved beach. Although there was a good breeze, the heat blasted her now that she wasn't on the water. Harry was waiting at the shore end of the jetty. It was four years since Louisa had seen her brother, she realized. She felt a pull of tenderness for him, for the little boy he'd been, the little boy she'd been so close to. She sighed, used the jetty rail to steady herself.

When Harry saw his sister, he took off his hat and used it to wave madly, reminding her of the guileless child he'd been. "Ho, Louie!" he called. "My but it's good to see your face."

As he approached, Louisa realized that if not for his posture, she might not have recognized her brother. He had changed so much. His face was more ruddy from the sun. His sandy hair was swept back, revealing the high Garrett forehead. He

looked more like their father, whom Louisa had adored, relaxed about who he was but with purpose now. Harry carried
himself with more intention, she thought, in just the way their
father had. He also looked more hearty, not the grieving wid-
ower she'd expected.

He came toward Louisa with his arms outstretched. They
embraced warmly. When she pulled away finally, she saw
tears pricked his eyes. Poor Harry, she thought then. He'd
suffered terribly, she knew. "Thank you," he said. "Thank you
for coming."

"Oh goodness, Harry," she said. "It's the least I could do.
And it's taken long enough." She smiled, holding on to his
hands, which he seemed in no hurry to free from her grasp.

"Yes, it has," he said, returning the smile with a boyish grin.
"But I'll forgive you as it's an awfully long way." He let go of
her hands and then took her arm to lead her off the pier, taking her portmanteau in his other hand. He was quite cheerful,
Louisa thought.

Only a year separated them, Louisa older, and they'd grown
up like twins, although Harry always towered over his sister
physically and Louisa worked harder at her studies. Left largely
to their own devices—their mother had taken up her post at
the London School of Medicine for Women before Harry was
walking; their brother Alexander was six years older than
Louisa and off at school—they'd always been close.

Harry had been adored as a child, in the way of blond-
haired, blue-eyed boys with dimples. Elizabeth was forty-seven
when he was born. "What a dear little man," visitors to their
house at Aldeburgh in Suffolk would say of him, or, "Imagine
him in a sailor suit. Goodness, wouldn't he be a picture?" When

Harry first smiled, you'd think the world had only then started turning. The entire household was in love with him, Cook, Nanny, even the two Scotties they had in those days, but no one loved him better than his big sister, Louie. Nanny was happy enough. For her part, Louisa couldn't imagine what she'd done with her time before Harry came along. She adored him too.

As Harry grew older, Louisa tried her best to be stern with him, but he'd look at her seriously for a moment and then grin as wide as the sea and she'd be away on some adventure, forgetting sternness altogether. She taught him to cook, although she hardly knew how, herself. They made toffee but they used bicarbonate soda instead of cream of tartar and the toffee bubbled over the stove and nearly burned the kitchen down. Cook was furious when she saw the saucepan. She made Louisa, not Harry, get up on a stool and scrub the stove. That was what it was like. Harry was excused for everything. You just wanted to love him. He was spoiled, Louisa knew, they all knew, but there was nothing to be done. At any rate, it seemed to make him more generous-spirited than anything else.

It was Elizabeth who noticed, suddenly, and not until Louisa's tenth year, that her daughter's lessons were giving way to time spent with Baby, as they still called Harry, now nine. Louisa's French was appalling by her tutor's account, and she'd given up on mathematics altogether. Elizabeth had spent the weekend at home, her first for months—she'd been at the hospital or medical school every weekday and weekend—and had seen how much Louisa was doing to care for Harry. "You shouldn't be doing all that," she'd said. She'd talked to Louisa's father, also home, and on Saturday night they'd given Louisa the verdict. She would go to Glasgow to board at the Canterbury School, Elizabeth's old school.

On the Sunday Harry came out to the back garden. "What's wrong, Louie?" he said. She'd been crying, and he could see the tear lines on her face.

"Oh Harry, Mummy says I have to go to school and I don't want to."

Harry sat down beside Louisa and took her hand. "You mustn't worry, Louie. They can take you away to school but they can't take you from in here." He touched his own chest and then took her hand and put it on her chest. "And they can't take me from in there. We're always forever friends." This only made Louisa cry more and he hugged her tightly. "I love you best of all, Louie. But don't tell Mummy."

Harry, now a grown man, was tall like their father, George, and he still had the curliest hair of the three children. When he was a child, it was like wires sticking out of his head, and red like their father's had been, though it was tamer now, Louisa noticed, and more sandy. He'd been the favorite of their grandmother in Edinburgh; she always made Napoleon cakes especially for him.

After he married, Harry had distanced himself from the Quicks and from Louisa in particular. She never understood why, and since he'd moved away to the island, she couldn't easily address it with him. He'd first visited Australia with Alexander, after their father died and Alexander took over the family shipping company. They'd extended the mail service, which meant their ships passed through the Torres Strait to Australia's north. Harry and Alexander stopped at the port at Thursday Island and then spent a month in Cairns. Alexander wanted Harry to go into the business with him, Louisa realized later, but Harry was set on following his mother and Louisa into medicine. The visit to the island only cemented his plan. When he came home, all he talked about was the hospital they were building on Thursday Island and the marvelous Torres Strait Islanders. He finished his medical studies and then spent six months training at Johns Hopkins in America, where he met Julia Freebody.

Besotted was the only word for it, Elizabeth had said when Julia first came on the scene. "Our Harry is besotted with an American girl." Elizabeth had gone over to America for the wedding. Louisa was still finishing her surgical training in Edinburgh. "Delightful," Elizabeth said. "Absolutely delightful people, even if they are Catholic."

They married so quickly that Louisa had wondered if Julia was pregnant, but Catherine was born eleven months later, after they'd left for Australia and Thursday Island, where Harry had secured the post as hospital doctor. So it had been a love match. And Julia was more than happy to go to a remote place, Elizabeth told Louisa when she came home from the wedding. "Aren't they marvelous, Louie? Aren't they just?"

Louisa wondered at first when Harry stopped writing if Julia was one of those possessive types—some of Louisa's friends had married men like this—but Julia hadn't seemed that way the one time Louisa had met her. They'd come to England on the way through to Australia. Louisa had traveled down from Edinburgh to Aldeburgh to see them. Harry was as besotted as Elizabeth claimed. Julia was polite, smiled a lot, but she wasn't really there. She seemed an uncomplicated girl to Louisa; a bit lost, if anything. She had no interest in the vote, or medicine, or any of the issues of the day, as far as Louisa could tell.

After they left, Harry rarely wrote home and never came back to visit, even after Catherine was born. Louisa asked her mother if there was something she, Louisa, had done to offend him. They'd always been so close and now he hardly even acknowledged his sister. Elizabeth said he was just getting on with life. "He's married with a family now." Louisa had missed her brother, and the opportunity she might have had to be an aunt to the child. She sometimes wondered if Elizabeth had breached Louisa's confidence and told Harry what had happened. Perhaps he knew and judged Louisa harshly. Alexander had always blamed her, so perhaps Harry did too.

Harry held a parasol over her head as they made their way to the buggy now. He didn't look like he was judging his sister. He looked relaxed, happy to see her. "Florence said to bring this," he said, twirling the parasol before handing it to her. "You'll burn in a minute otherwise." The cream linen suit and broad-brimmed hat suited him. Louisa didn't know who Florence was but didn't ask. Had Harry met a woman on the island? It would be no bad thing if he were to remarry, Louisa thought then.

They took a dirt road toward the town center, sitting up front in the open buggy, Harry gently guiding the horse. Oh, the heat of the place. While the horses moved quickly enough, the breeze they created was as hot as the air. It could make a person want to kill themselves, Louisa thought. She nearly said so, until she realized that, given his loss, talk of death probably wouldn't do Harry any good. But surely he noticed the heat. She looked across, but he appeared oblivious.

Louisa had expected the island to be populated by those natives she'd seen on the ferry. Back in London, she'd gone to the library and located in an atlas the islands to Australia's north. They were home to the Papuans, the atlas said, and the Papuans were cannibals. The people on the ferry didn't look as if they'd eat each other. What's more, when Harry took her through the main street of the town, it was full of Europeans rather than natives, men in suits like Harry's, arm in arm with young women in colorful dresses with parasols for the sun, workers in shirtsleeves and knickerbockers, girls and boys in cotton shorts or skirts.

Harry laughed when she asked him about the cannibals. "Wrong islands," he said. "New Guinea is north of here, and I didn't know the Papuans are cannibals. They come across in canoes sometimes to Saibai or Boigu in the north of the Strait when they're sick. Occasionally the native healers bring them to me. Blood poisoning, a labor that goes on too long—but I've never heard of them eating each other." He laughed again, as if Louisa had made some great joke.

Under the trees along the street she did see more Islanders, their skin as dark as coal, the little children running naked and laughing, soft voices drifting over to her on the breeze.

"These people are peaceful, more or less, as far as I know," Harry said. "And who wouldn't be, living here?"

She looked out toward the turquoise water. It drew her in.

"There used to be different groups on the different islands," Harry said. "Depending on geography more than anything. They were all linked by trade. Some had rock for tools, some had wood for boats. There's a fellow at Cambridge I met after I came here the first time. He's studied all the different cultures. The Islanders are mostly Christian now, but we English haven't always understood their ways of doing things. Those canoes you might have seen down on the beach, they can get anywhere in them. They're beautiful boats.

"There was a magistrate here on Thursday, John Douglas. He had a lot of respect for the Islanders." Harry looked at her. "I do too. But there's a new system now since Douglas left. They can't even travel island to island as easily."

Farther along the main street, she noticed a group of young men outside one of the stores. They had sun-browned skin and short black hair and they all wore cotton shirts and trousers. Louisa thought they might be Chinese.

"Japanese, actually," Harry said when she commented. "Good lung capacity."

"Lung."

"Pearls," Harry said. "They're divers."

"Pearls," Louisa said.

"Mother-of-pearl," he said. "The shell. We supply half the world's buttons."

They turned out of town and up the only hill on the island, a gentle incline of red dirt from which you'd be able to survey the sea on all sides. Harry pointed. "That's the house."

From a distance, it looked like a castle, Louisa thought, built from stone, a bell tower on one side, flags flying from the front. "A stupid thing I did," he said. "I think I wanted to impress Julia." He winced.

"I'm so sorry for your loss, Harry," Louisa said, patting his knee. "I should have come sooner. Mama sends her love, dear boy."

"Well, you've come," he said. "And I'm very glad you have."

"Do you want to tell me about it?" Ruth had said it would do him good to tell the story.

"About what?" he asked.

"About Julia. What happened to Julia," Louisa said.

"Yes," he said. "When we get to the house. Later."

As they wound their way up the hill, Louisa thought Harry might come home now after all. He'd been quite adamant about the island, Louisa remembered.

As they drew nearer, the house was no less imposing. The roof was made of slate tiles and they were indeed stone walls, Louisa saw now—they must have carried it in boats from the mainland and then up the hill from the jetty. The whole lower floor was surrounded by a deep portico. Harry led Louisa up a small set of stairs and through the large front door. He left her bag in the hall and sat her down in the parlor while he went to fetch a cool drink.

It took some time for Louisa's eyes to adjust to the dimness. There were double sash windows onto the verandah on two sides, she'd seen from outside as they entered, but they were closed now, and covered with heavy velvet drapes of a deep moss green. There was a sickly smell of flowers past their time. Louisa had an urge to tear back the drapes. She felt as if she were suffocating in the humid air. Harry had lost his young wife to the sea outside the windows; perhaps that was why the drapes were closed.

"Lord, Harry, how do you survive the heat?" she said when he came back.

He smiled. "You get used to it," he said. "And there's the monsoon. It's that breeze you could feel from the shore. It brings the rain. Usually by this time of afternoon, we'd have a shower at least. That helps too. But you've come in a dry year."

Louisa's eyes had adjusted now. She could see the room was furnished richly, with two sofas and two big chairs. It was spotlessly clean but looked strangely uninhabited. There were no dead flowers, and yet the smell persisted.

They were sitting sipping their cold water when Louisa heard a voice outside. "Where is she? Where?" A moment later, the door burst open and filled the room with light.

She was a beautiful child, with long chestnut hair that fell down her back in a wave, green eyes and dark skin, a handful of freckles thrown across her cheeks, and wit, if the speed at which those eyes surveyed Louisa was anything to go by. She was a Quick, Louisa could see, even in the way she stood, toes out, ankles together, like Elizabeth and Louisa both. Harry, too, now that she thought about it. Duck-footed Quicks. A dancer, Mrs. Quick, one of Louisa's governesses had suggested to Elizabeth. Young Louisa could be a dancer. Hah! Elizabeth had crowed. More like a poor skeleton.

Louisa looked at Catherine's face and found herself feeling so tender she couldn't trust herself to speak. She stared.

"You must be Louisa," the little girl said, sounding grown up.

Louisa smiled. "And you must be Catherine," she said finally, tears pricking her eyes. She had an urge to touch the child, to take her in her arms, which she resisted.

Harry cleared his throat and Louisa took her eyes off the child, reluctantly, and looked at him. He looked so proud, and she knew immediately what had helped him through his loss. It was Catherine.

The little girl walked over and stood in front of Louisa and smiled. She took Louisa's hands in her own little hands. She leaned in and kissed her aunt on each cheek. Then she pulled away and twirled. She wore a blue-and-white gingham dress with white socks and little black boots, and a blue ribbon in her hair.

"She's so beautiful," Louisa said to Harry.

"We've done our best with her," Harry said, his voice gruff with emotion, looking from his sister to his daughter, tears in his eyes.

"I truly am beautiful," the little girl said, twirling again in the dress. "Florence made me put on a dress." She leaned in. "It's awfully uncomfortable, though." She smiled. "Florence is bringing the tea," she said. "I wasn't allowed to carry the tray. It's too dangerous," she added, opening her eyes wide.

As if on cue, a native woman came in with the tray. She wore a blue cotton dress with a white apron tied at the back. So Florence was the help, Louisa thought, although the way both Harry and Catherine spoke of her, she was more than the help too.

Catherine maintained a steady chatter directed at Florence. "She's here. It's Aunt Louisa, see? She's very beautiful, isn't she? And she's a proper lady, just like Sister Ignatius said she would be." The girl ran over to Florence and wrapped her arms around the woman's legs. Florence put her hand to Catherine's head. Louisa noticed the woman's long, delicate fingers.

"I should have introduced you," Harry said. "This is Florence, who saved us." He looked briefly at the native woman and away. "She looks after Catherine."

The woman nodded. "Pleased to meet you, ma'am," she said. She smiled gently with her mouth closed.

Louisa noticed a look pass between Harry and Florence then. She had a distinct impression of being shut out, as if there was something between the pair that they weren't saying.

"Catherine's been looking forward to your visit, haven't you?" Harry said, his eyes flicking to Florence again and then back to Louisa.

The little girl smiled and curtsied. "Where did you learn those lovely manners?" Louisa said. She still felt the urge to reach out to the girl, although it was fading now in the face of whatever was going on between Harry and Florence, which Louisa couldn't fathom. The looks between them were full of meaning. She recalled Alexander saying something about Harry and a native woman in Cairns, but Louisa hadn't listened. Alexander had never liked Harry, too many years between them and Harry so adored by their mother. Alexander had been concerned, Louisa remembered now. Could the woman have been Florence? Surely not.

"From Sister Ignatius," the girl said. "She said you would be a lady, and I must curtsy to a lady."

Louisa laughed. "I'm your aunt, Catherine, your daddy's sister. You don't have to curtsy to me."

Catherine smiled conspiratorially. "I know that," she said in a whisper. "But it was very important to Sister Ignatius." Then she ran to Florence. "Oh, Florence, isn't it wonderful to have Aunt Louisa here with us? Aren't we so lucky? Well, aren't we?"

"Yes, she's your family," Florence said, stressing each

syllable of the word *family*. Florence flashed Louisa a look. It was as if she were sizing Louisa up.

Catherine was prattling on about the shells she'd found on the beach yesterday. One of them, if you listened carefully, had kept the sea inside, and Catherine would show Louisa, if she liked, once they'd had some tea. But they were most definitely going for a swim that afternoon. Daddy had promised. And scones, there were scones, with real jam they'd made from the mulberries they'd grown in the winter, even though Sister Ignatius said you couldn't grow mulberries on the island. But Florence could grow anything: "Can't you, Florence?" Catherine said. Florence only smiled.

When Florence left the room, Catherine trailing behind her, Louisa said to Harry, "Interesting woman."

"Who?" he said.

"Your housekeeper, Florence. Catherine adores her."

"Oh," he said. "Yes. We'd be lost without Florence. She does so much around the house. And for Catherine."

"That must be a relief," Louisa said.

Harry looked at her. "Florence was the housekeeper in Cairns when Alexander and I were there," he said, as if reading her thoughts. "She's Islander. When we had Catherine she came back here and we . . . She helped and now . . . I can't do it all."

So Alexander was jumping to conclusions, as usual, Louisa thought, but, still, there was something.

"Of course you can't," Louisa said, noting how he skirted over the loss of Julia. Harry would tell her about it when he was ready. "You're the only doctor here?" she said, changing the subject.

He nodded. "I have a doctor who comes up from Cairns

once a month, but other than that it's just me," he said. "It's not as hard as it sounds. It's more like having a big family. You don't really take time off." Louisa knew exactly what he meant.

He frowned at Catherine, who had come back into the room quietly. She'd sat on the floor at first but then had moved to Louisa's lap. "You don't need to be bothering your aunt," Harry said, more sternly than needed.

"Oh, she's all right," Louisa said, putting her arms around the little girl. She smelled sweet, Louisa thought. Harry was still frowning at his daughter, preoccupied with his thoughts.

"Well, you're right at home, Catherine," Harry said. "Come, let's get down to the beach before dark." The girl sprang from Louisa's lap, just like the Scotties when Louisa mentioned a walk.

Louisa had no bathing suit to change into and wouldn't have dared try to bathe anyway. She remained in her woolen skirt and blouse, leaving the jacket in her room, which was on the upper floor next to Catherine's looking out toward the sea. Although the sun would soon set, the heat was relentless. It would never be cool here, Louisa thought.

Catherine had shed her dress and was wearing shorts with a boy's singlet that was too big for her. Harry was in trunks with an old button-up shirt and a wide-brimmed straw hat. They climbed down a path behind the main house that took them to a cozy beach scalloped by rocks at one end and palms at the other. There was a little boathouse above the beach itself. Catherine had scooted ahead, Harry following her. Louisa, who'd carefully picked her way down the path, took a moment to peer through the briny window. There was a sailing skiff on mounts inside. She wondered if this was the boat Harry had taken out when Julia drowned.

Catherine took to the water as if she lived there, running out alone into the sea and then diving under, terrifying Louisa. In the twilight, she watched her little niece swimming out into the sea and catching the gentle waves back in with her father. Catherine was not like a person, Louisa thought then. She was like a sea creature. That was what she smelled like. It was the sea, clean and pure and alive.

9

After returning from the beach, they'd eaten dinner—cold chicken and salad followed by jelly and cold custard—in the conservatory that opened onto the back terrace. They'd retired to the front parlor, which was marginally cooler. Catherine had fallen asleep in Florence's lap over on the sofa, and Florence was sitting there quietly stroking the child's hair while Louisa and Harry talked. The drapes and windows were still closed to the sea, although Louisa thought she could hear it in the distance. A breeze blew in through the front door of the house. "We were out sailing," Harry said suddenly, looking not at Louisa but at Florence.

Louisa was surprised that Florence had remained with them after dinner. She'd got up to leave and it was Harry who'd asked her to stay. Catherine, for her part, seemed accustomed to Florence being a part of their life together. Florence was just like a mother to the child, Louisa thought.

Harry had been drinking; whisky before dinner and now

a glass or more of port. Was that how he managed after Julia's death? Louisa wondered.

He smiled weakly now. "We'd taken lunch and headed for Banks Island, which is north of here. Florence's people are from there, aren't they?" he said, and she nodded gently. "I do a monthly clinic and I used to take them sometimes. Julia liked to get out and about."

The way he said Julia's name made Louisa look up. There was something in his voice. Was it anger? Louisa thought it might be.

"You have to understand the weather patterns here," he said, putting his glass down heavily on the table in front of him. "It can be fine, not a cloud in the sky, and you think you'll head out. It was a blue day, wasn't it, Florence?"

Florence didn't answer him, didn't even look up, only sat looking down at Catherine.

Harry turned back to Louisa. "Actually, Florence said there was a storm coming. Florence, do you recall?"

Florence looked up at him now and nodded slowly.

"You knew. I wish I'd listened. Later, I wished I'd listened. You understand the weather." He pointed at Florence, took another sip of his drink. Louisa had the urge to move the bottle away from him.

The clinic was soon dispensed with, he said, so they ate their picnic and afterward Harry and Catherine took a swim. "She couldn't swim," he said, referring, Louisa assumed, to Julia, and they made for home in good time. "Banks Island is a couple of hours away even if the wind is up. And we were lucky, I thought. The breeze was good. But then the sea got rough, and the wind whipped up the swell. Still no storm that

I could see, but I know boats. I know what you do. I did it all right. I did everything to stop it." He looked up at her. "I did my best, Louie."

"Of course you did, darling," she said, noting the awful anguish in his eyes. "God, it must have been awful, Harry."

He saw the storm front then, he said, approaching from the southwest, between their boat and Thursday Island. He pulled into a bay near one of the unpopulated islands, thinking they would be protected there until the storm passed. But even in the shelter of the bay the water was wild. "The anchor wouldn't hold and we were soon swept back out." He shook his head, looked as if he might cry. "She shouldn't have . . ." He stopped and sighed.

The storm was furious, he said. "When the mast cracked, I knew we were done for." He paused. "You can't do anything without a mast. We just had to wait and hope." He shook his head. "You've no idea what it's like."

He drank again then, pausing so long Louisa thought he might have forgotten he was telling the story. She looked across at Catherine, who twitched in her sleep, as if her father's telling was being lived in her very dreams. Florence was still stroking the girl's hair and Louisa had the strangest urge to tell her to stop. She's not yours, she's ours, Louisa wanted to say.

Later, after she returned home to London, Louisa told Ruth how she'd felt about Florence with Catherine. "Was it because the housekeeper was black?" Ruth had asked.

"Of course not," Louisa said. "At least, I don't think it was. I think it was because Catherine was family. It hit me very suddenly that she's bound to me. I could see so much of Harry in her. I knew she was ours."

Harry followed Louisa's eye to Catherine. "I couldn't provide comfort. That's the thing. I couldn't help her." He stared at Florence. "A boat overturns relatively quietly," he said. "It's as if nothing is happening and yet your whole world is falling apart.

"Catherine screamed when we went in the water." He swallowed hard. "She was tiny. The swell, Louisa, it's likely to tear anything out of your hands. I just held on to Catherine."

"Of course," Louisa said. "It's what anyone would do in your situation."

They only had the one life preserver, he explained. He left Julia the life preserver and swam with little Catherine for an island. The storm passed, he said. He was able to save his daughter but not his wife. The life preserver washed ashore the next morning. Julia was gone. "Why couldn't she just hold on?" he said, glaring now at Florence.

Florence was a study in repressed emotion, Louisa thought. Her face was set tight, her arms folded around Catherine. Louisa couldn't say what the other woman's feelings were, only that she was having trouble keeping them in check. Later Louisa said to her, "It was a shame my brother's wife didn't listen to you that day, about the storm." Louisa saw that tight mouth again before Florence replied, "Sad day, miss. Sad, sad day."

It was later that night. They'd gone to bed early, Catherine still asleep in Florence's arms, Harry exhausted. Louisa woke filled with fear.

The dream, she'd had the dream. It was the first time in months, since before she'd left England. But here, it was, back.

It was always the same. Someone was chasing her, chasing her, a pursuer whose face she never saw. She couldn't run, and she couldn't scream. But then she heard a child crying. At first she thought it must be Catherine but it wasn't Catherine. It wasn't any child Louisa knew. And then she was wide awake, and the feeling she had was sadness not fear, tears on her face she couldn't remember shedding. Her body was wet with sweat. She sat up in bed, made herself breathe slowly and steadily. The brain, in panic, will believe the lungs if you can force them to breathe slow and steady, she knew. It's something she would say to those poor soldiers whose minds remained full of the horror they'd seen.

It had been Louisa's own fault. Her mother had all but said so and she herself had come to believe it. It had been her own fault. But these dreams were such a punishment. They were so real, threw her into such a panic, they made her question her very sanity. She gathered her nightdress at the chest and bit down on it hard to calm herself.

She'd said, "Yes, I'd love you to walk me home." That was forward of her. She shouldn't have used that word, love, I'd love you to walk me home. Was that it? She shouldn't have been curious. Alexander had said that. You led him on, Louisa. Did she? Is that what had happened?

They'd both been at the meeting, organized by Jane Maxwell. It was the week after Mr. Baldwin had ordered the police to start force-feeding the hunger strikers. Louisa had gone to the meeting to see what could be done and had been surprised to see Jonathan Pyne there, seated near the front, offering to write to the Government, suggesting all his colleagues do the same. That was Elizabeth's view, that it was the meeting, Louisa involving herself with the Pankhursts. That's what led to trouble. It wasn't logical. It didn't have to be.

Jonathan Pyne was handsome and clever and, of all the Edinburgh surgeons, he was the one who was supportive of women in the profession. Oh, others spoke as if they would be, but as soon as you wanted an actual placement under their tutelage, they made themselves scarce.

Elizabeth had written Jonathan Pyne on Louisa's behalf. "Of course," he'd replied immediately. "She'll join a lively team." He'd accepted Louisa into the surgical training program and had been a marvelous tutor.

Louisa had liked him from the start. He was witty and self-deprecating, and if he hadn't been married—his operating room nurse; three sons—then any one of the women training with him would have accepted him as a suitor.

Yes, she'd said that night, I'd love you to walk me home. And then, at her door, he'd said, "I'll see you inside." Louisa knew he was married, knew he had children. If she'd thought about it at all, she'd have said she knew it made her safe.

"Where did you study medicine?" he'd asked. He was in her sitting room.

She'd started at the University of London, finished at the School of Medicine for Women.

"Did you take lovers in medical school?" he said then.

It was an impertinent question, she knew. She wanted to meet his audacity with her own.

"I would try to impress suitors with my wit," she said. "But wit is not such an impressive quality in a woman, it turns out."

"It impresses me," he said.

There was a silence.

"Then you, Jonathan, are easily impressed," she said, attempting to laugh off his comment.

"On the contrary," he said, moving toward her.

Later she would tell Ruth, "I let him kiss me. I know I did wrong. I let him kiss me but then I told him to go and he would not. And he . . ." She could not bring herself to finish. And dear Ruth would hold her friend and let her cry, tell her, This wasn't your fault, Louisa. It wasn't your fault at all. Ruth was the only one who said that, the only one.

He told Louisa he wanted her. She was shocked, said something stupid like, "I beg your pardon?"

He leaned in and kissed her and she could smell rich tobacco and feel the scratch of his beard on her cheeks. She responded without thinking, her arms around him before she knew what was happening. He was not a tall man, but he was broadly built and strong. He held her in his arms and for a moment she forgot herself. But then she pulled back from him. "Dr. Pyne," she said. "I don't think . . ."

"You must indulge me," he said, his voice rough. He was pulling at his collar. "I cannot bear it any longer." He moved toward her then and Louisa found herself afraid. It was still fun, in a way, a game of cat and mouse, she told herself, but panic was rising like bile in her throat now, despite her attempts to reassure herself. Louisa was twenty-five, a good doctor, but totally inexperienced with men. The truth was she'd taken no lovers in medical school. There had been no one, not ever.

He advanced toward her and she retreated, until suddenly

the wall was at her back. Still he kept moving toward her. She was afraid now; a hard, relentless fear that made her breath come in short gasps and her vision blur. It was the expression on his face, the same expression she'd seen just before he began to cut a patient.

It was from here that her memory always fractured, coming back only as single sensations, unrelated to one another, that never collected themselves into an experience she could relate to. She might recall a smell of sweet fruit, dark hair on a wrist, or a damp chill in the air, but not put these individual sensations into a context. This was what was most unnerving.

The next morning, Jonathan himself gave her a version, and for many years it was easier to accept his memory. It seemed so sure. "How are you today?" he'd said, just before he was to go into surgery, a sly smile on his face, his hands in the air in front of him, clean. He'd winked. As if they had been lovers. That's what his smile said, the wink. Was that what he believed? she wondered. Was that what he believed they had been to one another?

Now, with the intervening years, she blamed memory entirely. She told herself of course she wouldn't be able to summon the details. Of course they would be blurred. Still, the incomplete images came to her, harmless ones and some that were not harmless, and she would do her best to remain calm until they passed. They always passed. And for that, she could be thankful. And the dream. The dream was the most unsettling, the faceless monster catching up, catching up.

Now, in her bedroom down the hall from Harry and Catherine, she could hear water lapping at the beach below. It was the sea at peace, no hint of a pursuer, no crying child, just birds greeting a new day. It was so incongruous with the dream. She lay back down in the bed and waited for the sun and the comfort it would bring.

They took breakfast in the dining room off the kitchen. Louisa could feel the blast of heat when they opened the French windows to the back terrace. She'd slept so poorly and the awakened house felt more oppressive not less, despite the bright sun that came in through the windows when she pulled open the drapes. Downstairs, she noticed the windows in the back wall of the house, built against the hill, were open. They were the only windows that didn't look at the sea.

Catherine was in the yard with Florence, who was hanging out the laundry. The little girl was running between sheets and Florence was pretending she couldn't find her.

"She's bright, Harry," Louisa said. They were still sitting at the table. "What will you do about school?"

"She already goes to school," Harry said. He didn't look any worse for the night's drinking. Perhaps he hadn't had as much as Louisa thought.

"Here?"

"Yes, here," he said. There was a touch of argumentativeness in his tone. Louisa didn't know why. "By rights, she shouldn't start for another year or two, but she was so keen and the nuns all know her from the hospital. So she started early."

Louisa sat forward in her chair. "That's all very well for the basics. But what about if she wants to go on, Harry? Surely they don't have the subjects she'll need."

"The nuns are French, so Catherine's already learning the language. One of them plays piano and Catherine's keen to learn. She'll read with me, write, mathematics, a bit of science. There's nothing wrong with the school here, Louie." He looked at her. "And here is where her mother . . . Here is where she started."

"Of course," Louisa said. "I'm just worried about you. If you were at home, I could help with Catherine."

He sighed. "Louisa, I'm sorry. But the island is the safest place for Catherine."

Later, she thought about his use of the word *safest*. It was an odd word, she thought, and how he reckoned his daughter would be safe on an island surrounded by the sea that had taken his wife, Louisa hardly knew.

"And she's happy—aren't you?" Catherine had run up and jumped into her father's lap. He smiled and nuzzled his face in her hair.

"I most certainly am," Catherine said, in that little adult voice of hers. And then suddenly, as if to confirm she was still a child, she jumped down and dipped her finger into a bowl of cream and put it in her mouth. She watched Louisa as she did this.

Harry looked at his sister. "I suppose I should tell her she's not to do that," he said, "but I don't seem to have the necessary . . . will, I suppose, to correct her. She's so very precious." He patted his daughter's head. Again, Louisa thought of Julia, of Harry's loss. No wonder he clung to his daughter. Catherine was still focused on that creamy finger, sucking the life out of it. After she removed it from her mouth, she smiled widely.

"Come with me," she said to Louisa, offering the sticky hand, which Louisa took.

Catherine led her back inside and out onto the front verandah. "You'll feel better out here, Aunt Louisa. Daddy thinks it keeps the cool air in to have all the windows shut, but Florence says it just makes it hotter."

"I think I'd have to agree with Florence," Louisa said, thankful for the moist breeze that came from the sea, "although I don't know that anything would make it comfortable." She regarded the child. "You like Florence, don't you?"

Catherine nodded. She sat down facing Louisa. "I don't have a mother." She sighed, another adult gesture, as if she'd learned this was how she should act.

"I know. That must be very hard."

She nodded. "You could be my mother."

Louisa smiled. "No, I can't be your mother." The breeze was delightful over her face.

"Why not?"

"Well, for a start, I live in England. And second, I'm your aunt."

"You could come here and be a nurse and be my mother. Also, I know third comes after second." She smiled as if the matter were now settled. "And you need to take off some of your undergarments or you'll simply boil to death."

Louisa laughed. "How do you know?"

"Sister Ignatius told me. I don't wear any unders but bloomers." She leaned forward. "It's all right for ladies in the heat."

"Catherine, about what you said before, I wouldn't be a

nurse. I'm a doctor. If I came here, I'd still be a doctor." It was important, Louisa thought, that girls understood from an early age that women, too, could be doctors.

"Oh very well," the little girl said. "But then we'll have two doctors and who will do the nursing?"

10

Louisa spent the day exploring the island with Catherine and Harry. They took the trap down to the town center, and from there to a church built in memory of lives lost when a ship struck a reef and sank. They went to the Catholic church, too, next to the school Catherine attended. There was a service being held. The Islanders were singing. Their harmonies were beautiful, Louisa thought, and the church was filled with light. She asked Harry if they could stay awhile and listen. He just smiled.

In the afternoon, they went down to the beach again. Louisa could see what appealed to Harry about his life on the island. Many people stopped to greet them, but it was more than being a big fish in a little pond. He felt at his ease here, Louisa saw. And the island did have a strange charm, she thought. He'd found a home.

That night, Louisa slept a dreamless sleep, waking once more to the sound of the sea.

After breakfast, Harry asked her to walk Catherine down to the school. The day before, she'd taken Catherine's advice, removed her corset and camisole, leaving only her brassiere and linen blouse. Today she took off her heavy wool stockings and petticoat, too, but had to wear the wool skirt as she had nothing cooler.

They walked through town, the heat becoming increasingly oppressive with every minute in the sun. Louisa thought she might die in her skirt and boots, the sun beating through the parasol she carried. She could almost feel the top of her head burning. Catherine was oblivious. She was like a tree, Louisa thought, taking her energy from the sun.

As they walked along the waterfront, Catherine pointed out three children about fifty yards from the shore. "They're the Walton boys," she said, "from Hammond Island. I don't like them. They pull my hair."

Farther out in the water from the Walton boys Louisa saw a woman in a dinghy. She was standing up, brandishing a very large rifle. "What's she got a gun for?" Louisa said, horrified.

"Sharks," Catherine said matter-of-factly. "That's their mother."

The schoolhouse was a single room in a little timber cottage with window openings that had no glass and a doorway with no door. Louisa met the nuns who taught Catherine. The one Catherine had mentioned, Sister Ignatius, was one of those wise old owls, with bright eyes behind wire-rimmed spectacles and a veil crooked on her head. She seemed pleased that Catherine had her aunt visiting. "We worry about the child too," she said, as if Louisa had expressed anxiety, which she hadn't. There was another young nun, a Sister Ursula, who'd studied science in Brisbane, Sister Ignatius told Louisa. "We're very proud she's chosen a vocation." She was a dear, the younger nun, Louisa thought, reminding Louisa a little of herself in her early twenties, more interested in science than in people.

After leaving Catherine, Louisa went on to the hospital, where Harry had agreed to meet her. It was a sprawling building, two rooms in front, a built-in verandah down one side and extensions to the rear, on the edge of the peninsula.

They treated Europeans and natives both, Harry said. "On the mainland, they split them, the natives in one place and the whites in another. We don't do that—and I'm against it. A patient's a patient, don't you agree?" Louisa smiled. He knew she did.

Louisa met the nurses and then toured the two wards. Harry said the work varied. Pearl divers suffered the bends. Occasionally, there were shark attacks. "They're usually dead before they're pulled from the water," Harry said, "but we've had a couple of bites you wouldn't have thought anyone could survive, but then the natives do. They don't always come to me. They like their own healers. Other than that it's just run-of-the-mill."

Afterward, they shared lunch in Harry's office. It was Louisa who brought up the future. She'd decided to be open about her purpose. "Harry, the truth is I came here to convince you to come home," she said.

He shook his head. "I won't come back to England. I'm happy here, Louie. So is Catherine. And it was the last place we . . ." He didn't finish. "But I did want to talk to you. There's something I really need to tell you." He breathed in, out, regarded her carefully.

"At the hospital here, we need nurses," he said finally, "and I agree Catherine needs her family. She needs a woman in her life, actually. I thought you could . . ."

"You thought I could what?" Louisa said.

"You could come here and take up one of the nursing positions. With your training you'd be ideal." He thrust his chin out, as if making his point more strongly.

"You thought I could just give up medical practice, drop everything and come to the island for you?" She tried to keep her voice level but failed. She expected this kind of attitude from Alexander but never Harry, who'd always respected her vocation. "You weren't thinking I'd just up and leave my practice?" So this was where Catherine had got the idea.

"Well, I was, actually. She's just a baby." He swallowed hard and blinked, perhaps to stop the threat of tears, but Louisa found it hard to sympathize. The nerve of her brother, thinking she would give up everything. She couldn't just give it away. How dare he expect her to? Really! Louisa was a doctor, same as he was.

Louisa left the island two weeks later. Harry had made it clear he would not come home to England under any circumstances, and Louisa made it clear she had no intention of uprooting and moving to Australia. She'd done the right thing, she told herself. She'd visited her brother. She'd asked him to come home. He hadn't agreed.

All the same, Louisa had felt awful leaving the little girl. Catherine had jumped into Louisa's lap on the ferry—they'd come on board to help Louisa with her things—and had thrown her little arms around Louisa's neck. Louisa had been quite chirpy until then. "You could stay," Catherine said, tears in her eyes. "You could say and we could be friends."

Louisa had held back her tears. She'd forced herself to smile and handed Catherine off to Florence. She'd told herself she didn't feel anything. But of course she did. After she departed the island, she could still smell Catherine's hair in her clothes, and it brought tears to her eyes. On the ship home, she often found herself crying. Ruth Luxton would surely have approved. She was always one for expressing strong emotion. But not Louisa. She'd stand out on the deck alone and the tears would come unbidden. This won't do me any good at all, Louisa thought. Still, the tears would come.

And there things had stood. Louisa wrote at Christmas every year, and for Catherine's birthday in August. She had clothes made for her niece. She had to estimate Catherine's size because Harry never responded when she wrote and asked. She had a dressmaker run them up: a blue-and-white gingham dress with a red sash, just like the one Catherine had worn the first time they met, and a pretty hair ribbon to match; a green silk dress, although Louisa had no idea where Catherine would wear it; gloves and shoes, skirts, blouses, socks and stockings. Louisa would keep them for a week or so, looking at them each day, and then send them, always with a little message.

She never heard back from Catherine, and from Harry she just had the most general news, nothing about the clothes, and not even much about his daughter.

Louisa thought of Catherine often, it was true. She'd experience that familiar aching in her chest, not really for Catherine, she knew. For another child, a child who never was.

She told no one, not even Ruth, not until she was sure. The tender breasts, the missed menses, the nausea. She'd heard enough women report the symptoms.

She debased herself further, went to see him. "Of course," he said. "Of course I'll help. We'll get rid of it."

"Get rid of it?" she said. "I don't want to get rid of it. I love you."

How could she say that after what he did? She felt sick when she thought of this later, telling him she loved him.

"You must understand," he said. "I'm married. I have a family. I'm unable to . . . You know that, Louisa."

That was the moment she realized how very alone she was.

The pregnancy was too far along, she knew, and soon it would be obvious to everyone. She went to her mother, who was not unkind. Louisa told Elizabeth lies, protected him. He'd been such a cad and she protected him even still. She couldn't understand herself. A medical student, she said. The father was a medical student she knew.

"Good God," her mother said. "Won't he do the honorable thing? All that study, Louie. How could you?" Her mother blamed the protests. "If you'd kept your head down, and done as I said, we wouldn't be here." Louisa blamed the protests too. If she hadn't gone, if she'd done as her mother said, he never would have walked her home.

Her mother soon stopped asking about the medical student, came up with another plan. Perhaps she guessed the truth. Louisa would go through with the pregnancy, her mother said, and they'd find a family through the local doctor at Aldeburgh who could be trusted to act with discretion.

The birth was mercifully quick. She'd hardly felt the first contraction before she was on the floor in the bathroom. She knew her blood pressure was high, had told her mother so. Her mother called the midwife as arranged. "All these doctors in the family and we're calling the midwife," was the last thing Louisa said before she lost consciousness. She remembered something; a loud voice. The baby, we're losing the baby.

When she recovered, it was Elizabeth who sat at her bedside, held her hand. "The child," she said. "We lost him. A little boy. A perfect little boy, Louie, stillborn." Tears in her poor mother's eyes. The cord had been wrapped around his neck. There was nothing to be done.

Afterward, Louisa would think of the boy as he might have been at various ages; a scallywag, clever, big green eyes. Was it wrong that she felt relief more than sadness?

PART III

London, August 1925

11

Catherine woke to the sound of a bird in the back garden. It was one she'd heard before, and she'd been meaning to ask Nellie what it was. Its song was so long and sweet, nothing like the parrots back on the island that screeched and squawked the morning awake.

She got up from her bed and looked out the window for the bird, but all she could see were the motor cars on the street and people hurrying along the footpath on their way to work. A soft rain fell. It would be cold on the way to school, she thought.

This was Catherine's life now: the city, the school, her aunt and Nellie. At first, she'd been able to conjure up the smells of the island—the kelp growing near the rocks or drifting in after a storm, the coconuts the boys threw down from the trees and cracked, the sun itself, which had a smell like hot linen—but all that was gone now. And she couldn't remember the colors, only that they were much brighter.

Catherine opened the window wide and put her head outside. There was the little bird, in the tree in the back lane, tiny beak, neat little tail, a well-mannered bird, Catherine thought, the kind of bird her aunt would like Catherine to be. But Catherine was more a screecher and squawker, however much she wished she could be a quiet little singer. It *was* cold, she thought then. To her right, the construction noise on Commercial Road had started up. It was later than she'd thought, the morning sun hidden behind clouds. But at least she'd been wrong about the rain. Catherine jumped down the stairs two at a time. Why hadn't anyone called her?

"Have you made your bed?" Nellie said when Catherine found her in the kitchen.

"Of course," Catherine said. "Is Louisa gone?"

"Yes, and you're lucky. She's fit to fry a cat this morning."

"What does that mean?"

"*Furious* would be my summary. Now, go back up and make your bed and then we'll have some breakfast. And a talk."

"Is there any mail for me today?" Catherine said. She was expecting a letter from Michael. His last letter had been an angry one. He blamed her for leaving the island, she knew, for leaving Florence and him.

Nellie frowned. "Why? Are you expecting something?"

"No, I just wondered," Catherine said.

"Hasn't been yet," Nellie said, still frowning. She was such a sweet person really, Catherine often thought, but she seemed to think she had to be in charge. Catherine considered refusing about the bed. What could Nellie do? And how did she know Catherine hadn't made her bed? She was pondering this on the way up the stairs when she stopped suddenly.

She remembered.

Yesterday she'd swum. For the first time since she'd left Australia, she'd swum. And she'd managed that swim, the swim Darcy said Catherine couldn't possibly do, the swim to prove whether she was a Henley girl or not. That's what Darcy had said, hadn't she? And then Darcy hadn't even turned up. Catherine had shown them, she thought. She'd made it across, landing exactly where she'd intended. Miss Anderson, the principal, had seen her. The girls had seen her. Louisa had seen her. But Darcy hadn't even shown up.

Swimming was something the children did together on the island. They sometimes went to one of the islands nearest Thursday, or if they were out in the canoes, they might swim to an island to explore. Swimming was part of their lives. But at Henley, no one swam, although their English teacher, Miss Proud, personally knew Miss Gleitze, she'd told them, who was going to be the first woman to swim the English Channel. Miss Gleitze is an example to us all, Miss Proud said.

Catherine had tried to fit in at Henley, the school where, Louisa said, she would be challenged. It was going to be different from the little island school, her aunt said, and Catherine would have to use her brains. Nellie had taken her to buy the uniform: a gray wool pleated skirt, a white linen blouse, a tie, blazer, gloves and hat. They were like restraints, Catherine thought, the skirt so tight around her legs it was difficult to move, the hard shoes that hurt her feet and clacked against the sidewalk. But the worst thing was the stockings. Catherine could not for the life of her see how Nellie gathered them into a little foot that you could poke your own foot into. When she tried to pull them on, she tore them. "Never mind, I can darn them," Nellie said, smiling kindly.

It was Nellie who took Catherine on her first day, walking the mile from Wellclose Square to the high gates that fronted Henley. Even Nellie looked unsure, Catherine thought. There were tight groups of girls on the footpath outside the gates. Some of them turned and stared as she approached. Even though Catherine looked the same in her skirt and blouse, she also knew she was totally different from these girls with their fair skin and English accents. She was new. She was one of the tallest too, which only made her stand out more. She felt self-conscious. How strange to come from the island, where she was one of few whites—many of the European children were off at boarding schools on the mainland, so that most of the students at the local school were natives—to a place where everyone was white and yet feel she was the one who was different.

Catherine went first to Miss Anderson's office. She was put in with the juniors for her lessons, since—as the teacher said to her on the first day—she'd have learned nothing much among the savages. The littler girls were kind but Catherine felt like Gulliver in Lilliput among them. At lunch, she sat with the older girls. Ivy Somerville was nice to her from the start, offering her a place at their table, and Darcy, almost as tall as Catherine, gave a little speech of welcome.

After a week, Catherine moved up to the class with the bigger girls. They were reading *Jane Eyre*, which Catherine had already read, and doing French verbs Catherine already knew. She didn't find the work difficult, although her new teacher, Miss Mason, said her handwriting was atrocious. She had trouble with needlework, and the ball games they played weren't familiar. But school in London wasn't harder than it had been on the island, Catherine quickly realized. It was just different.

It was after they'd had the English lesson where Miss Proud had mentioned Mercedes Gleitze. It might have been Ida who'd mentioned swimming, but it was Darcy who'd urged Catherine on. Darcy's father had read about it in the paper. Catherine had said she, Catherine, might swim the English Channel too. She didn't know why she'd said it. She had no idea whether she could actually swim the English Channel and she wasn't normally someone who told untruths or even exaggerated. But she wanted them to know she could do something. She could swim.

Catherine had seen the picture of Mercedes Gleitze in the newspaper, a small, dark-haired girl they called the mermaid typist. Mercedes was seen as daring and courageous, wearing a swimming suit that Louisa said was immodest. In the picture, Gleitze was wading out into dark water. Cold, Catherine had thought. The water looked cold.

Darcy had called Catherine a liar, said she couldn't possibly swim the Channel. This was what Darcy was like, sometimes kindly, more often cruel. Darcy said Catherine couldn't even swim the Thames. Of course I could, Catherine had said. She might not know the Channel but she'd seen the Thames. She'd thought it would be easy.

But the Thames was a tidal river, she soon learned. She'd watched the river rush in and out over several weeks. There were all those boats. And the water, when she went down and put a hand in, was like ice. But having made the claim, Catherine knew she had to prove herself now.

Ida and Darcy couldn't swim at all, Catherine knew. Most of

the girls couldn't here at Henley, which surprised Catherine. She'd never met anyone who couldn't swim, except her aunt, who was so afraid of water she never even put her toes in, she said.

Darcy had befriended Catherine at first. But then there was a day when she changed completely. She was sitting in the dining room with the older girls and Catherine came in and they all went quiet. Catherine had a sense they'd been talking about her. Darcy looked at Catherine and said, "You look like a boy." A few of the other girls giggled. Catherine didn't know what to say. Darcy said it again. "Are you a boy? Are you secretly a boy?" More giggles. Catherine shook her head.

"Don't mind her," Ivy said later. "She's just jealous. You got a higher score than her on the spelling." It was true Catherine had done better than Darcy in the spelling. But Darcy was the most popular girl in the class, a prefect. Why would Catherine's doing well in spelling bother her?

The Islanders were not like this, not ever. Catherine really was different from them, in skin color if nothing else, but Catherine was accepted as one of them. Catherine's teachers on the island, the Sacred Heart nuns, were kindly. Her teachers at the new school, and especially Miss Mason, were not. "Did they not teach you this?" she'd say, even when Catherine knew an answer. Catherine quickly stopped speaking up in class and became wary around Darcy, who was sometimes friendly and sometimes not.

Miss Mason taught them French. Catherine had taught French to the younger students on the island. But instead of this helping, it only seemed to make matters worse. One day when Ivy was worried because she'd forgotten her French copybook, Catherine had offered to swap. Catherine gave Ivy her own copybook, which she'd already filled in, thinking she could manage getting into trouble better than Ivy since she'd never forgotten her own book before and Ivy forgot hers regularly. "Miss Mason won't know," Catherine said as she scratched out her name. But Miss Mason did know, and blamed Catherine. "You think you're very clever, young lady," Miss Mason said. "But we'll see who feels clever soon."

When Miss Mason brought the cane down on Catherine's open palm, the physical pain was excruciating. No one had ever hit Catherine before. The nuns on the island were gentle, and Catherine's father would never have dreamed of striking her. But worse than the pain was what Catherine saw, the look of satisfaction on Miss Mason's face. Why would the teacher enjoy hitting her? Catherine wondered. It shocked her that someone could enjoy another's pain.

As well as the caning, Catherine had to visit the principal's office to tell Miss Anderson what she had done.

"We don't like liars here, Catherine," the principal had said. "Did you lie?"

Catherine only nodded, still smarting from the cane on her fingers, unable to trust her voice.

"Would you like me to speak to your aunt about this?" Miss Anderson said. Catherine didn't answer. "I didn't think so. Well, I'm willing to let this incident go, but you must never be a liar again. Do you understand?"

Catherine only stared at her. She was still upset and now she was angry as well. How dare they? she thought. How dare they hit someone for helping a friend? What kind of place was this?

"Very good," the principal said finally. "Dismissed." Catherine stood there for a moment, staring at the principal, and then turned and walked out.

Catherine thought of telling Louisa what was happening at the school. But when Louisa asked how school was going, Catherine found herself saying it was going well. What would she say to her aunt? Louisa was always so busy. She wanted to please Louisa, who'd made so much of how carefully she'd selected Henley. If Catherine wasn't fitting in, it must be Catherine's fault. And what would Louisa do? She might blame Catherine too.

But swimming, Catherine had thought, was something the girls at Henley would value. And Catherine could swim. If she could swim across the river, she'd thought, it would show them—those girls, her teachers, even Louisa and Nellie—that she could do something that mattered. She hadn't thought through what might happen next, but at least something would be different, she thought. It would say to them, "This is who I am. This is what I can do."

But it hadn't been like that at all. Louisa had been angry. Miss Anderson had been angry. And as for Darcy, she hadn't even turned up to watch. It was the worst possible thing to have done, Catherine thought now. Darcy had known exactly what would happen. How could a person do that to another? England wasn't just another country. It was a whole different world.

Catherine looked in her closet. At least she wouldn't be putting on her white blouse and tie today, or that awful wool skirt that stopped her from running. Not the blazer, nor the gloves, nor those horrid shoes. She sat down heavily on the bed. She knew she'd come to London to go to the school. That was the reason. Louisa had once told her that education was the way to freedom. And now, Catherine had failed at the school.

She made the bed, after a fashion, pulling the eiderdown over the disorderly sheets, and went back downstairs. "Nellie, I don't have to go to school." She was trying it out.

"No, you don't," Nellie said as she put a plate of buttered toast and a glass of milk on the table. "What a little idiot you are."

Not Nellie too, Catherine thought then.

"It's a stain on your character. Have you seen this?" It was the morning paper. There was Catherine on the riverbank.

"That's me!" she exclaimed. "I'm in the news!"

"For goodness' sake, don't let your aunt hear you talking like that. Look at you—you look like a harlot."

Catherine had no idea what a harlot was, only that it was something you shouldn't be. She'd heard the word once before. It was what one of the nurses at the clinic called Nellie herself. Nellie and Catherine had gone to Princes Square. Nellie was in picking up Louisa's gowns to have them laundered. "You know she was an East End girl before she met Dr. Louisa," one nurse said to another. "A harlot," the other nurse whispered. "I never knew."

Later, Catherine had asked Nellie what they meant.

"East End girl is a working girl," Nellie said. "Did they not have them in Australia?"

Catherine shook her head.

"I had to do bad things, Catherine, very bad things." Nellie's voice, normally loud and clear, sounded small and afraid. She didn't sound like bossy Nellie at all.

"Oh, Nellie, you're a dear," Catherine had said. "There

might be badness in the world. But not one bit of it was done by you."

Catherine looked at Nellie over the newspaper now. "I don't much care what they think of me," she said bravely. "If it means I never have to go back to that awful place, I don't much care."

"Yes, you do, Catherine. I know you do. Now, sit down and tell me why you did it and we'll work out what we can do from here to fix it."

She explained to Nellie what Miss Proud had said about swimming and what a great achievement it might be, what the girls had said, especially Darcy and how she'd planned out the swim. "It wasn't actually all that hard, Nellie, but for the cold. The water was colder than I expected. But the swim wasn't hard."

Nellie asked a few more questions about Darcy and the other girls. "So you thought it would make you popular to swim across the river?"

"No," Catherine said, angry now. "I don't like it there. I've tried. I really have. I'm just not what Louisa thinks I am."

Nellie shook her head. "Don't say that. Louisa . . . She's just not used to you. She doesn't know how best to help you. You're not having any trouble with your studies, are you?"

"No."

"I mean, was the schoolwork hard? That was always my problem. I couldn't do the math."

"No, it's not that," Catherine said. "It wasn't hard."

"These girls sound like right little misses to me. Let me talk to Louisa. Your swimming, though, Catherine, has really caused a problem."

Catherine felt like crying then. How to explain to Nellie.

Swimming wasn't the problem. It just was. Swimming was the island. It was Florence. It was her father. It was Michael. It was everything about the life she'd left, the life she'd been taken from and wanted so much to return to. Swimming was Catherine herself.

12

The headline, THE SPEEDY QUICK, was designed to grab attention, Louisa thought, but they hardly needed it with those legs. Louisa looked more closely at the photograph of Catherine in her swimming suit. The blanket was still wrapped around her shoulders, but those legs were totally exposed. Catherine was surrounded by men, the builders, all grinning. Her name was in the headline, Louisa's name. The story that followed was more muted than the photograph but no less damning.

At just fifteen years of age, Australian-born Catherine Quick successfully crossed the tidal Thames yesterday.

Miss Quick is the niece of London doctor Louisa Quick, who has been outspoken in these pages about support for women's health in London's East End, where she operates a hospital and clinic for families. Perhaps her niece is showing her aunt's fiery nature, making her plunge in the narrows from the Globe Wharf to Ratcliffe.

According to ferryman Stan Grant, who watched the swim, most who try have no idea of the pull of the tides. "That river's a snake, she rises twenty feet every day, a sly mistress. But this were a canny lass, swam at the turn and made it in good time."

Amateur Swim Club President Colonel Reg Maudsley said it was a reckless swim for a girl. "Make no mistake. She has none of the strength of lads who've got into trouble. I say she was lucky and she should be charged with recklessness. Imagine if other girls followed her example. Then where would we be?"

Asked if Miss Quick should try out for the Olympic team, Col. Maudsley said, "Certainly not. We want swimmers, not posers, and if I had my way, those girls would stay covered up in the house where they belong."

But ferryman Grant, who's been on the Thames since his boyhood, said he'd never seen the likes of Miss Quick. "She swam a way I'd never seen before," he said. "Using her two arms like windmills and her feet like paddles. She was fast."

Louisa left for work soon after, telling Nellie to wake Catherine by nine. "And get her to write a letter to the principal apologizing for what she's done."

"A letter," Nellie said, looking at Louisa.

"Yes, a letter," Louisa said curtly.

"You don't think, Louisa, that you should stop for a minute and consider whether it's the right school?"

Louisa was standing at the front door. She turned back to look at Nellie. "The school. The school is fine, Nellie. It wasn't the school that swam in the river yesterday."

"No, I suppose not," Nellie said. "But . . ."

"But what?"

"She's a good girl, Louisa."

"No doubt," Louisa said, looking at her pocket watch. She softened. "I must run." But she turned again and looked at Nellie.

"What?" Nellie said.

"I have to tell you something, and I need you to be understanding." Nellie tilted her head, as if asking a question. "I don't want Catherine sending any more letters to Australia."

"What do you mean?" Nellie looked truly confused now.

Oh, Nellie would never understand, Louisa thought, but Louisa must make her.

"I mean, she gives us her letters to mail. I want to make sure they don't get mailed." Louisa smiled a tight little smile, the smile she might give a child who was about to be vaccinated. Don't be afraid, the smile said. I'm in charge.

"Whyever would you do that?" Nellie said.

"It's time for her to move on, Nellie. She's too attached to the past; it's time for her to realize that her future is here. With us." Louisa was nodding.

"They'll write and say they haven't heard from her." Nellie was still looking shocked.

Louisa would need delicacy here, she knew. "I will keep their letters," she said, narrowing her eyes.

"You will what?" Nellie said. Oh, the look on her face. Louisa felt afraid suddenly, as if realizing for the first time what she'd actually done.

But what she said was, "Nellie, this isn't something I'm going to discuss. I am going to hold letters from Australia, just for a few weeks until all this business blows over. And then she can get a stack all at once and we'll send hers. I don't want to go into details but I have reason to believe that Catherine is in danger in her relationships on the island." There, that would do it, Louisa thought.

"What danger?" Nellie said, her voice raised now. "You can't do that, Louisa. It's dishonest. She asks about those letters all the time." Nellie stared at her. "You've started already. You're already holding letters. She'll be asking. Oh, Louisa, you can't be so cruel."

"I have one letter," Louisa said, feeling unsure again suddenly. If Nellie pushed back like this, how would Catherine feel? she thought suddenly. Had she misjudged the situation? No, she'd acted appropriately to protect her niece. Why couldn't Nellie see that?

"No, Louisa, I won't do this," Nellie said. "No good will come of it. She's not a child. She's near grown. She has a right."

Louisa put her hand up to stop Nellie from continuing. "I knew you'd be like this. But many things are not black-and-white in life. There are shades of gray. As a doctor, I deal with them all the time. I don't plan to keep her letters forever, just until we work out what happens next with Catherine, until she has a clear future. Weeks, that's all. Will you help me?"

"Are you sure it's for the best?"

"I am," Louisa said.

"Well, all right," Nellie said. "But only for a few weeks. Then we pass them on."

"Of course," Louisa said, believing that this was what they

would do, not letting herself face the fact that when you begin a deception, it rarely finishes anywhere near where it starts, and it even more rarely has only the consequences you intend.

⟨⟨⟨⟩⟩⟩

Louisa found Ruth in the little office mid-morning with the newspaper open on the desk. Ruth looked up, a quizzical smile on her face, her soft eyes. Louisa grimaced. The reception nurses had seen the article about Catherine too, as had the patients Louisa saw in her first session. She felt like crying suddenly. "Oh God, Ruth, it's terrible, what she's done. I just don't know what she was thinking." She was about to tell Ruth about the letter from the boy Michael and her concern for Catherine now. If anyone would understand, Ruth would, although Louisa wondered if, like Nellie, her friend would take a dim view of Louisa keeping Catherine's mail. But surely she'd see Catherine was in moral danger.

"Why terrible, Louisa?" Ruth said. "It says here she's a born swimmer. I say good for her."

In Catherine's first month in London, Louisa had brought Catherine into the clinic over a few weekends. Catherine had worked with two of Ruth's children, painting an old lockup in the back garden where they now stored medical supplies. Ruth had told Louisa she thought Catherine had tremendous spirit, "Just like you," she'd said. The two of them had got on well.

"Besides," Ruth said now. "It's you who always say women should be able to do whatever they want."

"Don't be ridiculous," Louisa said to her friend. "You

sound like Catherine. Yes, women can do anything, but why would they do this?"

"Hold on. This Grant fellow says he's never seen the likes of her. He sounds like he knows his river."

"The workmen standing on the bank with her were not celebrating Catherine's achievement," Louisa said, thinking suddenly of the letter from the boy, Michael.

"How do you know?"

"Oh, you are being naive on purpose, Ruth. Those builders weren't interested in her achievement. They were interested in her legs."

Ruth smiled. "You are too disbelieving in goodness, Louisa."

"And you are far too trusting," Louisa said. "Just like bloody Catherine."

Ruth looked at her. "Are you all right? You look exhausted."

"Oh, Ruth, this is so much harder than I thought it would be."

Ruth shrugged. "Do you think perhaps you're underestimating the upheaval she's been through? Coming to live here was an enormous change, and it's not that long since she lost her father."

"Now you sound like Nellie. Why can't she just be a good girl like I was at her age?"

Ruth laughed. "You just rebelled a bit later, Louisa." She stared at the photograph then looked at Louisa again. Her face softened again. After a moment, she asked, "Is she happy at the school?"

"I thought so, but now she says not. And there was a boy on the island."

"A boy."

"A native boy. You know, Florence, Harry's housekeeper. Her son. It's possible he and Catherine . . ."

"How do you know?" Ruth said calmly, looking less worried that Louisa would have expected.

Louisa looked at her friend, thought again of telling her about the letter. I read Catherine's mail. No, she wouldn't tell Ruth that. Ruth would think less of her, she was sure. "I don't know for sure. I just . . ."

"Do you talk to her, Louisa?"

"Of course I talk to her."

"I have wondered why you're finding it so difficult with Catherine," Ruth said. She put her hand on Louisa's.

Louisa pulled her hand away abruptly. "Perhaps I'm brusque," she said, too sharply. She sighed. "I'm sorry, Ruth. That swim was just unthinkably stupid. The water is cold, and what if she'd been run over by a boat?"

"That is a good point. But she wasn't," Ruth said. "She's just a girl, Louisa, like you were once, darling."

Louisa took a breath in and blew out. "It's the mail from Australia that's the problem. They never leave her alone."

"Who never leaves her alone?" Ruth looked confused then.

"The family she was staying with. There are letters every week, sometimes two. The boy is writing her. His mother. No wonder she's not settling in."

Ruth looked at the newspaper again. "I suppose I'm not as worried about it as you seem to be, Louisa. What on earth is wrong with that Helen Anderson these days? I always thought she was quite progressive. But if she's expelled Catherine, I don't know what I think. If I were you, I'd be quite proud of her, actually. Perhaps Henley's not the school for Catherine after all."

Ruth had been supportive of Louisa's decision to send Catherine to Henley but now she was blaming Henley. "After all, she's had an odd childhood, to say the least. But that's where I'd start. You have to take some time with her, I think, to get to know her."

Louisa thought again then of telling Ruth about the letter, but she knew Ruth would judge her for interfering. "You're right," she said. "I need to spend more time with her. If only the day had an extra twenty-four hours!"

13

It was in October of the year before, 1924, that Louisa had received the wire. HARRY PASSED STOP LOUISA GUARDIAN CATHERINE STOP CONTACT WITHERSPOON CAIRNS ASAP STOP ENDS. When she first read it, Louisa thought Harry must have passed some test. It was the shock, she supposed later. She was in shock. It was only when she reread that she understood. Her brother Harry was dead.

Heart failure, Alexander told Louisa when she visited him at Southampton. Alexander came out to meet her in the foyer and they embraced briefly and stiffly. He took her back to his office, which looked out over the keel of a ship in dry dock below. The office had always seemed cold to Louisa. Alexander had nothing personal on the desk, and there was no view to speak of. He gestured for Louisa to sit down in the only visitor chair, in front of the desk.

Alexander wasn't as tall as Harry. Like Louisa, he took

after their mother's side rather than their father's. He had their father's curly hair, though—blond rather than red—and George's fine profile and sharp eyes. He'd followed their father into the shipping business. Now it was his whole life. On that day, he wore an expensive suit, cut perfectly around his muscled frame. He'd taken off the coat and had hung it on the back of his chair, before sitting down and facing his sister. Gold cuff links and a silk-backed vest completed the picture of a successful man in his prime.

Alexander was named executor in Harry's will, he said. He'd had word from Harry's solicitor too. Harry had been in Cairns, Alexander told Louisa. He'd been at the hospital in the morning, to assist in surgery, and had been about to set out on the return journey back to the island. His heart stopped just like that. One minute he was alive, the next he was dead, according to Alexander. Their father had died of a heart attack. Alexander was older than Harry by seven years. It had shaken him, Louisa could see.

"Harry's named me Catherine's guardian," Louisa said.

"I know. You'll have to go for her," Alexander replied.

"Someone will," she said. "I've got the clinic."

"Well, she can't stay on the island, Louisa, and she can hardly travel unaccompanied. We can sort out the house and estate later, but you must go for the child, and soon. She's terribly exposed there."

"To what?" Louisa said.

Her brother looked at her.

"I know she can't stay there, Alexander," Louisa said, annoyed. "I'm not totally without wit. But I can't leave at a moment's notice."

"Surely the poor can survive a couple of months without you."

Alexander had always been like this. He saw himself as the one in charge in a way even their father didn't. When Louisa had been arrested during the protests for the vote, it was Alexander who'd told her she should be ashamed. He said she'd worried their mother unnecessarily: "And for what, Louisa? Some stupid idea about the vote."

Louisa regarded her older brother now. He was probably right. She would have to go to Australia. It was a six-week journey at the minimum, which would take her through to the end of the year. She didn't want to feel resentful of Catherine, but she hardly knew the girl. Why should Louisa now drop everything in order to care for Harry's child, the child he'd made it impossible for Louisa to be close to? Harry should have come home. "I'm not inclined to motherhood, Alexander."

Alexander only shrugged. "Well, you're a woman, which puts you in a better position than I am to go, and to be a mother."

Alexander knew what had happened to Louisa. Elizabeth had confided in him, against Louisa's wishes. He'd blamed his sister. She looked at him now. "I have my work," she said, "just as you do."

"Yes, I know, your work. But now Catherine Quick is officially part of your work—it says so here." He'd picked up the telegram and handed it back to Louisa. "I really must go." He stood and took the jacket from the back of his chair, put it on in one fluid movement and started toward the door.

"What about the funeral?" Louisa said.

"They're having something on the island, the solicitor said.

There's that native family Harry was close to." Alexander looked hard at Louisa. "A total Harry mess." He stood at the door, waiting for his sister.

"What do you mean?"

Alexander shrugged.

"The native family—that's the housekeeper, Florence, you're talking about?"

Alexander shrugged again.

"I did notice that Harry seemed very close to Florence," Louisa said. "But you don't think . . ."

Alexander held his hand up. "I'm not saying anything," he said, "except that Harry was Harry. Just go and see what you can do. You can have an island Christmas."

On the train back from Southampton, Louisa had sat by herself and looked out the window at the bleak winter landscape. Oh, Harry, I wish it had been different, she thought. I wish . . . Just what did she wish? That he'd come home when she'd asked? That she'd gone to Australia, as he'd asked, to help with Catherine? Perhaps.

Louisa's life had been a series of decisions, she thought, that had left her just a little stranded. Sometimes she felt as if the life she might have lived was there, just off to the left of the life she was living. It was as if the things that had happened had altered her life course and not necessarily for the better. Two lives, the one she was heading toward and then, after a single night, the one she'd moved to, the smaller, more frightened life. And then, even after Jonathan, after everything, she might have stayed on the island, mightn't she? She might have cared for the child. It would have helped ease her own pain, surely. But she hadn't.

Louisa had done something useful with her life since then. She and Ruth had run the hospital during the war, and then they'd opened the clinic. And the clinic was marvelous. Everyone said so, even those who hated the poor. Louisa cared for so many families now. But not your own family, she thought, with a bitter taste in her mouth. It was Ruth she imagined saying that, although Ruth had never said it and never would, Louisa knew. Ruth had been a good friend, Louisa's best friend. But Ruth had her own family, and they'd always come first.

Louisa and Harry had lost one another along the way. "And now you're gone," she said out loud to herself. She sat there as the countryside chugged by, raindrops rolling down the windowpane.

At home that night in London, Louisa had looked at the telegram again. Alexander was right. Someone would have to go for Catherine and Louisa was named. And then Catherine would have to live somewhere. She couldn't stay on in Australia alone. She couldn't really go to Alexander, a confirmed bachelor. There was Julia's family, but Julia had been gone for years now. She'd been an only child with parents, in Canada now, who would be aged. Her father had a sister, Louisa recalled, who had children. They were in New York, or Long Island. Those children must be grown now, must have children of their own. Catherine could go to one of them, it occurred to Louisa, to someone who'd been a mother already. Catherine would surely fare better with an experienced mother.

The next morning, Louisa told Nellie about her visit to Alexander. She said she might contact Julia's family about Catherine going to America to live. Nellie had stared at her open-mouthed. It would be wrong, plain wrong, she said finally, to send Catherine to Julia's family, whom she hardly knew. Nellie didn't care what sort of family Julia came from. "She's your blood, Louisa," Nellie said. "You can't just refuse her. And it's your side she knows best."

How could Louisa explain to Nellie that of all the things Louisa felt she could do in life, mothering was not among them?

Louisa asked Ruth later that day at the clinic, but Ruth was surprised too. "She's your kin," Ruth said. "Of course you must take her in. And you'll never regret it if you do."

There it was. The world would be happier if there were not only more children, but if those women who hadn't had children would just go and have a few. "You'll never regret it," was their song. Louisa didn't believe them. Not everything you decide in life comes without regret, she'd found. There were more than enough experiences that led to much regret. And many mothers' lives, as far as Louisa was concerned, were full of regret.

Still, Ruth and Nellie were right. Whatever else she was, Catherine was her kin. Louisa would have to go and fetch her niece and bring her home. She'd have to do the best she could.

PART IV

Thursday Island,
October 1924

14

I t had been a day much like any of the others in the months since his death. People had stopped leaving food at the house, although one of the mothers, Mrs. Watson, had asked just a week before what Catherine was going to do now. She'd accosted Catherine in town. While Florence was seeking green beans, Mrs. Watson asked Catherine when the family was coming.

At first, Catherine had been confused. As far as she was concerned, the family was Florence and Michael, and Florence was just getting beans. When Florence returned, Mrs. Watson smiled and left.

Florence asked Catherine what Mrs. Watson had wanted, but instead of telling Florence the truth, Catherine said Mrs. Watson had wanted to know about her daughter's spelling. "She can't spell very well at all," Catherine said, "but I didn't tell Mrs. Watson." By then, Catherine had figured out what Mrs. Watson actually meant. When were Catherine's father's family, the Quicks, or her mother's family, the Freebodys, coming? For surely they would come.

Catherine didn't know her mother's relatives, now living in Canada, and she'd only ever met her aunt Louisa once, when she was little. She couldn't even remember her, except that she'd smelled like flowers. There was her father's older brother, Alexander, but she didn't know him well either. He'd always seemed stern when he visited them on the island, as if he were judging them. He was nothing like her father; that's what Catherine remembered about him.

She'd been out swimming with Michael in the morning and then Florence had made breakfast for them, bubble and squeak using last night's veggies. Michael had walked with her to school. In the afternoon, he'd left early to go home and help Florence take some cakes back down for a bake sale the next day. Catherine had stayed back to help Sister Ursula with the younger ones. She'd been helping teach for over a year now. Sister Ursula was trying to convince her to sit the university scholarship exam. She could go to Brisbane, Sister Ursula said, board with Sister Ursula's family there and go to the university to study science. Sister Ursula was trying to get Catherine to think about her future. Catherine hadn't been interested before but now she wondered if that was what she should do after all. Her father had talked about the university too. She didn't want to leave the island, but now she knew she'd have to do something. If she went to Brisbane to study, she thought, she could come back to the island as a teacher.

Catherine had left the school around four and hurried up the hill, intending to have another swim before dinner. She ran up the path, opened the front gate and stopped.

There was a woman seated on the verandah, perched forward in a canvas-backed easy chair, Catherine's father's chair. The woman was dressed in a pale linen blouse and a long dark skirt, and her feet, clad in boots, were crossed at the ankles. They didn't quite reach the floor. She had a hat pulled over her head but you could see wisps of hair sneaking out. When she stood Catherine saw she was tiny. She came forward, said Catherine's name.

Catherine realized she must be the woman from the government, the one Florence had said would come. "They won't let you stay with us," Florence said. It was what Sister Ursula said as well. "You're a white girl, Catherine, and they won't let you stay with a black family." It's what Mrs. Watson had meant too, Catherine knew. But Michael isn't black, Catherine wanted to say to them all. If skin color was the determining factor, Catherine was nearly as dark as him.

When Catherine was small, she didn't even know Florence had a child. If anything, Catherine assumed *she* was Florence's child. But one day, just after Catherine's fourth birthday, they were at the harbormaster's office, waiting to meet the ferry to pick up the mail. Someone had left a newspaper on the bench in the waiting area. In the top left-hand corner of the page was a photograph of a group of children, four in dresses, two in pants too big for them, all holding toys. Above was a headline: HOMES ARE SOUGHT FOR THESE CHILDREN. Half-castes, they called them, and quadroons. Catherine remembered the words because they were words she didn't know.

Catherine was about to ask Florence what a quadroon was but Florence had turned and was rushing outside. Catherine looked at the newspaper again. Underneath the picture was an advertisement for White's Jelly Crystals, which were Catherine's favorite.

She found Florence on the steps but Florence wouldn't speak, and she was shaking as if cold. Catherine went back inside and asked the woman behind the counter for a glass of water for Florence. While she waited, she studied the newspaper. Someone had handwritten a note below the photograph. "*I like the little boy in center of the group but if taken by anyone else, any of the others would do, as long as they are strong.*"

The photograph had affected Florence but Catherine didn't know why. Before she went back outside with the water, she tore the photograph from the newspaper and shoved it in her pocket. They walked home together, and by the time they'd gotten to the top of the hill Florence was better. Catherine didn't mention what had happened in the harbormaster's office for fear of upsetting Florence again.

"They took him away, I think," Catherine's father told Catherine later that night when she asked him. Florence was downstairs. Catherine was in bed. "I don't know all the details, but I think they took a baby from her when she was living in Cairns."

"What do you mean?" Catherine said, not understanding. "What's this?" She pointed at a word.

"'Quadroon,'" he said. "It means a quarter black and three-quarters white. 'Half-caste' is half black and half white."

"They took Florence's baby?" Catherine said.

Her father nodded. He looked at the clipping again. "Did Florence say anything about it?"

Catherine shook her head. "She was crying, Daddy, and Florence never cries."

"No, she never does," he said absently, still staring at the picture.

The next morning Catherine's father came to her room and sat on the bed beside her. He'd spoken to Florence. The Protector had taken Florence's child when she was in Cairns, Catherine's father said. "The baby's daddy was white, so the child wasn't as black as Florence."

"I thought I was Florence's children," Catherine said.

Her father smiled. "No, darling, you're not Florence's."

"Will they take me away?"

"Of course not."

"How do you know?"

"It's different for the natives."

"Why?"

He didn't answer straightaway. "I think they want the children to grow up with our values, not the native values."

"Was my mother native?" Catherine said.

"No," he said emphatically. "Why do you ask that?"

"You said they took Florence's child because he looks white. They want children who are white."

"Your mother was American. You know that." He looked upset suddenly. "Anyway, I wouldn't let anyone take you away." But Florence was the most fierce person in Catherine's life. If Florence couldn't stop them, then no one could, Catherine thought.

"They take the children to families who can provide schooling," Catherine's father said.

"But we have a school."

"Yes, we do," he said. "And they've left the Islanders alone until recently, but Florence was on the mainland. It's different there for the blacks."

"Why?"

"I don't know," her father said. "The government says the blacks are less civilized than white people."

"Florence?"

"No, not Florence."

"Then why did they take her baby away?"

"I really don't know," Catherine's father said, sounding exasperated now. "I'm telling you this because I promised you I wouldn't lie, not about important things." He patted her head and smiled. "Stop asking questions now," he said.

Three days later, her father came home early. He found Catherine playing out on the back lawn. He spoke quietly. "I'm going to tell you something, but you're not to tell Florence." He narrowed his eyes, looked serious. Catherine sat down and looked up at his face. "You know my friend, the doctor in Cairns who comes here, Dr. Andrews?" Catherine nodded. "Dr. Andrews says there's a new Protector in Cairns. I have an appointment when I go there next week. It may be that Florence can see her child. But you mustn't tell just in case. You must tell Florence I'm going to Cairns for work." He put his finger to his lips and bent down and kissed her hair. "I love you so much, Cate."

The next week, he went to Cairns and Catherine knew not to say anything. A month later he went again and she'd all but forgotten their conversation.

Florence and Catherine were on the verandah shelling peas, and they'd been talking about whether or not to go back down to town to meet her father on the evening ferry. But then she saw him walking up the path. There was someone with him, Catherine saw, a child. She looked harder. It wasn't anyone she knew.

Florence began to moan softly and then cried out. They weren't words Catherine knew. The child—a boy, Catherine thought, judging by the shorts—broke free from Catherine's father and ran toward Florence. They met at the gate and she gathered him up in her arms, his long legs on either side of her hips. He had snot coming out of his nose, Catherine noticed when she caught them up, a nasty, brown-colored snot that Catherine knew from her father meant an infection. He was nearly as big as Catherine, with black hair and blue eyes, and he was skinny. His eyes darted around nervously, and he wouldn't let go of Florence.

When Catherine's father reached them, he stood a few feet away from Florence; he was out of breath but staring, a look of concern on his face. The child, still in Florence's arms, was sobbing too.

"Dr. Harry, how have you done this?" Florence was saying.

Catherine was confused. Who was this child?

And then she remembered. This must be Florence's child, the one her father had mentioned. Her father had found him and brought him back.

"He's back to stay," Catherine's father said.

The boy, Michael, two years older than Catherine, wouldn't speak. He was sick in his kidneys, Catherine's father told Florence later that night. But they'd get him well. They surely would. Florence fussed over him. Catherine watched as his frightened eyes took in the scene around him. Catherine's father stood in the background, watching them.

The doctor in Cairns knew the Protector, and they convinced him to release the child, Catherine's father told Florence. "I had to imply that I'm the boy's father, but never mind. He's here to stay, that's the main thing." Michael had been placed with a new family. Before that, he'd been with a family outside Cairns. Catherine's father didn't know much more than that, and Michael wouldn't talk that first night, nor for many nights that followed.

In all the commotion, Florence hardly noticed Catherine, who had a bath and put herself to bed. That's where she was when Florence came to tuck her in. "It's my baby back," Florence said. "This is the best day of my life."

"Yes, I suppose it is," Catherine said, not looking up.

"Are you all right?"

"Of course I am," Catherine said. She knew she should be happy for Florence, but for some reason she just wanted to cry. She focused on her hands outside the covers and said nothing.

Florence sat down. "So many changes," she said. She stroked Catherine's hair and then took the girl's hands from the covers and held them. She regarded the little fingers. "You know, don't you, that you're my spirit-child?"

"Am I?" Catherine said. Her mouth turned down, even

though she tried to stop it, and tears filled her eyes. She shook her head.

"Oh yes. I knew you first time I saw you. We've been in the world a long time, you and me. I saw you in your daddy's arms and I knew you were my spirit-child. It's good my boy's home. This is where he belongs. But you're still my spirit-child. I couldn't have come through without you. I won't forget that."

"Will you go away now?" Catherine asked, her bottom lip quivering as she spoke.

"Go away? What for? Who's going to look after you if I go away? Oh no, we're all going to live together. It's going to be fine. There's enough for everybody here. You know that."

And all at once, it was like the sun coming out. Catherine had thought, without even knowing she was thinking it, that Florence would leave her now, just as her mother had gone. But Florence wasn't going. It was just like the sun coming out after rain.

It wasn't all smooth sailing. It was a long time before Michael would leave the house. And Catherine, who'd always been the center of everyone's world, was suddenly on the edge. She was one of those who was trying to help instead of being a child herself. It was Catherine who enticed Michael to school finally. He was up the mango tree in the front yard. "What you doing up there?" she called one morning, bored with his silence. He didn't answer. She climbed up to a branch below his. "Come on, I'll take you to school." He looked down at her, his eyes wild. "You think they'll take you away?" He nodded slightly.

"Nah, not Sister Ignatius. She won't let anyone take you away. Promise. Come on."

And to everyone's great surprise, including Catherine's, he climbed down from the tree, took her hand, and went with her. From then on, it was settled: they were a family.

~

The little woman on the verandah sitting in Catherine's father's chair came all the way forward into the sunshine now. "Hullo," she called. She was English, or Scottish, like Catherine's father.

"Hullo," Catherine said. She remained at the gate.

The woman came out to the steps. "Catherine, my dear, it's me. Do you remember me?"

Catherine shook her head. The woman took off her hat. She looked familiar, kind gray-green eyes the color of the sea on a cloudy day, and little spectacles she peered through, dark brown curly hair going gray. "I'm your Aunt Louisa, Harry's sister."

The relief! She wasn't from the government after all.

"Oh," Catherine said. "What are you doing here?"

Louisa laughed. "I'm here to . . . After Harry. Come up out of the sun, my dear. Let me look at you. Goodness, you're a giant." She looked genuinely glad to see Catherine, Catherine thought. She looked like Harry too, which made Catherine miss her father suddenly.

Louisa's blouse was light blue, the same color as Catherine's, and they both wore gray skirts, Catherine saw now. And Louisa must have purchased her hat in the little shop in Samson Street in Cairns. It was the same hat Catherine had chosen, straw, with a wide brim and a wide black band. "At least we're in uniform," Catherine said, gesturing to her skirt and top and grinning.

Louisa laughed, looking up at Catherine. "Yes. Do you think they'll mistake us for twins?"

Catherine laughed too then. Louisa had stood back to make room for Catherine to come up the stairs. They stood facing one another. Catherine was a head taller than her aunt. Neither made a move to embrace.

"I've been at school," Catherine said, and felt a sudden urge to cry. Louisa was so obviously her father's sister, a tiny version of him, like him in the face most of all, especially her eyes. "I teach the little ones now."

"Well, isn't that wonderful?" Louisa said.

Catherine looked down at her shoes, not sure what else to say. She'd only started wearing shoes to school this year— Sister Ursula's idea—to set an example for the younger ones. The year before, she'd graduated from dungarees and a shirt to a skirt and blouse. It was Florence who insisted on this. When you didn't have a mother, Catherine had learned, everyone was your mother.

Later that afternoon, Catherine and Michael went for their swim. They saw the turtles on the far reef, the same two they'd been seeing all year. Will your aunty stay with us? Michael had asked Catherine afterward. I think so, Catherine had said, at least for a little while. She wasn't sure what would happen next, she said.

But after dinner, Catherine realized Louisa may as well

have been from the government after all. Her plan was to take Catherine away. Louisa and Catherine were out on the front verandah. "This is where you and I sat when I came to visit when you were small," Louisa said. "Do you remember?"

"No," Catherine said.

It was then that Louisa told her. "You don't need to worry, Catherine. I'm going to take you back to London with me." She was smiling.

"London?" Catherine said. Louisa nodded. "I can't leave the island. I'm needed at the school."

But Louisa had been to the school, she said, screwing up her nose as if it itched. She'd spoken to the nuns and they'd agreed—even Sister Ursula. They all agreed, Louisa told her. Catherine needed to leave the island and go to a proper school. "Of course it's for the best," Louisa said. She seemed very sure, Catherine thought.

"I'm at a proper school," Catherine said.

"You can't stay here without your parents, Catherine," Louisa said. "And that's final." She ran her hands over the cloth on the table, as if smoothing it, although there were no wrinkles, and smiled weakly.

"I have Florence."

"Florence can't look after you properly. She . . ."

"She what?" Catherine said.

Louisa didn't respond. Catherine knew the way the natives were viewed. Florence had talked to her about it. "They think we're idiots," Florence said. "They speak slowly, as if we might not understand them otherwise. They're the stupid ones, eh?" Catherine laughed. "They don't know how to catch a fish like Michael does, or make a roast chicken like I do. Oh, actually, I think they do know how to make a roast chicken," Florence corrected herself. "I think I learned that from Julia, now that I come to think of it." Florence had a habit of shrugging and covering her mouth when she said something incorrect or funny.

But in the end, even Florence had taken Louisa's side. After Louisa spoke to Catherine, Catherine had gone immediately to tell Florence but Florence already knew.

"You have to go," was all Florence said. "I don't like it, but Louisa is right. She spoke to me. That's your future, not here. And Louisa, she didn't get to have children. She should have you." Florence looked at her intently.

"No," Catherine said. "I'm not going. I'm happy here. I'm going to teach. You don't really want me to go?" She was almost in tears.

Florence was fiddling with her hands in her lap. She looked down at them. "Louisa is your people," Florence said firmly. "It doesn't matter how much we love each other; I'm not yours. And Michael's not either." She looked hard at Catherine. "You and my boy—you couldn't have children, Catherine. It would be wrong. You wouldn't be allowed to keep them. The Protector will take them. And there's no Dr. Harry to help us. You know as well as I do what that means."

"You think they'll take Michael again?"

"No, he's too old for the Protector. But if you and Michael . . . you know what I'm talking about."

Catherine blushed.

Florence looked at her sharply. "You must go. You have to trust me. You must go." She softened then. "You like your aunt. And she's a doctor, like your daddy. She's giving you an opportunity that you could never get here, Catherine."

"But, Florence, what will you ever do without me?" The tears came now, falling down her face.

"Oh goodness. You mustn't worry about me." Florence smiled, but her face was tight, controlled, Catherine saw. With her big warm hands, she wiped Catherine's cheeks, smearing the tears there. "I got the prize, Catherine. I got to raise you. I got to work for Dr. Harry. I got given a second chance with my boy. No mother gets all that without having to pay something back."

15

Thursday Island was much the same as it had been eleven years before. Louisa had left London as soon as she reasonably could, but she'd had to recruit another surgeon for Princes Square and that took a month, and then transfer her surgical patients at the practice to another surgeon. She didn't get away until December. She was on the *Oriana* this time, which sailed through the Torres Strait en route to Cairns. The journey seemed to take longer but perhaps it was her frame of mind, wondering what she'd find in Australia. She'd seen the islands in the distance, worried then about what was happening to Catherine.

She had to stop in Cairns to meet Harry's lawyer, Mr. Witherspoon, who was older than she'd expected and rail-thin, with sharp eyes that regarded Louisa as if she might be plotting to steal her brother's estate on the spot. Not that the estate was worth much, the house and whatever Harry had put away of his government salary. Louisa did her best to assure Mr. Witherspoon that she had Catherine's best interests at heart.

Witherspoon's concern seemed to be that Harry had left his estate to Louisa outright rather than in trust for Catherine. Louisa agreed this was odd but not all that odd. Harry knew he could rely on his sister on that score. On the other hand, even her own solicitors had said there would be a trust. It didn't much matter, except that Witherspoon seemed worried on Catherine's behalf.

As he'd been going through the file, Witherspoon had said something was missing. He located a document number but no corresponding document. He remembered something, he said, and he'd ask his clerk to do a search. He'd find it, he assured Louisa, and if it included instructions to set up a trust for Catherine, Louisa could be very sure that's what he would do. But for now, Louisa just needed to sign papers to make her Catherine's guardian.

Louisa saw a copy of Julia's death certificate. Harry had certified the death, which was most irregular. Her brother would know he shouldn't certify the death of a relative.

But Mr. Witherspoon was unperturbed about it.

And drowning was given as the cause of death, Louisa noted, but she also knew that Julia's body had never been found. It should have been Missing, Assumed Drowned, which would have triggered an inquiry. It was strange, she thought, but perhaps Harry wanted as little fuss as possible.

Louisa read the documents she had to sign, feeling for the first time the weight of the responsibility she was taking on. She had to guarantee to care for the girl, to be "totally responsible for the minor's welfare," the agreement said.

The trip north from Cairns did nothing to ease Louisa's mind and, she realized, it had taken her three months to get here. Harry had died in October and now it was early February. They'd had word through the solicitor that Catherine had stayed on in the house with Florence, the housekeeper, and was still attending school. The police officer on the island, a Sergeant Macklin, had been appointed guardian pro tem, although he hadn't done much as far as Louisa could see. Now Louisa had signed a document that gave her full responsibility for this fourteen-year-old girl of Harry's.

As the buggy had come through town on Thursday Island, Louisa noticed the native children under the trees in the main street, just like all those years ago, only these ones wore dresses instead of shorts and shirts. There was what looked like a green silk dress in the oriental style Louisa remembered well—how dear it might have been with Catherine's eyes—and a linen blouse and skirt in blue. They were the clothes Louisa had been sending for Catherine over the years, worn by the native children. No wonder Harry had never answered when she'd asked about the clothes. Louisa wondered if he'd even given them to Catherine or had just handed them around. The children did look lovely, she thought, even if that bow around the boy's arm should have been in his sister's hair.

After she'd met with Sister Ursula from the school, who, eleven years on, was now in charge, Louisa went up to the house. Florence answered the door. She looked taken aback by Louisa's arrival, as if she hadn't been expecting her, although

Louisa had wired ahead. Florence didn't look a day older than the last time Louisa had met her. She was polite but far from friendly now, eyeing Louisa carefully as if Louisa might be planning to make off with the silver any minute, not unlike the lawyer Witherspoon.

"Dr. Louisa," Florence said. "You've had a long journey. And Michael wasn't with us last time you came. He's my son."

Michael was tall and slim, with a body that communicated strength, soft blue eyes and a smile that made you want to smile back. He was carrying a basket. He didn't say much to Louisa but he did take her offered hand. He leaned down to her in a kindly way and told her that Catherine was teaching down at school but was sure to be home soon to go for a swim. "We go every afternoon," he said, smiling. "She likes to beat me out to the reef."

Louisa said she'd wait on the verandah where it was cool and, yes, a glass of cold water would be lovely. He was a delightful young man, she thought then. She didn't know where he'd been the last time she'd come to the island. He'd have been a child.

Catherine came bounding through the gate about half an hour later. She was older, of course. She had Harry's eyes and her mother's chestnut hair combined with the Quick red and darkened to auburn, her skin browned by the sun. Across her nose and cheeks was still that band of freckles. She looked straight at Louisa. She was much calmer and more demure than Louisa had expected she'd be. The wild creature Alexander described had grown into a thoughtful young woman, Louisa saw. She was tall, too, like Louisa's father and Harry.

While Catherine and Michael were still down at the beach later that afternoon, Florence came out to the front verandah, which overlooked the sea, flecked with gold in the last of the sun. "Dr. Louisa, if I may have a word." Her tone was polite, but she looked afraid.

"Of course, Florence. Sit down." Louisa gestured to the chair opposite. Florence remained standing.

"I'm not sure what your plans are, but I do know that Catherine is keen to stay on the island."

"Catherine doesn't know what she wants right now," Louisa said, surprised at Florence's frankness. "Things have been very hard for her, and it's up to us to make them easier."

Florence narrowed her eyes, setting her jaw tight. "I've been with Catherine her whole life. I'm the only one now who has. And Dr. Harry did something for me I'll never forget. My boy Michael, they took him, and Dr. Harry got him back. If Catherine wants to stay, it would be fine with me, more than fine. I have some money saved. I just want to make sure you know that."

"But, Florence, you're not thinking she could spend the rest of her life here, on the island? What about her education?"

"She's at the convent."

"That's not what I meant. Look, you can help Catherine right now, or hinder her. It's up to you. I know that the best place for her is England, where she can develop to her fullest potential." Louisa wanted to ask who had taken the boy, Michael, but held back.

"How do I help the child most?" Florence said. "The Protector said my son was better off with a white family, and I was so young I believed him." She paused, looked out at the water. "Dr. Harry couldn't know he was going to die, that's the thing. And I need to have Catherine's best interests in my heart too. That's why I don't know, Louisa." She looked as if she wanted to say more but pressed her lips together.

"Well, I'm very sure," Louisa said, too sharply, she thought. Florence shook her head and didn't respond. Louisa waited and then said, "I can assure you there's nothing to worry about. Catherine will be with her family. She'll be happy, I'm very sure. And you have no blood tie to the girl." Louisa paused but saw no flicker of feeling on Florence's face. She still stood there, saying nothing.

Louisa sighed. "I'm sorry, Florence, but Catherine must come to England. It will be easier for her if you and your son let her go with your blessing." She looked at the other woman. Florence's face was hard to read. She watched Louisa for a moment more and then turned and went back inside.

~

"I want to stay here," Catherine said. They were sitting together in the parlor, which was so stuffy the first time Louisa had visited. Now the windows were all open, the drapes pulled back. They looked out into the deep of evening, the sound of the native crickets heavy in their ears and, beyond, the sound of the sea. Catherine said she wasn't prepared to go to London, almost before Louisa had finished explaining what was to happen. Her mouth was set in a line and she glared at Louisa as she spoke. They were alone, but Louisa had the feeling that Florence and Michael weren't far away. She wondered then if Florence had already spoken to Catherine, had warned her.

"Well, that's not possible, dear," Louisa said. "I know you've had a difficult time. But you can't stay here. There's no one to look after you."

"Florence will look after me," Catherine said. "She's always looked after me."

Louisa had watched from the house that afternoon as Catherine and Michael had run down the hill together and dived into the sea. They were like puppies, bumping into one another as they raced, his naked chest, her bare legs. Louisa had never thought of herself as prudish, but in that swimming suit, a man's suit, Catherine's knees and shoulders were exposed. She showed no modesty whatsoever. And with a boy close to her own age. Louisa had been worried. She knew what could happen in these situations, what men were capable of, even seemingly nice young men like Michael. It sent a shiver through her.

"They're natives," Louisa said to Catherine in the parlor, knowing this wasn't what she meant. The girl only looked confused. "They're not your people."

"Yes they are," Catherine said. "Of course they are. I've grown up with them."

Louisa sighed. "Catherine, I'm your guardian. I'm named in Harry's will. I can't fail in my responsibility here."

"I have to go?" Catherine said.

Louisa nodded.

Catherine thrust her chin forward, a gesture Louisa would get to know well, avoiding the tears that threatened. She made her mouth into a tight line and stood and left the room without saying anything more. Oh dear, Louisa thought. I'm worse at this business than even I expected I would be.

⌇

"We love Catherine," the woman was saying. She was too close to Louisa's face. "In fact, if she were to remain on the island, we'd be more than happy to help with her management." Louisa was racking her brains for a name. She'd met this woman the day before. Catherine didn't like her, Louisa had thought at the time, and then Louisa had forgotten to ask why. Was it Wharton? Or Smithson? It was a name like that, she was sure.

Now, the woman had accosted Louisa and Catherine in the main street. Louisa had come to send a wire to Alexander, confirming their departure date, although given Catherine's reluctance, she was already thinking she might need to revise it. Catherine was still insisting she could stay on the island, but Louisa was more certain than ever that the correct course was to have her come to England, where they'd find a good school. Catherine knew Louisa was right too, Louisa was pretty sure. But getting her to say so was proving very difficult.

Louisa and Catherine had met this woman—Watson, yes, Mrs. Watson—who was staring at Louisa now, waiting for a response. Management, she'd said. She'd be happy to involve herself in Catherine's management. The look of hope on the woman's face made Louisa uncomfortable. Why would she want Catherine to stay on the island? What was it to her?

"I've tried my very best to get her to see," Mrs. Watson said. "But she simply will not, Dr. Quick. Can I say what a great honor it is to have you among us? I feel I am in the presence of a giant of the movement."

She had particularly red cheeks and Louisa was finding it difficult to know if they were rouged. She reminded Louisa of those patients with no real ailments to speak of other than the experience of an average life. If they paid on the way out, should she care? That's what Ruth Luxton said. But Louisa was a surgeon, unaccustomed to doing nothing. She was happiest in an operating room, where patients didn't talk, where she could fix their problems without having to spend hours listening to their complaints. She was disinclined to be tolerant of Mrs. Watson.

"I appreciate everything you've done, Mrs. Watson," she said, swallowing the name in case she still had it wrong.

"The girl is living with natives currently, which we, Jack and I, feel is compromising her reputation."

Louisa shook her head. "As I say, I appreciate everything you've done, Mrs. Watson, but you will be aware that Florence Cunningham has been in Catherine's life since Catherine was born. Florence is like a member of the family."

It had crossed Louisa's mind again since she'd arrived on the island that Florence and Harry might have had some sort of tryst. This was what Alexander had implied that day in Southampton, although he'd never made anything explicit and he probably had no evidence. It wouldn't do to dwell on this notion, Louisa knew, but Catherine's skin was as dark as some of the natives', almost as dark as Michael's. Could there have been some relationship that Julia agreed to cover over? Or worse, could Harry and Florence have conspired to harm Julia, poor young thing that she was? Well, that was ridiculous.

Harry didn't go to the island in time to impregnate another woman and then bring his American wife into the picture. And even if the timing added up, Harry would never have acted so dishonorably. But he had brought the boy, Florence's son, Michael, home to the island. Catherine had told Louisa the whole story. Why had he done that for a child who wasn't his? At the very least, Harry held Florence in high regard. Was Michael . . . Louisa put any thoughts of Harry's relationship with his housekeeper away, stared at the block of a woman in front of her. "So I would think you might think twice before you would say something like that," she said.

Mrs. Watson left them soon after, but Louisa could see there was something changed in her niece. Catherine had looked angry as the woman spoke, and Louisa had realized the girl would have defended Florence. Now she looked at her aunt with a small smile on her face.

"Why did you say that to her about Florence?" Catherine asked.

"Because Florence *has* been like family to you. I didn't like what the woman was implying, that there was something wrong with that. Did you tell me yesterday you know her daughter?"

"Yes," Catherine said. "I teach her reading. She's a sweet little thing. She comes to school looking like a little princess and goes home looking like a street urchin. I'm surprised her mother would trust me with her, frankly. I lead her astray."

"I think the plan is to bring you back to the straight and narrow, Catherine, and have you caring for her children."

"Oh," Catherine said. "I never thought of that."

"And if that's the alternative, surely you'd prefer to come back to London," Louisa said.

"I can't just stay here?"

Louisa and Catherine had spoken twice more since their first conversation and while Catherine continued to resist, Louisa had seen the girl was becoming less firm in her view. She'd even asked Louisa about the schools in London and the subjects she would do there. "I think you know the answer to that in your heart, dear," Louisa said now.

Catherine looked sad then, but also as if she did know the answer.

Louisa was relieved. She'd been worrying about what she'd do if Catherine refused outright to come to London. "It must be nice to be so wanted, sweet girl," Louisa said now. "Florence means well and she's a good woman. She's been wonderful to you. I have no doubt of that. But I visited the school again. They can't do for you what you need. You could be anything, Catherine—a doctor, a lawyer. There are no limits for women, not anymore. You must see that."

"Are you sure, Aunt Louisa?" Catherine said.

"Of course I am," Louisa said.

On their last full day on the island, Louisa watched Catherine swimming out beyond the break, beyond the jetty, so far out Louisa lost sight of her. There was a reef three miles out, Catherine had told her. It was nothing for the girl to swim that far in a day. Catherine was so at home here, and the beauty of the place, the green of the water, the easy way the natives had with one another, affected Louisa too. She'd ended up staying for a whole month. It was true she had to finalize Harry's estate and clear the house of his personal effects. But the island had a way of slowing a person down. It was quite delightful, even with the heat, Louisa thought. Perhaps Catherine should stay here after all and Louisa should stay with her.

Oh good Lord, your brain is melting, Louisa told herself. Of course the girl should come to London. What on earth would she do for the rest of her life otherwise?

Before they boarded the ship in Sydney, Louisa took Catherine to a seamstress in the city to have dresses made up. Catherine agreed the materials were lovely, ran her fingers over the silks and velvets, but Louisa could see she had no interest in fine dresses. They'd packed what they could of the clothes she wore on the island, but mostly she'd worn Harry's old shorts and a man's shirt with her big straw hat. Only on school days did she even bother with shoes, so they didn't take much in the end.

Louisa had three plain woolen skirts and three linen blouses made, along with two dresses in the new style, hemmed just below the knee—which Louisa agreed to on the seamstress's advice; she herself was against the shorter skirts, which she felt were unnecessary—and an evening dress in a dark green silk that set off Catherine's hair.

Catherine wanted to go to a beach before they left for London and so Louisa arranged for them to visit the little seaside village of Coogee. The beach had a small headland at one end and a pier at the other. Louisa and Catherine walked out on the pier in the afternoon and bought ices. Catherine wanted to swim, so while she was changing into a bathing suit Louisa rented for her—Louisa had made sure to leave Catherine's men's swimming suit back on the island—Louisa watched two little girls in white dresses, long socks and black leather shoes. They looked so dear, Louisa thought to herself.

"Look at those girls, Catherine," she said when Catherine returned. "Aren't they sweet?"

Catherine smiled. "That's how you'd like me to look," she said. "But I look more like him." With the girls was a boy of around twelve in a button-up cotton shirt and serge shorts, socks falling down around his ankles, scuffed brown leather shoes.

"Yes you do, I'm afraid," Louisa said. "Did you not want to get new clothes for England?"

"I don't much care," Catherine said, and ran off and leapt into the sea.

On the journey back to London, Catherine either sat in their stateroom staring out the porthole or went up on the main deck to stare at the ocean from there.

"You like the sea," Louisa said one afternoon when she found Catherine on the deck.

"When I was a little girl," Catherine said, "I told my father that I loved swimming so much I wasn't sure if I was a boy or a fish. He said I was neither. I was a girl who loved the water. I said I most certainly wasn't a girl and since he was sure I couldn't be a boy, I might have to be a fish. That was my name on the island, Waapi. It's the word for fish."

"What was it about the water you loved so much?"

"I still love it," Catherine said, looking squarely at Louisa. "I could dive in here. Sometimes I feel I could swim forever."

"We used to go to the beach at Aldeburgh, where my mother's family lived," Louisa said. "We had our holidays there every summer. I used to go into the water to paddle but I couldn't swim." Louisa had never learned. When they went to the seaside her brothers would swim. Louisa wore a swimming skirt and blouse. Even if she'd known how to swim, she couldn't have carried the weight.

When she was very small, Louisa remembered, her father would throw a rope out and she'd hold on while she bathed. Once she'd let go of the rope without thinking and had been swept out with the current. Before she knew it, the water had overwhelmed her. As she bobbed up, she could see her father stepping out of his shoes and throwing off his jacket and hat. It was as if he were moving very slowly, but he must have been going fast for he soon reached her and lifted her up and told her to make herself floppy.

"Can you hear me, Louie?" he said, his arms tight about her.

"Of course I can hear you," she said. "Don't be scared, Papa."

"I'm not," he said.

"Then why are you hurting me?"

He stopped squeezing so hard.

They came up onto the beach a long way from where they'd left their towels and he carried her all the way. He said they weren't to tell Mama what had happened.

Louisa smiled at Catherine now, looking from her niece

out into the calm sea. "My mother was a great fan of children being outdoors, but I was never taught to swim. Harry was a fine swimmer."

"He was very keen for me to be able to swim well," Catherine said, "and more proud of my swimming than anything I did at school."

"Yes, he was," Louisa said. They were exposed to the oncoming breeze, which was building as the afternoon progressed. "Come in now, and we'll get ready for dinner."

"You go in," Catherine said. "I'll just stand here a while."

Catherine had none of the training most young women had for life, Louisa thought. Perhaps that was a good thing, although it would always make her stand out. The fact that she seemed not to care was probably a blessing.

16

They were leaving, leaving the island, the only home Catherine had ever known. She'd said good-bye to Florence at the ferry, a quick hug in the end for there was no time for more. It all happened too quickly, she thought. Florence shook her head. Catherine saw there were tears in Florence's dear eyes.

And then, as the ferry pulled away, Catherine saw Florence's frame slump over on the jetty, as if someone had punched her. She was supporting herself against one of the pylons. Catherine couldn't bear to see her so upset.

"We knew the day would come," she'd said to Catherine the night before. "It just came too soon."

Catherine wished more than ever now that Michael had come to say good-bye, that he'd been there to look after his mother. Catherine couldn't bear it. She looked away from Florence and toward the sea.

Two days before, Michael had gone swimming alone. A dolphin had swum with him, he said. "I asked Bid to watch over you. He said you'll come back." Michael leaned in. They hugged one another, Catherine reluctant to let him go.

"We could run," he said. "Take a boat up to Saibai. They'd never find us."

But Catherine knew that would be wrong. She felt it was her duty to go with Louisa now. Here was an opportunity to go to a school, a real school where she would learn the ways of the wider world. That's what Louisa had said. Catherine's future for now lay in London. If she was to come back to the island, if she was to have power over her own life, she needed to go with Louisa and learn how.

Michael looked upset then. "You do want to go," he said. She didn't answer him.

"Fine," he said. "Go. But don't expect I'll wait around for you to come back."

She looked back toward the jetty once more now to wave to Florence, and thank goodness, there was Michael. He ran down past Florence toward the end of the jetty. "Waapi!" he called out. "Come back to us, you hear? You come back to us, or I'll come get you." He waved then and grinned. She didn't call out but waved back, tears streaming down her cheeks. He turned and went back to Florence, put his arms around his mother.

After Catherine left the island, after she was all those thousands of miles across the sea, it would be Florence she'd think of at night before she slept: Florence's soft, kind voice, her smile, her smell, which Catherine never smelled after she left

Thursday Island, of coconut and frangipani, luscious and safe. She'd think of her last swim with Michael, his laugh, and she'd remember that view of the two of them, Michael and Florence, together at the ferry as Catherine sailed away from them. I'll be back, she said to herself. I will.

PART V

London, August 1925

17

It was four in the afternoon and Louisa was about to leave the practice for the day. She'd arrived late from the clinic and had seen a run of surgical patients—an excised tumor post-op, excellent prognosis, a tiny woman heavily pregnant booking for a cesarean operation to deliver her of the giant she was carrying, and an unmarried woman of breeding with a fiercely unwanted pregnancy. Louisa came out to the waiting area to let the nurse on the desk know she was planning to go home. The nurse pointed toward the office. "There's a man to see you, Doctor," the nurse said quietly.

Louisa frowned, whispered, "I've finished my list." She wanted to get home early so she could talk with Catherine again. Whatever the swim in the Thames meant for the future, Ruth was right about one thing. Louisa had expected too much of Catherine. And she hadn't worked hard enough to understand why Catherine felt the way she did, to help her move forward, leaving the island behind and finding her new life here in London. Louisa needed to understand what was driving Catherine, why she wasn't settling. She had to give the girl a chance to do better.

The nurse shook her head. "Not a patient," she said quietly. "An American." Louisa looked at the nurse, who only shrugged.

She went into the main office. Sitting in the chair by the large oak desk was a middle-aged man with wavy silver hair combed straight back. He looked vaguely familiar, Louisa thought. "I'm Dr. Quick," Louisa said. She could smell a fragrance. There were no flowers here. Was he wearing perfume?

The office was still furnished in the dark timbers Louisa had inherited from her predecessor, a dour surgeon who'd finally retired at the age of eighty-six. Louisa and Ruth had taken over the offices but they hadn't bought new furniture and equipment, as they'd needed everything they earned to establish the clinic. There had never been any spare money since to refurnish.

"Dr. Quick." He stood and walked toward her. He was a head taller than Louisa, a compact man of slim build with a kind of pent-up energy to him, as if he might be called upon to sprint at any moment. At the same time he seemed perfectly at his ease, comfortable in his skin. It was an alluring combination.

Over one arm he had a dark overcoat and in that hand, his left, a dark gray trilby. He smiled, held out his other hand. It was one of those disarming smiles that expected to be returned, more on the left side of his face than the right.

Louisa smoothed her hands on her skirt. They were still damp from washing after the final patient. He took her hand in his and for a moment she thought he might kiss it. But he shook it instead and stood there. "I'm Manfred Lear Black." His voice was soft, his accent stretching and accentuating the "a" in Black. He smiled again, and Louisa saw the flash of white teeth, creases at his dark eyes.

"Mr. Black," Louisa said. She knew the name, Manfred Lear Black. He'd been in the papers. The mad American, they called him. Something about an aeroplane. "Do sit down." She flicked her eyes up to the clock on the wall above the desk behind him. He turned.

"I'm sorry," he said. "I had intended to make an appointment but when I telephoned I was told you are booked solid for the next month. I took the liberty of popping by." He said "popping" as if trying the word out.

His accent was strong on certain words, like the accents of the Americans she'd worked with in Baltimore. "Well, Mr. Black, you're here now. How can I help?" She smiled gently, the way she did for patients who had something difficult to tell her. She assumed he would be coming about a wife or daughter with a medical problem. Sometimes the men came first, especially if it was an unwanted pregnancy.

"Yes, I'll come straight to the point." He smiled. It disappeared quickly. "I've been told you are immune to charm." Louisa didn't respond to this. "I have a clinic in Baltimore not unlike your Princes Square, linked to Johns Hopkins. I believe you know Dr. Emily Masterton."

"Emily, of course," Louisa said. Emily had studied at Johns Hopkins University and had stayed on at the hospital when she finished. "We trained together." Louisa had gone to Johns Hopkins after she'd completed her surgical training in Edinburgh, following in her brother Harry's footsteps. Being at a hospital that cared for the poor, with doctors who were committed to helping others, had helped Harry decide on Thursday Island, and it had helped Louisa decide to start the clinic at Princes Square. The Johns Hopkins approach, where doctors respected patients and one another, had been healing for Louisa herself, if she was honest. It was a gentle place, a gentler place than the hospital in Edinburgh, and Emily and Louisa had been friends.

"Emily is now our chief of medicine," Manfred Lear Black said. "We're quite similar to your clinic, a kind of social experiment, or so Emily and the other doctors tell our board. The clinic is doing its best to stop people getting sick in the first place: better food, better hygiene, vaccination."

If only they were doing that at Princes Square, Louisa thought, but they didn't have the time or the resources. "Yes, Emily was very interested in public health," she said, glancing up at the clock again. "And how do you fit into a medical clinic, Mr. Black?" she asked.

"My family has an interest in shipping. In truth, we've benefited substantially from the industry. I have always been of the view that we should give something back. A little like Johns Hopkins himself, although I don't pretend for one minute to fill those shoes. But the clinic." Black put his hand to his face, wiped it across his mouth. Louisa didn't know where this was leading. "I have a proposition to put to you, and I thought I ought to come in person so that you'd see I'm sincere."

"Go on," she said. There was something in his expression, something she liked.

"I want you to come to Baltimore and spend some time with my doctors. We're planning to offer a major shift to confinement care in hospital. Most women deliver at home, which is not ideal, according to my doctors. We wanted a family specialist to provide us with up-to-date advice on women's health."

"Me?" Louisa said. "I'm a surgeon." Was he being coy about abortion? Louisa was one of the few doctors willing to be outspoken on the issue and on others besides. Princes Square was shameless, an editorial in *The Times* had claimed recently. Girls the Sally Ann had rejected as amoral had been provided with succor by Louisa Quick and her doctors. Louisa, who tried hard to stay out of the newspapers, couldn't bear this kind of self-righteousness. The Sally Ann refused pregnant women a place to stay if they were unmarried, turned them out on the street. That was what was shameless, as far as Louisa was concerned.

"Your clinic offers family medicine," Black said. As he spoke, Louisa noticed his hands, long, graceful fingers.

"But if it's medicine, you'd be better off talking to my colleague, Dr. Luxton." Louisa glanced at the desk, the mountain of paperwork she hadn't managed to clear from yesterday.

"Well, I'm talking to you," he said. He smiled. His smile was quite irresistible, Louisa was finding. She found herself returning it, despite the fact he was keeping her late. "My doctors know you. They know your work. They'll listen to you." The smile again, winning.

"But they're in Baltimore," Louisa said, returning his smile again.

"Yes, that's what I'm suggesting. If you could find a way to visit us later in the year, you could advise us."

"Visit Baltimore?" Louisa said. "I can't possibly leave here."

She thought of the clinic, and now Catherine. She gestured to the paperwork on the desk. There was no way she could go abroad in the foreseeable future.

"Of course, we would pay all your expenses," he said, looking at the papers she pointed toward, "*and* make a contribution to cover your absence. I know there are moves afoot here in London to require establishments such as yours to meet new health standards. I'd envisage that would involve some additional costs for you. I could be helpful." There was a twinkle in his eye then, as if he expected the mention of money might win her over.

Louisa nodded. How did he know about the new health standards? There had been another letter from the Inspectorate. They were finalizing details of a visit. Louisa knew her clinic didn't have a chance of passing the inspection. If they closed the clinic, what would happen to all those families?

"We don't have to decide anything today," Black said, regarding her carefully. "But if you want to test my bona fides, perhaps you might speak with your brother."

"You know Alexander?" Louisa said. She sat back in her chair.

"We're about to invest together in a new line. Four more ships, London to New York. Alex is good on the money side."

"Yes he is," Louisa said.

Black smiled, tilted his head and regarded her. "I must say, he's not nearly as charming as his sister."

"When Alexander told you I was immune to charm, Mr. Black, did he also tell you that I once split his lip for calling me a sissy-girl?"

"No, he didn't," Black said, chuckling. "As a matter of fact, Dr. Quick, we've never discussed you. It was a staff member of mine whose family knows you who gave me that warning, not your brother. I'd hate to be the cause of a second split lip for Alex, although I imagine he could hold his own." He laughed. "Come to think of it, he has been a tough negotiator. More than once over the years, I've wished he was on my side of the table, not the other. So perhaps another split lip wouldn't worry me unduly. But we must stick to the truth. It wasn't Alex."

He sat forward in his chair, regarded her more carefully. "The name, Quick. Now, tell me, am I right in assuming the swimmer I saw on the Thames yesterday is related to you?"

"My niece," Louisa said, "Catherine. You saw the news-paper?"

He nodded. "I saw the swim itself," he said. "Is she Harry's daughter?"

"You knew Harry too?"

"Through Alex. Harry helped me set up the clinic when he was at Johns Hopkins. I should have said at the outset, I'm sorry for your loss."

Louisa nodded. She'd hardly thought of Harry these last months. "Catherine lives with me now."

He nodded. "Harry's wife, Julia, awful business. I intro-duced them, you know."

"Harry and Julia?" Louisa said.

"Yes, she was a Freebody. My mother was a Freebody. Harry came to a little party I had at my house on Long Island. But I lost track after they left Baltimore. I knew they'd had a child, of course. As I say, awful business about poor Julia." Louisa saw the look of pain on his face, the lines down his cheeks. "Harry did some wonderful work to set up our clinic.

He was one of the most egalitarian fellows I've ever had the privilege to know. A good man."

"Yes," Louisa said. "We were very close growing up, and I'm now Catherine's guardian. You said you saw the swim?"

"I was at a meeting at Globe Wharves to do with this deal we're negotiating. We were called to the window to see this slip of a girl crossing the Thames. Just extraordinary, dodging barges and ferries, swimming against that tide. And then this morning when I saw the name in the newspaper, I put two and two together. My, what spirit she has. She must take after her father," Black said. "It's a heck of a swim, you know."

"Perhaps," Louisa said, feeling the weight of responsibility for Catherine.

"You don't approve, Dr. Quick?"

She sighed. "Actually, Mr. Black, the swim was not sanctioned by me or by Catherine's school." She frowned. "Especially by Catherine's school. As a matter of fact, Catherine is at home right now, waiting for me to get there and tell her what we're going to do. And I have absolutely no idea." He looked concerned. "There's no defense I can think of to remedy the situation. She was supposed to be in school. She took eight students with her to watch and now she's been expelled." Oh goodness, Louisa thought then. What was she doing telling a perfect stranger about Catherine? She must be more frazzled than she'd realized.

He laughed loudly suddenly.

"You think this is funny?" Louisa said.

"Oh, I'm sorry," he said, becoming serious. But then he started to chuckle again. "I mean, can't they see the merit in what she did? How does a girl manage a swim like that? I'm no champion myself, but you could see the way she glides through the water. The girl's born to it."

Louisa hadn't really thought about how Catherine had managed to do the swim. How did she manage it? "It was a thoroughly irresponsible act."

"Do you think?" he said. "Strikes me as a thoroughly courageous act. She swam the Thames, Dr. Quick. How old is she?"

"Fifteen."

"Could you have managed something like that at fifteen? I couldn't."

"I suppose that's one way of looking at it."

"I have some contacts in swimming, as it happens. We're hoping to support a young swimmer to attempt the English Channel next year." He pulled at one of his earlobes, a gesture Louisa found vaguely attractive. "Not here but back at home. Do you think Catherine might be interested in that?"

"Swimming," Louisa said.

"Well, I'm just thinking out loud here but there's a swimming group in New York—Charlotte Epstein, the Women's Swimming Association. I give them money."

"Women's swimming."

"Yes. They teach girls to swim. They trained last year's Olympic team. They won everything. I want one of our swimmers to be the first woman to swim the English Channel. It could be Catherine."

"You give them money?" Louisa looked hard at him.

He put his hand up and flicked the air, dismissing his largesse. "A little," he said. "I lost a sister to drowning." A look of pain crossed his face then. "Couldn't swim. Girls didn't in my day."

"I'm sorry," Louisa said. They didn't swim in Louisa's day either.

He shook his head. "It was a long time ago. Anyway, it's just an idea. Your niece could come with you—to America, I mean—and swim with the Association while you're in Baltimore. She's at least as strong as Mercedes Gleitze, maybe stronger. I'd be willing to back her as my swimmer."

"Mercedes Gleitze?" Louisa knew the name, vaguely.

"You don't know who Mercedes Gleitze is? You don't know the story of the Channel?"

Louisa shook her head. "Assume I don't."

"No woman has yet swum across the English Channel. Heck, only five men have succeeded. Mercedes Gleitze has come the closest so far. She's trying again this year, and one of our swimmers—that is, the WSA swimmers—Gertrude Ederle, plans to beat her. Matter of fact, Trudy's swimming right now, as we speak. She set out at first light today. Surely you saw that in the paper?" Louisa shook her head. She hadn't seen anything about it. She didn't have time to read the real news, let alone anything about swimming. "It's an exciting battle between England and America, and it may be over tonight. But your young niece would have given both of them a run for their money, I'd warrant. If they fail, I'd be more than happy to look at Catherine to sponsor in July next year."

Louisa stood. "I'm sorry, Mr. Black. This has been very illuminating, but I'm afraid I really must go. Your proposal is . . . totally unexpected. Give me some time to think and perhaps I can write you here in London." What a ridiculous notion, Louisa thought, running off to Baltimore while Catherine swam. She'd write a polite "no" after a decent interval.

"Of course." He stood too. "Dr. Quick, can I say it has been an honor to meet you? Emily speaks so highly of you, and I know my doctors would value your help as we go forward." He took a breath in and out. "I had hoped to tempt you with the challenge I presented but I can see you have a full dance card when it comes to challenges with your own clinic and now your young niece. And given that our time is up, I shall have to be the crass American your newspapers love to paint me as."

He gathered his coat and hat from the chair beside him, put out a hand. She took it. He held it. "The truth is this: I am a man of considerable means, Dr. Quick. I can help you in your work if you can help us in Baltimore. We need you. If I may be so bold," he said. "Is that how you English put it? If I may be so bold, I will pay whatever it costs. I would venture that your own clinic is going to require substantial work in order to pass the coming inspection. I do want you to know that the money isn't going to be the issue here." He still had her hand.

She was shaking her head, about to let him know she couldn't possibly leave the clinic, when it occurred to her that she could. Of course she could. She could go to Baltimore and visit Mr. Black's clinic. She could take Catherine, just as he suggested, and Catherine could swim with this New York group, which was what Catherine wanted to do. She wanted to swim. And why shouldn't she swim? Oh, Louisa didn't like swimming, or the reasons those men ogled the girls at any rate. But if Catherine wanted to swim, it might take her mind off Australia and the island and wanting to go back there. Ruth didn't have a problem with swimming. Nellie didn't. It was only Louisa, who was occasionally odd about things, she knew. Louisa could take Catherine to America where Catherine could swim with this swimming group of Mr. Black's. Louisa could visit Emily and see the clinic setup, and then Mr. Black could give them the money they needed to upgrade the clinic. How marvelous. She felt her head nodding, almost in spite of herself.

"Sit back down, Mr. Black," she said suddenly. "How would this work? When?"

He smiled but didn't sit, released her hand. "Ideally, before the end of this year," he said. "I go back in November, and any time after that would suit us."

She regarded him. Gardenias, that was the fragrance. "For some reason, I find myself liking your idea, Mr. Black, and there is nothing crass about money as far as I'm concerned. We run a clinic for the poor. They have no one but us, and if we were closed, they'd have no one."

"You're a lot like your younger brother, Dr. Quick. And actually, if you are thinking of bringing your niece, I've realized that the winter swim season is much easier in New York than here, as we have so many heated tanks.

"Say, I'm giving a little party this Saturday. Perhaps you could attend and bring your niece. I'd like to meet her." She was about to decline but he held up a hand. "No need to answer now. There's been a lot to digest. I'll have my man pop by with an invitation tomorrow. May I say again it's been an honor, Dr. Quick."

"Mr. Black," she said, walking him to the office door. She looked behind her at the clock. Five o'clock. Normally to get home from the office, Louisa would take the train from The

Regent's Park to Waterloo and transfer. She could walk from Aldgate. But she'd still be late.

"Let me drive you home," he said when she turned back to say farewell. "I have a car outside." She started to protest but lamely. He shook his head. "Truly, it's the least I can do."

Black's car was a Daimler, parked right outside Louisa's building. When the driver opened the door for her and she stepped in, she felt like the other Harley Street doctors who cared for London's well-to-do. They were driven around in cars like this. The rich smells of leather and cigars reminded Louisa of her childhood in Edinburgh, at her grandfather's house, when the men would sit around telling stories and smoking cigars. She'd fall asleep in her father's lap, the men's soft, low voices drifting into her ears.

Black opened the other rear door, got in and sat beside her. She could smell that fragrance again. He was easy company for the journey, making jokes at his own expense about his reputation in the English papers as the mad American, which amused him greatly. He owned a newspaper himself in Baltimore, he said, so he knew the business. But they'd be proven wrong one day, he said. He was sure flight was the way to travel anywhere, he continued, pointing out the traffic they encountered; nothing like New York, he said, but it still takes an age to get anywhere in a motor car. "And yet, you Londoners don't think we'll take to the sky." If he'd flown her home, she'd be there now, he said. Louisa should come up some time, he added, and she'd see what he meant. She looked out the window and up into the sky, couldn't quite picture herself in flight.

As they'd pulled up outside her house, Louisa found herself

in a happy mood, to her surprise. What a delightful person, she thought. The driver opened Louisa's door for her. Black got out on his side and came around to her on the footpath.

"I'm sorry that I can't ask you in, Mr. Black," she said. "I need to talk with my niece about the Thames business and it may be quite delicate."

He waved her away. "Wouldn't think of imposing, Dr. Quick," he said. "My, you have me in good cheer, though. No wonder your patients speak so highly of you." He leaned down and kissed her cheek and while she found herself shocked at the intimacy, he leaned back out and smiled and she couldn't help but return his smile. "Be kind to your niece," he said. "She really has done something extraordinary."

Talk about extraordinary, she thought on the way up the front path. She could still feel the warmth of his breath on her cheek.

18

She found Nellie in the kitchen in a great storm of activity. She was wearing her maid's uniform, a gray skirt, good white apron and bonnet. Her face was flushed pink. "We have the Yardsleys coming," Nellie said.

"I completely forgot." Louisa looked at her watch. It was just past six. "There was a fellow . . . Oh, never mind now. What time?" Louisa said, all thoughts of her pleasant drive home disappearing in a panic. How could she have forgotten Lord Yardsley?

"Seven," Nellie said. "I've made a roast and fought Catherine off the lemon delicious but I wondered what you want to serve for drinks."

"Something from the cellar. Let me go. Lord Yardsley needs to give me more money, and he won't want to. We'll ply him with drink. You, Nellie, are a gem."

"He's rich then?"

"Don't you know him?"

Nellie shook her head. "I don't meet all that many lords, I'm afraid."

"Oh, well, he is rich, yes. And his wife is so very tiresome. I always have the strangest urge to giggle when she speaks to me. She couldn't be ruder if she tried."

"And that makes you want to laugh?"

"As a matter of fact it does. Where's Catherine?" she asked just as her niece came in. Louisa found herself smiling. "Well, Catherine, what are we to do with you?" She tried to say it gently.

Nellie looked at them both. "Louisa, if I may, and I know we're busy getting ready and we don't have time to talk now, but I did want to make sure you know that there was a girl at the school who's been right nasty to Catherine. I hope Catherine won't mind my saying that this girl was the one who not only urged Catherine to swim the river, but also told the principal. A real piece of work, to my mind."

"Really," Louisa said. "Is that true, Catherine?"

"It is," Catherine said. "But as Nellie said today, what I did—it was very irresponsible. And I'm sorry it caused so much trouble, Aunt Louisa. I didn't think about it being wicked. I thought it would show them what I can do. I can't do so many other things at that school, but I can swim."

"You can swim," Louisa said. Catherine nodded, looked a little perplexed. Louisa only smiled. "Yes you can, Catherine. You most certainly can."

Louisa could take Catherine to America. Catherine could visit the women swimmers Black spoke of, and then she and Catherine could go on to Baltimore and spend some time together. It would give Catherine a break after the unpleasantness at Henley, and when they came home they could find a more suitable school. And Catherine would forget the island in all the excitement, Louisa felt sure. Let Mr. Black think of his Channel champion. Catherine could swim, build her confidence and come back to school and all the unpleasantness would blow over. Not only that. What better way to forget her old life in Australia than a holiday in America? "Well, Catherine, we don't have to worry about it right now," Louisa said. "You weren't happy there anyway, by Nellie's account, and I don't think every school in the world would make you this unhappy."

"Yes," Catherine said, looking even more confused by Louisa's seeming change of heart. "I was happy at school on the island. I loved it more than anything."

"Yes, well, we'll talk again, my dear. But for now, the Yardsleys are coming."

"Which means I have work to do," Nellie said. "Off now, Catherine, and set the table."

Louisa followed Catherine into the dining room where the cloth had already been laid. "We haven't shown you how we set the table here, have we?" Louisa said. "It's probably different from what you did on the island."

Catherine shrugged. "I don't really remember anyone setting the table."

"Well," Louisa said, "it's useful information. Do you know what goes on the outside?"

Catherine shook her head.

"The first thing you use—which tonight will be the soup spoon—on the side you use it, which is mostly the right. And then you just work your way in. It's very sensible, really." Louisa opened the drawer on the sideboard and pointed out the silver.

She had intended to set one place and then leave Catherine to do the rest, but she ended up doing them all. "See, easy?" she said, and smiled. Catherine just looked at her.

"I can't thank you enough for getting us ready for tonight," Louisa said to Nellie when she returned to the kitchen. "I can't believe I forgot the Yardsleys, but I did. And thank you, Nellie, for letting me know about Catherine. I need to do more. I know that now." She left Nellie to the rest of the preparations.

Catherine came down soon after, in one of the blue woolen skirts and cream blouses they'd bought in Sydney. She looked presentable enough, except for her hair, which hadn't seen a brush all day. "Catherine, you could have done more with your hair."

"If I spent hours," Catherine said. "And it would still be hair at the end of it."

It reminded Louisa of an interaction she'd had with Elizabeth when she herself was a girl about Catherine's age. Brush your hair, or you can't come down to meet the visitors, Louisa's mother had said. Louisa had refused, and had stayed in her room through a luncheon. Ruth was right. Catherine was young and finding her way. And Louisa hadn't always been as compliant as she told herself she had. Elizabeth met Louisa's attempts at self-assertion firmly. Had it helped? Not really, Louisa thought now. She said, more gently, "I want us on our best behavior this evening. I need Lord Yardsley to give me money."

"Oh, Louisa, is money all you care about?" This was Nellie, who'd come up behind Catherine.

"As a matter of fact, it is," Louisa said. "Half of my patients depend on my being able to attract money from the likes of Lord Yardsley." She thought of Mr. Black then, who'd said he'd pay whatever it cost. Imagine having money like that so that you could just do whatever you wanted. Louisa had spent her adult life barely getting by. Although her father had done well in shipping, it was Alexander who'd made the most of the family business, and Alexander who'd inherited the wealth. He'd never offered to help Louisa with the clinic and she'd never asked him. Oh, he'd not leave his sister destitute, of course, but he didn't see it as his responsibility to provide for what he saw as a pet interest.

Louisa had loved being able to practice to the full scope of her training as a surgeon during the war, so afterward she came up with the idea to establish her own hospital. They'd started a day clinic. Other doctors had joined them, all women, and Louisa wanted more than anything to be able to offer surgical services. Eventually they set up an operating theater and opened the inpatient service. Now they had the clinic, hospital, and a hostel for pregnant women who couldn't afford to go anywhere else.

Some of the women Louisa treated at the Harley Street practice were generous enough to donate to the clinic. Others were not. The one thing Louisa had learned from working between London's well-to-do and London's poor was that poverty was not the characteristic that made people ugly. Poverty did not discriminate between good and bad, clean and dirty, caring and uncaring, or intelligent and stupid. It only changed things like having a roof over your head or not, having enough to eat each day or not. Women in the East End had nothing to fall back on. Many had lost husbands and sons to the war. Even families that were still intact suffered unemployment, which left them destitute. Sometimes it felt to Louisa that the world must change soon, for it was impossible to have so many living so poorly while others lived so well.

Lord and Lady Yardsley were estate owners from Surrey with three grown daughters, all now married with their own families. The Yardsleys had known the Quicks, and Louisa had asked them for money before. Lord Yardsley had always obliged. While the dinner was a thank-you, Louisa was also hoping to secure funding for a new X-ray machine; though she needed more than just an X-ray machine now that Princes Square was to be inspected. While Mr. Black might provide for this larger cost, she still needed to push Lord Yardsley to help where he could.

The doorbell rang and Nellie bustled down the passage to answer it. She always greeted guests and took their coats and sat them in the parlor.

When she came back to the hallway on this occasion though, she was as white as a sheet, her palms flat against her apron. "Whatever's the matter, Nellie?"

"Nothing, miss. The guests have arrived. Actually . . . No, nothing." Nellie's face was pale.

"Are you quite sure you're well, Nellie?" Louisa asked. "You look like you've seen a ghost."

"No, miss. I . . . The visitors . . ."

"All right," Louisa said. "But if you're ill, go to bed. I can look after the Yardsleys."

But Nellie just shook her head and hurried back into the kitchen.

As Louisa turned to go down the hallway to greet the

guests in the parlor she saw Lord Yardsley himself next to the hat stand. He was looking at Louisa wide-eyed, as if he'd had a blow. And then she knew. He must have visited Nellie when she was on the street. Louisa took a moment to compose herself, looked at him incredulously. How could he? she thought. He was someone she respected, even admired. How *could* he?

"Oh, Lord Yardsley," she said finally, in a loud voice, "clearly you've met our wonderful Nellie." Nellie was a child even now, Louisa thought. She turned her face away from Lord Yardsley, repulsed. "And where's dear Lady Yardsley?" she managed to say.

He turned behind him dumbly and there she was, a jewel in emerald green silk. "Oh, Lady Yardsley," Louisa said, staring now at Lord Yardsley. "Have you met Nellie? She's been with us since . . . We won't speak of that here." Louisa held Yardsley's eye until he looked away.

"Dr. Quick," she said. "So kind of you to invite us. And your little house. It's so . . . quaint." Lady Yardsley looked up and down the tiny hallway. The paint was peeling from the ceiling, and the rug in the hall looked like a team of hounds had slept on it every night for a decade. At least the lights were dim, so the scene was somewhat softened. The bulbs were blown in the electrical lamps and Louisa hadn't brought the ladder down from the attic to change them, so they had a gas lamp instead. She saw their home as Lady Yardsley might. At least the Scotties were shut up in the upstairs bedroom.

Louisa introduced Catherine, who was standing at the bottom of the stairs. The girl was staring.

"Charmed, I'm sure," Lady Yardsley said in a way that suggested she wasn't at all charmed. "You must be the one from the colonies." Catherine raised her eyebrows in a quizzical smile.

Louisa ushered them into the parlor.

"And you have a tiger," Lady Yardsley said.

Better than the wolf you have, Louisa might have said but refrained. Instead she smiled at Lady Yardsley. "We put everything toward the clinic, Lady Yardsley, and there's not much left, I'm afraid. Home is where the heart is. Now if you'll just excuse me a moment . . ."

Louisa went into the kitchen. "I can serve up if you're not well, Nellie."

Nellie looked up, her jaw set. "No," she said. "I want to."

"Do I have to sit through this?" Catherine whispered when Louisa was on her way back to the parlor. She'd come out to the hallway, leaving their guests alone.

"For the clinic, my dear, for the clinic," Louisa whispered. And then she thought better of it. "Actually, can you go and talk to Nellie? She's upset. She'll talk to you, I think."

Lord Yardsley was usually an improvement on his wife, but tonight he was without his unusual bonhomie. He was standing in the middle of the parlor still in his gloves and hat. He cleared his throat loudly. "And so, Louisa, we hear wonderful things about your work."

"Hat, Yardsley," his wife said.

"Oh, yes," he said, removing the hat and gloves and handing them to Louisa, who deposited them in the hall.

"You know," Louisa said when she returned, "it's the generosity of folk like yourself and Lady Yardsley that makes the clinic possible."

"Of course," he said. "But we're not doing the work. You are." He cleared his throat.

"Oh, you're doing quite a bit," Louisa said, narrowing her eyes as he flinched and looked away. "But you're right. We always need more."

Lady Yardsley spoke then, about someone Louisa didn't know, or perhaps she did, but she lost the beginning and was finding the story difficult to follow now, something about a fish having a spike that someone may have got in their foot. Was it a health story? Perhaps it was.

Catherine came back in. She had a fierce look on her face. "Catherine, dear," Louisa said. "Nellie's made a wonderful dinner. We'll make sure we thank her."

Catherine nodded tightly. She looked as though she wanted to give Yardsley a piece of her mind. Louisa hoped her niece would be able to hold her tongue.

The dinner was interminable, and Louisa felt for Nellie, who came out to serve as usual but looked mortified each time. Lord Yardsley was uncharacteristically quiet throughout the meal, which meant his wife spoke incessantly about nothing. Catherine continued to fume.

Louisa saw her chance. "Catherine," she said after the plates were cleared and Lady Yardsley was refreshing herself, "I worry that Nellie is unwell." She looked straight at Lord Yardsley as she spoke. "Go in and help her, my dear. Perhaps you could bring dessert and Nellie could retire early tonight."

"All right," Catherine said.

When Catherine left, Louisa turned her eyes to Yardsley but she didn't even need to speak.

"I know your clinic does such excellent work for those less fortunate than the rest of us," he said. "And so, with this in mind, I have decided to donate once again."

"Oh, Lord Yardsley, if only you knew what a difference your support makes."

He held up a hand to stop Louisa saying any more.

"I haven't yet spoken with Lady Yardsley about a further contribution," he said. "So best not mention it. Last year, we were able to give a hundred pounds, I believe. This year, we are able to double that amount because of our good fortune."

"That will go toward a much-needed X-ray machine. If you were able to bring yourself to give another two hundred, making the total four hundred pounds, you've no idea the help we could offer to those less fortunate than yourself."

He agreed so quickly Louisa wondered if she should have asked for more.

The Yardsleys left soon after dessert, declining port, for which Louisa was thankful. Nellie had retired, as Louisa suggested, and Catherine had done an adequate job of serving the lemon delicious, although the portions might have been more suited to dockworkers.

When Louisa returned to the kitchen after seeing the visitors off, Catherine was waiting for her. "You stay here," Louisa said. "I just want to check on Nellie."

She went upstairs quietly, stood at the door of the room and heard sobbing. She went in. The lamp was out and Nellie was lying on her cot, her face turned to the wall. She must have heard Louisa come in, though, because she said in a voice thick with tears, "I'm so sorry."

Louisa sat on the bed. "Turn around now and look at me."

Nellie half turned and sneaked a glance at Louisa before turning back.

"Oh, Nellie, you mustn't worry. I don't. Please."

But the poor girl wouldn't be consoled. Louisa talked a while more and then offered her a sedative to help her sleep, which she accepted. Once she was settled, Louisa went back downstairs.

Catherine had been tidying in her absence. She was still angry. "He'd been to visit Nellie," she said accusingly.

"I know."

"Why didn't you confront him then?"

"To what end?" Louisa said flatly, looking at her niece.

"Louisa, Nellie's our friend. He'd . . . taken advantage of her."

"Well, she can go to school next year with his money." Louisa felt proud of Catherine then, that the girl saw Nellie as someone they should defend. It showed her strength of character.

"I thought you needed the money for the X-ray machine," Catherine said.

"Well, of course we do. But you judge me harshly, Catherine. Nellie must go to school or she'll be back where she was if anything happens to me."

"Is that true for me too?" Catherine said. "If I don't go to school."

Louisa nodded slowly. "I'm afraid it is, yes," she said. "It's important to have an education, Catherine. And if you're a woman, it's the key to the door."

"The door to where?"

"Freedom," Louisa said. She sat down opposite her young

niece. "Catherine, I'm not sure I've looked after you very well these six months. I . . ."

"I'm sorry about the swimming. I shouldn't have done it," Catherine said. She looked genuinely upset.

Louisa put her hand up to stop her speaking. "No, Catherine. You haven't done anything wrong, not really. I don't think I've quite understood how hard all of this change has been for you. And I'm not very good at listening sometimes, or at understanding things the way I ought to. Can we try to go forward from here on a different footing? I'll try to be more understanding, and I promise I will do my best in future to make sure you are looked after." Louisa felt tears welling in her eyes. "I'm just sorry, Catherine."

"Me too," Catherine said.

19

Catherine and Louisa had tidied the kitchen after dinner and finished washing the dishes together. Now it was the middle of the night and Catherine was at Louisa's bedroom door. "There's someone on the telephone, Louisa, who says you must come."

"Yes, yes," Louisa said, groggy with sleep. She was still in a dream, quite a pleasant dream, already fading, a little shocking when she realized Mr. Black was in it. She stopped thoughts of the dream and went downstairs, her feet cold on the tiles in the hall. Her eyes wouldn't stay open, the dream pulling her back to bed.

"I've been asked to say sorry for waking you up," a little voice said when she went to the telephone.

"That's all right," Louisa said.

"Sally said to tell you it's a beach." Sally was one of the midwives. "You need to come, she said. She's worried about the footings."

"Where is she?"

"Do you know Danby Road?"

"Yes."

"We're the house at the end of the last row on the left off the road, the river end. We're the one with a light on, Sally said."

"Tell her I'm on the way."

Louisa surmised the lad meant a breech, footling, and the midwife needed help with the delivery—quickly.

Nellie was asleep but she found Catherine in the kitchen. "I have to go out. Do you want to come?"

Catherine nodded.

Louisa went upstairs to dress. When she came down, Catherine was back downstairs, dressed, ready and making tea. "You won't have time for that," Louisa said.

"It's for you. I'll put it in a flask," Catherine said. "The driver's waiting."

"Grab the whisky," Louisa said. Catherine looked at her in horror. "For the mother, dear."

They came to the house at the end of the row and the light was indeed shining out into the night. Louisa knocked on the door and they were admitted by a girl who looked like she should be asleep. The house was tiny; it made Louisa's seem palatial. There were two rooms, one a kitchen and eating space, the other a bedroom. The kitchen was filled with small children, none older than six. The boy who'd telephoned, knowable by his face, still flushed with the cold he'd been out in, couldn't have been more than five. Their father was working on the subway, the boy told them.

Louisa could hear moans coming from the bedroom. They went in.

"Nancy, is it?" Louisa said to the woman. "You remember me from the clinic? I'm Louisa. We're going to help you now."

Sally, the midwife, stood to go and see to the other children.

"Sally!" Nancy called out in alarm. "I don't want no doctor." Many of the East End women were suspicious of doctors, especially women doctors.

Louisa took Nancy's hand. "I know what you're going through. I've had a child, too, you know, Nancy," she said quietly. "But the baby's coming feetfirst, which we'd rather he didn't. You'll need two of us. Sally won't go anywhere, dear." She turned to the midwife. "Stay by her side," she said. Then she noticed Catherine standing there behind her. "You go and look after the other children, would you, Catherine?" Louisa said.

Louisa was thankful Sally had been able to keep the mother calm; it was worse when they panicked. As the contractions intensified, they waited, hopeful. If worse came to worst, Louisa could do a cesarean operation, but she'd do everything to avoid it here in the home.

As Sally comforted the mother, Louisa listened to Catherine out in the kitchen. One of the children said, "We've had no tea, miss."

"Are you hungry, then?" Catherine replied.

"Oh my, yes."

"Let's see what we can find." There was a pause, then Catherine said, "There's flour and an egg. A treasure trove. What's your name?"

"Alice."

"Well, Alice, do you know how to make pancakes? I think the two of us might be able to work it out together. What do you say? Do you have a skillet?" Louisa heard the clatter of pans. Then the contractions became more intense and she stopped noticing the sounds outside.

By the time the baby came, another boy, Catherine and the children were clearing the dishes and tidying the kitchen. When Louisa emerged, one of them said, "We're cleaning up for Mummy, so she doesn't feel so bad."

"She's feeling much better," Louisa said, "now that baby's here." The largest one squealed. "Is it a girl?"

"Why don't you come in and see for yourselves? Softly now."

Louisa looked across at Catherine then. She'd put the kitchen in order, wiped all the children's hands and faces, and now she was sweeping the floor. She'd started chopping vegetables for a soup, she said, and would like to get it on before they left.

"I'm just not quite sure what goes in soup," Catherine said. "I assumed water because you drink it."

Louisa laughed. "Maybe Sally can finish the soup," she said. "She'll stay now for the rest of the day."

There were five of them, Catherine told Louisa on the way home: Alice was six, Tom five, the twins three. "And there was a one-year-old who sat in my lap while I gave him milk from a cup. But they were lovely children, and Alice so grown up. She told me it was her baby coming. The others weren't old enough to look after a baby but she could. How sweet."

"Did you enjoy going?"

"Oh, yes," Catherine said. "It's the first time I've felt . . . useful. I felt useful."

"Well, you certainly were useful," Louisa said. "Normally there's no one there to help with the children. Sally would have gone to them, but it was better to have her with me when we told the mother her baby was breech. She knows Sally."

"Aunt Louisa, I didn't know you'd had a baby."

Louisa stared at her for a moment. "Oh, that," she said, forcing a smile. "A white lie. I just wanted to reassure the mother," she said quickly.

"So you haven't?" Catherine said.

"Of course not," Louisa said, more sharply than she intended. She felt fear suddenly, as if she were about to be found out doing something she shouldn't. She made herself calm, looked at her niece squarely.

"So that was a lie?" Catherine said.

"Well, strictly speaking, yes. But as I say, a white lie."

"What's a white lie?"

"One you tell to help someone." Catherine nodded, seemingly satisfied with Louisa's answer. Changing the subject, she explained why a breech birth was a concern. "It's mostly straightforward, like today, but when it's not, it can be awful."

Catherine seemed hardly to hear Louisa. She was so full of energy. "And when their mother was crying out, the little ones looked frightened," she said. "And I was scared, too, because I thought she must have been dying from the sound of it. But Alice, the one I told you about, just said, 'Babies hurt coming out.' It settled the rest of them down."

"Those children loved you," Louisa said. She regarded her niece. "You were marvelous, Catherine, just marvelous. And to think it was your first-ever birth!"

"Thank *you*, Louisa," she said. "I loved it. But I've been to births before."

"You have?"

"Oh yes, on the island, all the time."

The first time Florence had taken her to Badu. When a new baby came, there was always a feast. And after the feast, the baby would be given to the parents, Florence told Catherine on the boat going over.

"The mother and father?" Catherine had said, confused.

"Not always the first parents. This baby we're visiting, he's my sister's baby, but he's going to my brother." Florence nodded confidently so Catherine just nodded, too, although she hadn't really understood.

When they arrived, Catherine went with Florence into the hut where the men pointed. Inside were half a dozen women sitting quietly. In the back of the hut, behind a screen, was Florence's sister Mary, who Catherine knew. She was kneeling on all fours, rocking back and forth, moaning, and when she looked up she smiled weakly, but her eyes didn't really seem to see Catherine. Florence went to Mary, put her hand on her lower back and began to sing in a low, soft voice. One of the other women came to stand with Catherine. "Baby's coming," she whispered. "Very soon."

They helped Mary on to her haunches, with a woman on each side of her shoulders holding her up. She took Florence's hand and began to cry out. Florence sang in Kulkalgal Ya language. "Baby coming, baby coming. Sing the song, sing the song." Mary's eyes looked afraid.

And then the child had come out in a rush into Florence's

arms. Catherine saw dark curls and then limbs unfolding like a package. They lay the mother back down and put the baby straight up onto her belly. All the women were singing now. The little child raised his head, so big compared with his body, and sniffed, dropped his head, crawled, sniffed, crawled up his mother's belly toward her breast. There was still a string tying the baby to his mother, Catherine saw. Later she asked Florence what it was. "It's so wherever baby goes, his mother knows him."

At the feast that followed later that night, the baby was given to Florence's brother and his wife. Catherine continued to watch the first mother. She looked sad, Catherine thought, but maybe she was just tired.

When they returned to Thursday Island the next morning Catherine pulled off her pinafore and camisole and stood there in her pants and studied her belly button. She too had a line to her mother somewhere. Her mother knew where she was, but Catherine didn't think the line would last beyond the grave.

The next morning, Saturday, Louisa was in the parlor reading case notes. Nellie was dusting and Catherine was reading a book. Louisa looked over at her niece on the lounge. She'd stopped reading and was sitting there looking into the middle distance, listening to a song she'd put on the gramophone.

"You always play that song on the gramophone," Nellie said.

"It's beautiful," Louisa said. Catherine had told her the night before about the first birth she'd witnessed. It had sounded so different from what happened to Louisa's patients, and yet, so much the same. Louisa wasn't sure what she thought about Florence taking a girl to see something like that. And did Harry know? Louisa hadn't asked. She hadn't said anything to Catherine about her concerns but looked at her now with new eyes. Perhaps Catherine was more worldly than she'd realized. Perhaps the relationship with Michael was normal among the Islanders. Oh Harry, Louisa thought, I have no idea what to do with her. But I'm going to do my very best.

Nellie looked at Catherine too. "It's not so beautiful when you've heard it a hundred times this week."

"It's still beautiful," Louisa said. "What's it called, Catherine?"

"I don't know," Catherine said. "I bought it at the Camden Market."

"Is he singing 'where dreams come true'?" Louisa asked.

"He is," Catherine said.

"In dreamland," Louisa said. She smiled. "I can see why you'd like it."

Catherine smiled and it filled Louisa with warmth.

"The pair of you are beyond me," Nellie said. "I'm going to clean the stove. I can't think of anything I'd rather do right now." She took up her dusting cloths and left them.

Louisa smiled at Catherine. "I think Nellie grew up in a more industrious household than you or I," she said.

"Do you think?" Catherine said. "You manage everything."

Louisa laughed. "If only," she said. "Why do think Nellie's here?"

"She said it's because you're a Christian woman."

"Hah. For a start, I am anything but a Christian woman. And

second, Nellie's here because if Nellie wasn't here, I wouldn't manage. I don't know the first thing about running a household."

"But you're a surgeon, Louisa. You don't need to be able to do those things."

"And what would stop you being a surgeon?" She put down her pen and looked at Catherine.

"I couldn't do that. I can't even get through school."

"Of course you can," Louisa said. Catherine's confidence had taken a blow, Louisa realized. "You're a Quick. You can do anything. If you want to succeed in school, you'll be able to. We just have to find the right kind of school."

"You thought Henley was the right kind of school."

"Yes, I did," Louisa said. "But I was wrong. Or the timing was wrong. Whatever it was, you didn't fit in there. We need to try somewhere else. Even Ruth Luxton is disappointed in the school. But not in you." She smiled.

The song had finished and Catherine went over to play it again.

"But for now, give me a hand with this case, would you?" Louisa said. She wanted to take the girl's mind off the school. She went back to her report. "I'll tell you about it and you tell me what I should do."

Catherine looked at her aunt, sniffed. "Are you serious?"

"Of course. Come, sit down with me."

Louisa explained the details of the case. A young man who'd been superficially injured in the war had ever since experienced a range of odd symptoms: facial tics, involuntary vocal sounds, sometimes foul language. He'd been referred by a physician in Harley Street and Louisa wanted to help if she could. The physician was suggesting there might be a tumor.

Catherine thought for a moment. "Well, is there a risk that if you operate you'll harm the patient?"

Louisa nodded. "There most certainly is."

"And don't you promise not to do harm?"

"Hmmm."

"So maybe don't operate."

"That's what I think too. So what if the man swears too much? I doubt we'll find anything in his skull that causes it. Harry's taught you very well. Most of my work is like this, deciding not to do anything. And when I *do* do something, it's usually relatively straightforward. See, you could be a surgeon. You could be anything, my dear."

"Even a swimmer?"

Louisa smiled. "Yes, even a swimmer." She looked at her niece. "But I'm not sure that swimming would be enough for a life, to be honest. I can't help thinking you'd want more."

"Me too," Catherine said. "I don't think swimming is anything like what you do. Or Papa. Or even Sister Ursula. It's really just for fun.

"Aunt Louisa, when you said you weren't a Christian, did you really mean it?"

Louisa nodded. "I did."

"Do you believe in God?"

She thought about this question. "I don't know, Catherine. I really don't."

"I don't know either," Catherine said, swallowing hard. "Florence is Christian. I liked Sister Ursula a lot. I thought at one time I might be a nun."

Louisa smiled. "I think every girl thinks that at some time," she said. "I know I did. And I wasn't even raised in a Christian household."

"Were you and my father close growing up?" Catherine said then.

"Oh my, yes," Louisa said. "They called us the twins."

"What was he like?"

"Harry? Well, he was unexpected. My mother lost a child, a girl before me, Margaret, and when I came, I think she and my father were overjoyed, a girl to replace her. But then, just a year later, along came Harry. Our mother was very busy. She was involved in the London School of Medicine for Women and then she found out she was pregnant. It wasn't easy for her. She had her work and then these two babies. He was happy, though. Harry was always happy. That's what I remember."

"So you looked after him?"

"I don't know about that." Louisa thought back. "They were different times, Catherine. My mother was trying to do something so important." She regarded her niece. "When I was your age, my mother drove me mad. My sister who died, Margaret, had tuberculosis. Mama was convinced it was hereditary and that I would die too. I was sick when I was about ten, after they sent me off to boarding school, which didn't help. Mama was wrong, we now know. Margaret died because she had cow's milk from one cow only, which was what was recommended at the time. It gave her tuberculosis over and over. If medical science had inched just a little further along, perhaps Mama would have worried less. But it drove me to distraction the way she ran my life."

"Did you know my mother?" Catherine said.

"Hardly at all," Louisa said.

"Do you know if she was happy?"

"I don't," Louisa said. "Did she seem unhappy to you?"

"I don't remember her," Catherine said. "It was just . . ."

"Yes?"

"Nothing. Just my father never talked about her. And I wondered, you know, if they were happy. I don't feel anything about her."

"Oh, I do know they were happy," Louisa said. "Harry adored Julia. In fact, it was quite a joke in our family. Harry was smitten. And he loved you very much, as you know."

There were tears in Catherine's eyes. "Aunt Louisa, I'm glad I came here. I mean, I miss the island. I miss Florence. But I'm glad I'm here."

Louisa swallowed hard. She couldn't trust her voice to answer.

20

Catherine was sitting at the table in the dining room writing a letter to Florence—she still hadn't heard from Michael—when she heard the doorbell. She knew not to answer it—Nellie had scolded her before. Catherine was supposed to understand that Nellie was the help, whereas Catherine was the mistress. "Well, if I'm the mistress, why is it you don't ever do as I say?" Catherine had said to Nellie once.

"That's another matter altogether," Nellie said. "But you have to start acting your station, girl, or you'll never be like your aunt."

That morning, before she'd left for work, Louisa had said that Catherine mustn't worry herself. We'll find somewhere to go, she'd said, almost gaily. She'd even sat at breakfast in the kitchen with Nellie and Catherine, sipping coffee and talking about the days ahead. She thought perhaps Catherine could come to visit the clinic while they were sorting out what to do next. Would you like that? she'd said. Catherine said she would, unsure about this new Louisa, who seemed more relaxed than the old one but not quite real yet.

I haven't heard from Michael, Catherine had written, *and you can imagine I am a bit worried. Please write again and let me know you are both safe. Ask him about the turtles.* If anything would get him to write, their turtles would.

Now Nellie was at the door. "There's a messenger for you."

"What sort of messenger?"

"One that has a message, I'd warrant. Quick sticks. Get your pinnie off and out you go. Quite sure of himself, said he must see Miss Quick and I wouldn't do. Come on now. I haven't got all day."

Catherine rose, pulled her pinafore over her head and draped it over the chair. As she was walking toward the kitchen, Nellie said quietly, "Parlor, dear."

Catherine turned and went to the little sitting room at the front of the house.

On the sofa was a young man dressed in a dark brown suit, his long legs crossed at the ankles. He had a hat in his lap, which he held in his hand as he stood. "Miss Quick, it's so kind of you . . ." Something went wrong as he moved toward Catherine and he fell forward. Catherine caught him just as he was going over, holding him up under the arms.

"Goodness," Catherine said.

"I'm so sorry," the young man said as he righted himself. "Are you all right?" He had an accent that was not quite English or, if it was, there was something else in it as well.

"Of course," she replied. "Are you?"

He was at least a head taller than Catherine, willowy with

fair skin and dark brown hair swept back from a high forehead, accentuating soft dark eyes. He smiled. "Yes. I must have caught my foot in the rug, I think." He smoothed his jacket and looked behind him at the tiger. A lick of hair had fallen forward and he pushed it back. He smiled nervously and looked at the rug again. "That's a tiger," he said. He seemed a little flustered now. "I come on behalf of Mr. Manfred Lear Black, whom you may have heard of."

Catherine shook her head. "I haven't," she said.

"He's American, staying here for the summer."

"Oh, the mad American," Catherine said without thinking.

"Quite. The journalists are fond of calling him that."

"I'm sorry. I didn't mean to be rude."

"Don't worry. Mr. Black enjoys our English press immensely."

"Let's sit down," Catherine said, taking a seat herself on the chair, "if you feel that might be safe now, Mr. . . . ?"

"Oh God, Mackintosh, Andrew Mackintosh. Lovely to meet you, Miss Quick. I'm sorry. The tiger has quite done me in. Mr. Black is my employer. That is, I am his confidential secretary. And so." He returned to the sofa and then, as if suddenly remembering what he was there for, took from inside his suit pocket an envelope and handed it to Catherine. It was addressed to Dr. Louisa Quick and Miss Catherine Quick.

"Should I open it?" Catherine said.

"Perhaps wait for your aunt. But I can tell you its contents. Mr. Black would be delighted if you could attend a little party on his yacht, the *Aloha*, this coming Saturday, to celebrate the marvelous Captain Bone, who brought Mr. Black safely to our shores from the great state of Maryland, the United States of

America." This last was said with an accent that perhaps was supposed to be American, Catherine wasn't sure.

"The *Aloha*."

"Yes, that's Mr. Black's yacht. It's moored in the Thames."

"Captain Bone?"

He nodded.

"Does Mr. Black know my aunt?"

"I believe he does, and I understand you are intimately acquainted with the Thames." He smiled gently, a sparkle in his eyes now.

"Yes." Catherine found herself blushing.

"Oh, I'm sorry," he said. "Is it not widely known?"

"No," she said. "I got into trouble at school."

"I bet," he said. "But *The Times* says you're a champion."

"Are you a swimmer?" she said.

He laughed. "I like the bath," he said. "And at Eton, I fell in the pond and a teacher had to fish me out. No, I'm not fond of water. But I saw you in the newspaper, Miss Quick. Mr. Black says it was a fine swim and he *is* a swimmer."

"Really," she said. She stood up. "Well, I'll give the invitation to my aunt."

"Good then," he said, standing when Catherine did. "Delightful. I'll very much look forward to seeing you again." He put out his hand to shake hers. "I'm quite safe when standing still," he said.

"That's a relief," she said, taking the offered hand. "And it's been lovely to meet you, Mr. Mackintosh."

21

L ouisa did a run of routine excisions, then saw three patients and caught up on paperwork. She looked at the
clock. It was just past eleven. She went out to the waiting
room and said to the nurse at the reception desk, "Can you
ask Dr. Luxton to pop into the office as soon as she's free?"

Then she returned to her desk and started writing up case
reports on the morning's patients.

Ruth soon came in. "You were right," Louisa said. Ruth
looked a question. "About Catherine. I talked to her and I do
believe, Ruth, I've been unkind. Too busy, and thoughtless.
I've been quite unkind to her."

Ruth smiled. "Not unkind, Louisa, not you. But sometimes, our demons get in the way of our better angels. And
your demons are worse than most."

Louisa laughed. "Then pity poor Catherine. But today, my
dear, I have another problem."

"The inspector."

"Two problems, then. Do you know an American business-man, Manfred Lear Black?"

Ruth shook her head.

"He seems to think I should go to Baltimore to visit a clinic he funds. He knows Alexander. He also saw Catherine's swim. He says it was extraordinary. They swim in America, appar-ently. Women, I mean. They won at the Olympics. One of them's trying to swim across the English Channel, apparently."

"They did win the Olympics," Ruth said. "Last year, yes they did. You didn't notice?"

"No," Louisa said. "I don't keep up with women's swim-ming. Anyway, he seems to know about swimming, and he has a group in New York that Catherine could swim with."

"And?"

"I can't leave here."

"Why not?"

"What would happen to the patients?"

"They'd see another doctor? If the clinic's all that's stopping you, Louisa . . ."

"He's offered money."

"Who?"

"Mr. Black. He's rich, and he's virtually told me to name my price. We'd have a chance with the inspector coming."

"I see. So a wealthy American has offered you an oppor-tunity to help him with a clinic. He also knows a way to help your niece to swim, which, apparently, is what she loves to do. And he's offered to get us out of a real pickle we're about to be in. And you can't make up your mind about going."

Ruth looked at Louisa over the top of her spectacles. She al-ways did this when she wanted to make a point.

Louisa nodded. "I see what you're saying."

Ruth broke into a smile. "Louisa, darling, this is a marvelous idea. I agree. You haven't had a proper vacation, ever. When you went off to get Catherine, you had all those worries about what it would be like. Now, you're finally learning what she needs. Of course you should go. You should go for six months, a sabbatical. There's a young doctor I've been trying to convince to come to us. She wants full-time work. So we'll give her full-time work. Easy. Mr. Whatsit can pay her salary."

"Women's swimming is the next thing, apparently," Louisa said, not really listening.

"Well, perhaps it is. Wouldn't that be marvelous?"

"Would it?"

"Oh, yes, wouldn't it? I mean, for Catherine, if there were only something she could find her place in. Do you remember Lily Smith?" Louisa shook her head. "Before your time, the swimming suffragist. Her idea was that she'd swim the English Channel to prove women could do whatever men could do and so should have the vote."

"Mr. Black said something about the Channel. No woman has ever swum it. He thinks Catherine could be the first."

"Yes, well, Lily Smith was going to be the first. She wasn't, in the end. She came out after just a few hours. But he thinks Catherine has that sort of ability. Goodness me, Louisa. How marvelous. I mean, it's true Lily put the cause behind by ten years because she failed so early on. But her failure was an enormous success. It got women swimming. My daughters all swim. I insisted. It's something about our bodies being able to do things. And also, floating. I think floating is important, don't you?" She tilted her head and regarded Louisa. "New

York! I'll tell you something. That young American girl, the one your Mr. Black was talking about, was within shouting distance of Dover when they pulled *her* out of the Channel yesterday, apparently, and look at Gleitze. She'll manage it one of these times. She's a typist, you know, who saves up enough money each year to get herself a coach and tugboat . . ."

Louisa hadn't really been listening. She'd been thinking about Mr. Black. The American girl, the one he'd sponsored, had failed, according to Ruth. He'd said Catherine might swim the Channel. That would be a very different path for the girl.

Earlier that morning, Louisa had telephoned Alexander, who'd said that yes, he knew Manfred Lear Black. "Outstanding fellow," Alexander said. "Big in the Democratic Party, I believe. They say he might run for high office one day. We're about to propose a major partnership with his Baltimore company. It will bring us into the U.S. passenger market. But why do you ask?"

"He's interested in our clinic," she said.

"Oh, yes, he has a similar setup in Baltimore, I think. Harry did some work for them. It would be great for me if you could help him, Louie. He's a tough businessman, ruthless on price. Maybe you can charm him." Alexander laughed as if the notion that Louisa might charm anyone was a hilarious joke.

She told Alexander that Mr. Black wanted her to help with his clinic. "I'll take Catherine out of school, I think," she said slyly. Alexander didn't say anything. He'd seen Catherine's picture in the paper but hadn't realized Catherine had been expelled. Louisa decided she'd rather keep it that way. The last thing she needed was Alexander on her back.

"I had a meeting this week," she said to Nellie that evening after Catherine had gone to bed. "A man named Black, an American businessman, wants me to go to America. He has a clinic and he needs advice. It would be for a month or two, probably early next year. Catherine's father did some work for them, and this Black fellow knows Alexander. I'd want you to stay here and take care of the house and dogs, just as you did when I went to Australia."

"Of course," Nellie said. "But what about Catherine?"

"That's the thing. Mr. Black is interested in women's swimming."

"Oh, yes," Nellie said with a look.

"No, not like that. I think he may be quite sincere. He seems very certain Catherine could be a competitive swimmer."

"Where would she swim?"

"There's a group of women in New York, apparently. It's not what you're thinking, Nellie. I think he may just be a good person."

"Do you believe in fairy godmothers, Louisa?"

"No, Nellie, I don't."

"Neither do I," Nellie said.

22

The deck in front of them was lit up with strings of colored lanterns, each one reflected as hundreds on the water. The weather had held through the week and tonight it was warm enough to go out in summer dresses, Louisa had told Catherine before they'd left. Best take a shawl in case, though, she added. It can be chilly down on the river.

Catherine was excited. Louisa had decided they would go to the party. They were to meet Mr. Black, Louisa said, who had asked Louisa to visit his clinic in America. And Louisa had said yes. She was going to take some time off from the clinic, she'd told Catherine. Dr. Luxton and the other doctors would look after her patients. She would take Catherine with her. "You'll be able to swim there," Louisa said. "If swimming's what you want to do, you'll be able to swim more easily there. In America, women can do more things."

But all Catherine heard was that they were going to America. America, where her mother's family had come from. Oh, yes, she could swim, and she truly loved to swim. She'd never had to consider not being able to swim until now. But perhaps, too, she could find her people. Mr. Black was related to her mother, Louisa said. His mother had been a Freebody, "or something," according to Louisa. Julia was a Freebody too, Catherine knew. Her mother's family. She might get to meet her mother's family.

Louisa had also said that, in the meantime, Catherine wasn't going back to school. She could come to the clinic and help the nurses some days, and once a week, if she wanted, she could go with Nellie up to Hampstead ponds to swim. When they were back from America, they'd sort out what to do about school. Catherine wasn't to worry, Louisa had said. She was sure they could get through this difficulty.

In front of them now was Mr. Black's ship, the *Aloha*, its main deck festooned with those lovely lanterns. Mr. Black had sent a car for them. The driver had opened the door for Catherine and had called her Miss Quick. Now they were met by a footman who led them down a small gangway and along the deck to a set of wooden doors. Catherine could hear a band playing and when the footman opened the doors the music was suddenly louder, like someone's face lighting up when they noticed you. Jazz, Louisa said, that's the new jazz music. You can't help but feel happy when you hear it. They were both smiling widely.

They went inside and found themselves on a landing looking down into a room the length of the entire deck. There were more than a hundred people downstairs, men in tuxedos, women in long gowns, and waiters in white jackets with trays.

Red, white and blue streamers were strung from a central

chandelier to each corner. A red carpet led down the stairs. "It matches your red dress," Catherine said to Louisa. Her own dress was made of velvet in a deep shade of green. Catherine had never felt anything so soft that wasn't alive, she'd thought when she first tried it on at the dressmaker in Sydney. She wore ivory slippers and a wrap they'd borrowed from Ruth Luxton's daughter May. When she'd come down the stairs before they left home, Louisa had said, "You look beautiful, my dear."

Louisa looked so graceful, Catherine had thought, the red silk dress, her hair piled into a chignon, a simple string of pearls around her neck. She was the one who looked beautiful. It was her eyes. They shone. But when Catherine said this aloud, Louisa laughed. And then Louisa had asked if she was happy. Catherine had said, "Yes, I am," because she saw the look on Louisa's face, of expectation, desire to please, and she'd felt sorry for her aunt suddenly. And she *was* happy. She was looking forward to tonight. Andrew Mackintosh would be here, he'd said, and Catherine hoped she'd see him again.

At the top of the stairs was a fellow in tails and white gloves. He had a staff in his hand, and as Catherine and Louisa approached he struck the staff on the floor three times. The crowd hushed. Then he boomed, "Ladies and gentlemen, I present Dr. Louisa Quick and Miss Catherine Quick of London."

People looked up and smiled, then the party resumed and the footman led Louisa and Catherine down the stairs. "Oh goodness," Louisa said. "It's quite an affair, isn't it? Mr. Black said it was a little party. I'm glad now we dressed up."

Just then Catherine saw Andrew Mackintosh heading toward them from the other side of the ballroom. She waved.

"Who's that?" Louisa said, frowning.

But before Catherine could respond he was with them. "Dr. Quick, Miss Quick. Mr. Black is so terribly sorry he's not here to greet you." Andrew looked flustered, Catherine thought. "He's been called away temporarily on an urgent matter, and he's asked me to look after you. Come over and we'll get out of the way and find the waiter with the drinks." As he said *drinks*, his eyes widened and he smiled. He turned to Catherine. "Did you swim here?"

"Of course," Catherine said.

Louisa looked at Andrew Mackintosh. "Have we met?" she said curtly.

"Oh, yes, yes we have," he said. "But I was about this tall." He used his hand to gesture at knee height. "I'm so sorry. It's been quite a day. You know my mother, Dr. Quick. Ada."

"Ada Mackintosh?" Louisa said, smiling suddenly.

"The same."

"Donald." Louisa's face lit up then, as she recognized the young man.

"No, Donald's my brother. I'm Andrew, the younger one."

"Of course. You were the handful."

"I was the bright spot in my mother's day was the way she mostly put it. But you're quite right. She told me not to touch anything on your desk."

"And you broke . . ."

He was nodding. "A vase, yes, expensive. And we bought you a new one and you said it was better than the old one, which was terribly kind of you."

"It's possible the new vase was actually better," Louisa said.

He laughed. "Ah yes, entirely, if my mother was involved in its purchase. She has marvelously good taste, unlike her offspring. Come, here's a man to fetch us a drink, which will make everything better."

He'd led them over to one side of the room, with doors out to the deck. "Just give me a moment to figure out what I do here. I'm not used to all this." He took from his pocket a wad of bills and peeled off two to give to the drinks waiter, who smiled widely. "Mr. Black insists I take care of 'tipping.' Do you know what that is?" Catherine shook her head. "We give money to the staff. I have a hundred pounds, which I'm to ensure everyone gets a little of. I'm not very good at it, I'm afraid. I gave the same fellow a pound three times. Thank goodness he's honest. Anyway, it's so lovely you could both attend. I know you're busy, Dr. Quick. Mr. Black very much wanted to be here to greet you himself." He turned to Catherine. "And so, have you been back in the river?" he said.

"You know Catherine too?" Louisa said to him.

"I delivered the invitation for tonight. I work for Mr. Black," he said, gesturing for them to go through a doorway out onto the deck. "Quieter out here," he said. There was a gentle breeze now that made the little lanterns swing from side to side. It was all so beautiful, Catherine thought. The white-coated waiter was back and Andrew took a glass of champagne for Louisa, punch for Catherine, and champagne for himself. "Sláinte, as we say in the old country," he said, taking a sip. "I love an employer who appreciates the finer things of life."

"Catherine mentioned someone had delivered the invitation," Louisa said, "but she didn't say the name. Ada's boy." She shook her head. "I thought you were at Oxford."

"Past tense, I'm afraid. I just wasn't suited to the life, I suspect," he said. "And the week I came down, Mr. Black was inquiring about recruiting an Englishman to help him while he's here. One of my father's friends put two and two together. I must say, Dr. Quick, Mr. Black is awfully glad you could come. And he is amazed by Miss Quick's achievement, that's certain. He's been following the Channel swimmers these last weeks."

Black had bought the *Aloha* from the U.S. Navy, Andrew told them. "But he came across on the *Transylvania* with Captain Bone, which is why we're having this party, to thank the good captain, who's somewhere over there, I think"—gesturing to the left of the ballroom—"and the captain's brother brought the *Aloha*."

Just then, the crowd parted and through the gap Catherine saw a middle-aged man with silver hair slicked straight back from his forehead, a lick falling forward onto his face. He was frowning slightly, as if concentrating on something down and to his left. He was about Catherine's height, small next to Andrew.

"Now, Mr. Mackintosh," he said, "are you taking good care of my special guests?" His eyes, a deep brown, sparkled as he smiled. Around them, Catherine saw, conversations had paused as people watched him. It was Manfred Lear Black.

"I'm doing my very best," Andrew said. "Mr. Black, Dr. Quick, whom you know, and her niece, Miss Quick."

"Dr. Quick," he said, leaning in to kiss Louisa on the cheek. Catherine was surprised. She'd never seen anyone kiss her aunt. He turned toward Catherine and nodded. "Miss Quick. It's my great pleasure to make your acquaintance."

His smile, from his eyes mostly, made Catherine feel at ease. "Mr. Black," she said. "Thank you so much for inviting us this evening."

"This is quite a party," Louisa said. "My mother used to say she didn't often throw parties, but when she did, they were good ones. But this is extraordinary."

Mr. Black surveyed the room. "Well, thank you, Dr. Quick. We're very honored to have you among us." His eyes flicked to Catherine again. "And to have a swimmer of such caliber. You," he said, smiling. "What a swim! I couldn't swim like that, Miss Quick." He smiled widely. "And now that Trudy Ederle has failed, the Channel is still there for the taking."

Catherine was confused momentarily.

"You," Mr. Black said. "You're going to swim the English Channel next year. I can feel it in my bones." He stared hard at her, broke into a smile. "Don't worry. You'll be ready."

"I wasn't worried," Catherine found herself saying. "It was just all news to me."

He laughed.

"Mr. Black flies, Catherine," Louisa said, looking at her niece.

"Well, I do, Dr. Quick," Mr. Black said. "But at functions like this, I keep my wings tucked under."

Louisa laughed. "Well, Catherine doesn't show her scales either."

"Of course not. She'd be smarter than that. That would be showing off. But you have the makings of a champion." He was still looking at Catherine. "What do you think of that?" He raised his head slightly, as if peering over spectacles, although he wore none.

Catherine didn't know what to say.

"Catherine is a little embarrassed, Mr. Black," Louisa said. "We're still discussing with the school what might be done." This was what Louisa had told her they would say.

"I'd give them a piece of my mind if you were my daughter," Mr. Black said, still looking at Louisa. "Schools here in London wouldn't know what to do with you, Catherine. And I have some sympathy with that point of view."

"You didn't enjoy school?" Louisa said.

"I did not," he said. "I failed mathematics, as it happens, and yet I'm a banker. I failed English and I'm a newspaper publisher. I think schools are overrated, Catherine. What do you think?" He was still looking at Louisa.

"Well, I didn't much like Henley," Catherine said, wishing he hadn't raised the matter of the school. Since she'd been expelled, her relief to be away from the place had given way to an awful feeling that she'd lost her one chance. "I guess I didn't fit in there."

"We're considering other schools," Louisa said to Black. "I do think Henley was less academic than I'd imagined it might be."

He laughed. "Good attitude, Dr. Quick. The school's the problem, not this one. My daughter's in France. She loves her school because all they do is ride horses and play sport and cook and eat. They even swim, Catherine. But you don't need school when you swim like you do. And as I say, the Channel is still there for the taking, girl," he said. "Gertrude Ederle was within sight of Dover when she stopped. You could give her a run next year if you trained. That's what I think. 'August '26' has a nice ring, and my newspaper would love it. What do you say about that?"

"Can a woman actually swim the English Channel?" Louisa said. "I mean, physically."

"Listen to you," Black said. "And I heard you were in favor

of women's equality." He pointed his finger at her. "Course a woman can swim the Channel—and the first one who does will be remembered forever.

"Dr. Quick, can I say again what a great honor it is to have you, and your niece, at our little party?" he continued. Louisa smiled up at him. She was blushing, Catherine thought. How odd. "I'm so pleased you could attend. And, Catherine, what you did was an amazing feat and don't let your aunt tell you differently." He grinned. "There is nothing finer in the world than a champion. In the newspaper business, we love them. And you, my dear girl, are a champion. I know it. And, as I understand it, we might be seeing more of you?" He gave Louisa a quizzical look.

"Yes," Louisa said. "I'm just finalizing arrangements for the clinic and then I'll be in a position to talk to you more. But I'm very hopeful we can come to an agreement."

"Well, that's fine news," he said. "Now, you were asking me about flying, Dr. Quick. Catherine, as your aunt already knows, I happen to believe that flying will one day be as normal as taking a train or ferry. It gets your newspapers very excited when I say things like that. Perhaps you've heard of the mad American?" He smiled as he said it. Catherine nodded. "Have you ever been up?" he said then.

"Up?" Catherine said.

He pointed toward the ceiling. "In the sky."

"No," Catherine said, smiling suddenly at the thought. Imagine being able to fly.

"Dr. Quick?" Black said.

Louisa shook her head. "I'm afraid of heights."

"Hah," Black said. "Me too. But when you're up there, you're so high it doesn't seem high at all, if that makes sense. Andrew here will vouch for that." He smiled slyly.

"Mr. Black is referring to the fact that I suffer dreadfully from air sickness," Andrew said, grinning. "I'm not at all frightened by how high we are, as I'm too focused on being ill."

Catherine looked at Andrew. "Oh dear, that sounds like no fun at all," she said. "But I think I'd love flying, Mr. Black."

"Say, why don't we take these two gals with us?" Black said to Andrew, looking from him to Catherine. "We're off to Paris the first weekend of September."

"No, I really don't think . . . ," Louisa started to protest.

"That settles it. I'll leave Andrew to tell you where and when. We'll send a car. Paris, so pack your glad rags." He looked at his pocket watch. "Now, you'll have to excuse me; I must get back to my meeting, unfortunately—an urgent matter. But I did want to make sure I welcomed you personally. It's been a great pleasure to make your acquaintance, Miss Quick, and to see you again, Dr. Quick." He smiled at Louisa, turned on his heel and left them, Andrew following behind him.

"He's quite singular, isn't he?" Louisa said once they were out of earshot. Her eyes were following his back across the room, Catherine noticed.

"Yes," Catherine said, smiling widely. "Did you hear what he said, Louisa? About flying? So can we go to Paris?"

"Can we go to Paris?" Louisa said. She was still looking after Black, watching the crowd parting again to let him through.

"Yes, can we go to Paris?"

"I don't see why not," Louisa said. "It might be fun." She

looked back at her niece and smiled, screwing her nose up as if they were two young girls planning a midnight feast.

It was late, after eleven. Louisa was on one side of the ballroom, watching the dancing. Most of the women wore full-length evening gowns, but there were some in the modern style whose dresses only came to mid-calf.

"They do whatever they like," Ruth Luxton had said to Louisa when women who came to the surgery began dressing in the style, showing their legs, their arms. "They're just like men."

"If they wanted to be like men, they'd wear trousers," Louisa had said. Sometimes she found Ruth exasperating.

"Some of them do," Ruth said, smiling. "Trousers and a shirt. Aren't they daring?"

"But why would they want to look like men?" Louisa said.

"To have the freedom of men. I think they're gorgeous, like flamingos."

"Flamingos are stupid," Louisa retorted.

"It was a metaphor, Louisa. No need to be so literal." Ruth smiled.

Now it occurred to Louisa that they didn't look like men at all; they were like boys with their flat chests and short hair. And why not? Boys, she thought: that's where freedom is.

Andrew and Catherine were among the dancers, laughing and chatting as they tried one of the new dance steps. He was a lovely young man, kind eyes, and Louisa could see that Catherine enjoyed his company. Ada Mackintosh, his mother, had been one of Elizabeth's patients. Elizabeth had delivered the two boys, and Louisa had inherited the family after Elizabeth retired. The other one, Donald, had been lost in France in the war, Louisa remembered now. Poor Ada. She adored her sons. Andrew had grown into a fine young man, Louisa thought, still getting used to his adult limbs by the look of him on the dance floor now. He'd be trustworthy in relation to Catherine, Louisa was sure. It was a relief, really, to see her with a local boy. He could do with a bit of fattening up, though, Louisa decided.

She was about to go over and tell Catherine it was time to go home when she heard a quiet voice behind her. "Dr. Quick?"

She turned around. It was Black. He had that little smile, more on one side than the other, his head tilted as if listening to a songbird a long way away.

Louisa had seen him once or twice during the evening, standing at the side of the dance floor watching the couples as the band played. On another occasion, he was looking out at the water. She didn't know what he was looking at, but he looked tired, worn down.

"Louisa," he said in his slow drawl. "May I call you Louisa?"

"Of course," she said, "if I can call you . . ."

"My mother used to call me Lear but everyone else just calls me Black."

"Lear then," she said. "It suits you." Louisa had had two glasses of champagne, and as a waiter approached she began to contemplate a third.

"A mad king?"

"Perhaps. Or perhaps Black, for you strike me as a definite kind of person." The champagne must have gone to her head, she thought as she turned down the third glass. She should have eaten.

"That I am," he said. "I want to talk about Catherine."

"Catherine?"

He took a long time to respond, so long she thought for a moment he'd forgotten he'd initiated a conversation. Then he looked sharply at Louisa. As he met her eye she felt a shiver. Not drunk, then, but hesitant, unsure about something. Those dark eyes—sad eyes, she decided when she thought of him later. There was something compelling about his sadness.

"Catherine," he said again. He was smoking a fat cigar, drinking what looked like scotch. "The swimmer." He smiled, but his face looked as if it might at any moment crumple into tears, or laughter. "The Thames is a terrible river. The tides, Louisa. She may be the best swimmer we've ever seen. Certainly better than Ederle. In my view."

Louisa put her glass on a nearby table. Why on earth would you care? she wanted to say. "You probably already know that Catherine grew up on an island very remote from the world," Louisa said. "She arrived in London with no idea how to behave, and now she is . . ." Louisa trailed off, looked over toward Catherine and Andrew, who were still dancing. He had his hand on her back. Louisa wondered should she intervene. "Please be assured that I will be most happy to come to Baltimore and help you with your clinic in whatever way I can. I would certainly want to bring Catherine as I am very worried about her future, and particularly . . ." Louisa couldn't go on.

She thought of the boy Michael, the letters. There had been another, this one in a different hand, from Florence, Louisa guessed. And Nellie had held one Catherine had asked her to mail. As Nellie handed it over, she gave Louisa a look. But

Louisa must take care of Catherine and the island was a danger to the girl.

He smiled, took a long sip of his drink. "Let's take some air," he suggested, and started toward the doors out onto the deck.

Outside it was chilly and Louisa felt herself shiver in her sleeveless dress. Black took off his jacket and put it over her shoulders. She found herself drawn to him.

He looked out toward the water, a dark force beneath the ship. "Ah," he said. "Later. We'll talk about all this later." He went to take her hand. She let him. At first she thought he was about to lead her somewhere, but instead he shook her hand, as if they'd made a deal. "My doctors will be pleased to have you come and visit us, Louisa, and I will wire Charlotte Epstein and make arrangements for Catherine to join the Women's Swimming Association.

"Meantime," he smiled again, "let's pack for Paris."

PART VI

Paris, September 1925

23

Catherine rubbed the window and peered out. Mr. Black had sent a car for them again, this time to take them to the airfield at Croydon. They'd had to get up at four in the morning and she'd had trouble getting off to sleep the night before with excitement. They were going in the aeroplane. Louisa had said yes! Now Catherine wished she'd eaten something as her stomach was beginning to growl. Nellie had offered them breakfast but Catherine had been too excited, Louisa too nervous.

In the pre-dawn light, Catherine could make out a long, faded track with a light at the far end. In shadow and mist was what she assumed was their aeroplane. It looked like a giant insect from here. Oh goodness, she thought. They'd be going up in the sky. She looked up through the car window.

Andrew emerged from a squat building to their left and walked over to them as they got out of the car. It was frightfully cold now, overnight rain having cleared to leave an icy chill.

"Is it safe today?" was the first thing Louisa said when Andrew reached them.

"No," Andrew said. "It's never safe. I can't stand it. But you'll be able to say you've flown in an aeroplane."

They made their way across to the building. "Our honored guests," Mr. Black said when they got inside. "Did you see the aeroplane?"

"No," Louisa said. "There was an aeroplane?"

"I did," Catherine said. "It's very fine, Mr. Black. But it doesn't look strong."

"Hah," Mr. Black said. "Your aunt's infected you with her fear. Don't worry. It can carry all of us and more besides."

He introduced them to the two pilots when they came in. The senior of the pair was Heindrick, a big man with a barrel chest and booming voice. "These are the girls, then," was all he said.

The second pilot, younger, blond hair and blue eyes, was all the way from Canada, Mr. Black said. "His name is Sam. Just don't call him an American. It upsets him."

Sam came over to Catherine. He wore dark brown wool pants and a leather jacket. He was about Catherine's height. "Have you ever been up?"

"No," she said. "I can't wait." Catherine was grinning, she knew. She couldn't believe it was actually happening. "Just like swimming, only in the air," she said.

He smiled. "Yes," he said. "A lot like swimming, really. This is an easy flight," he said. "We'll be there in a couple hours—although Mr. Black sometimes takes a detour, so you just never know what's going to happen. But make sure you look out the window once we're up." He had awfully straight white teeth and kindly eyes.

Heindrick went out and came back. The luggage had been loaded, he said. "We go."

They walked along the airstrip to the end. There was their aeroplane. It looked more sturdy closer up, Catherine decided, a large propeller in the front where the mechanic stood, and a ladder to take them up into the cabin. It was a dark blue, Mr. Black's favorite color, Andrew whispered to Catherine.

They climbed the ladder up into the aeroplane, the pilots first followed by Louisa then Catherine. The pilots went into the front of the plane, which was separated by glass doors from the cabin where half a dozen canvas chairs had been nailed to the floor for passengers. Black took the first row, Andrew beside him, Louisa and Catherine behind. Behind them was the spare tank of fuel—the smell was overpowering. Their luggage was piled on the sides of the plane. The bath-room was a bucket in the back.

Catherine could see the backs of the pilots' heads. They wore leather caps now, and she watched as Sam put his head out the window, signaling to the mechanic below. After a few minutes, the engine sputtered into life.

"Goodness me, it's loud!" Louisa shouted. It *was* loud, Catherine thought. They tracked along at ground level, slowly at first, then turned, picked up speed, the noise of the engines earsplitting. Catherine could feel the vibrations in every bone of her body. It shook you half apart. They bumped, rose, bumped, rose, bumped and finally rose and were airborne. It was like magic then, the engine still so noisy but the noise somehow less intrusive, the vibrations calming suddenly.

The strange feeling in her stomach as they ascended soon passed. The sun was rising and Catherine could see the earth below them recede. She could make out landmarks, now totally transformed. A farm, which from the ground might include a farmer with a wife and children, became squares of crops and a little red roof. It made everything simpler, Catherine thought. It was the most extraordinary thing she had ever seen.

They banked and came back around over the city of London and passed over the Thames. It was like a long highway of gold in the morning light.

When she saw the Tower Bridge, Catherine thought of the swim she'd done and all the trouble it had caused. She looked over at Louisa. Her aunt looked so fearful, her hands clasped together in her lap, her mouth set, her face pale. Louisa looked frail suddenly. She'd always seemed so strong. Catherine felt a pang of tenderness.

Catherine looked out again at the river, which wound its way through the countryside. The sun had disappeared behind a cloud and the river was the only detail she could make out now. It was gray, like the city itself, nothing like the sea at home, whose water was a pure blue-green from a distance and as clear as glass up close. The Islanders believed the sea was alive. But the river, Catherine had found, was a different kind of creature altogether, not wicked, she thought now, and alive, certainly, but dark and mysterious.

Andrew soon stood, ducking his head because of the low ceiling, and went to the back. Catherine could hear him retching.

She looked out the window again. They were flying over the English Channel. From here it looked so small, as if you could swim it in minutes, she thought. It would be an achievement to be the first woman to swim the Channel, Mr. Black had said at his party. Catherine looked down again. It really did look small, for already she could see the green of France.

Before long, they were over what must be Paris. She saw the Eiffel Tower she'd seen in books.

"Good Lord, we're there already," Louisa said. Her color was back, Catherine thought.

"Ain't it great?" Black turned around and said. "Now, tell me again this will never catch on as a way for getting around the place."

They passed Paris to their left and flew to Versailles—to visit his daughter's school, Mr. Black told them. But it turned out that by "visiting" he meant flying low over the ground. They could see the roof of the convent, the spires of the church. And sure enough there were the young women of Saint Marcel's waving to them. Mr. Black dropped bunches of flowers that had been packed for the purpose and then they climbed again, at Mr. Black's request, to "go over some Alps, please, fellas, to show the girls," before heading back toward Paris.

When Heindrick came back to talk to Mr. Black, he asked Catherine if she'd like to join Sam up the front. She went into the cockpit. You could see the whole world, she thought. The mountains in front of them were covered in white. Snow, she realized. It was snow. She'd never seen it before. "Oh, it's so very marvelous," Catherine said.

She took the seat next to Sam and he delighted in her sense of wonder. He said he never got sick of it. He'd learned to fly in the last months of the war. "In the end, I didn't get to do much flying," he said. "But I haven't been home yet. Plenty of work for pilots now."

"Do you miss home?" Catherine said.

"Oh, yes," he said. "I live in mountains like those ones down there. It's nothing like England. We get so much snow through the winter and even the summers are cold. It's beautiful. But you're not from England either if that accent's anything to go by."

"I grew up in Australia."

"Do you miss home?"

Suddenly Catherine thought she might cry. She nodded. She hadn't heard from them, not for over a month. She was worried. Michael hadn't written. He'd been angry at her for leaving. But Florence hadn't written either. Had they forgotten Catherine?

"I'm sorry," he said. "I didn't mean to upset you."

She shook her head. "I . . . It doesn't usually upset me so much." She swallowed her tears. "Tell me more about the mountains," she said.

In the summers, he said, he and his brother had set a goal to climb every mountain you could see from the town. "We'd nearly done it too. I'll finish if I ever get back there."

"I think you will," Catherine said.

Just then, Andrew poked his head into the cockpit. "Here you are. I thought you might have jumped in to swim the rest of the way down the Seine."

Catherine turned to him and smiled. "You must be feeling better. You're making bad jokes."

"Better enough," he said. "You know she's a swimmer?" he told Sam. "I'm surprised we're not down in the drink."

"Thank you so much," Catherine said to Sam before she left the cockpit. She felt strangely light, as if she'd been sitting in the kitchen on the island with Florence rather than up in the sky with a perfect stranger from a country she'd never seen.

Louisa was feeling better too. "This is not what I expected," she said.

"I love it," Catherine said. "Sam showed me how he flies the aeroplane. He's from the mountains in Canada. It sounds like magic."

"Aren't there bears in Canada?"

"Louisa, you make everything something to be afraid of."

"Do I?"

"No, but it was just lovely to . . ."

"To what?"

"Nothing. Anyway, we're landing in fifteen minutes. In Paris, Louisa."

They came down quickly and landed at the little airstrip with three bumps, a perfect landing, Mr. Black said.

They caught taxis from the airstrip to the Hôtel de Crillon as the light was fading, passing green fields in late sunshine, cows still out in pasture, little villages. As they approached the city itself, Catherine's eyes couldn't take it in fast enough. Andrew was glib, chattering constantly about what they'd do the next day, pointing casually toward the Arc de Triomphe and the Place de la Concorde as they passed. Catherine was in awe. It was as she'd thought London might be, she realized, everything related to everything else, the bridges across the river, the buildings, the trees, even the color of the sky, so pale and beautiful. It was perfect.

In the hotel lobby, Catherine was struck by the French speakers. She'd learned French from one of the nuns at school, a native speaker, and was surprised at how much she understood.

She and Louisa were sharing an apartment that looked over the Place de la Concorde. They'd giggled when they first saw the bathroom. It had a bidet and Catherine had said there were two toilets, in case they both needed one, she guessed, not knowing what a bidet was for. Learning its function didn't make it any less funny and the two of them collapsed on the beds, laughing at nothing. For Catherine, it was lovely to see Louisa happy, to see her laughing and enjoying being away from her work. They unpacked their things, dressed and went down for dinner in the hotel dining room.

The next morning Catherine was in the dining room late for breakfast. She'd been for a walk on her own earlier in the morning and had just kept walking, under a gentle fog. She went down toward the river and through a park where the trees were dropping their leaves. She'd crossed over the river and back, mesmerized by the beauty of the buildings. She'd come upon Notre Dame Cathedral, not knowing what it was at first. She'd gone in and sat for a few minutes. The silence reminded her of nights on the island.

Mr. Black came into the dining room now. He saw Catherine and smiled. "Miss Quick," he said.

"Hello, Mr. Black. I've been out walking."

"Do you mind if I join you?"

"Of course not. But you're supposed to call me Catherine. I'm just a girl, you know."

"Catherine, then," he said, and smiled. "But you're not just a girl. You're a champion. You hear?" He waggled a finger and looked at her mock-sternly. He was very sweet, in his way, she thought. The day before, when they'd dropped the bunches of flowers for his daughter, she'd seen him lean against the window and wave madly. Then he wiped his eye. Catherine had thought it was a tear he wiped away. It had given her a sudden feeling of sadness, missing her own father.

He called the waiter over, ordered coffee for himself and a hot chocolate for Catherine, and milk toast and two-minute eggs. Even with Catherine interpreting it took some minutes for the order to be understood, as Catherine herself didn't know what milk toast and two-minute eggs were.

"I used to eat my eggs like that," she said when the waiter had gone. "But we didn't call them two-minute eggs."

"You did?" he said, smiling. "Well, isn't that something?"

"I wouldn't eat the whites, only the yolk, and then Florence stopped making eggs for me because she said it was too wasteful."

"I still don't eat the whites," Mr. Black said. "An indulgence."

He was in his dark gray suit, his hair neatly combed back from his forehead. It wanted to spring up, by the look of it. His face was pink, like her father's just after he shaved in the morning and once again Catherine felt a pull of sadness in her heart.

"So, how are you liking Paris?" he asked.

"Oh, it's so beautiful," she said. "Thank you so much for inviting us."

He waved away her thanks. "Your aunt does a fine job with

her clinic, a fine job that should be recognized. I'm thrilled she's going to come and help us out in Baltimore. Whatever small thing I can do to make her life more pleasant, I'm more than willing. But you want to swim." He raised his eyebrows. "And as it happens, I have an interest in swimming. And I want a swimmer who can conquer the English Channel."

"Mr. Black, swimming got me in an awful lot of trouble."

"I know that."

"You don't understand. I was expelled." Louisa had said they wouldn't tell anyone this, but Catherine wanted to tell him. He was a link to her mother, to the people who might be like her.

"Yes, I know," he said, as if being expelled were nothing. Louisa must have told him. Catherine was surprised. "But I also saw you cross that river. And while I am not a betting man, I would bet anything you are the fastest and strongest woman swimmer on earth."

She didn't respond.

"So what do you think, Catherine?"

"I don't really know," she said. "Swimming isn't something I've ever had to think about. It's always been part of my life. It just is."

He laughed. "That will be great with the reporters. I've never thought about swimming. It just is." He chuckled again. "You think about it. You hear? I'll be sending one swimmer to France next year and it will not be Gertrude Ederle. You know who I want?"

She blushed, shook her head no.

He pointed gently. "You," he whispered, and then smiled. "I'll stop embarrassing you now."

"Thank you," she said. "It's not that I don't want to swim."

"What is it then?"

"My aunt . . ."

"Forget Louisa here, Catherine. Do you know what I'm saying?"

"I do," she said. "Do you really think I'm that good a swimmer?"

"I know it," he said. He put out his hand. "So, English Channel. August '26. We have a deal?" She blushed again. "We have a deal?" he said.

She nodded slowly. "Yes, we do," she said, "if you think I can do it."

"Then shake on it." They shook hands. He looked satisfied.

"Mr. Black, you knew my mother," she said, relieved to be able to change the subject now. She was embarrassed about him telling her she was a champion.

He looked at her. "A little," he said.

"What was she like?"

"Julia? Oh, they moved away when she was young, so I hardly knew her as a child. I saw her again with your father. She was very pretty, a lot like you." He smiled. It disappeared quickly. "Her mother was my mother's cousin, if that makes sense. We were second cousins."

Catherine nodded. She felt disappointed for some reason. She had hoped . . . Just what had she hoped for? That Mr. Black might lead her to her own people? That she might find a home in America? "I don't remember her and I was thinking that in America, I could meet more people from her family as well as swim."

"Her parents are still in Canada," he said. "But I'm sure we can get in touch with them. Julia was an only child, wasn't she? There might be others on that side. I should know, I suppose, but I don't." He eyed her carefully. "You do want to swim as well, don't you, Catherine?" he said.

"Of course." How could she explain to him that his question made no sense? It was like asking if she wanted to breathe.

"Well, let's see if we can work on your aunt so that you can." He stood then. "August '26. English Channel. You. But now, I must go. I'm glad you're enjoying the trip."

After he left, Catherine noticed that he'd eaten hardly any of his toast and eggs.

24

S he could be the one, Louisa." They were sitting in the little bar across the square from the hotel. Louisa and Catherine had spent the morning with Andrew. In the afternoon Louisa had gone to the Sorbonne, where a doctor she'd served with during the war was now working. They'd spent a couple of hours reminiscing about those days when they thought the sky would be the limit for women doctors from now on. Oh my, Louisa could have said now. What young fools they were.

Black had spent the day in the hotel, staving off a bid to buy his newspaper, he said. He looked tired around the eyes.

"And she wants to swim," he said. "The Channel. She wants to swim the Channel. It takes a special kind of courage to want that."

"Well, of course she'll want to swim. She also wants to go back to the island." Louisa thought then of the letters from the island. There had been a third in the week before, in different handwriting, perhaps from Florence. Louisa hadn't read it—she'd decided that would be unethical—but she hadn't given it to Catherine either.

It was September. Louisa's plan was to take Catherine to America in the new year. Catherine could meet the swimmers Black had spoken about and then come home and Louisa would find a school. His talk of the Channel was just that, Louisa thought. Catherine wouldn't swim the English Channel. It was a pipe dream. Maybe she could board at school in Glasgow, Louisa thought, or go to the Spitalfields public school. She needn't go back to Henley. As for the letters, well, Louisa would see.

"I don't think any of us know what we want at fifteen," Louisa said to Black. She thought of her own girlhood and felt a stab of something. Regret? There was never any question for Louisa. She was going to do medicine. She looked squarely at him. "I want Catherine to go back to school. It's the only thing that will secure a future for her."

The waiter came over and Black ordered another martini for himself. Louisa was still working on her first. The hotel's bar was cozy and looked out onto a little square. "Do you know, I've never really noticed this," Louisa said, "but Paris is terribly beautiful."

"You've never noticed?" Black said. "How did you miss it?"

"I don't know," she said. "I just didn't take it in, I suppose. Always something else to be thinking about." She took a small sip of her drink. "Lear, I understand you want advice for your clinic. But why Catherine? Why swimming?" In truth, she was beginning to feel a little uncomfortable. He'd originally come to see her about the clinic, getting her advice, but now he seemed more interested in the swimming. He'd approached Catherine that morning, Catherine had told Louisa.

"My reasons are quite selfish," he said, watching her carefully. "I mentioned I've had some interest in my newspaper business back in Baltimore. The paper I own, the *Baltimore Sun*, is not the oldest or most distinguished newspaper. I bought into it when it was in trouble ten years ago and found I like being a newspaperman. Our main competition then was the *News*, which was recently bought by Mr. Hearst. They have a longer history than we do, and they've modernized better. And Mr. Hearst is very good at this newspaper business.

"There's a third paper, the *Baltimore Daily Post*. It's a bit like your *Mirror*, lots of pictures, gossip—things, it turns out, readers want. The *Post* is better than we are at creating stories people want to read, and the *News* is better at reporting. So we're a bit betwixt and between. All of this is a way of explaining that I do understand why my advisers are urging me to sell. I bought a lemon." He took a sip of his drink, examined the back of his other hand.

"It's possible I've been a bit slow to realize that the people who want to buy us out are quite serious. I'm under pressure now, you see."

"I don't see how this is relevant to Catherine."

"No, I don't imagine you do." He fiddled with a jar of toothpicks on the table, straightening them. "It's funny the way things happen. I told you about the Women's Swimming Association. I've been able to support the Association over the years." He took a cigar from his pocket. "Do you mind?" She shook her head. He lit up, blew smoke into the air above them. "And it's become very obvious to me that women's swimming is of interest to readers."

"Women's swimming," Louisa said. "So your newspaper needs women swimmers?"

"Yes, the blasted *Post* has signed up Lillian Cannon." Louisa must have looked confused. "She's a Baltimore girl who swam Chesapeake Bay last year, with a big burly lad who gave up in bad weather. She's a tiny thing, but she's the one who kept going, real spunk. The *Post* is financing her attempt at the English Channel next year. They got to her before I did. And she has those dogs."

"Dogs," Louisa said.

"Chesapeake Bay Retrievers. Everyone loves them."

"You think Catherine could beat her?"

"Oh, I know Catherine could beat Lillian Cannon. But the Association has another swimmer, a little older than Catherine, Gertrude Ederle. I told you about her. She's the one they fished out of the water last month and it caused a hoo-ha. I've met her. She's not what I want."

"Is she a good swimmer?"

"Yes, but it's more than swimming. Gertrude's from New York, which won't go down well in Baltimore. And she's from German stock, which isn't quite what I want either. And I want someone who can communicate."

"Catherine?" Louisa was astonished that someone with his wealth and power would care this much. It was the same with the party on his yacht. Every last detail, Andrew had said. He wanted to supervise every last detail.

"Yes. She grew up on an island, learned to swim from natives, and she's British stock but colonial, which is about perfect. She can talk. If she made good in America, the land where anyone can succeed, wouldn't that be marvelous? She's exactly what I want." As he spoke, he raised his eyebrows, used his hands to gesture. He was clearly taken by the idea of a swimming champion and he thought Catherine would fit the bill.

"Well, you have a whole plan, don't you?" Louisa said, taking another small sip of her martini.

It still made her uneasy, she realized. Black had invited them to the party on his yacht. Now he'd paid their way to Paris. He was footing the hotel bill; insisted on it, in fact. Dinner last night and tonight, the accommodations. He was taking them to America, all expenses paid. He was going to contribute to the clinic—they'd come to an agreement. He was going to fund a major upgrade to the Princes Square building. They couldn't do without him now, Louisa realized. Catherine seemed excited by his idea that she could be the first woman to swim the English Channel. But Louisa felt uneasy.

As if he read her thoughts, he said, "Louisa, I'm not going to push anyone around here. But when I found out who the swimmer I saw was, when I found out that her guardian was you, Dr. Louisa Quick, who I'd already intended to visit, I thought something was acting on us here. I am a great believer in serendipity."

He paused, took a puff of his cigar. "You know, when I was Catherine's age, I worked hard. I left school, went into banking. And then it became a habit, I suppose. I didn't ever get used to not working hard." Louisa noticed the look on his face, the momentary sadness—it was this she liked in him, this sadness that he wore with such dignity. It was still there when he smiled. It made him more human. Oh, there was the charm, the power of the man, but it was this sadness she could relate to.

She smiled. "I know what you mean," she said. "My colleagues sometimes ask if I have regrets. They mean not having a husband, not having children. But you see, I don't regret it at all. I have my work. Why would I want children?"

"You have a child now," he said, narrowing his eyes.

The waiter came with more drinks.

"Yes, I do," she said after the waiter withdrew. "And Mrs. Black. Is she back in Baltimore?"

He smiled. "You're thinking of my daughter, of course. Well, there is no Mrs. Black. Adeline is the product of an affair I had with a singer here in Paris." He looked at her squarely. "Are you shocked?"

Louisa smiled. "I'm a doctor, Lear. It would take more than an unwanted pregnancy to shock me." The truth was she was a little shocked. He hadn't seemed the type to go for an affair with a singer. It made her think a little less of him. At least he was owning up to his responsibilities, she thought then. "And Adeline's mother?"

"Died ten years ago," Black said. "I sent Adeline to school. But you are the conundrum, not me. Men don't marry because they don't marry. But women marry. And yet, you never married?"

"No," she said curtly. "Do you have siblings other than your sister?"

He shook his head. "And you, just the two brothers?"

"Yes. My mother lost a child, another girl, after Alexander and before me. She died in my father's arms." Inexplicably, Louisa found tears in her eyes, thinking about the sister she never knew, taking her last breath, her poor father seeing his child out of life. She breathed in sharply. "I'm sorry. I don't quite know what's come over me." His eyes were so soft.

"Anyway, I had two futures to live up to, my sister's and mine. Alexander followed Papa into the business, so he was allowed certain concessions. Harry more or less did as he pleased and nothing he did worried our mother. Were you close to your sister?" He kept switching the conversation back to her, she noticed, and she wanted to know about him, especially as he was now so interested in Catherine.

He nodded but didn't speak, looked out toward the street. "Do you know, I made a little fun of you before for not noticing the beauty of Paris," he said finally. "But when I think about it, I don't believe I've ever noticed it much either." He smiled. "I'm not very good at enjoying myself."

"That's what Nellie, my housekeeper, says about me—that I can't enjoy myself. I enjoy work."

"Me too," he said. "And we could drink to that. But here we are, two lost souls in their sunset years looking for some sort of life."

Louisa smiled. "I'm not quite sure I'm ready for sunset yet." She sipped her drink again. "And I have a perfectly acceptable life."

"Well, we could drink to a perfectly acceptable life. You're still worried about Catherine, though."

Louisa smiled, for this was exactly what she was worried about. Black had a directness she both liked and feared. You never knew where he was going to go next.

"That's good," he said. "It's what you should be doing." He drained his glass and called the waiter to order another. "You're a good guardian of the child. But I think I understand someone like Catherine better than you realize. I know how it feels to lose your parents at a young age. It knocks you off your feet, the loss of security. I was at school when my father died. They called me home. I never went back to the school. We didn't have the money." He frowned. "I lost my mother not long after, and my sister, and I was on my own."

"Catherine's not on her own."

"No," he said. "She's not. But it has been difficult for her, and she needs to find her own place. She needs to find her confidence. I'm pretty sure she'll find it in the water." He shook his head. "What do I know? Anyway, Louisa, swimming is what I can help with, and that girl is a swimmer. I'll put you in touch with Charlotte Epstein. You'll like her, and you can be sure that she'll take good care of Catherine. Charlotte's always hosting visiting swimmers. Catherine will be fine."

Louisa eyed him carefully.

"We're going to have to trust each other if this is going to work, Louisa."

"Yes, quite," she said. And she told herself she had no reason to doubt him.

PART VII

New York, March 1926

25

Catherine watched from the upper deck as passengers began to disembark, to be met by family and friends. Many embraced warmly, and tears filled Catherine's eyes. As they'd come into the harbor, she'd looked toward the tall buildings on Manhattan Island like Mr. Black had told her to. She'd never seen anything like them, not in London, not in Paris. She saw too the Statue of Liberty, much smaller than she expected, a woman out on her own in the water. The statue was supposed to represent freedom, she knew, but Liberty didn't look free to Catherine, anchored there to the rock. The chains at her feet were supposed to be the chains she'd broken. But she looked as if she couldn't get away even if she wanted to. She looked as if she might like to dive in and swim rather than hold a torch but the rock was keeping her there.

Catherine wore a long wool coat and a scarf, which she pulled up around her neck. She had mittens somewhere but for now just put her hands deep in her coat pockets. It was a different kind of cold from London. A pale sun shone over the water and turned it gold.

It had taken nearly six months to get here. Ruth Luxton's daughter May, a violinist in her middle twenties, was coming to New York to attend the Juilliard School. Originally Louisa was to sail with Catherine, but then Louisa had to defer her own travel for a further month—to make sure the refurbishments at Princes Square were satisfactory—and so Dr. Luxton had suggested that Catherine could travel with May, a quietly spoken young woman a lot like Dr. Luxton herself. Catherine would be chaperoned by Miss Charlotte Epstein in New York, who, Louisa said, had hosted young swimmers from all over the world.

On the ship, Catherine and May had a lovely room with a porthole, and for dinner they'd sat most nights at the captain's table because the ship was one of Catherine's uncle's line. Catherine had to wear the dresses Louisa had bought for her. It was supposed to be an honor, to sit at the captain's table, but Catherine had longed to be free of the confines of the ship and in particular the nightly ritual of dinner. Perhaps that was why she wished Liberty would hoist her skirts and dive in.

May Luxton didn't seem to mind the ship journey. She sat in the cabin and read or went to the engine room, where she could practice her violin and no one would be bothered by it. She gave a little performance one night during the trip. Catherine had loved the music. She'd never heard anything like it, she said later. Other than that, May left her alone. For all May knew, Catherine might be off swimming in the ocean every day.

May had disembarked in Newfoundland to visit the Canadian Luxtons before coming down to New York, so Catherine had been alone for the last few days of the journey. She wished she could have stopped in Canada too, to find the Freebodys, her mother's family. And then she could go across Canada and see the mountains Sam the pilot had told her about. She wondered would she see Sam in America. Was he still flying Mr. Black around? It was a little daunting to be traveling alone to a strange place, but exciting too. She'd never felt so far from home and so alone. And yet, strangely, she was sure she would be all right.

In the months they'd been planning the trip, Louisa had corresponded with Charlotte Epstein, who was the director of the Women's Swimming Association in New York. The summer had ended and, after an autumn that felt all too brief to Catherine, they were back to winter, London's favorite season. Christmas, New Year, sleet, rain and, finally, Catherine set off in February. Now it was early March, but spring still seemed a long way off.

In all that time, Catherine hadn't heard from Michael or Florence. She'd written to ask them if they were all right. Still they didn't write. When she asked Louisa, Louisa had said they'd probably just moved on in life, as people did. Catherine felt perhaps Louisa knew more than she'd let on. You should stop pestering them, Louisa had said, and so, reluctantly, Catherine had decided not to continue writing.

But she missed Florence terribly now, in another new place, and wished Michael was with her looking out at this new water. What would he think of Lady Liberty? Catherine wondered. She imagined he'd see her just as Catherine did, anything but free there on her lonely rock.

Catherine heard a voice behind her suddenly, a woman's voice, but when she looked behind her on the deck of the boat, there was no one there. She always said she never missed her mother. When one of the teachers in London had described Catherine as an orphan, she'd been on the verge of correcting the woman. "That's not true," she wanted to say. "I have my father and Florence, and Michael." But the teacher had been right. Catherine was an orphan, all alone in the world. She had no one. Her father was dead, and Florence and Michael had forgotten her. She had Louisa, but Louisa was hard to fathom, even now. Catherine had become quite fond of her aunt, although still there was a distance that separated them that Catherine didn't quite understand.

When Catherine had still been in London, they'd started a little nursery school of sorts in the waiting room at the clinic. Children accompanying their mothers could stay with Catherine and hear stories or sketch. Ruth Luxton had convinced Louisa to buy some art materials, and they'd designated a corner for them. "I just love her," Dr. Luxton told Louisa on Catherine's last day. "But onward, young woman of the sea," she said. She hugged Catherine warmly and there were tears in her eyes.

Catherine had felt sad leaving someone who'd been so kind.

During the summer and autumn, Nellie had gone with Catherine to the Hampstead ladies' pond. The English swimmers mostly wore the same kind of suit Catherine had bought, although some wore a more revealing costume, tight to the skin and without a skirt. They swam differently from Catherine too, she noticed, with their heads out of the water, either breaststroke or a strange sidestroke Catherine had never seen before.

Catherine became adept as a cold-water swimmer. Strangely,

now she preferred it; the sting on her skin when she first jumped in, the slow warming up, even the shivering afterward. And, oddly, the pond reminded her of the island. The water was much colder, of course, but like the island it was an ancient place, a place where many spirits dwelled, as Florence might have said. Catherine wished she could have shown Michael the pond. She wished they could have swum there together. Every adventure of her young life had been shared with Michael, and made richer. Now, he was no longer part of her life. He might not have liked the pond, though, even if he'd been allowed to swim there. Too cold, he'd have said. Too many reeds under- neath the surface. She could hear his voice. Could be crocs, his eyes wide.

For the first two visits, Catherine swam on her own. Nellie couldn't be convinced to try it. The water was like silk, Catherine said, softer than the sea or the river farther down. Catherine soon came to love that feeling when she first jumped in and the blood rushed out to her skin and prickled.

Nellie sat and watched her swim. Why don't you try? Cath- erine said. Nellie only shook her head. But on the third visit, Nellie surprised Catherine and said she'd try it. Catherine con- vinced her to leave the overdress of her swimming suit and just wear the suit itself. "You'll never learn otherwise." Nellie eased herself into the water from the ladder, holding on all the while. The other women swimming stopped and clapped for Nellie.

"Oh dear, there are creeping things," Nellie said. She looked so afraid, Catherine thought, feeling such tenderness for her friend.

"They're just reeds, I think," Catherine said.

"Oh, how disgusting. They tickle. Are there fish too?"

"Perhaps," Catherine said, trying to coax Nellie to let go of the ladder. "Or maybe eels?" Nellie looked aghast. "They won't hurt you. Come on, I'll show you how to float."

"No thank you," Nellie said. "I'm fine here."

"Isn't it beautiful?" one woman said. She was elderly. They watched as she pushed off and swam on her back across the pond.

"That," Nellie said, pointing to the woman. "I want to be able to do that."

"And you will, Nellie," Catherine said. "But first you have to let go of the ladder." Nellie did and grabbed on to Catherine, almost pushing them both under.

"Oh dear," Catherine laughed. "Just relax, Nellie. I've got you, see?" Catherine was treading water.

Over the next several visits, Catherine coaxed Nellie to float on her back, to put her head under and to trace a kind of breaststroke through the water. They were the most enjoyable days she spent in London, swimming up at the ponds and teaching her friend.

But now standing on the upper deck of the *Whyalla* that had brought her from England, Catherine faced an uncertain future. She was totally unmoored—from her family, her home, from everything familiar. Mr. Black was the only person she knew in America. She and Louisa had seen little of him before he'd left London. He and Andrew had gone off flying, to Cairo, then Johannesburg. Then they'd attempted Java but they crashed somewhere in Asia. No one was hurt, but the aeroplane was left behind and then Mr. Black had to find another. He visited at Wellclose Square, and had Louisa and Catherine over to visit at the house he rented on Alderson Street. But Catherine hadn't seen that much of him.

Catherine liked Mr. Black, though, and she wanted to swim well for him. He'd mentioned the English Channel again, always when Louisa was out of earshot. Once he'd said it might have to be their secret, as he and Catherine understood swimming but Louisa didn't. He was odd, Nellie said, but Catherine liked him. He was interesting, always on to something new and exciting, and he believed in Catherine's swimming. She was glad she'd see him again here in America. She'd see Andrew too, she knew, because Mr. Black had found a job for him at his newspaper. She was looking forward to that too.

The sun had gone behind a cloud momentarily and the softened light gave the pier building before her a gentleness. So here I am, she thought to herself, in America. Perhaps she'd find something of herself here, as well as the opportunity to swim.

Catherine realized she didn't know what she was supposed to do. She hadn't thought of the end of the journey at all. In all the rush to pack and leave, she hadn't asked who would be meeting her. Louisa may have said something, but Catherine had been too excited to take it in properly. Oh, I should have listened, Catherine thought now. I don't even know what to do. She thought then of Louisa saying good-bye at Southampton. Catherine had seen tears in her aunt's eyes, which surprised them both.

"Just remember, dear," Louisa had said, "you can do anything."

"I'm a Quick," Catherine replied. She found she felt sad too.

"You certainly are," Louisa said. "And I'll be right behind you." Her aunt swallowed then, and tried to smile.

Catherine was just about to go to find a steward to see whether there was a message for her from Mr. Black when she saw Andrew, his head well above the crowd, in a long coat and black hat. She waved wildly when she saw him. He held his hat to his chest, waving with his other hand, a grin on his face. His dark hair was slicked back from his forehead, just like Mr. Black's, Catherine realized.

When Mr. Black had packed up his London home to return to America, he'd offered Andrew a job. Banking or newspapers? he'd said. Newspapers, for sure, Andrew had replied, he told Catherine afterward. And so he'd left with Mr. Black to start at the *Baltimore Sun* as a reporter.

Catherine was soon down the stairs and along the gangway onto the pier. A minute later, Andrew was with her. "Mr. Black sent me," he explained. "He wanted to come himself but, as usual, he's terribly busy." Andrew embraced her warmly. "You're here. How did we manage this?" He grinned.

"It's so grand," she said, looking up and along the pier.

"That's the only word for it," he said, recovering himself. "New York is the grandest place I've ever been." He'd changed, she thought, grown into himself more. He was even taller, she thought.

There were windows in the roof of the terminal building and soft light spilled onto their faces. Catherine could still smell the sea but it was mixed now with a smell of fuel and wet wood. She looked around her. Just for a moment, the light above them changed and everything softened. The moment passed, the faces brightened again, and the loud noises resumed. A boat blew its whistle. There were engines and horns sounding constantly from the street outside, and people everywhere shouting to one another. The pier was probably no busier than Southampton, but it seemed busier, more alive. It even smelled busy.

They collected Catherine's suitcase. "Is this all you've brought?" Andrew said.

Catherine smiled. "You don't need much for swimming." Everything was bright to Catherine, more colorful.

"I brought three trunks," he said. "And you need even less for being a reporter; just a pen and notebook, apparently."

"How is the reporting?" she said.

"Oh, you have no idea what a life I'm leading. I'll tell you about it over lunch." He looked happy to see her, she thought, although there was something smart-looking about him now, a glibness in his manner that hadn't been there before. Catherine wasn't sure she liked it. It was a little like Mr. Black, she thought, but didn't sit well on Andrew. Perhaps it was a way to get by in America.

Catherine soon cleared the Immigration Center for first-class passengers and found herself on the street. Andrew took her arm and they walked together happily. The salty smell of the water was soon enhanced by richer smells, earth like the island, rich and full of possibility. Andrew hailed a taxi, put a bill into the driver's hand through the window and then opened the door for Catherine. "I've become better at the tipping business," he said quietly.

They went to a café that had a row of tables alongside a long counter with stools. "Baltimore Dairy Lunch." Andrew pointed to the sign in the window. "Mr. Black's favorite, of course." He parked her suitcase at the front entrance and took her to a table in the back. He ordered soup and sandwiches for both of them. "Trust me, it'll be delicious," he said.

The sandwiches were the most enormous things Catherine

had ever seen. The soup was warm and flavorful, with lots of vegetables. "I've never had soup for breakfast," she said.

"Well, where you've come from, it's probably dinnertime, and I'm more in the mood for lunch right at the moment," he said. "And anyway, it's eleven-thirty, well and truly lunchtime."

"There are so many people here," she said, looking outside at the people hurrying by.

"As it happens, it's all over the news at the moment: New York's population is bigger than London's," he said. "If you sit here and count, you could probably prove it."

She laughed. "Well, they're all out on the streets today," she said.

"It's like this every time I've been," he said. "I have to come up when Mr. Black does. I'm still working for him when needed. Last weekend we had another party for Captain Bone, who very kindly brought Mr. Black home. Mr. Black had a bell made for the *Transylvania*." Andrew was shaking his head softly. "I don't know how many nights we sat up working out the most appropriate words to speak at the ceremony to commission the ship's bell. Finally Mr. Black just said, 'May it ring true,' and that was it." Andrew smiled. "He's just the same."

"So, the reporting?" Catherine said, smiling. "It makes you smoke those cigarettes?"

Andrew had just lit up. "It makes you stay up until three in the morning," he said. "Taking of the demon drink."

"I thought drink was banned here," Catherine said. "That's what Louisa said."

"She'd be referring to the Eighteenth Amendment. We call it the Eighteenth Pretendment. Yes, liquor is banned. But there are the speaks, you see, and they are the bane of my existence currently. It's a bar without a front entrance. You have to know the password. The beer's terrible, and it's laced with ether, which is the real problem. It makes you sick the next morning. And the gin is younger than tomorrow. To be honest, I don't usually surface until eleven or so. I work nights at the *Sun*."

"Well, you've done well to come for me," she said. "And I very much appreciate it." She smiled. "But it can't be very good for you if it makes you sick. Don't the police prowl around looking for drink?"

"The police are the first through the door," Andrew said. "They're looking for drink, all right—to drink it. Soon as the sarge gets off duty, he's down there with us."

"And how is your mother coping without you?" Catherine said. Andrew had been worried before he'd left that his mother would miss him.

He didn't answer straightaway. Then he said, "Not well, frankly. She wants me home, keeps sending job notices from *The Times*. Awful, really. I suppose I won't stay here forever."

Catherine nodded. "It must be hard to be away from her."

"Oh, goodness me, no. Not for me. But it's hard on her." Catherine knew that Andrew's older brother had been killed in the war. "But you—here you are in New York. And I cannot get over how you've grown up." The way he said it made her feel heat rising in her throat. "I'm sorry. I'll stop embarrassing you." Had she grown up in those months? Perhaps she had. "At any rate, I've been given strict instructions in relation to you."

"And what are they?" she said.

"Well, first was your aunt, who told me she was only letting you come to New York unaccompanied because Ada Mackintosh's son would be there to watch over you. And she knew

I was a gentleman, she said. Then Mr. Black told me that if there are any shenanigans in regard to you, I'm to let him know straightaway. He said I'm to be your big brother and if you get into trouble, it will be on my shoulders."

"And what exactly are shenanigans?" Catherine said.

"I'm glad you asked, because I asked Mr. Black that very question. He said, 'Look here, Andy, you know what I'm talking about? You young folk get up to all sorts of capers.'" It was a good imitation of Mr. Black. "I told him I'd watch over you." He became more serious now. "And I will, Catherine. You can be sure of that."

She returned his gaze. There was the Andrew she knew, back again for that moment. "Thank you," she said.

She looked out to the street again while Andrew went to order more coffee. New York, more than anything, was intense living, she thought. And there were more women, or at least she noticed them more. Their coats were shorter and their heels higher but it was more than that; they were more confident, more alive. A city of lipstick, Louisa had told Catherine. She smiled now to think of her aunt's take on New York.

Andrew came back to the table. "Charlotte Epstein is supposed to come and meet us." He looked at his watch. "She must be running late. Well, we'll just have to wait, although I must get the train back to Baltimore by one."

"I can wait on my own," she said.

He smiled. "Having just explained to you the many and varied responsibilities I now have for your general welfare, I'm not going to leave you to your own devices in New York."

"Andrew!"

Catherine turned to see a tiny bustling woman with dark

hair and eyes coming over to their table. She wore a coat to mid-calf, tightly belted in the middle. On her feet were bright red boots. She had a toothy grin.

"Here we go," he said to Catherine as he stood to greet the woman. "Charlotte, my dear—I have your girl."

"So you do," the woman said, holding out her hand to Catherine. "I'm Charlotte Epstein, hon, but just call me Eppy. Welcome to America!" Her voice was loud but no one seemed to notice.

"Oh, hello," Catherine said. "I didn't expect you'd be so . . ." she wanted to say small but thought better of it, ". . . young." It was true, she had assumed that Charlotte would be older, but here she was, a woman in her thirties at most.

"Aw honey," Charlotte Epstein said. "What did you expect, an old troll?" She laughed loudly. "So, you guys had your lunch?"

"We've just ordered coffee," Andrew said. "Sit down, for goodness' sake." He got up and took a chair from the next table for her. Andrew had written a story about the Association's swimmers for the newspaper, he said, "which meant I spent a week in Charlotte's sparkling company."

She looked at her watch. "Can't stay. I'm on my own lunch break and I hiked up from the courts." She sat down anyway and turned to Catherine. "I work as a court reporter. Okay, I imagine you're keen to get swimming." She put her hand on Catherine's arm.

"I am," Catherine said. "And I saw the harbor coming in." She opened her eyes wide.

"Of course, Catherine nearly dived in to swim to shore," Andrew said.

Charlotte Epstein laughed again. "I heard about you." She pointed a finger at Catherine, but she was smiling. "The Thames, huh?" She shook her head. "You don't want to swim in the harbor, hon. Well, not right at the moment." Charlotte's eyes seemed to bulge as she spoke.

"Why not?"

"Too cold. Now, listen, Andrew is going to take you to my apartment, where you'll be staying. Don't mind the cats. They won't hurt you."

Catherine nodded.

"And then tomorrow we'll get up together to go to training. How does that sound?" She put a set of keys on the table.

"Wonderful," Catherine said. "But where do we swim?"

"Mr. Black rents an indoor tank for us. We'll be back in the open water next month, if you're still here." She smiled warmly. "I won't confuse you now, but the girls are just dying to meet you, and we'll do a whole lot of lovely things while you're here."

"We must take good care of little Catherine, Charlotte," Andrew said.

Catherine didn't like him describing her as little Catherine. It made her feel like it was a joke about her. "I'm hardly little," she said.

"No, you're not," Andrew said. "But we still have to look after you. I've just finished explaining to Catherine that I have instructions from her aunt on exactly what my duties are in relation to her care and supervision. Charlotte, be warned. She is quite difficult, apparently." Catherine didn't like him saying this either. It made her sound badly behaved.

"I'm with Catherine here, Andy," Charlotte Epstein said. "She's not little. What a thing to say. And why we're picking on little people is beyond me. Catherine, I must go. And I'm off to New Jersey straight after work for a swim meet. I thought of taking you but decided it would be better to wait for the training session in the morning. I left a snack in the icebox and the guest bed is made up."

"Thank you so much," Catherine said. She stood when Charlotte did. Andrew joined them.

"Thank *you*, honey. We're all looking forward to having you at training tomorrow. I'll wake you at five."

"Well, what do you think of your new mistress?" Andrew said after Charlotte left.

"She's lovely," Catherine said.

He collected her bag at the door and they set out to find Catherine's temporary home.

26

Charlotte Epstein's apartment was on the third floor of a building on West 14th Street that, from the outside at least, reminded Catherine of the apartment buildings she'd seen in London, plain brick with few adornments and pull-up windows facing the street. From the café, Andrew had taken her in a taxicab and Catherine couldn't figure out the direction with all the high buildings and turns. They were still near the river, she was sure, because she could still smell the rich mud.

Andrew said they were at the market end of Chelsea, where he'd been once with Mr. Black. There were crowds of people on the street, Catherine noticed, all walking quickly. Some were carrying baskets laden with provisions, green leaves, bread. She could hear vendors shouting, just like they did at the markets in Cairns. She felt the pull of home.

Andrew took her suitcase up the three flights of stairs. They left it outside Charlotte's door and Catherine went back down to the street with him. They said good-bye and then he disappeared into a sea of heads, his own poking up every now and then until he disappeared for good. Well, she thought, standing there on the steps, here I am.

Catherine went back upstairs and let herself in. The front door of the apartment led into a small vestibule that opened into the living room. It was cold inside, although not as cold as the street. There was no fireplace, so Catherine kept her coat on.

Though the apartment was smaller than Louisa's house, it was sparsely furnished, so it felt quite spacious. There was a plain rug on the parquet floor in the entry, soft electric lights, a sitting room with a couch and two comfy chairs. The cats were both black, one enormous, one not, and in the kitchen Charlotte had left salted crackers, bread, something called nut butter, and cake. In the icebox was a salad.

The sitting room overlooked a building site and beyond, Catherine was sure, were the docks and the river. She opened the window and smelled the air. It wasn't clean but it was interesting, smoke from engine exhaust, and underneath that the salt and mud of the river. The smell of salt water was so familiar it made Catherine ache for home.

It was a year now since she'd left the island. It seemed so very far away. Michael had been angry about her leaving. He'd told her she should stay, that she owed it to Florence to stay. You're my sister, he'd said in the last letter she'd had from him, but then he'd forgotten her altogether. And Mr. Black, who'd wanted her to come to America, who was her only link to her real family, hadn't even come to meet her today. Catherine found herself feeling very alone. She took in the smell of the sea, the smell that reminded her of home.

It was still dark when she heard Charlotte Epstein in the kitchen the next morning. She got up, dressed quickly and went out, stopping in the bathroom to splash water on her face. The apartment looked different. Catherine wondered if that was because she wasn't as tired. Or perhaps it only came to life when its owner was in residence. Charlotte was small, but she took up space. Her face lit up when she saw Catherine. "Aren't you good to get up without being called? My mother will love you. I've been instructed to bring you over there for dinner tomorrow night. Did you sleep well?"

"Oh, yes," Catherine said. "Very soundly." She felt shy in her pajamas.

"I came and looked in on you about ten and you were fast asleep. That's good. But you didn't have your dinner. Have some oatmeal now and then we'll head off to the tank."

Catherine sat at the little table in the kitchen, adorned with a red-checked cloth and salt and pepper shakers shaped like cats.

"You like it here?"

"Oh, yes," Catherine said. "Thank you, it's lovely."

"My father liked that it's not far from the courts. My mother liked that it was three floors up." Charlotte smiled. "But I like that if you look around the corner you can see Lady Liberty. Now, I'll have to go to work after swimming but one of the girls will help you find your way back here. You can stop at the markets if you like. I'll show you where they are on the way. Do you need some money?"

"I have some American money my aunt gave me before I left."

"Good. We can buy you a subway ticket and you can get anything else you might need at the markets later. Don't worry too much, though. Mr. Black has given us more than enough to accommodate you, so don't be at all concerned about any of that. He's very excited about you coming. He's told me he wants you to be our contender next year for the English Channel." Charlotte looked at Catherine sharply. "We're an independent association, though." Catherine didn't know what she meant.

"Mr. Black must love swimming," Catherine said.

"Yes," Charlotte said. "He does." She smiled tightly.

After breakfast, Catherine dressed and packed a bag—the swimming suit she'd bought in London, the cap, and a towel. Charlotte was wearing a long skirt and blouse, with a woolen hat over her hair. She had an enormous satchel over her shoulder. She put on mittens at the door to the apartment building, and made Catherine do the same.

The grass crunched under their feet as they walked across a small park. Catherine was glad then that they wouldn't be swimming in the harbor after all. It would be frozen over, she thought. When she breathed in, the air hurt her lungs. "Chilly," was all Charlotte said. She'd pulled her scarf up over her mouth.

Morning seemed forever away but the city was already waking up, cleaners in the shops and factories, cafés preparing the day's meals, bakers about to go home, boys with milk or newspapers to deliver. They went down into the subway, Charlotte navigating the maze of dimly lit corridors and stairs effortlessly.

They caught a train that came out of a tunnel and then crossed a bridge—you could just make out the glint of the water and ferry lights beneath them. "My grandfather danced across this bridge the day it opened," Charlotte told her.

They alighted from the train on the far side of the bridge. It was quieter here. Catherine could hear the heels of Charlotte's boots click on the sidewalk. "Where are we?" Catherine said.

"Brooklyn," Charlotte said. "The tank's on the next corner." They took another right turn down a smaller street. "We can't get access to many tanks because they won't have women."

On the train, Charlotte had talked about Mr. Black. "Catherine, you need to understand that Mr. Black is our patron," Charlotte said. "I don't mean to disrespect him. And we take everyone, good swimmers or poor, so you don't have to worry about being the best." She nodded as if to herself. "Frankly, I don't care if you can hardly swim at all. You can come to the WSA.

"But you won't be the first swimmer Mr. Black has brought to us. And while we want to encourage the champions, we also want everyone to have an opportunity to swim. Anyway, you swam the Thames. Mr. Handley says you must be able to do something in the water." Catherine had no idea who Mr. Handley was. "But the English Channel. We only have the one chance left really before Mercedes Gleitze or someone like her beats us. It's very important that we succeed. And you're not New York." She was nodding to herself, as if it would help Catherine to understand.

As they turned the next corner, Catherine saw a dozen young women in long coats with bags slung over their shoulders, waiting outside a three-story building. They were lit softly by an overhead streetlamp. As she approached, Charlotte called out to them, "Hey, gals. You are the best girls in the world. What are you?"

"The best girls in the world," they said in a chorus, and then broke into laughter. Catherine smiled along with them, although she wasn't sure why.

When they reached the group, Charlotte said, "Girls, this is Catherine, the one I told you about. She's come all the way from London to swim with the Women's Swimming Association. Apparently, she's going to be our secret weapon."

"What about me?" This was from a small, slim girl with square shoulders, in a long pair of pants and jumper, blond hair cut short, sheepskin boots.

"Well, you're no secret weapon, Aileen. You're more like the cavalry."

The girl, who was more than a head shorter than Catherine, laughed. "You tell my father I'm the cavalry, Eppy. He thinks I'm wasting my time."

"Your father needs to come and see me, Aileen. I told you that."

Charlotte Epstein rummaged in her bag for her keys, then opened the front door to the building. It was warmer inside the foyer. There was a sign on the wall that read HOTEL TOURAINE. There were lounge chairs and lamps on one side and a front desk, unattended now.

"I'm Aileen Ryan," the small girl said to Catherine, and smiled. "Swimmer or diver?"

"I beg your pardon?" Catherine said.

"Are you a diver, or just a swimmer?" Aileen said more slowly.

"What do you mean, 'just a swimmer,' Aileen?" Charlotte said. "Swimming is plenty good."

"I'm a swimmer, I think," Catherine said. "I don't even know what diving is. Do you mean for pearls?"

Aileen smiled. "You know, from a board into a tank." She gestured with her hand.

"What's a tank?" Catherine said.

"Where do you swim, then?" Aileen said.

"The sea," Catherine said.

"You're from London?"

"Yes, but before that, Australia. In London, I didn't swim very much."

They'd gone through the lobby and were walking along a corridor.

"We swim in the sea too," Aileen said. "Just not at the moment."

"On the island, you swim year-round," Catherine said.

"Keep moving, girls," Charlotte said. "Mr. Handley doesn't like you to run late, and you'll all catch cold and your parents will blame me."

They followed Charlotte down the narrow corridor to a stairwell. They went down two flights and emerged into a hot, low-ceilinged room with what looked like a giant bathtub along its length.

Catherine stared at it. "What's that smell?" she asked Aileen. It was something between rotting oranges and kelp.

"Chlorine," Aileen said. "It's what they use to keep the tank clean."

"Is the water warm?" Catherine said.

"Oh, yeah." Aileen nodded. "Hey, girls," she said to the others. "Catherine is here all the way from Australia and she's never swum in a tank."

Two girls came over to them. "I'm Meg Ederle," one said,

"and this is my sister Trudy." Trudy nodded. "She don't hear so good," Meg said. "You never swum in a tank?"

Catherine shook her head. She was nervous, she realized. She was thinking of Darcy. But these girls were nothing like Darcy, she thought. They were kindly.

"Trudy don't like the tank either," Meg Ederle said.

Trudy smiled, a lovely, open smile, Catherine thought. This was Gertrude Ederle, Catherine realized, the nineteen-year-old who'd attempted the English Channel the year before, the one Mr. Black said Catherine could beat.

Their accents were all the same and all different. Meg Ederle sounded almost like an East Ender, but with a twang and some-thing else. German, Catherine learned later; Meg and Trudy's father, who often came to training, was German. There were five girls in the family, and three of them were swimmers.

Aileen's accent was more subtle, only apparent on certain words. "Trudy's the second youngest in our team," Aileen said as she led Catherine to the change room. "How old are you?"

"Fifteen," Catherine said. "Sixteen this year."

"Well, you're the new youngest then—of the advanced swimmers, I mean. There's lots of younger ones in the junior team. Trudy's nineteen, I'm eighteen." The girls were all strip-ping to put their suits on. They wore the new style, woolen swimming suits cut off at thigh level with straps over their shoulders, rather than sleeves. Catherine's suit was more mod-est. "We're all champions."

"Eppy doesn't swim?" Catherine said, noticing that she hadn't joined them in the change room.

"Not competition. She started the WSA. She's famous."

"We got to be the best," another girl said.

"The very best," still another said.

"My aunt thinks swimming might be a waste of time," Catherine said. "I hope she meets Eppy."

"My father hates swimming too. Don't worry about it," Aileen said.

"And do you know Mr. Black?" Catherine said.

Aileen shook her head. "Do you live with your aunt?" she asked.

"In London, yes."

"Where are your parents?"

"My mother died when I was little, and my father last year," Catherine said.

"You're an orphan, like Anne."

"Anne?"

"In *Anne of Green Gables*, the book. You haven't read it?" Catherine shook her head.

"Her parents have died and she's in an orphanage and these people adopt her. They'd meant to adopt a boy so he could help on the farm, but they keep her, even though she's a lot of trouble, and then she goes to school and meets her best friend. She has red hair like yours, only she hates it. Your hair is beautiful."

"Well, like Anne of Green Gables, I don't exactly like it," she said. "It makes me stand out in a crowd. And at school . . ." She didn't finish the sentence. She hadn't met a best friend. "I think I might be about as much trouble for my aunt as Anne was."

"Nah, you're not trouble," Aileen Ryan said. "I have a special sense for such matters."

When they went back outside, Charlotte Epstein was standing next to a compact man in shirtsleeves and a vest, with thinning silver hair and a neatly trimmed silver moustache.

"Here she is," Charlotte said, smiling at Catherine. "Catherine, this is our esteemed coach, Mr. Louis de Breda Handley. Mr. Handley, may I introduce you to our visiting swimmer, Catherine Quick."

The man greeted Catherine formally, bowing and taking her hand. "You will wait here," he said, "while I get the other swimmers started on their routines. And then we'll get properly acquainted. Is that all right?" Catherine nodded.

She watched as he went and spoke with each of the swimmers before they started. They swam in four rows, different strokes, two on their backs, a few doing frog kicks, four along one wall kicking their legs, and another two, Aileen and Trudy, swimming a crawl.

After a few minutes more, the coach returned.

Standing there in her suit, Catherine felt self-conscious as Mr. Handley looked her up and down.

"You need some muscle to swim," he said. "May I?" He brought her hands forward. "Flex."

She flexed her arms.

"Here," he said, grabbing her upper arm. "You need some muscle. But let's get you swimming. The muscle will come."

He led her over to the tank. They had a section to themselves, roped off from the others.

The coach gestured to the water, and Catherine jumped in. It was like getting into a warm bath, and the smell was overpowering. She began swimming. He walked along the pool deck beside her. She could see his pant legs each time she turned to breathe.

She finished a length and stopped.

The coach was frowning. "Well, you have a style I've never seen," he said, shaking his head. "Watch Aileen there." Catherine looked across toward the other swimmers. "Do you see that we kick six beats to the stroke and bring our arms up high?"

She nodded, although she didn't know what he meant about the kick. "You only do two beats to the stroke, or perhaps four. Did you know that?" He used his fingers like kicking legs. "You'll be faster when you learn to do six, like this"—kicking his fingers faster—"and when you can get your arms higher." He made windmills with his arms.

For the rest of the session, Catherine had to kick her legs without using her arms. She didn't enjoy it at all, the smelly water, the small space, the other swimmers, and her kicking seemed to get her nowhere. It was nothing like swimming at all. Before she knew it the session was finished, and Charlotte and Mr. Handley called her over.

"Well, you've had a great first day," Charlotte said, looking at the coach. "But you've learned some bad habits that you'll have to break, I'm afraid."

"Will we swim in the sea soon?" Catherine asked.

Charlotte smiled, looked at the coach. "We've entered the Battery to Sandy Hook in May. That's our first ocean race this year. We'll train in the harbor beforehand." She looked at Mr. Handley again. "Catherine, for open water we only take the fastest swimmers. And your aunt hasn't said how long you'll be with us yet."

"Yes, one step at a time," Mr. Handley said. "Where did you learn your crawl?"

"Pardon?" Catherine said.

"You swim a crawl, same as my girls, but it's different."

"On the island," Catherine said.

"Like I said, she's from Australia, Lou," Charlotte said. "She swam there, same as Annette Kellerman."

"Annette never swam the way this one swims," Mr. Handley said. "You don't get as much chance with your legs when you only kick two beats for each arm stroke, although your legs are strong, and I can see it gives you a very good balance position in the water. You get a lot of mileage from slow kicks. It's those feet." He looked down and then laughed at his little joke. Catherine had always had big feet.

She went to the change room to get out of her swimming suit.

Aileen Ryan had waited for her. "Are you staying with Eppy?" she said.

Catherine nodded. "Just until my aunt arrives," she said.

Catherine was hoping she'd remember how to get back to Charlotte Epstein's apartment. She had a piece of paper with directions to the train. She took it out now.

"Oh, don't worry," Aileen said. "I'll go with you. I don't need to be at school until ten today and Eppy asked if I'd mind. I'd love to take you."

"Oh, would you?" Catherine said. "I'm quite bamboozled here. The buildings make it hard to see where I am." They came back out past the tank. "It's so small."

"It's not much fun, is it?" Aileen said. "Still, when we were in Paris we swam in the river and it was really disgusting. And in Antwerp, it was so cold they had to put me in a warming room every time I dived. On account of my small size. I was only fourteen then."

"Were you at the Olympics?"

"Yep. At Antwerp, I got silver in the diving. We nearly weren't allowed to compete because they didn't want women. But don't worry too much about the tank. Once summer comes, you'll be sick of the water."

"What's the Battery to Sandy Hook?" Catherine said.

"We swim from Manhattan, near Eppy's place, to Sandy Hook Beach. The WSA is organizing it. We're the favorites, me and Trudy—if she's in the mood. She did it last year and beat everyone. That's why we all thought she would swim the English Channel. I didn't finish Sandy Hook last year because I hurt my shoulder. Helen Wainwright came second. She's away at the moment, thankfully. Helen is my big rival. But they're taking three swimmers to the Channel this year, whoever does best at Sandy Hook. They really want to make sure we're successful. So it will probably be the three of us—me, Trudy and Helen. Are you swimming Sandy Hook?"

"Apparently not. I don't kick correctly." Catherine realized if she didn't swim in the Sandy Hook race, she wouldn't join the team that was swimming the English Channel. This was why Mr. Black had brought her here, she thought, and already, Charlotte Epstein had implied, she wouldn't be included.

Aileen saw the look of concern on Catherine's face. "Don't worry about it. That's just Mr. Handley. He'll get used to you. He really is a dear—such a gentleman, as my mother would say. He never likes to let anyone do anything except his way. He loves the youngest swimmers best because they haven't learned any bad habits, he says. So Trudy is his total favorite because he had years with her to teach her his way. He played water polo, and water polo players all have to do the same thing."

"I can't swim the way he says, kicking so much. It feels wrong."

"Don't do it. He'll stop noticing soon. That's what happened with me. He gave up eventually. Then you can do what you like. Swimming isn't really a team thing like water polo. Hey, do you want to come to our beach place at the weekend? We might even be able to dip in the water."

"Oh, that would be so wonderful," Catherine said.

"Cold, okay? It's going to be cold."

"I don't care. I really don't." It didn't matter if she had to swim through icebergs; anything would be better than that stupid tank.

27

Catherine spent the remaining days of her first week in New York traveling to and from the tank twice each day. She'd gone on Wednesday to the YMCA pool to swim and watch the divers. She'd met Charlotte's family that night. Charlotte's mother was an older version of Charlotte, and her father kept calling Catherine Katrina. They told her she mustn't ever be lonely in New York. She could always pop in to see any of the Epsteins who seemed to live at regular intervals all over Manhattan. They gave her a map showing where all their homes were. Never too far away, Mrs. Epstein said. They were very kind.

Aileen's mother picked Catherine up from Charlotte's apartment block after Aileen finished school at noon that Friday. Catherine and Aileen sat in the backseat as they drove out of the city to Long Island. Late in the afternoon, they pulled up a long drive lined by pine trees to a white weatherboard house with green shutters and a slate roof. In the soft light it looked magical, the expanse of the bay behind, lit up by the afternoon sun.

"You girls must be positively starving," Aileen's mother said. "I meant to pack some snacks but clean forgot. Let's hope there are cookies left over from last weekend!" She laughed. Mrs. Ryan had the most marvelous laugh. Mr. Ryan, who Catherine met later that first night, was quiet and very serious. He spent most of the weekend behind a newspaper. But Aileen's mother—"Do call me Dotty, Catherine"—was as much fun as Aileen herself, and Catherine loved her immediately.

"She's a daughter of the American Revolution," Aileen said at dinner that first night, as if it explained why her mother went into fits of giggles at her own jokes.

Aileen's father looked up over his newspaper. "She really is," he said.

On that first afternoon, the two girls helped to unpack the car and went into the large kitchen at the back of the house. It had doors out onto a terrace that overlooked the water. They ate a box of cookies and then Aileen asked if they could go down to the beach.

"Daddy will be up at six for dinner and it's already late," Mrs. Ryan said. "Why don't you take Catherine for a walk along the point and dip your toes in? And tomorrow you can have the whole day on the beach."

Aileen's mother had been a runner, Aileen said on their walk, but she'd been stopped from competing. The Amateur Athletics Association wouldn't let women run in competitions. Aileen's mother could have gone to the Olympics, Aileen's father had told Aileen. Women couldn't swim in those days either, Aileen added. When Eppy started the WSA, she said, women were not allowed to swim in competitions at all. "There was a president of the Association who didn't believe women should compete. And neither did the president of the Olympics. Antwerp was the first time we were allowed to swim. And we very nearly weren't even then."

Mrs. Ryan was all for Aileen's diving, but Aileen's father thought it was nonsense.

"My father is a lawyer, and his father was a lawyer, and so I am to be a lawyer," Aileen said. "And if I am to be a lawyer, I must apply myself to my lessons." She sighed. "I love diving more than I've ever loved anything. Don't you love swimming that way?"

"I never had to imagine not swimming until I left Australia," Catherine said. "It's always been part of my life. I do love it, yes."

For most of the girls she'd met so far at the WSA, Catherine had realized, swimming was a sport, something they'd learned to do so they could compete and win. Catherine had never thought of swimming as a way to compete. It was so much a part of her she couldn't imagine being without swimming until it had happened.

~

The next morning, Catherine and Aileen ate a hearty breakfast of ham and eggs and fresh bread baked by Mrs. Ryan, then set off to explore. They found a cave Aileen had never seen before in the rocks at the point and ate their sandwiches while looking out to the water.

"Eppy says they're putting off deciding about the Channel swim until after Sandy Hook," Aileen said. "They sent Trudy last year but when she didn't make it, Eppy was devastated.

She wants a WSA swimmer to be the first, and so this year, they're being more careful. Eppy really wants three swimmers to go if there's enough money. It's very exciting. But Trudy's father is angry. He thinks it should be Trudy automatically. So Trudy might make another try on her own. They say one of the newspapers will pay for it."

Catherine knew Trudy's story now. She'd very nearly swum the English Channel the year before, but nine hours into the swim her coach had pulled her from the water. He said she was drowning, and the swimmer who was pacing her agreed. But afterward Trudy herself was furious, the newspaper report said. She told the reporters the coach had fed her something during the swim that had made her groggy. She said there was nothing wrong with her and she could swim the Channel any day of the week. She would be back, she said, her father and sister on either side of her. Trudy's father often came to training. He yelled at the girls to swim harder. It made the tank even more unpleasant.

Mrs. Ryan said the newspapers had been unthinkably poor in their treatment of Trudy, who was "just a girl, really. Swimming gets people so worked up," she said. "There were writers even here in America who said it was unwomanly to swim the Channel. They put Trudy in with the flappers. For goodness' sake, she's the butcher on Amsterdam Avenue's daughter. She's no flapper."

When Andrew had come up to see Catherine during her first week in New York, she'd asked him about Trudy Ederle's swim. Trudy's outburst had won her no friends in England, Andrew said, where they called her a sore loser. "Nobody likes a bad sport," he said. Trudy didn't strike Catherine as a bad sport.

Andrew said Catherine should be the one to swim the Channel. "Mr. Black says you're a champion, and Mr. Black knows these things. You could beat the Americans, the Germans and win the Channel for England, our England. Mr. Black says you will."

Catherine already knew Mr. Black had brought her here so she could train to swim the English Channel. The last time he'd seen her, before he came to America, he'd told her he was counting on her. She hadn't felt nervous. She'd smiled and told him, yes, of course she would swim the Channel. No talking to your aunt about it, he'd winked. She'd agreed to that too. She'd assumed she could swim the Channel, of course she could. The distance didn't faze her, and the cold wasn't something she minded. But now it was the way everyone talked about it. Rather than a swim, it was something terrible, something to be beaten. She wondered if there was some aspect she didn't understand, and it might be too difficult after all. Mr. Handley had been telling her all week she needed to change her swimming style. It had been exasperating. And the stupid little tank was not fun at all. It wasn't swimming.

"It's not my England," Catherine had said to Andrew.

"Oh, yes it is," he said. "If you win, we'll say you're English. Of course we will."

Now on the beach with her friend, Catherine looked out to the dark sea. Aileen said she didn't believe Trudy was aloof. "She's just in her own world. I don't think she can hear people very well, so she does her own thing."

A group of dolphins swam past out in the sea. "Porpoises," Aileen said, when Catherine pointed them out. They watched them playing in the waves while they shared the last of the soda with cheese crackers.

"Are you scared of swimming the Channel?" Catherine asked.

"Oh no," Aileen said. "They have a boat beside you the whole time. There's nothing to be scared of. I might not make it. But that would be okay. Have you ever swum that far?"

Catherine shook her head, looked out at the sea. But I could, she thought. Of course I could.

"Have you ever had a beau?" Aileen asked then.

"What's a beau?" Catherine said.

"A boyfriend, silly."

"No," Catherine said. She thought of Michael. "Well, maybe."

"Maybe what?" Aileen said.

"Well, not so much a boyfriend, more like a brother. He's not my real brother but back on the island there was a boy, Florence's son. Florence was our housekeeper who helped looked after me."

"Blech," Aileen said. "You can't kiss your brother. Did you kiss?"

Catherine shook her head quickly. "Of course not. Michael's not like that." She blushed. "There's also another fellow," she said. "I knew him in London. He's here now, or in Baltimore. But I'm not sure he's a beau. He's more like a brother, too, I think. How would I know?" Catherine thought about Andrew. She was fond of him, and was glad he was coming to see her. It was someone from home, or from London anyway. When she'd first met him, he'd been so sweet. She'd liked him straightaway, and his slight awkwardness had been part of his charm for her. Now, though, he'd changed. He was a reporter for Mr. Black's newspaper, smoking those cigarettes and drinking the beer. He'd hardened toward life, she thought, although she wondered if it was just an act. Every now and then his old sweet self would poke through. She wasn't sure of his feelings for her, and she wasn't sure of her own feelings. How would she know? she thought. "What about you?" she said to Aileen. "Do you have a beau?"

"Well, there's this boy who lives a few streets away. I'll take you past his house. He's twenty-three and he works at the club at the end of the beach. I don't know if I'll be able to go on without him." Aileen held her palm to her forehead in mock upset. "But seriously, he's handsome," she said, "with the blondest hair that flops onto his large forehead—lots of brains, I think—and muscles on his muscles. He swims in the afternoons, so let's keep an eye out, just in case." Her eyes widened. "Daddy hates him, of course, without even knowing him. I don't dare tell Daddy, actually, for fear he'll go over there with a gun.

"Oh, I'm so glad you're here, Catherine," she said. "My best friend, Marlene, left last term, and I've been lonely. But you're just like Marlene—a real friend."

The next morning, they got up early and headed for the beach again. The day was fine and warm, and they decided to swim out to a shipwreck a mile from shore. They raced each other to the water and it reminded Catherine of swimming with Michael back on the island. Until they were in the sea, that is, and the cold hit her. The water was freezing, colder than the ponds at Hampstead, but so long as Catherine kept swimming hard, she could manage. The bow of the old ship jutted up out of the water, and the rusted keel was visible, covered now in barnacles. Catherine swam as hard as she could to get warm and soon reached the keel.

She looked around her. The sun was shining on the water, and the sea seemed to go forever, meeting the sky seamlessly on the horizon. This was what she had missed, being in the sea, alone in all the world.

"Oh, Aileen, what a wonderful place." Her friend had caught up with her.

"Holy moley," Aileen said. "I couldn't keep up with you. Boy, you can swim!"

They didn't tread water for long, as they started to feel the cold, so they swam back to shore and dressed quickly, and ran along the sand to warm up in the sun.

They didn't see Aileen's "beau" that day, but they had enormous fun looking for him.

The rest of the weekend was full of good food and fun. The time she spent with the Ryans, on that weekend and a number that followed, would remain with Catherine. It wasn't like being with Florence on the island, but it wasn't like being with Louisa and Nellie either. It was just normal, Catherine thought later. She could have settled in and become part of the Ryan family quite easily. It gave her a notion she'd never had before: that she might be able to live somewhere other than the island and it would be all right.

The truth was that Catherine was starting to forget the island. She'd try to remember the smells, but it was difficult. You never smelled coconut in London or New York. It was the strongest memory she had, but she couldn't quite recall it. It was a hot smell, she knew, a wholesome smell that made her think of goodness.

On her last afternoon on Long Island, Catherine watched

the sun set with Aileen. They held hands. I could be happy, she thought. I could be happy with these people, with swimming in New York. No one was more surprised to discover she felt this way than Catherine herself.

In the weeks that followed, Catherine and Aileen spent time together when Aileen wasn't at school. Catherine fell into an easy routine of swimming morning and evening and spending her days exploring New York. She liked the library on Fifth Avenue, where she could stay all day if she wanted and read newspapers. Outside the library was an ice-cream vendor. The worst of the cold weather was over and there were tiny buds on all the trees. Sometimes she'd get one of those ice creams—vanilla or chocolate—and go and sit in the park and eat it while she watched the people go by. Soon Louisa would come. She'd put off her trip twice now, but she'd wired Catherine that she was finally getting away. When Louisa came, Catherine would leave Charlotte Epstein's apartment and she and her aunt would move into a hotel together. Louisa's last telegram was typical Louisa. MAD HERE STOP SAIL 26TH STOP. That was all. LOVE or even REGARDS probably wouldn't have cost any more, Andrew observed when he saw the telegram. Catherine couldn't imagine Louisa using those words.

All the same, Catherine found that she was looking forward to seeing her aunt again. She was glad to be swimming, she really was, but the tank wasn't what she'd expected. It was so small, like trying to swim in Louisa's bathtub. Catherine would hardly start out before she'd have to turn around. And

Mr. Handley still said she wasn't swimming properly. The American girls kicked more frequently, while Catherine kicked in rhythm with her arms. She tried hard to do as he said, but it didn't feel normal, and then she would lose speed and he'd tell her to swing her arms higher. She only had one way she could go forward, she told him, and that was the way she was going. He smiled. "That's good," he said. "One way forward."

Charlotte had been lovely, and Charlotte's and Aileen's families had made sure Catherine felt welcome. She also saw Andrew every week. He came up on the train. Mr. Black didn't come, and Catherine found she was disappointed. She told Andrew she'd hoped Mr. Black might help her meet her American family but Andrew said he'd hardly seen Mr. Black either. There was some trouble with a shipping company he was involved in. Andrew didn't know the details. Catherine worried that perhaps he wasn't coming because Charlotte and Mr. Handley had told him she wasn't as good a swimmer as he thought. Perhaps he was disappointed in her, and felt he'd wasted his money.

Aileen came with Catherine to meet with Andrew one day. After he'd gone back on the train, Aileen said Catherine definitely had herself a beau. As he'd been leaving, he'd shaken hands with Aileen to say good-bye and then he'd leaned in to embrace Catherine.

"He's a dish," Aileen said. "And he speaks like a prince. Oh, oh, oh," she said. "I love him even if you don't."

Catherine just laughed. "Oh, Aileen, Andrew's like a big brother. He's not a beau." But afterward, she wondered too what his feelings were, what her own feelings were. It was confusing.

Catherine had come to know Charlotte Epstein better. She told Catherine that her experience with court cases had trained her well for the many battles she'd fought to get the Women's Swimming Association up and running. Like Louisa, Charlotte was always doing something. She came to swimming training at six o'clock every morning and then left the girls at eight to go to work. She came back in the evenings for training and then went home to work some more.

The girls all wore WSA suits to training. They were more revealing than the suit Catherine wore in England, with straps over the shoulders and cut off higher at the thigh, Catherine told Louisa in a letter. *You'll hate them*, she wrote. *They don't even have a skirt!* They were more like the suits the men wore, Catherine thought, more like what she herself had worn at home. Charlotte said if they all wore them to meets, there would be no problem. The girls were used to one another in the new costumes, but some worried they'd be in trouble once they were swimming competitively again on the beaches, which still imposed strict dress codes, policed by beach officers.

"If we get arrested, we'll all get arrested," Aileen said bravely.

Catherine had laughed. "They can't arrest me. I'm not even an American."

"You think that will stop the police?" Aileen said. "Hah! They arrested Ethelda Bleibtrey on Manhattan Beach, and all she did was take off her stockings. They'll deport you back to Australia, or wherever they like. You might have to become Canadian." They'd arrested Annette Kellerman for wearing a suit just like these, "although it's true that was before the war," Aileen said.

Charlotte Epstein, who had been listening to them talking, smiled. "The charge was indecent exposure, if you can believe it. Miss Kellerman gave a great speech in the court about what she needed in order to swim, how you could be pulled under by all those clothes and drown. She said they expected women to go around looking like clotheslines."

Aileen took a bite of the apple she'd brought with her to training, and then offered Catherine some. Catherine shook her head.

"The judge was livid at the beach police," Charlotte said. "He threw the case out. They'd never arrest you now, but only because of what Annette Kellerman did."

One morning in her fourth week, Mr. Handley asked Catherine to remain after training. Charlotte hadn't gone to work yet, which was unusual, and the two took her into the small room beside the pool which doubled as the office. Mr. Handley took the chair beside the desk and Charlotte sat behind it, gesturing for Catherine to take the chair that faced her.

"Catherine, as you know, the WSA has decided that if we can raise funds we will send three swimmers to attempt the Channel this year."

Catherine nodded.

"And," Charlotte continued seriously, "we have to consider a number of factors—not just ability, but also seniority and likelihood of success."

Mr. Handley was silent, though Catherine was aware of him watching her intently.

"We've decided to use the Sandy Hook swim to confirm the decision."

"Yes," Catherine said eagerly.

"But we don't think you should be in the Sandy Hook team."

Catherine stared at Charlotte. She heard the words, but her brain just wasn't making sense of them. "I beg your pardon?" she said.

"You're not ready, Catherine," Mr. Handley said. "You need to improve your style and, so far, you haven't made as much progress as I'd like. In my opinion, as the coach, it would be too risky to allow you to take part in an open-water swim."

"Risky?" Catherine said. She didn't understand. Were they worried about sharks, crocodiles? Where was the risk?

"Well, we can only do so much to keep our swimmers safe in the water," Charlotte said. "So, after taking advice from Mr. Handley, the board has decided that you shouldn't swim with the team."

Catherine was about to speak, to protest that there would be no risk, when she realized what they meant. They were saying she wasn't a good enough swimmer. "Oh, of course. Oh. I thought . . . I . . . of course. I'm sorry. That's great news. I mean, that you're sending swimmers to the Channel . . ." Catherine was devastated. She'd failed. She'd told Mr. Black she could do this swim and now she wouldn't even be in the group they selected the swimmers from. She had failed. Again.

Charlotte's face softened. "There will be other years, other attempts. And you're still so young." She put her hand on Catherine's and patted it lightly. "We had enormous trouble in Paris with Helen and Aileen, and I don't want to go through that ever again."

Catherine wanted to pull her hand away from Charlotte's and tell them to leave her alone. Instead, she sat there with a stupid grin on her face, trying to pretend that she understood, that none of it mattered.

Mr. Handley stood up to leave. He nodded to Catherine then looked at Charlotte, shook his head.

Charlotte sighed. "Catherine, I have many things to balance, as you can well imagine. You are a promising swimmer, and Coach sees that. And you are willing, if not yet able, to master the stroke . . . But as I say, I have competing priorities. I have to do what's best for the WSA, what gives us the most chance of a win . . ."

But Catherine wasn't listening. All she was aware of was that she'd failed. She'd been expelled from school because of swimming—and now she'd failed at that. Her aunt had only gone along with the whole idea of her swimming because Mr. Black said she would be a champion. Mr. Black had said she'd be the first woman to swim the English Channel and it would be great. But Catherine wasn't a champion. She wasn't even on the team. She thought she'd found a place here in New York, but it was no place for her. It couldn't be worse.

She went back into the change room cubicle and locked the door. She sat on the floor and cried as silently as she could.

28

It's because you're not American," Aileen said when Catherine told her the next morning before training. "Imagine if we took a Brit over there and they did the Channel first. We have to have an American."

"I thought they took all swimmers. Anyway, I'm not a Brit."

"No, you're not. And yes, they do take anyone, but not for this. This is the most important thing ever. This is the English Channel. I don't think they're scared you'll fail. I think they're scared you'll succeed. I've seen you swim. And I told Eppy; I told her you could beat everyone."

Catherine didn't believe Aileen. She didn't even think Aileen believed Aileen. But it was awfully sweet of her to say it.

After the session, in which she didn't even try to swim the way Mr. Handley suggested, Catherine was in the change room when she heard voices in the office, Charlotte's and another. Aileen had left to go to school and there was only Catherine and two other girls still getting dressed.

"It appears you may have overestimated your charge," Eppy was saying, her lovely loud voice clear through the thin wall. "Coach says she doesn't take instruction."

She couldn't hear what the other voice, a man's, much quieter, said in reply.

"Swimming is swimming," Eppy said.

"I want her to stay here," Catherine heard, the male voice raised now. It was familiar. Oh, my goodness, she thought. It was Mr. Black. Catherine felt her heart pumping in her chest. She leaned toward the wall to listen harder.

"Of course," Charlotte said. "I understand."

"And I think my contributions buy me the right to a view." It was Mr. Black, Catherine was sure now, and they were talking about her. Oh, how awful. Eppy had told him Catherine wasn't a good swimmer. He'd spent all that money bringing her here for nothing. It was the worst possible thing to have happen.

When Catherine came out of the change room, hoping to get away without being seen, Charlotte was there waiting for her. She beckoned Catherine to come into the office. There was Mr. Black sitting in the chair by the desk. Catherine just wanted to disappear.

He stood but didn't move closer to her. "Catherine," he said gruffly, and nodded. "How are you?" He sounded angry and he looked disappointed, reminding her suddenly of her father when she did something wrong.

"Mr. Black." She was on the verge of tears.

"I hear you're not swimming at your best. You make me look like a liar. Or a fool."

"I'm sorry, Mr. Black," she said, keeping her tears in check as best she could. She looked at Eppy. "I'm doing my best, though. Eppy, I'm doing my best, aren't I?"

Eppy nodded. "Of course you are. Manfred, that's not what . . ."

"You know I brought you here," he said to Catherine. "You know I'm counting on you."

"I do," she said. "I'm so sorry."

"Miss Epstein tells me you've been complaining about the tank."

"I'm just not used to a small space," she said.

"Well, maybe that's the problem," he said. "What if I found you a bigger space? Would that help?" He came over and stood close to Catherine. Eppy was behind her.

"Yes, I think it would," she said as confidently as she could muster.

He nodded slowly, looked at his watch. He picked up his hat and coat from Charlotte's desk. "Let's you and I have a little chat now," he said to Catherine. "Charlotte, I'm sure we'll be seeing one another. I go back tomorrow but I'll pop in this evening." Charlotte stepped out of the way to let him through. Catherine stood there. "Come on," he said. "Charlotte, always a pleasure."

Charlotte bade Mr. Black farewell. Catherine looked behind as she walked along the tank deck with him. Charlotte was standing at the door of the little office, frowning.

When they reached the hotel foyer, Mr. Black turned to her. "Catherine, I'm sorry if I was too direct with you." He looked upset too, Catherine thought. Oh, what a disaster. As if it wasn't bad enough being left off the team. Now she'd disappointed the person she most wanted to please.

"I'm so sorry, Mr. Black." She felt like crying again.

His face softened. "Please," he said. "Don't be upset. Have you had some breakfast?" She shook her head, not trusting her voice.

He took her to the diner across the street from the Touraine. He picked a table in the back and pulled out a chair for her, sat facing her. He called the waitress, ordered his usual toast and eggs and she ordered oatmeal with cinnamon and sugar. "I *am* sorry," he said. He looked at her intently. "But I'm not used to losing, and I'm not very good at it. And I hope you're not either." He paused, ran his hand over his mouth. "I didn't like them cutting you from the team without talking to me first. That's what I was mad about. Charlotte shouldn't have done that. She knew my view. I found out quite by accident and I was livid. I came down last night. I'm sorry if I took that my anger on you. It hadn't been my intention. I was furious, but not with you."

"Mr. Black, I'm really not as good a swimmer as the others. Charlotte was right . . ."

He waved at her to be quiet. "I don't want to hear that talk, you hear?" he said firmly. "Look at you," he went on. "You have the entire world at your fingertips, girl, and you don't even see it." He grabbed her hand.

She felt so ashamed. "Mr. Black, I . . ."

"Don't," he said. "Let's just let the swimming worry about itself. All right?" He let go of her hand. "All right?"

She nodded.

"That's my girl," he said. "You may not understand this but I lost someone a long time ago, and you very much remind me of her. I want you to be everything you can, Catherine.

Do you understand that?" He took a breath in, out. Looking at his face, Catherine thought he might be about to cry.

"I think so," she said.

"You're a great girl." He patted her hand again. "Now, can you find your way home from here all right?" She nodded. "That's the way." He stood and looked at his watch. Their food hadn't yet arrived. He threw a bill on to the table.

"Louisa is here next week. I'd very much like to take the two of you to lunch at my club." He smiled. "Swim well. I'll see you then." He stood there a moment more, then he turned and walked away.

They were sitting in the café Andrew had taken her to on her first day in New York. Mr. Black had sent him up "to check on our champ," Andrew told Catherine. It was the Monday after Mr. Black himself had come to New York. Charlotte had told Catherine she'd be on the Sandy Hook team after all. She was only on the team because of Mr. Black, she knew, and Charlotte was angry, Catherine thought. It had been an awful few days.

As she'd walked along 23rd Street with Andrew, she'd seen the buds on the trees, some with leaves unfolding.

"I don't really know why I'm here," she said.

"Lunch," he said matter-of-factly.

"I meant in a more fundamental way."

"New York?"

She nodded.

"Well, you don't need a reason. You're in New York because it's New York. And because you swim. Isn't that enough? Louisa will be here soon. She's sure to have you busy rolling bandages in Baltimore or something."

They'd had their boiled eggs and toast for lunch as the weak sun crept over the top of the building and into the window.

Andrew drank coffee with everything now—a thoroughly Continental sensibility, he called it. He'd lit a cigarette, offering her one and then withdrawing the offer. "I keep forgetting you're so young," he said. "Do you want to try one? I'm sure you could now."

Catherine was wearing a light blue sweater and gray skirt. She needed to gain weight for the Sandy Hook swim. Mr. Handley had told them they'd need a good layer of body fat, that the swim would be cold even in May.

She shook her head no about the cigarette. "I'm not as good as the others," she said, her mind still on swimming. "When we race, I come last. I hate that stupid tank."

Andrew shrugged. "When I first came to Baltimore, they all hated me because I'm English and I was forced on them by Black. They got over it, and now I'm the star."

"They don't hate me," she said, "although there's a couple who really wonder why I've been picked for the race."

"Whatever do you mean, darling? You're a marvel. Everyone says. Anyway, who cares about the silly WSA? You could swim for England. You're our marvel, not theirs. That's what's really going on here. They don't want England to pip them to the post when it comes to the Channel."

"Am I a marvel?" she said. She didn't feel like a marvel.

She wasn't even that good a swimmer, she thought now. She'd swum on Thursday Island, but who said the Islanders were good swimmers? She was a good swimmer in London because she was the only swimmer. How did she come to think that swimming would help her? "The only one I can beat is Aileen, and she's a diver, not a swimmer."

"Well, Mr. Black must think you're a winner. He told me he's put a thousand dollars on you to win."

"He's what?" Catherine was shocked.

"He says you're a sure thing. He's wagered a thousand on you for a win. If you lose, he'll give the money to the Association. If you win, well, I don't quite know. But anyway."

"Oh, goodness," she said. "That's just awful. Why did Mr. Black do that?"

"Faith, he told me. 'You gotta have faith, Andy.'"

She shook her head and sighed. This was harder than she'd thought it would be. "Do you miss home?" she said.

He smiled. "I miss my dog. And I wish I'd brought my ukulele. But I love America. It's so exciting, the mood here. It's not all covered over like home is. Everything's opaque like a London fog. When I was at Oxford, it was like I wasn't really alive, or like I was observing everything from a long way away. With Mr. Black, everything came to life. I just worry about Mama. She's so lost without me there."

The waitress came over to the table. "You folks all done?"

"Yes, the check, please," Andrew said. After she'd left, he continued, "You have to be picked for the Channel."

"Why?"

"Because then Mr. Black will find a reporter to go with you. And I hope it will be me. I can visit Mama and Papa, to keep them happy, and then have a month in France." He smiled again. "You really are in the doldrums today, aren't you?"

She looked at him.

"You're like the ugly duckling in the fairy tale," he said.

"How?"

"You're becoming a beautiful swan but you don't know it. You still think you want to be a silly old duck."

29

London, April 1926

Louisa had papers all over the table in the dining room, things to be handed over or finished before she left the next day. It was late. She'd been held up at Harley Street that afternoon, finalizing details of the transfer of her patients to the other doctors, and then she'd gone back to the clinic to finish up there. Nellie had gone to bed. The Scotties were on the floor. She should stoke the fire but she'd go to bed herself soon.

On the table in front of her was the pile of letters she'd collected. And today, Nellie had handed her two more, one addressed to Louisa herself. Nellie had asked Louisa was she planning to take Catherine's letters to America and give them to the girl. Was she planning to mail Catherine's letters to Australia now?

"Probably," Louisa had said.

"You have to," Nellie had said. "You can't do this, Louisa. You can't keep them from her. You said weeks. It's been months."

Louisa had let the time slip by. She should have done something about the letters before Catherine left for America but she hadn't. Things had been so much better between them. Louisa had taken the letters out the night before Catherine embarked, but found her courage failed her. How could she give her these letters? How could she say she hadn't sent Catherine's on? Catherine would never forgive her, and the truth was, Catherine had forgotten Florence and Michael now. She'd been so excited about the trip. She'd been busy at the clinic. She'd been positively bright. It was best now, Louisa thought, to let it go. They'd become close. Once Catherine didn't have the island as a constant reminder, they'd become close.

Except for Nellie.

"Those people—I met them," Louisa had said to Nellie. "They may mean well, Nellie. But they are not Catherine's future. They are her past. Her future is here with us. Surely you, of anyone, can see that."

"What do you mean me, of anyone?"

"You lost your family, Nellie, and I know you've settled here with me. I know you'll go on to do something great with your life. And while you would never have wanted to lose the baby, your life now is so much more."

"What baby?" Nellie said.

"Sorry?"

"What baby are you talking about?"

Had Louisa mentioned a baby? Perhaps she had. "I meant your brother—the baby of the family," she said.

"I swear to God, Louisa, I do appreciate all you've done for me. I do. I feel blessed that you saw me and decided to help. But I would give it all up to have just one day with my family.

I would give it all up in a minute. So, Louisa, you need to think about what you're doing to that girl. And that's all I'll say on the matter."

"Well, it just upsets her to hear from them," Louisa said, feeling heat rise in her neck. "Why do that? She's not going back there. She needs a chance to start a new life."

Catherine had found a place for herself in the clinic before she'd left for America, and Louisa was sure they could get her back to school after this trip. She could finish her formal schooling and go on to university. She might even become a doctor, Louisa had thought, and wouldn't that be marvelous? Louisa didn't want to tell her the truth now.

The swimming didn't worry Louisa as much as it had in the beginning. Black seemed to think Catherine had the makings of a champion and Louisa could tell that being in New York with other swimmers was doing Catherine a world of good. She'd made a friend, a young diver whose family had been terribly kind. Charlotte Epstein seemed a very good role model for a female swimmer, and Black had made sure Andrew visited every week to look out for Catherine. Her letters to Louisa were bright and full of interest. Swimming might build Catherine's confidence just as Black had suggested.

Louisa found herself thinking about Black, his laugh, low and from his chest, when he saw something that amused him, especially if it was something about the English. Truthfully, she thought of him more often than she'd have liked. She'd see him again soon. And there was probably nothing but childish fancy in her thoughts of him. But still, that smile. He'd been true to his word too. He'd funded an upgrade to the Princes Square facilities—additional bathrooms, an extension of the surgical ward, a new waiting room—to meet all the requirements the inspector had listed. They'd passed the inspection without qualification. It never would have happened otherwise.

The two letters joined the other six Louisa had in front of her. She sat there looking at the envelope addressed to herself and then opened the letter.

Dear Dr. Quick,

We have not heard from Catherine in months, and the last letter she sent asked why I had not written. I can only assume she is not getting our letters for some reason. You cannot think that we would ever do Catherine harm.

I encouraged her to leave the island, and I trusted you because you are Dr. Harry's sister.

My son Michael and Catherine are very close to one another. He is very distressed not to hear from Catherine, and worried. I am worried about both of them.

Please let me know that Catherine is all right.

Sincerely,
Florence Cunningham

Louisa would have liked to take the moral high ground. How dare Florence suggest that Louisa was doing something untoward? But she was doing something untoward, so the moral high ground would remain unoccupied on this occasion. Louisa knew she couldn't easily recover the situation now. At any rate, Catherine had moved on. She'd done exactly as Louisa thought she would, and she was much better for it.

Florence wasn't giving up, though.

It was the second letter, which Louisa also opened, that gave her pause.

> *Dear Catherine,*
>
> *I hope this letter finds you well. I am writing because I am worried about Michael. He went down to Cairns a few weeks back with a group of boys from here, John and Charlie Mackie, who you know, and some others who've come these last months from Badu. He's been staying with my sister but I got news from her daughter that he's left there and they're not sure where he is.*
>
> *He has been trying to get work. The thing is, he wants to come to you. He's worried because we haven't heard. I don't like him being in town by himself, and I'm thinking if you just wrote and said you were all right, he might come home. My sister said there's a bad group of boys he's been spending time with. Michael's a good boy, and I don't want any more trouble.*
>
> *I remain your loving Florence*

The notion that Michael would come to London worried Louisa. She would have to tell the truth about the letters. She'd never considered they'd go to such lengths. He must hold Catherine in high regard, Louisa thought. Perhaps it wasn't as she'd assumed. Perhaps he wasn't taking advantage. Oh, there was so much Louisa didn't know.

Never mind. Once Louisa was there with Catherine in America, she was sure, this would be so much easier. She put the letters back in the drawer, where they belonged.

30

New York, May 1926

New York Harbor smelled of peanuts and dirt. London smelled of the cold, Louisa had often thought, a rather clean smell, one she liked. But peanuts and dirt made her think of childhood, the few times they'd gone to fairs, the smell of the hay for the animals, the roasted peanuts their father would treat them to. That's what America was, she'd thought the last time she'd been here, an almighty fair from which no one seemed to want to go home.

Louisa looked toward the dock where people waited for their loved ones and felt a pang of loneliness. It was the first time she'd taken a break from work since she'd gone to bring Catherine home, and that was hardly a holiday. She couldn't remember when she'd last taken time for herself. She didn't have much use for holidays, she'd said to Ruth Luxton when she told her she was going to America. "I don't know quite what I'll do."

"You'll find something," Ruth had said, crisply but kindly. They'd survive, Ruth said. They really would.

"It was easier when I didn't have time to think," Louisa said to herself now, causing the young man beside her to look at her askance.

"I beg your pardon?" he said.

"Nothing," she said. "Just talking to myself."

He smiled. "I usually don't admit it," he said. "First time?"

"I beg your pardon?"

"New York. Is it your first time in New York?"

Louisa looked at him. He was young, perhaps middle twenties, with sandy hair and blue eyes. He wore a long coat made of some sort of animal hide and a broad-brimmed hat. "No," she said. "But the first time in a long while."

"Marvelous," he said. "Anything can be possible here."

Louisa looked at him squarely. "It's attitudes like that that see people disappointed by life," she said. The young man looked as if he might argue but thought better of it, smiled weakly and turned and walked away.

Catherine had wired Louisa that she would come to meet her at the dock and, look, there she was. What a sweet girl, Louisa thought, although Catherine didn't look like a girl anymore. She'd grown. Louisa shouldn't have left it so long, she thought, but there had been so much to do in the end to set up for the trip, and she'd had to stay through the health inspector's visit.

Catherine was wearing a pair of long trousers and a cotton jumper. She was back in those silly trousers, Louisa thought. Her cheeks were ruddy and she grinned as she threw her arms around her aunt.

"Just a minute," Louisa said, trying to hold Catherine at arm's length then wishing she hadn't.

But Catherine didn't seem to care. She held on to Louisa and hugged her warmly.

Louisa put her arms around the girl and embraced her.

"Oh, I missed you, Louisa." Catherine laughed and her aunt joined in.

"I missed you too," Louisa said, finding tears in her eyes. Where did those come from? she thought. Oh, the girl was dear. And her smell. It was the smell of sunshine, Louisa thought, recalling her first visit to the island. She smelled like sunshine.

"Mr. Black's coming," Catherine said. "He's going to take us out to some fancy club. He came to see me, and he shouldn't have done this but he's bet on me to win a race, Louisa."

"He can afford it," Louisa said. "But I didn't realize he'd been to see you. You've been seeing Andrew too, haven't you?"

"Oh, yes, but I do want to do well for Mr. Black, Louisa, and I'm very worried that I won't. The coach says I don't swim properly." Louisa looked at her niece. She did look worried. Louisa must talk to Black, make sure he wasn't putting pressure on Catherine. That would do her no good at all.

Catherine took her aunt to Allerton House on East 57th Street, where they'd stay together before Louisa went on to Baltimore. The hotel had been recommended by Charlotte Epstein; it was one of the new women-only hotels in New York, Catherine said. Catherine had already left her suitcase at the front desk, she said. She talked all the way in the taxicab, about the awful tank she had to swim in, the trains that were so much more efficient than in London, the wonderful diners with their sandwiches, and her new friend, Aileen.

The hotel had a simply furnished lobby and a lounge off to one side where guests could entertain. They took an elevator to the twelfth floor. Their room looked over the park across the street. On the top floor was a gorgeous little roof garden, Catherine told Louisa, and a solarium. "And there's a tank, Louisa. It's small, but bigger than the one we train in, so I'll swim while I'm here."

That afternoon, Andrew came on the train from Baltimore and took them for tea, on the basis that Louisa wasn't yet ready for an American diner experience. He was affable as ever, if slightly removed from the world. Louisa had gone to see his mother, Ada, after he left for America. She was a strong woman, and she'd loved her two boys so fiercely. And now she'd lost them both, Donald to the war and Andrew to life. There was not much happiness in motherhood, Louisa thought.

Ada had told Louisa that Andrew was engaged to be married to an English girl, a girl his older brother had known. Louisa wondered had he told Catherine this. They were close, she could see, and she worried for her niece, who seemed to be keen to find her moorings in New York.

In the evening, while Catherine was at the YMCA pool, Louisa had dinner with Charlotte Epstein in the hotel dining room. Charlotte was exactly as Louisa expected, smart and strong with a hearty laugh. She'd been a chaperone for Catherine in New York, although, she said, Catherine was so well behaved she didn't need much in the way of guidance.

Charlotte was clearly less enamored of Catherine's swimming than Black was, and her view matched Catherine's self-assessment. "I'll be honest with you, Louisa," Charlotte said. "As you'll quickly learn, I don't know how to be any other way. Delightful young woman, but Catherine isn't the swimmer we'd hoped she'd be. She's welcome to stay, of course, but, really, she needs a lot of work before she'll be at competition level."

They were eating fish in a white sauce; overcooked, Louisa had thought. Nellie was good with fish—good with everything.

"Black's wrong, then," Louisa said. Why the devil bring her all this way?, she wondered. "Frankly, I can't say I'm terribly disappointed."

Charlotte smiled. "You're not a fan?"

"Of swimming? I suppose I've never seen where it leads, especially for women. And perhaps I'm from an old world. I do think you've done a marvelous job to make a place in sports for women. And I'm all for Catherine having this time, which I hope will help her mature and grow in confidence. But I'd love to see her back in school. She's bright."

"I know you were very active in the women's suffrage movement," Charlotte said. "So were my swimmers."

"And?"

"Swimming isn't all that different from any number of things women have been shut out of."

Louisa thought about this. "We're also shut out of bars. But I don't intend to campaign any time soon to have us established there. Some things matter less. As I say, I think I may be something of the old guard. I don't even like the suits they wear, and I particularly don't like the idea of men coming to watch them."

Charlotte nodded. "Granted about the men. But until 1920, there was no Olympic swimming for women. We changed that. Us, the WSA—we did that."

"But that's not why your swimmers get their pictures in the newspaper." Louisa wondered if Charlotte could possibly believe women's swimming was growing in popularity because they were good swimmers.

"I don't care."

"You don't? It's lascivious."

"Well, it's lascivious of the fellows who ogle the girls, but it's nothing to do with my swimmers." Charlotte regarded Louisa.

"Black."

"What about him?" Charlotte said, a little smile at the corners of her mouth.

"He intrigues me."

"He intrigues us all, honey."

"Not like that. I mean his interest. He seems terribly interested in Catherine. He wired me about all this, said he'd had to intervene so she can swim in some race. I am sorry he did that."

Charlotte shrugged. "Oh, that didn't worry me so much. He'd probably give us the money anyway if we needed it. You don't have to worry on Black's account. It's the swimming. He's brought us many Catherines over the years." There was no hint of scandal in Charlotte's voice, Louisa noticed.

"He has? Why?"

Charlotte took a sip of her wine. "Did he ever tell you about the *Slocum*?"

Louisa shook her head.

"It was a passenger ferry that caught fire in the East River

twenty years ago. The *General Slocum*, one of the last big paddle steamers. It was a terrible accident. A thousand died."

"Oh, how awful."

"And it was because they couldn't swim. I remember the
Slocum," Charlotte said. "They were pulling bodies out of the
water for days. I'll never forget it."

"And what does that have to do with Black?"

"His mother and sister were on board. They were with
him. He was separated from them. He survived because he
could swim. They didn't."

"Oh," Louisa said. "So he supports women's swimming?"
Heartbreaking, Louisa thought. Absolutely heartbreaking.
Why was the world so sad?

"Yes. You see, a boy like him would have been taught to
swim but not his sister and not his mother." Like Louisa herself, she thought. "It's a tragic story. His father had died not
long before and so he lost his whole family in the space of a
year. Once the association started attracting attention, he came
to see me about helping. We couldn't have survived without
his support. For him, perhaps it gives him comfort.

"It was his lawyer who told me about his mother and sister.
We were drawing up the contracts. It was a warning, really,
that we shouldn't take advantage of Black."

That night, when Louisa was alone in the hotel suite—
Catherine having gone back to the Ryan house from the
YMCA—she thought again about what Charlotte had told
her. Poor Black. To lose your family like that. He'd been so

young when it happened; Nellie's age. When Louisa was that age, she'd had everything to look forward to. Oh, later, she'd had troubles but at twenty-one, she was looking forward to a bright life. And what happened to her couldn't compare to what he'd lost.

Poor Black. He saw Catherine as his lost sister. Was he trying to help his sister to swim? Is that why he wanted to believe in Catherine? Oh, how harsh.

Still, it was all very well for Black to assuage his grief and guilt through swimmers, but it might not be the best for Catherine. Louisa was relieved to hear Charlotte say that Catherine wasn't a strong swimmer. It would make it easier to finish up in America and make their way back home. Catherine would surely be more ready for school now.

Louisa felt a twinge then. She hadn't told Catherine about the letters from Australia. She'd told Nellie she would but then she hadn't. Oh well, she thought. There was nothing to do now but go on as she'd started.

And anyway, the letters were still tucked up at Wellclose Square. She and Catherine might laugh about them one day. Remember that family? I hid their letters.

No, now that she thought about it, she and Catherine would never laugh about them, Louisa realized. Best to keep secrets secret, she decided.

31

Twenty-one young women had gathered at Battery Park at the end of Manhattan Island ready to start their swim. The sun was up but the day wasn't yet warm and Catherine knew the water would be cold. The swim route was marked. It would take them to Sandy Hook at the north end of New Jersey.

It was a cracker of a day according to Aileen Ryan, who thought everything was a cracker. It was her favorite word, Catherine said.

"So?" Aileen said. "It's better than saying everything's dull."

"Do I say everything's dull?" Catherine said.

"No," Aileen replied, and laughed. "I just meant I'd rather be positive than negative."

"I agree," Catherine said. She was looking forward to this swim, she realized. There had been all the trouble about the English Channel and she knew that no matter what happened today she wouldn't be selected. She might have hoped Mr.

Handley and Charlotte would change their minds but that wasn't going to happen, she was sure now. So today, she could enjoy the swim and not have to worry about what happened next. Louisa had told her that they'd soon be returning to England and that she could go back to school after the summer break. Catherine felt this was for the best, although she worried about how much she'd disappointed Mr. Black.

Meg Ederle joined Catherine and Aileen. "How's it looking?" she said, a frown on her face as she looked out at the water. Gulls were wheeling overhead, crying like children for the scraps people threw. A small crowd had gathered in the park behind them, mostly families of the swimmers. Louisa was up there somewhere with Charlotte Epstein but Catherine couldn't see her.

"It's a cracker," Catherine said. "An absolute cracker."

Meg looked at her. "What's that supposed to mean?"

Catherine looked at Aileen.

"I give up," Aileen said. "Let's get ready."

The tide would be against them for the start of their course, Charlotte had told them, but not to worry; it would soon be in their favor—although, depending on their timing, they might have a struggle at the end.

The dories were lined up along the edge of the pier, one for each swimmer. There were the six girls from the WSA, including Catherine. The others had come from Florida and Texas.

Catherine knew she was only swimming because of Mr. Black, but Mr. Handley had acted as if it had been his decision. He'd said they changed their minds and decided to give her some experience of open-water swimming after all. He looked happy about it, Catherine thought.

Catherine and Aileen had been swimming at the beach every weekend, and they'd swum together in the harbor a few times too, but this was Catherine's first race. It was just like trying to beat Michael out to the reef, she thought to herself, and smiled.

A light breeze blew and the tide ran the way of the swimmers, not against them, Catherine thought, watching the water. It would be a day to set a world record, she'd heard someone say in the morning. "You're our best hope," Charlotte had said to Meg Ederle. Trudy was the better swimmer, Catherine knew, but Trudy was sick today. Her father was taking her to swim the Channel on her own this year, funded by a New York newspaper. He didn't need the Association, he'd told Charlotte Epstein. All the girls had heard his booming voice in the office. Poor Meg and Trudy had been embarrassed.

They stood along the pier together in the early-morning light now. There were newspaper photographers. Aileen and Meg Ederle posed for the cameras, giggling in their swimming suits. Then the starter told them to take their marks and they lined up again. He fired his gun. Catherine dived in with the rest, into the blinding cold, emerging to sunlight on the water. Even in this cold, it was beautiful. There was nothing about the water that was not beautiful, Catherine thought.

She knew the race would be long—twenty-two miles on a straight course, and the waters might be kind or otherwise—but she felt more ready to swim than she'd ever felt. Her body opened up to the sea and welcomed it.

As long as she cleared each buoy, she could take whatever course she wanted, Aileen had said. The other swimmers, she knew, were planning to swim through the Buttermilk

Channel past Governors Island, but Catherine had decided to swim to the right, toward Liberty, and then come back in toward Sandy Hook. Partly it was because she wanted to go close to Liberty, but it was more than that: the way the sea looked, Catherine thought, it wanted them to go that way. When you swam in the sea, the sea made most of the decisions, Catherine knew.

She settled into an easy pace. Arm up and over, breathe, arm up and over, breathe. After a while, she couldn't see the other swimmers, and she had to look to find the dory that was accompanying her. She became oblivious to time, nothing but swimming now and the occasional correction when she stopped to check the next buoy. The water was cold, the light was soft, but she could be home on the island instead of here in New York Harbor. The sensation of leaving herself behind, of being nothing but her body and the sea, was still the same. "I swear you came from the sea, Waapi," Florence always said.

"Do some humans come from the sea?" she asked.

"We all do," Florence said. "We're all water babies. But some go back there."

Charlotte had arranged for a car to take Louisa from Manhattan, where they'd watched the start of the race, down to Sandy Hook in New Jersey, so they could watch the finish on the beach there. You could almost swim it faster than you could drive, Charlotte said.

There had been a small crowd for the early start, including

reporters and photographers. The swimmers had looked so vulnerable out there in their costumes, Louisa thought. There was a bigger crowd here at the finish, and, Louisa noticed, there were many young women as well as the families and groups of men. They were not all the oglers she'd expected.

She couldn't see Andrew. Black was in Baltimore. He'd planned to make the race but couldn't at the last minute. He wired to say he'd see her next week. She'd been disappointed not to see him again but relieved he wasn't going to be there putting Catherine under unnecessary pressure.

They were up on the lifeguard stand above the beach.

"Swimming," Louisa said to Charlotte. "I'm sorry if I was rude about it."

"Oh, I don't mind," Charlotte said. "You don't swim, so you can't know what it's like to want to and not be able to."

It was a beautiful day, Louisa thought, warm and sunny, and the water made long, lovely waves on the way into shore. Charlotte pointed to the right of the shoreline, where swimmers were just coming into view.

"Oh, yes, I see," Louisa said. She felt quite excited now. "So who's the favorite?" she asked.

"Well, Aileen Ryan is swimming well, and so is Helen Wainwright. They're at loggerheads, those two, always have been. There's another swimmer, Gertrude Ederle, whom you might have heard of, but she's not swimming today. Her sister Meg is in the team, very strong at the moment. They're good in these open-water swims." She pointed out Aileen and Helen, who were in the lead, along with the British swimmer Hilda James. "It's going to be very close," Charlotte said. "If they stay in front, I hope it's a tie. I couldn't stand to have Aileen and Helen at each other again."

These three swimmers were ahead of the pack, the rest some way behind. Louisa was looking for Catherine among the swimmers at the back but couldn't see her. She knew Catherine was in a dark cap—Charlotte had pointed her out at the start. When Louisa couldn't find her niece, she became worried. She started counting heads. "Where's Catherine?" she said to Charlotte.

"She'll be here," Charlotte said. "All the swimmers have a boat with them. Don't worry." They watched a few minutes more, the lead swimmers rounding a buoy and picking up pace now for the final run into shore, all the other swimmers in view. Catherine must be a long way behind, Louisa thought.

Now Charlotte was looking too, scanning the sea.

"I'd better alert the lifeguard captain," she said. Louisa could hear the fear in her voice.

And then Louisa saw her. "There she is! By God, she's ahead of them all!"

Catherine wasn't at the back of the pack. She wasn't with the group to the right of the shore. She'd come from farther away, on the left. And she was in the lead—a long way in the lead—on the far side of the group of swimmers. She would beat the others by a mile.

"Is that Catherine?" Charlotte Epstein said.

"I believe it is," Louisa said. "Yes, yes, it's her!" Louisa watched her niece increase her lead with each stroke. She looked so strong, so free, in the water.

Louisa saw then for the first time what she hadn't seen, or

hadn't let herself see, that morning on the Thames. Swimming was a part of Catherine, and to take this from her was to take her life from her. How could I have been so stupid?, she thought then.

Catherine surfed in on a wave, which took her almost to shore. She stood and was pushed over by another wave. Oh, the cold. Her hands and feet were totally numb and her lungs hurt. But she was laughing. If this was a calm day, she'd hate to see rough seas. She couldn't believe the race was finished already. The fellow in the boat had kept offering her food, chicken broth, chocolate cake, but she hadn't been hungry.

There was a crowd gathered above the beach, cheering. A dozen ran down the sand to meet her. Mr. Handley hurried over with a towel. "Why didn't you tell me you could swim like that?" he said. His eyes were open wide and he was shaking his head slowly.

"What?" she said. "Mr. Handley, you were right. The water isn't so cold if you don't think about it. I'm actually sort of warm, to be honest." She smacked her lips together. "But my mouth isn't working very well."

Mr. Handley was laughing as he wrapped the towel around her. Everyone was smiling. The photographers were taking pictures. "I saw fish, a big school of them in front of me. I tried to follow but they were too fast. I've never seen fish like that before, green and black and yellow. They were very beautiful."

"You know, you won, Catherine," one of the photographers said. "The Australian won. What do you think of that?"

She looked at Mr. Handley. They were taking pictures of her and she didn't know what to say.

He smiled at Catherine. "All right, boys," he said, "that's enough. You'll terrify the poor girl. My, Catherine, I never expected you could do that."

In the back of the group, she saw Andrew smiling and waving.

"Andrew!" she called. "Andrew, it's you!"

He came over. "Well, that was a sight to see, Catherine—you coming in way ahead. There's no one else even finished yet."

"Really?" She looked around and realized that what the photographer had said was true: there were no other swimmers on the beach. She had won.

"You're going to be famous, girl," Andrew said. He leaned down and kissed her softly. She pulled back, surprised.

"Andrew," she said.

"I'm so sorry," he said then. "I don't know what came over me."

"No," she said. "I really won?"

He nodded, smiling.

"Goodness," she said. "I didn't think anything like that would happen."

After the swim, Catherine collected her trophy. A reporter from the *Daily News* asked her how she'd won by so much.

"I was lucky," she said. "I picked the tides, so that when all the others were swimming against, I was being pulled to the shore and I looked faster. But it's always luck," she said honestly.

Aileen was there. "She's being modest," Aileen said. "She's a cracker."

"But you were the fastest swimmer too," the reporter said.

Catherine thought about this. "Being fast isn't anything out there," she said. "It's the water that gives or not."

The photographers took pictures of her getting out of the water, getting her award, toweling dry and then once she'd dressed.

Louisa had come down the beach to Catherine after the swim. "I'm getting sand in my boots," she'd said first. "Oh, I'm terrible at this. Well done, Catherine. You've swum amazingly well. You won!"

Catherine smiled.

Her aunt stepped forward to embrace her.

"I'm all wet," Catherine said.

"Oh, I don't care, darling. You're just a marvel," Louisa said. She hugged her tightly and didn't let go until Catherine did.

Catherine was exhausted by the end of the post-race celebrations, happy to get in the motor car that would take them back to the hotel in New York. The photographers hadn't let her alone all afternoon.

Andrew and Louisa came with Catherine in the car. Charlotte had gone back with Mr. Handley.

"Oh my," Charlotte had said when she'd greeted Catherine. "You've managed to make fools of us all."

"I'm sorry," Catherine said. "I didn't mean . . ."

"No," Charlotte laughed her off. "I mean, we watched you in the tank. Turns out, Mr. Black knew his swimmer."

When they arrived at the hotel, there were more photographers, sent by the local papers. Catherine could smell the magnesium from their flashbulbs on her clothes for hours after.

Finally they went inside. She'd been seven hours in the water and three hours on the journey back, by which time the evening papers were reporting Catherine's feat. She'd set a new record.

"Is that what reporters do?" she said to Andrew. "Follow girls like me?"

"It could be worse," he said. "Once I had to follow this prize fighter who was a terrible drunk. I think you'd be easier."

"I didn't mean for them. I meant for me."

"For you? You're the star, darling. We all adore you!"

The next morning, when Catherine left the hotel to go to the WSA pool, there were half a dozen reporters and twice that many photographers waiting for her. It was strange that they were so interested in her, Catherine thought. All she'd done was swim. "Can you tell us what you'll do today, Catherine?" one of them said. He had slicked-back dark hair and a dark brown suit, the tie off to one side. Catherine disliked him for no reason she understood. His eyes were too bright. He licked his lips when she looked at him.

"I'm going to the tank to train," she said, and smiled. "And maybe I'll swim in the harbor with my friend this afternoon." When she smiled they took pictures, so she smiled some more.

"Hey! Honey!" the photographer in the brown suit shouted after her. "Come and let me get another picture." He took three large steps to her and grabbed hold of her arm and turned her to face him. He smiled, but his smile was not kind. His touch on her bare arm shocked Catherine. Their eyes locked.

"Let go," she said quietly. He stepped back. She continued to look at him. He frightened her.

"What's next?" another one of them asked.

She was shaken by the photographer who'd grabbed hold of her and it took her a moment to compose herself. "I think we swim around Manhattan next Saturday," she said. She was still looking at the photographer in the brown suit.

"Are you going to France?"

"No," Catherine said. "I haven't been selected."

"How does that work? Didn't you beat everyone yesterday?"

"Yes, I did," she said. "But the WSA will select American swimmers." She smiled and they took her picture again. They seemed to want to take her picture doing just about anything.

It was the next day at training that Charlotte Epstein asked Catherine to come into the office. "What were you thinking?" she said, throwing a newspaper onto the desk.

Catherine looked at her in astonishment. "I don't know what you mean."

"You told them you weren't selected for the Channel."

"Well, I wasn't," Catherine said. "I told them the truth."

"This looks dreadful for us. I've had Black and our chairman on the telephone this morning asking me how we made such a blunder. Black says I promised we'd put you on the team if you won Sandy Hook. He's threatening to withdraw his support. We were going to fix it, Catherine. I would have talked to Mr. Handley and . . ."

Catherine shook her head. "I really don't know what you mean, Charlotte. I just told the truth."

32

Louisa had found herself looking forward to seeing Black. While she was getting ready—the blue scarf or the red one? Oh really, Louisa, does it matter at your age? The red one then, with matching lipstick.

They met in the lounge of her hotel. They'd decided to take a walk in the park across the road. There were new leaves on the trees, and the world would seem more hopeful, Black had said.

"I'm so sorry I missed the race," he said. He embraced her lightly. He smelled fresh.

"Oh, it was something to see," Louisa said. He opened the door of the hotel and held it while she walked through. In the street, he took her arm gently. They crossed over and into the park. He'd been right. It was hopeful.

"You look wonderful," he said.

"It's just lovely to be here," she said. "Thank you for suggesting it."

"I bet Charlotte was surprised," he said. "I knew Catherine was the one." He smiled.

"Yes," Louisa said. "We all were pretty surprised, I think." She'd been thinking since the race. It was going to be harder to extract Catherine now. Would Black want her to do other swims? Louisa wasn't sure it was best for Catherine. She'd had a clear picture on the day of the race, of Catherine and swimming. It wasn't anything like what Black wanted, a champion for his newspaper.

"Not me," he said. "I know my girl." The way he said it irked Louisa—my girl.

"So now she can come home happy, triumphant and confident," Louisa said. "We're very appreciative of what you've done for her."

He smiled, stopped and turned to face her. "Louisa, she really could be the first woman to swim the Channel, you know."

"But she's not on the team."

"She doesn't need to worry about the WSA. Let them take the Ederle girl. We'll take Catherine."

"We?"

"Me. And you. I'll get her a coach over there. She can go home with you and then train."

"Lear . . ." Louisa wanted to mention his family but thought better of it. "I'm not sure anymore that this is what she wants, and it's never been what I want for her," she said firmly.

"Of course it's what she wants," Black said. "She was born to it. Anyone can see that." He thrust his jaw out, a gesture she'd not seen before. "I didn't mention this before because I knew you'd be against it." They'd come to a pond in the middle of the park. Children were sailing little boats across.

"But you think she should go on with swimming," Louisa said.

"I really do," he said. "Louisa, she'll be the first woman to swim across the English Channel. She'll never have to worry about money or anything. She'll be feted for the rest of her life."

Louisa looked at him. "Perhaps she will," she said. "Let me think about all this."

When they returned to the hotel, Catherine was waiting for them in the foyer. She grinned. She was wearing trousers again, Louisa noticed. Charlotte Epstein encouraged the swimmers to wear long trousers to keep their legs warm after swimming.

"So you did it," Black said. "I just knew you would. I just knew it. You're my girl."

He embraced Catherine. Again, Louisa was bothered by the familiarity in his tone, and his embrace was warm. He was staring at Catherine now and the look on his face was hard to read. Pride, Louisa thought. He was proud of her. When he looked at Catherine, he was thinking of the sister he'd lost. It worried Louisa.

Louisa switched her gaze to Catherine and smiled. "Catherine, you are in all the papers," she said. "And this time, they've actually got pictures of you swimming." She showed her the pile on the coffee table. "Mr. Black says you could swim the English Channel next."

Catherine smiled. "Do you really think so? Do you think I should?"

Black didn't give Louisa a chance to answer. "Of course you should. You're going to be the greatest swimmer in the world. You'll see."

The Association made the announcement the next morning. The three swimmers to attempt the English Channel would be Trudy Ederle and Helen Wainwright from the WSA and the Australian Catherine Quick, funded jointly by the Association and Mr. Manfred Lear Black. The Association had decided to support Trudy Ederle after all, but some of her funding would still come from the New York newspaper.

Catherine had thought Aileen would be selected over Helen Wainwright. She was a better swimmer, and a much better diver. Catherine was going to Aileen's for the weekend but now she worried Aileen wouldn't want her to come. She'd pushed Aileen out of the Channel swim, after all. When she arrived at the house, she hugged Aileen and burst into tears. "I'm so sorry," she said.

"Oh, fally-bally! Don't worry, Catherine," Aileen said. She grinned. "I don't mind, really I don't." She was grinning through tears, Catherine saw then. She did mind, but she loved her friend. Catherine was lucky to have her.

"Oh, Aileen, look at me. I'm the one who's going and you have to stay and I'm crying."

"Well, that makes perfect sense to me. You're going to leave us, and we don't want you to. You've been the best friend. Will you come back?"

"Oh, I do hope so." They were sitting out on the porch on the swing chair.

"You know, I wasn't going anyway," Aileen said, smiling

through her tears. "I'm starting Georgetown in the fall. Daddy wouldn't have let me swim, even if I'd been picked."

"You're going to university?"

She nodded. "We visited last week. I'll be in college, with a dorm mate, and the only thing that would make it better would be if it was you. I'm allowed to keep swimming through the rest of the summer, though, and diving. And I'll be watching you. You bet I will."

When they went inside, Mrs. Ryan embraced Catherine warmly. "You have to come back to us, Catherine. You're our family now. Don't forget that."

33

After Louisa left to go to Baltimore, Catherine was worried whenever she had to leave Charlotte's apartment because she might see the photographer who'd grabbed her. At first she had liked it when they took her picture. It had felt like they were her friends. They called out after her in the street: "Give us a smile, Catherine." She quickly got used to the noise of the flash behind her, the smiles on their faces, the big eyes of their flashbulbs staring coldly at her. But they never left her alone now, and she kept thinking of the fellow who'd grabbed her arm. There was something about him, something unpleasant. She came to think of all of them this way. They wanted something other than an image but she didn't know what.

Catherine had come to hate seeing her image looking back at her from the newspaper page too. While others would say, "Don't you look beautiful?" she felt anything but beautiful.

They photographed Trudy, too, and other swimmers. Mr. Black's newspaper had a big feature article, written by Andrew, on the Channel contenders of 1926. He put his money behind Catherine Quick, he said, "the Australian girl who'd made good in America."

She walked past the newsstand at the station and saw her own face looking out at her, a pasted-on smile. When she arrived at the tank, Charlotte said, "You're on page three again."

"I know," Catherine said. "I saw."

"It's great for us."

"I hadn't even been swimming," Catherine said. "I put my costume on and stood there. I hadn't even been in the water."

"That doesn't matter," Charlotte said. "We need to stay in the papers, Catherine. It's for the sport."

"Is it?" Catherine said. "Is it for the sport? Andrew told me it's for the legs." She thought of Louisa suddenly, what her aunt had said at the beginning about swimming. She'd been right. "Why do they do that?"

Charlotte shrugged. "Perhaps it's not ideal, but if it helps us grow our membership and increase donations, then I don't see the harm."

"It's not your picture."

In the change room, she asked Aileen, "Do you think it's right that the papers print pictures of us in our swimsuits even when we're not actually swimming?"

"I've never thought about it," Aileen said. "They don't put my picture in the paper very much. They seem to like you the most." This was said without any ill will, Catherine knew. "I suppose diving isn't like that swim you did. They're mad

keen on the Channel, and it will surely be you or Trudy."
Aileen looked at her more closely. "But you're crying, Catherine. What's wrong?"

She'd put her suit on and was about to go outside. She sat down heavily on the bench. "I don't know," she said. "I thought it was all good fun at first. But it's all the time, Aileen. I can't go out of the hotel without seeing a photographer. Charlotte said they'd leave me alone after Sandy Hook settled down but they just want to keep at me. Even Andrew."

"Well, it's his job," Aileen said. "He's supposed to do stories for the newspaper. Maybe you need to be more like that Lillian Cannon? She has the dogs."

"What do you mean?"

"In all the pictures, she has those two big dogs. They swim with her and then they put the dogs in the pictures. It's less about her, I suppose. Or maybe you need to get married and have some children. They're not putting Mille Gade in the paper so much. Or not in her swimming suit, at least. Mostly it's pictures of her hugging her children." Mille Gade was another New York swimmer who'd announced her intention to attempt the Channel. Her husband, a naval officer, was her coach. She said she'd be the first mother across the Channel. It was true they hardly ever pictured her alone in a swimming suit. She always had her children with her.

Catherine laughed. "You really think it's all right?"

"Of course it's all right. Eppy wouldn't let them do anything wrong."

Early one morning, before any of the photographers were awake, Catherine caught the trolley car down to the pier. She swam out past the first buoy, past the end of the pier, out farther toward the ships that were sailing away from New York. Take me home, she wanted to say, but she realized that now she had no home. Even if she could get back to the island, there was no one for her there. They'd forgotten her. She was completely adrift.

34

Baltimore, June 1926

L ouisa was staying at the Emerson, which had been built by one of Black's friends. The hotel was beautiful, its two-story foyer lined with white marble and ornate timber carvings. She was in a penthouse suite on the twenty-first floor and she had a view taking in the harbor, city and surrounds. The weather held while she was there.

Other than her visits to Black's clinic, Louisa was free to do as she pleased. She wandered Baltimore, a surprisingly pretty city that she'd somehow missed when she'd been there last. Where were you, Louisa? she wanted to ask herself. It was nice to come back now, after so many years had passed, and discover she could enjoy a place so much.

The city was different too. There were motor cars everywhere now, a lot like New York; horses and carts had disappeared. It was cleaner, Louisa noticed, and when she started at the clinic she quickly learned the diseases that were largely caused by unclean water, which had done such harm when she'd last visited, were unheard of now. Louisa had visited the new School of Public Health, the first of its kind in the world. Black's clinic had grown from that school's work. It was in the East Baltimore docks area and enjoyed much more money and equipment than Louisa's Princes Square clinic.

In her first week, Louisa attended a birth with two of the hospital midwives. They were against the doctors' proposal to move confinements into the hospital, which was one of the reasons Black had asked Louisa to visit. Louisa could see both sides. Catherine had talked to her about births on the island, where women were cared for by other women who'd already had children. Traditional midwives, Harry had called them. In the East End, Louisa had learned to respect the midwives who would form a bond with a laboring woman, help them through their fear. While Louisa would try to do this too, the midwives were much better at it. Perhaps they knew less of what could go wrong, or perhaps the type of person who did midwifery was suited to being with a woman giving birth.

From Catherine's description, birth on the island wasn't feared in the way it was feared by women in Louisa's experience. True, if Louisa was involved, usually something was already wrong and there was reason for their fear. But she was unsure whether the doctors at Black's clinic might be making a terrible error in judgment, if the hospital itself might cause women to fear. Hospitals were never happy places in Louisa's experience. And the one thing Louisa had learned from her years in practice was the fear was the enemy of a woman's laboring.

The woman whose birth Louisa attended in Baltimore

already had one other child, a little boy of four who had cerebral palsy. The mother was terrified it was something she'd done to him when he was born. Louisa tried to reassure her on that score. "We don't know why," Louisa said. "But giving birth is something we're meant to do." She'd smiled at the woman and sat while the midwives cared for her.

They were wonderful, the two young midwives, soothing her, sitting with her. The husband was outside with the little boy, a sweet child whose whole life would be determined by his condition. But Louisa had no reason at all to believe that if he'd been born in hospital, anything would have been different.

Soon the baby came, a little girl this time, a perfect screamer with no indication of the condition that beset her brother. Louisa soon took her leave. Why would you put that poor woman in a hospital? she thought. Surely she was happier at home.

Through the rest of the week, Louisa met with the clinic doctors and nurses. The emphasis was very much on medical care, although Louisa's friend Emily Masterson was doing her best to encourage a public health approach, prevention as well as cure. But even Emily was keen to move confinements to the hospital setting. "Women are safer with us," she said. She and Louisa had dinner the night before Louisa finished so that Louisa could talk informally about what her report might say. Now they were nutting out details.

"Yes," Louisa said, "I suppose. But fear is always subjective, even if safety is assured. And fear is the enemy of labor."

"You're sounding like our midwives," Emily said.

"Yes, perhaps I am," Louisa said. "I'm just not sure you're right on this, Emily."

On her last night in the city, before she returned to New York, Louisa had dinner with Black in the hotel restaurant. She'd given her report to Emily Masterton but Black wanted her to meet and tell him in person what she'd found. What she'd found was that his clinic wanted for nothing. She'd written warily about the move of confinements to the hospital, making clear that the midwives were against the proposal but not taking it further from her own point of view.

"You seem despondent," he said. They'd eaten local clams, and now they were eating lobster.

"I suppose I don't know why you brought me here. You have so much more than we do. That X-ray facility is extraordinary. And the operating rooms! I'd give my eyeteeth to have half the setup you have here."

He smiled. "Yes, we've done the great city of Baltimore proud," he said. "But there's a network of donors. They've been a great help."

"From what I hear, no one gives more than you do." The doctors Louisa met with, including Emily, couldn't speak highly enough of Black, who gave money and time to the clinic. Their success had largely been dependent on his support.

"Well, Louisa, when I think of giving, I only have to look at Johns Hopkins himself to realize I don't do nearly enough. He had the good fortune to be successful financially, and he gave back. It is incumbent upon those of us who are fortunate to do something for the less fortunate, don't you agree?"

"Of course," Louisa said. "And as I say, I really don't know what it is you thought I could do for you."

Black smiled. "You're too modest, Louisa. We have all the gimmicks, but your quality of care is better. I'm not a fool and neither is my board. That's what our doctors are telling us. They say your care is the best in the world. Your brother was immensely helpful when we were setting up, but I want you to make sure we're on track, especially as we move to confinements."

"Nurses and midwives," Louisa said. It was the most helpful thing you could do, she knew. His clinic relied heavily on doctors, with less emphasis on nursing care. And the plans to move confinements to the hospital setting should at least make sure midwives were involved in the care.

"Nurses and midwives?"

"Yes. When my mother did medicine, she had to start in nursing because there was no way for her to work as a trainee doctor. She always said it was her nursing training that made her a good doctor, and she always said if doctors thought more like midwives there would be a whole lot less unhappiness in the world.

"In medicine, we're so busy trying to work out how this bone connects with that bone that we forget sometimes that those bones connect to a patient. Nursing and midwifery start there rather than with the bones.

"I didn't put this in the report," Louisa said, "but I'd think twice about this whole idea that confinement belongs in a hospital. I'd look to bolster the care you can provide and make sure your midwives are well trained so that they see a situation where a doctor is needed earlier."

"That's just the advice we needed," he said, lighting up a cigar. He nodded, as if thinking about something.

"But that doesn't mean you just fill the place up with nurses and midwives. At Princes Square we recruited well. We have a physician, Ruth Luxton, excellent with people, who selects the nurses for our wards, our reception, our surgery. And they're very good. Our midwives are just as good."

"And ours are not?"

She smiled, took a sip of her wine. "I didn't say that. The Johns Hopkins Nursing School was set up with help from Florence Nightingale. It's a fine school, and if you recruit from the school and make sure you keep standards up, things will stay on track, as you term it. The midwives I worked with, in particular, were outstanding."

He leaned back in his chair. He was looking at her intently and seemed about to speak. But he stopped himself, leaned back in. "I want to thank you for trusting me," he said. "I'm very glad I was able to assist with your clinic, Louisa. You've had nothing to worry about on that score."

Whereas previously, Louisa might have been relieved, now his mentioning his help unnerved her a little. She had continued to feel uneasy about the way Black had become so proprietorial about Catherine and swimming. She'd tried to raise the issue with him during the week but he'd always skirted around it, changed the subject. It had even occurred to Louisa that his support for the clinic, even his bringing her to Baltimore to give him advice, was all a ruse to have Catherine swim. That was ridiculous, though, she thought now. He'd been proper in all his dealings with Catherine, hadn't he? Except in relation to the swimming, which he was obsessed with, he'd been entirely gentlemanly. Still, his obsessiveness, which probably contributed to his business success, was unnerving.

There was a piano playing somewhere and the music trickled over to them in soft waves.

"I've been wanting to talk to you," she said.

"About the clinic?"

She shook her head. "No, about swimming. I don't think Catherine wants it."

"Wants what?"

"The Channel. Charlotte told me you've assigned a journalist now to cover her swim."

He nodded. "I've got Andrew on it; Catherine feels comfortable with him. And it will get the others out of her hair if we have exclusive rights. That's all."

"But your paper stands to benefit."

He let out a short laugh. "You think my paper needs to benefit from Catherine? I mean, I should hope we'll benefit. I'm paying for the swim. I have some rights here. And yes, it will help circulation, especially given that the *Post* has Lillian Cannon. But I told you that already." He waved his hand, dismissing the notion. He looked at her. "She wants this, Louisa. Ask her yourself. She wants this."

Louisa saw that he could have anything in the world; that's what his money could do. She nearly told him that she knew about his mother and sister, but she felt he would not take kindly to being confronted with her knowing. It would mean she and Charlotte had spoken of him and Louisa felt sure he wouldn't like that. "Oh, Lear," she said, "I wish the world were a kinder place."

"What on earth does that mean?"

She looked at him for a long time. "Life's just not as easy as it could be," she said finally. And it really wasn't, she thought.

PART VIII

London, June 1926

35

Catherine hadn't expected anyone to meet them at Southampton, but there was Nellie, the dear, in a coat and hat, looking like she was dressed for winter although the day was warm. When she saw Catherine, she rushed over and hugged her.

"Oh, but it's sweet of you to come," Catherine cried.

"I swear you've grown another foot, Catherine," Nellie said, hugging her warmly. "Look at you now, though. You've lost weight. Are you all right?" She looked beyond Catherine, to Louisa, who stood behind her.

"Nellie, dear, it's good to see you," Louisa said.

"You must come to New York with me next time," Catherine said. "Mr. Black says I can run the table if I swim the Channel. Do you know what that is? It's a gambling term. It means running the gambling table because you've won so much. Mr. Black doesn't gamble, he told me, but he knows all about it. He's been so kind, Nellie. You were wrong to suspect him."

"Was I now?" Nellie said, looking at Louisa again. "Let me look at you properly," she said, stepping back and returning her gaze to Catherine. "Yes, you've grown. As for Mr. Black, I will reserve judgment, young lady."

"Listen to you calling me 'young lady.' You're only a few years older than I am."

"But they're the ones that count. Did you not miss us at all?" Nellie was smiling.

Catherine frowned. "Of course I did. Especially the food. How I long for one of your beef stews."

Nellie laughed. "Oh, that's so kind of you to say, Catherine." Nellie was proud of the way she looked after them. "And, Louisa, you're looking relaxed."

Louisa laughed. "I feel relaxed. Come, Nellie, let's get Catherine home, so she can show you what she brought you."

Catherine looked around. "Louisa, there are no reporters."

"No what?" Nellie said.

"Doesn't matter," Catherine said. "Let's get away."

They collected the suitcases and took a taxicab back to Wellclose Square.

"So was it very grand?" Nellie asked when she'd made tea. There was fruitcake too.

"Oh, Nellie, New York is so busy," Catherine said. "Everyone is going somewhere and has something important to do."

"And what we do in London isn't important?" Nellie said as she poured.

"It's different. It's just more easy. You know, it reminded me strangely of the island. There are the Negroes, of course. But it's more than the color of people's skin." She thought suddenly of one of the reporters on the day she'd left. He'd yelled out to her to show some leg. That hadn't felt free.

"Are you all right?" Nellie said.

"Oh, yes, fine. I was thinking about something unpleasant."

"What?"

"Nothing that matters now. Oh, it's a truly grand place, Nellie. You would love it. Everyone is free."

"I'm not sure the Negroes would agree about freedom," Louisa said. "When women fought for the vote they had to take the Negroes out of the equation or it would have failed."

"The Islanders don't vote in Australia," Catherine said. "I hardly think that makes a difference."

"Of course it does," Louisa said. "Voting's the one thing that you can make a difference with. Have I taught you nothing?"

"I couldn't care less for voting," Catherine said. "The people in New York are free. I could smell it in the streets."

"Have it your way," Nellie said. "Freedom's a smell then. So what did you bring me?"

Catherine went back out to the front hall and took from her bag the little statuette. She went back to the kitchen. "You come into New York Harbor and it's the first thing you see. It's freedom and it's a woman."

Nellie looked at Liberty. "I do like boiled sweets, you know."

Catherine laughed. "Oh, stop it, Nellie. Seriously, it's a symbol of freedom."

"In your last letter you said you were unhappy."

Catherine looked at Louisa. "I was. The swimming wasn't going very well until we could get out of the silly tank we had to swim in. Once I did that, we were fine. Except . . ."

"Except what?"

"Nothing. Oh, I sound ungrateful saying it but they kept putting my picture in the paper, and I didn't much like it. It's not at all private. It's like I'm everyone's." Catherine walked over to the back door. "I do like about London that no one knows me. And the dogs are glad to have me home."

"So am I," Nellie said. "I just don't run around your feet snorting. Come, sit and have some more tea. I made jam roly-poly, which is what the Scotties are after. No one will put your picture in the paper in this house. And jam roly-poly will put some fat on those bones. I'll go and get it."

"I'm going to swim the Channel, Nellie. Did you hear that?"

"I did. I think you're amazing, Catherine. But you still need jam roly-poly."

Oh, but it was good to be home, Louisa thought. Travel was all very well, and she'd had the most marvelous time in Baltimore, but Nellie had given her a warm hug and the Scotties had run around their feet, crying with delight, as they came in the front door. No, there was nothing like home. When Catherine came in and greeted Nellie, it was like she was coming home too. It was lovely to hear her chatter on, although she did sound anxious about the reporters. Still, Wellclose Square was her home now and that was a good thing, surely.

Louisa decided not to go to the clinic the next morning, but instead to spend some time in her little house. Catherine had gone in, "to see what they've done to my schoolroom," she said. Louisa was in the kitchen with Nellie.

"She has a hunted look," Nellie said.

"Those awful photographers were there all the time in New York," Louisa said. "You wonder what they do when there are no swimmers around to photograph. She was in all the papers when she won the race, and then again when they announced the Channel team. It's like a madness over there. But she's back here now and all will be well. You'd have to agree she's in better spirits."

"Yes, she is," Nellie said. "She's growing up." She looked squarely at Louisa. "And have you given her those letters?"

Louisa shook her head. She didn't respond straight away. Finally, she said softly, "It's been too long now, Nellie. I can't. And anyway, she's stopped asking."

"I can't help but feel we've done her wrong."

Louisa wanted to argue with Nellie but found she didn't have it in her to do so. Nellie was right.

"Did she like the swimming?" Nellie said.

"Oh, yes," Louisa replied, wondering if she should try to explain to Nellie what worried her. She wasn't altogether sure she could articulate it, but it had something to do with Black. "Anyway, she'll just go over and try the Channel. Mr. Black says she has a good chance. And then she'll come home."

Louisa had agreed to let Catherine try the swim. School wouldn't start until September, and by then the Channel season would be over. The plan was that Catherine and Louisa would go over together in July. They'd meet up with a coach Black had engaged, a Mr. Burgess, who'd swum the Channel successfully himself. Louisa had written to her old school in Glasgow before she'd gone to America and they'd written back and said they'd love to have Catherine. Louisa still hadn't talked to Catherine about it yet. She'd wait, she decided, until the Channel business was behind them. But everything would then be well. Catherine would go back to school, and life would go on.

"Won't that just make it harder?" Nellie said now. "Those Channel girls are in all the papers even here. Once they get wind of Catherine . . ."

"Let's worry about one thing at a time," Louisa said. "For now, it sounds like she's happy to be back. The clinic work is something she loves more than swimming. She'll go to France next month, swim the Channel or not, and come home and then go back to school."

Ruth Luxton was waiting for Louisa when she arrived the next day. "I'm very happy you went," Ruth said, embracing her so hard Louisa nearly fell over. "But, oh, we missed you. Just for your surgeon's hands as much as anything."

"Not for my surgeon's temperament?" Louisa said.

"Perhaps," Ruth said. "I think you get more done in a day than I do."

"But you do it so much more kindly."

They sat down in the little office. It was still early and Ruth made tea. "You're looking better," she said.

"I am," Louisa answered. "I think I've learned something about myself."

"And what's that?"

"I think I've spent my whole life since . . . since Edinburgh, working too hard."

"Well, that is good news. How did you come to that realization?" Ruth smiled. "Don't get me wrong, Louisa. I've always understood. But it's got to feel good to let that go."

"Who said anything about letting go? My intention is to hold on as tight as I can."

They both laughed.

"It was Catherine," Louisa said.

"Oh, yes," Ruth said. "I hear she's been a grand success over there. And the Channel now."

"It's not so much the success that struck me as the girl herself. Everyone else was so amazed when she won that race, but she didn't even care. She really didn't, Ruth."

"Well, of course, she's a delightful girl who doesn't care a fig for all that nonsense," Ruth said. "But what does that mean for you?"

"I think that's how I might have been too, before . . . . It's just been a very extraordinary experience to watch her, to spend time with her. Almost an opportunity to travel back in time, to see what might have been."

"Does that lead to regrets?"

"A little, yes," Louisa said, tears in her eyes. "But perhaps also, one day, peace."

"What a lovely holiday you've had, my dear. We don't get to plan when we're given insight. Now, should we tackle the mountain of paperwork over there?"

"No," Louisa said. "Let's not. Let's see some patients and worry about the paperwork later."

"Well, you really have been transformed. I've never known you to put off paperwork, given a chance!"

"There's something else," Louisa said.

"Yes?"

Louisa hesitated. "Nothing," she said finally. She had been going to ask Ruth about the letters, what she should do. Nellie was still insisting that Louisa give them to Catherine, but she didn't want to. It was too late. And what if Catherine didn't forgive her? Maybe after the Channel, when Black was out of their lives, she'd tell her. But maybe she'd just let sleeping dogs lie.

Two weeks later, Catherine left for France on the ferry with Andrew, who was writing the stories for Black's newspaper in Baltimore. Louisa intended to follow Catherine as soon as she could and stay until Catherine attempted the swim. She could work out what to do with the letters after that.

But then on her way home from the surgery one night, Louisa collected the mail and there on top was another letter, this one postmarked Cairns, not Thursday Island, addressed to Catherine, in Florence's hand. It was marked urgent.

Louisa decided to open it.

Dear Catherine,
I am writing with very bad news. Michael is in trouble. We've been in Cairns for a month. As I said in my last letter, he went down a couple of months ago to get work with some other boys from here. He was wanting to earn enough money to get over to you and find out what's going on.

He's been accused of a terrible crime. Someone held up a store in Samsonvale and they killed the owner. It wasn't Michael. I know it wasn't. But because he'd moved there with

*a group of boys, they've arrested them all and one of them has
confessed.*

*Michael says none of them did anything and you know he
wouldn't do that. But the charge is murder, Waapi. And he's
old enough to be hanged.*

*There's no one I can turn to but you. I don't know any
solicitors but Dr. Harry's, and he's said he can't help us
without money. He says you will help us, being your father's
daughter. I've never missed Dr. Harry more than in these
weeks. I don't know who else to turn to.*

Yours with love,
Florence

Louisa read the letter a second and then a third time. The
boy had been charged with a criminal offense. The letter would
have taken at least a month to get to London, and Louisa had
no idea what might have transpired since Florence wrote. Michael might already have been tried, for all she knew.

He'd been wanting to earn the money to come to London,
to come to London to see Catherine, who hadn't written.
Except Catherine had written. She'd written three letters, all
of which were in Louisa's possession, along with Michael's and
Florence's letters *to* Catherine. With a sick feeling, Louisa
knew that if he had stolen in order to come to Catherine, if
he'd killed another human being, she, Louisa, was responsible.
She remembered the boy, that lovely smile. She had never
meant for something like this to happen. She'd just wanted
Catherine to be happy in London. She'd wanted to protect her.

She went into the kitchen, poured herself a glass of scotch
and downed it. She knew if Catherine read the letter she would

not only want to help them, she would go to them on the very next ship. Oh, Louisa should have asked Catherine about the relationship rather than hiding that first letter. In fact, she wished now she'd just given Catherine the letters and let events take their course. Catherine would probably be forgetting the island in any event. She had a new life. She had the Channel swim coming up and after that, Louisa was sure, she'd return to school.

It had started as a small wrong, hiding one letter. But now it was so much more than that. That poor girl, Louisa thought. I was supposed to help her and all I've done is harm. Louisa sat and thought. And then, she knew what she must do.

36

Black must have heard the urgency in Louisa's voice on the telephone. He'd only arrived from America the day before. He'd come back to Europe to see his swimmer beat the rest, he'd told Louisa. He had a meeting he could cancel, he said, if she could come to the Carlisle at noon.

"She's going to do it, Louisa. My girl's going to swim the Channel." There it was again: "his" girl. Louisa wondered just how far he'd go to help his girl. She needed him to help her now.

Black was in the lobby waiting when she arrived, wearing his lounge jacket and pressed slacks. "Thank you for agreeing to meet me," she said.

He offered his arm, smiling hopefully. She didn't take it. "Are you all right?"

"No, I'm not," she said abruptly. "I have done something that I thought was in Catherine's best interests, but it's become complicated and I need you to listen."

"What is it, Louisa? You look like you've seen a ghost."

"Yes. Please. Just let me speak. Is there somewhere private we can go? Perhaps I don't want to walk after all." She had suggested on the telephone that they might walk in the park, but now that she was here, she didn't feel she could go any farther. She had a plan, she reminded herself, and she needed Black if she was to execute it.

"Of course." He gestured to the waiter, stood and spoke quietly to him. He came back to Louisa. "I'd invite you to my suite, but that might cause a stir, so our man here has arranged for us to use the private lounge." He helped her up and linked his arm in hers, then placed his other hand on her hand. She calmed a little.

They went into a lounge off the lobby. He closed the door behind him and she sat down at the table by the window. He poured her a drink, a neat scotch, brought it over, then poured one for himself. "Why don't you tell me what's wrong?"

"You know Catherine grew up on an island north of Australia?"

He nodded.

"There was a family there, a woman and her child, who were close to my brother Harry. The woman, Florence. My other brother . . . Oh, that doesn't matter now. Anyway, when Catherine came home to London with me after Harry died, she wouldn't settle at school. She just wanted to go back to the island. I began to despair. She and I didn't know each other terribly well, and I'm not used to children. I know it's no excuse. But it seemed to me that the thing that unsettled her most was news from Australia—from Florence and her son."

He nodded. "Of course," he said. "You might expect that."

"Yes. And then one day I collected the mail on my way to

work. And there was a letter for Catherine. And I read it." She raised her hand to stop him from talking. "Yes, I know it was wrong. I know it wasn't mine to read."

"No, I understand," he said. "I would have done exactly as you did."

The relief! He didn't think she was a terrible person. She continued. "When I look back now, I . . . I think I misunderstood something in the letter—although perhaps I didn't. But anyway, I made a decision; that is, I kept that one letter to see what happened." She explained then how one by one she'd kept withholding the letters, how Catherine had moved on from the island, was so much happier now.

There was a gardener outside in the drive, pruning something, rosebushes probably—she'd seen rosebushes on the way in. She could hear the regular snip of his shears, the click of the stems breaking.

"Well, that's probably good," he said. "Well done."

She smiled weakly and put her fingers to her eyelids, held them there for a moment. "No, you don't understand. There's been another letter. The boy, the boy Catherine was close to, is in terrible trouble and it's my fault."

"What boy do you mean, Louisa? Florence's boy?"

She nodded. "He's Catherine's age or a bit older. His mother says he went to one of the towns on the coast. He wanted to get a job, to earn money. He wanted to come over to see Catherine, to find out why she hadn't replied to his letters. I thought he'd forget. She'd forget. And it was for the best. And now he's in trouble. The boy. He's in trouble, terrible trouble, and it's my fault." Louisa explained briefly what had happened. She looked over at Black. His soft eyes normally calmed her but not today.

"I don't understand, Louisa. That's not your fault."

"Well, of course it is. The boy would never have been in Cairns if it weren't for me withholding the letters. And Catherine would never have stopped writing."

"You can't know that." He looked at her intently.

"Oh, for God's sake, I'm not seeking your forgiveness here, or some version of Maryland wisdom. Just listen."

She realized she was close to losing control, and he was doing his best. She needed to calm down. She needed him now like never before. "I wired Harry's lawyer in Cairns and got him to look into the situation. At first I was terribly worried, of course, because the letter would have taken some time to arrive and . . . Anyway, Mr. Witherspoon—that's the lawyer—has been able to reassure me on that score. The boy's in prison. He's been charged, awaiting trial.

"I thought of going to Alexander, but he and Harry . . . He won't be disposed to help. He'll say I did the right thing."

"And you think you didn't?"

"Of course not. If he's hanged, it will be because of me."

"Now, hold your horses there, Louisa. We went from trouble to hanged. Why hanged?"

"I'm sorry. It's just so awful. They robbed a shop. They shot a man. He's dead."

"This boy did?"

"His mother says no." Black looked at her. "And not just his mother. Mr. Witherspoon says she's right."

He nodded, breathed in and out slowly. "All right, Louisa, you need to look at me." He sat for a few moments, regarded her carefully. She felt like talking but stopped herself. "So you withheld some letters to help your niece. I don't see a problem with that. It's your job to care for her. And then this boy's done something wrong, or not." He took a sip of his scotch. "That's not your fault." He shook his head. "Not at all."

He spoke as if he was used to people agreeing with him, as if he could fix anything, teasing out Louisa's liability as if that would make it all right. And she imagined he mostly could fix anything. But no amount of clever description and running from liability changed what had now happened.

"As far as I'm concerned," he said, "you don't have to do anything."

"Of course I have to do something," Louisa said, exasperated. "I can't keep this from Catherine now."

"Why tell her?" he said. "Why does she need to know? There's nothing you can do about it now. Just let it go."

"That's just it. Witherspoon *can* do something," Louisa said. "He needs money, though. I've told him to go ahead on the basis that I will pay." She narrowed her eyes and looked at Black carefully.

"What for?"

"He says the police aren't terribly interested in the case. They want to solve it, and the three boys give them an easy way to do so. The other two have had some trouble before. To take the more difficult way, which means truly solving the crime, they need money." She felt tears threatening. "He's a lovely boy, Lear. I met him."

"How does Witherspoon know this boy didn't do it?"

"Michael. His name's Michael. He was working on a fishing boat. He wasn't even in Cairns when the man was shot.

The other boys say they weren't there either. Their alibis would hold in a fair trial, Mr. Witherspoon says. It's just an appalling place where some lives are cheaper than others.

"The owner of the boat has signed an affidavit to the effect that Michael was working on the day of the murder, but the police so far have shown little interest. We can take our chances with a trial, Mr. Witherspoon said, and he'll represent the boy. But that too is fraught. Witherspoon tells me the quickest way to convince the police to look at the affidavits he's collected is to give them money."

"A bribe."

"That's not the word he used."

"What word did he use?"

"Contribution."

Black smiled. "Ah, the world's the world. And I'm guessing that's where I come in—the money."

She nodded. "Yes, the money. I told him to go ahead, but I don't have a thousand pounds."

He took a sharp breath in. "Oh, that's a lot of money."

"It's less than you'd spend on one of your parties, I'd warrant, let alone those jaunts up in the aeroplane."

"Possibly," he said. "But those are my parties and my jaunts. This is to help a boy I've never met."

"It's to help me."

He took a puff of his cigar. "If I'm to help, you mustn't tell Catherine about any of this."

"I have to tell Catherine."

"Ah, we come to an impasse. You now want to unburden yourself of your dishonesty as a way of seeking atonement."

"No; if I don't tell her, Florence and Michael will." She was about to tell him how but stopped herself.

"Not if she never sees them again," he said. "Which is what you wanted in the first place."

Louisa didn't respond. She wouldn't tell Black the whole story. She wouldn't tell him what else she was planning to do. What had happened to Michael—and all because Louisa decided she knew best—made her realize she must now do the right thing. She must give Catherine a choice, to go to school in Glasgow, as Louisa wanted her to do, or to go home to the island. And in order to decide, Catherine needed to know the truth, all of it, and she needed to see her Islander family again. It was as simple as that.

Louisa had talked to Nellie, and Nellie agreed. If Mr. Witherspoon could free Michael, Louisa would wire Florence enough money to come across to England with him. Catherine could see them and decide what she wanted to do.

Louisa had also told Ruth Luxton what she'd done with Catherine's letters, and dear Ruth had understood better than Louisa thought she would why Louisa had done what she had. "But yes, you must tell her now," Ruth Luxton had said.

"Do you think I'll lose her?" Louisa had asked.

"I don't know," Ruth had said, her face creased in a frown. "But that's a consequence you have to be willing to contemplate now."

Ruth was right. Michael and Florence were Catherine's family more than Louisa was. Nellie had been right too. Catherine was cast adrift not because she was wild and uncivilized as Alexander had claimed, and not because she couldn't fit in at the school, but because she'd been taken from the only home she'd known. And, Louisa thought now, it may have been a good home. It was certainly the home Catherine herself would have chosen if Louisa had let her. The girl, at fifteen, knew better than her aunt what she wanted in life.

Louisa was going to do what she could to make up for the harm she'd caused—if only she wasn't too late, she thought now. If Catherine chose to go back to the island, so be it. Louisa would do whatever she could to make sure Catherine was safe there. But Louisa knew she wouldn't tell Black all this. He would never agree, so bent was he now on his own goal of making Catherine his champion.

"Are you suggesting I go on as if nothing happened?" she said to him. "I don't believe I can do that now, Lear. I just can't. It's wrong."

"Then you have a problem, Louisa. Because you absolutely must keep it from her now," Black said, a sense of urgency in his voice. "She mustn't under any circumstance know this, not now, when she's about to make the attempt on the Channel— not now, when she's left all that island nonsense behind."

"The bloody Channel is all you think of," Louisa said.

He looked surprised that she thought so poorly of him. "The Channel, Louisa, is going to be the best thing that ever happens to that girl." He sighed. "But I'll give you your money. Of course I will. I don't want to see a boy wrongly hanged. Of course I don't."

PART IX

Cap Gris-Nez,
July 1926

37

The weather had been fine for a week and Catherine thought they might try the swim—the sun shone and the water looked like glass day after day—but Mr. Burgess was waiting for the right combination of weather and tides. Catherine was still waiting for Louisa to arrive. She was supposed to be here by now but there was a problem, she'd written. She'd tell Catherine when she saw her. Catherine had never missed her aunt as much.

Catherine had left England a month ago and now she was restless to be done with the Channel swim. The longer they waited, the more daunting it became. And here in France, the photographers never let up.

Nellie had come to see Catherine off on the ferry. She'd wished her the best and said that when she came home, everything would be better. Louisa hadn't come to see her off. "She'll be over as soon as she can, I'm sure," Nellie said. Nellie looked worried for some reason. Louisa had had to go and see Mr. Black, who was now in London. "Don't worry. I'm sure everything will be all right." It had unnerved Catherine. Nellie was not a worrier.

About an hour into the journey across to France, a storm had come up, creating a huge swell. The ferry was tossed around. In the worst of the weather, Catherine had stood outside watching the water. The rain hit her face and ran down the oilskin coat a crew member had lent her. It was mighty, she thought; a living thing.

"The old girl didn't like us," Andrew had said. He'd taken the ferry with Catherine and was covering the swim for Mr. Black's newspaper. He'd been sick for the first half of the journey but was better once the sea calmed. "You can't be thinking you'll swim it?" he said to her when he came out on deck near Calais.

"Apparently," she said. "I think it will be easier on a body than on a boat."

Before Catherine had left England, Louisa had asked her again if she really wanted to attempt the Channel. With all the talk of how challenging it was, how it was a mental as well as physical test, of endurance, of courage, of strength, Catherine had become more nervous. Of course I want to do it, she'd said to her aunt, thinking of Mr. Black, who'd been so good to her. She wanted to make him proud. But the journey across was enough to make her pause.

After they landed at Calais, they took the train to Boulogne and taxis from there to Cap Gris-Nez, where swimmers gathered every year for the season. As they came down the hill and saw the water again the Channel was quiet. Gris-Nez was an unassuming place, two inns, a few houses, not even a store.

The beach was defined by the headland at one end and rocks that jutted out at the other. The headland did look a little like a *gris nez*, a gray nose, sniffing the sea. It was the closest land point to Dover, twenty-one miles away. Some swimmers still tried to go the other way, starting in Dover to finish in France, but the tides were kinder in this direction for the end of the swim. It was less distance for a swimmer than the Battery to Sandy Hook, Catherine knew, except that you could never plot a straight course. The water could be treachery or mischief, depending how the seas that ran into the English Channel were feeling on the day. They'd take you north or south at will. Trudy Ederle was within sight of Dover the year before when they pulled her from the water. The Channel had turned sour, and no matter how hard she swam, she could not make headway.

Had it not been for the swimmers who came every summer, the Cape would hardly have a visitor. Today the sky was a pale blue with a few clouds on the far horizon and Catherine could see the coastline stretch away and disappear into the haze. The water was softly kissing the shoals below and it reminded her of the island suddenly. She felt the pull of home.

Catherine was staying at the Hotel du Phare on the hill above the bay, named for the lighthouse that stood at the bridge of the gray nose. The three-story hotel was tired, with rickety stairs and creaking windows, no electricity or running water. It was run by a couple who'd made a business of accommodating swimmers and reporters every year. They closed in the winter and opened now when the swimmers intent on conquering the Channel came in. The larger Hotel la Sirène, halfway across the bay and just above the beach, was more popular, but Catherine was glad to be somewhere she might have privacy—the reporters would stay at the other hotel.

The Ederles had gone from Calais to Paris, which had left Catherine on her own at the Cape. Trudy was doing interviews. The English papers said she was the only one of the swimmers who'd even come close to swimming the Channel before. She was particularly disparaging about Lillian Cannon, for some reason, the Baltimore swimmer, claiming Lillian wasn't strong enough. She didn't mention Catherine at all— perhaps she thought Catherine wasn't even in the running.

Helen Wainwright, the third WSA swimmer, had pulled out at the last minute with a broken arm. Catherine had been secretly overjoyed, hoping that Aileen might join them in her place. But given the choice, Aileen had opted instead to prepare for university. Catherine was disappointed her friend wouldn't be with her. It also made her realize that the choice she'd made, to come here to swim, might mean she'd never get back to school, and school was why she'd left the island in the first place.

She'd tried to talk to Andrew about it. "Louisa's right," she said. "I should be at school. That's why I came to London."

"Oh, I wouldn't think too much about that now," Andrew replied. "Mr. Black says you can run your own school once you swim the Channel."

So far, Catherine had been swimming as an amateur, which meant she could not earn any money. After the Channel swim, though, she could turn professional. Andrew said there would be sponsors who'd pay for her name. "They get you to stand there next to the cars they're selling or wear the clothes."

"I don't think I'd much like that," she said.

Andrew had become so much more worldly since going to America. "What about you?" she'd asked. "What will you do next?"

He looked at her. "Yes. What about me?" he said. "Mama is very keen on a girl my brother knew. We had a big family discussion about it when I went home."

"A girl your brother knew?"

"A nice English girl."

"And you?"

"When Donald . . ." He smiled tightly. "He was the brave son."

"So, do you like this girl?" Catherine said.

"I do," he said. "I do." He looked awfully sad, though, Catherine thought, for someone who liked a girl.

"Well, good on you," she said.

"Is that how you really feel?"

"Why should I feel anything?" she said, trying the words out.

"No, of course you shouldn't," he said, smiling weakly.

Now they'd been at the Cape for over a month and still, they couldn't swim. Louisa had written that she'd been held up once again but would be over soon, very soon.

Early that morning, Catherine had walked down the little path to the sea. She reached the beach in five minutes but Andrew and the other newspapermen were already down there.

"How you feeling, Catherine?" one of them yelled.

She smiled. "I'm feeling like swimming," she said. They'd been there every day. She never felt like stripping down to her swimmers in front of them.

Andrew had said they'd leave her alone now that she was signed to Mr. Black's newspaper. Even in London, they'd started pestering her about this swim. The English papers had caught on to the fact that there was a challenger, and they all wanted to know what Catherine thought about what Gertrude Ederle was saying. Catherine replied that it wouldn't be up to Gertrude Ederle, and it wouldn't be up to Catherine Quick. "The sea makes its own mind up," she said. "It always does. There's no telling what will happen." But then they wrote that she was challenging Gertrude Ederle. Maybe Trudy didn't say the things they attributed to her either. Maybe they just made them up.

When Catherine read the stories about herself in the paper and saw the pictures, it was as if they weren't really writing about her. It was as if they meant another person altogether, a person she didn't know, a person she might not like very much.

According to the newspapers, one of them would be the first woman to swim the Channel. Mercedes Gleitze was planning her attempt from the English side. There were other swimmers too, and the newspapers couldn't get enough of them—or, at least, couldn't get enough of some of them. Another American, Clarabelle Barrett, was a strong contender, but she was never in the newspaper. Clarabelle came from a New York family and had been an early WSA swimmer. When her father died suddenly, he left them with little so she'd had to leave the WSA to turn professional and care for her mother. "One of our great losses," Charlotte said. Now

Clarabelle taught swimming in schools. She was the only one of them attempting the Channel on her own, with no funding for a trainer or even a pilot boat. She had no newspaper sponsorship, and her friends had lent her money to make the trip to France.

Aileen had told Catherine that Clarabelle was the swimmer with the most chance of success. She'd swum across Long Island Sound in May, when the water was freezing. She did look like a champion, Catherine thought when they met in France. She was taller than Catherine, over six feet, and strong.

Clarabelle had long auburn hair, which she wore tied back. At thirty-four she was older than the other WSA swimmers. She hated the photographers more than Catherine did. And they left her alone mostly, Catherine noticed. "Because she doesn't look like you," Andrew said, and smiled. "She's big and scary."

Clarabelle wasn't swimming for fame, and there was no one like Mr. Black or Gertrude Ederle's father encouraging her either. She wanted money because she wanted to become a professional singer. When her father had been alive, he'd paid for her to learn to sing, but after his death there was no money left for singing lessons. Clarabelle had seen the stories on the Channel swimmers and had decided she should at least try, that it was her best chance of singing. She'd been training all year, longer than Catherine had, longer than Gertrude Ederle or Lillian Cannon. She was desperate to succeed, and it made Catherine want success for her.

Catherine looked over at the group of photographers watching her. What she wanted more than anything was to take off her clothes and leave them here on the sand, and dive in and swim. She knew it would be cold, but even the cold wouldn't be enough to deter her. As she waited and watched the sea, photographers snapping their blasted pictures, she realized she would not go in while they were there. She saw Andrew farther up the sand, sauntering toward her. She shivered, remembered suddenly the photographer in America who'd grabbed her. She didn't know why it had affected her so much. It had been the first time she'd been afraid. Now they were all like him, it seemed.

"Good morning," Andrew said when he reached her. "Are you swimming or contemplating?"

"Both?" she said.

"Company?" he said.

"I don't want to go swimming with all these fellows here," she said.

"Why not?"

"I don't know. Can you ask them to leave?"

"Not really. They can snap whatever pictures they like in a public place. You could just strip down to your bathing suit and let them photograph you getting in the water. They'd love that."

"But I wouldn't love it," she said. "I don't want to, not in front of all of them."

Andrew looked over to the group of reporters and photographers and sighed. "Well, they won't be happy until they have something to send back to America. That's how the business is."

"Well, it's a terrible business," Catherine said.

"No it's not," he said, looking stung by her comment. "It's just the news."

"I'm not news," Catherine said. "And you know that as well as anyone. They're just . . ."

"Just what?" he said, grinning. He knew what she meant.

"I can't stand this," she said, and turned and walked through the crowd of reporters and back up the headland toward the hotel.

Mr. Burgess had been the second person ever to swim the English Channel, and Mr. Black had engaged him and paid his fee. "He's the best," Mr. Black had said before they'd left America to return to England. "Can't have my girl with some idiot."

He was a compact man with steel-gray hair and a gray beard, light blue eyes and dark leathery skin, as if he'd seen too many days at sea. Catherine felt comfortable with him. The photographers didn't bother her so much when Mr. Burgess was with her.

"If you know your swimming, Catherine, I know the Channel," he'd said on their first day. He'd tried to swim across eleven times before succeeding. "So I know it better than most men do." He had a full-throated laugh.

"I know my swimming, Mr. Burgess," Catherine had said, relieved he wouldn't be trying to change her stroke like Mr. Handley had. Catherine knew that all five swimmers who'd conquered the Channel to date, including Burgess, had swum the trudgeon, a stroke Mr. Handley had shown them that looked odd and was even more odd when you tried to swim it. It was a sort of scissor kick with frog arms. In America, many of the girls had started swimming by learning the trudgeon. It wasn't until Mr. Handley took over coaching that they swam a crawl. But Catherine had always swum a crawl, even if it wasn't quite how Mr. Handley wanted her to do it. She still kicked two beats for each stroke, or sometimes four, but never six.

"The Channel is in charge here, not us," Mr. Burgess said. "I thought you were the swimmer who already knew that. Anyway, the sooner you learn it, the better you'll be. The Channel tells us when she'll let us swim, and when she won't."

Now Catherine was standing on the beach with her coach. They needed perfect conditions, he'd said, but even if the tides were in their favor and the weather looked calm, the North Sea could squall at a moment's notice and ruin a swim.

"The English Channel, my girl, is the most difficult body of water in the world," Mr. Burgess said. "You're squeezing two grumpy seas into a too-narrow gap, creating a force that has to go somewhere. Often it goes on top of a little swimmer." It was notorious for claiming ships, and many a fine swimmer had failed, he said, sucking on his pipe thoughtfully.

Catherine had been spending time in the water every day. Acclimatizing, Mr. Burgess called it. She started at twenty minutes. She could have stayed longer. She didn't mind the cold at all, the thrill of the icy water on her skin, even the way it seeped into her bones. She loved the tiredness afterward, as she drank hot tea in front of the fire. She preferred it to swimming in warm water now, she realized, although Lillian Cannon, who trained with Catherine, told her she'd still rather swim in warmer water. Lillian was sponsored by the Baltimore *Daily Post*, and her dogs were to swim the Channel with her, although Catherine had read a story in *The Times* that said this was cruel to the dogs. The newspapers were just making a story of it, Lillian said. One of the dogs refused to get in the water anyway, Catherine had noticed—he just stood on the beach and howled—so she wasn't sure how they were planning to have them swim the Channel.

Lillian didn't seem to want to win anything. Like Catherine, she just enjoyed swimming. And there was a lightness about her that was lacking in everyone else here, Catherine thought, including Andrew, who was getting very serious about the challenge of the Channel and Catherine's chances. Even Clarabelle Barrett, whom Catherine liked, was serious when it came to swimming. Catherine had asked Mr. Burgess if Clarabelle could swim with them but he'd said no. When Miss Ederle arrives, he said, I'll have three swimmers, and that will be enough.

The newspapermen tried to get Catherine and Lillian to be mean about one another, but they had agreed they wouldn't say anything negative about the other. "Do the newspapers bother you?" Catherine had asked Lillian.

"Oh, no," Lillian said. "I don't mind so much. I just cuddle one of the dogs and think nice thoughts and then it's over."

"I wish they cared more about other things."

"Yes, it's odd. All we're doing is swimming. Before I left New York, I did a little swim for the newspaper in the river."

"I remember."

"And all those sailors from the *Illinois* came out on deck and cheered. You'd think I'd won the war. But do you know, I didn't really even swim. I just dived in with the dogs and then got out. My husband says they like me in my bathing suit."

The two swimmers often walked along the shore in the afternoons, sometimes followed by the reporters and photographers who Catherine did her best to ignore. If you didn't capitulate, give them a smile and turn their way, they wrote stories with headlines like SWIMMER SULKS or POUTING PRINCESS. You couldn't win, she knew that well enough now.

Lillian had met Andrew over dinner one night. When Catherine said he was a reporter, she noticed that Lillian and her husband, Eddie, became more careful with him. Lillian wasn't as open. One day on the beach, Catherine asked Lillian about it. "Oh, I would never talk openly to one of those fellows," she said. "The next day, it would all be in the newspaper."

"He's my friend," Catherine said.

"Yes, but he's not mine," Lillian replied.

Andrew did try to help. He told the reporters they weren't allowed to speak to Catherine because they didn't have an exclusive contract. But the photographers were the ones who took everything from you, and Andrew couldn't stop them. At any rate, Andrew himself was sending stories back to America all the while. He was in charge of writing a column in Catherine's name. Initially, she'd told him what things she wanted to write about, but he soon started coming up with his own ideas. Catherine wanted to write about swimming and how it felt, but he said no one would care about that. "They'll want to know what you're going to wear in the water," he said. "The men go naked, you know." He smiled slyly. Catherine disliked him for it.

The columns were running in the English papers too, and the French. Everyone knew now that Catherine Quick was up against Lillian Cannon and Gertrude Ederle to conquer the Channel. Clarabelle Barrett continued to prepare for her swim but the newspapermen didn't have any interest in her. To

Catherine, it was suffocating. It seemed like every day there were more of them ensconced in the other hotel down on the beach, or in the nearby village. What she would remember from those weeks was not the smell of kelp that drifted up from the sea, the smell of salt water on her skin, the smell of the sea air, all of which she loved. What she would remember was their magnesium flashes, which smelled of a match lighting.

Louisa still hadn't come over. Originally, she'd said she'd be over once Catherine was ready to swim, but now she said something had come up. Catherine was longing to have people she knew other than Andrew around her. In the hotel she could curl up in a chair and read a book without anyone bothering her. The food was wonderful—chicken in rich sauces, beefsteaks with creamy potato, roast lamb—but she wasn't hungry, she found, although she was supposed to be putting on weight for the swim. The problem for the reporters was that there was so little to report, Andrew said. They couldn't leave, in case Burgess suddenly decided it was time to swim, but there was nothing for them to do in the meantime. She knew exactly how they felt.

When the Ederles arrived—Trudy, Meg, and their father—the reporters had something new to focus on. Meg greeted Catherine warmly but Trudy was her usual self, quiet and withdrawn. And Mr. Ederle was furious, Andrew told Catherine, because Mr. Burgess was training other swimmers. "What's the problem with that?" Catherine said, not understanding.

"He's supposed to be Trudy's coach exclusively. Old Papa Ederle is talking to anyone who'll listen. What a bag of wind." Trudy wanted Mr. Burgess to herself, Andrew said.

"But aren't we both swimming with the WSA? I mean, Lillian's swimming with her dogs, and Clarabelle's on her own, but aren't Trudy and I with the WSA, more or less?" The WSA wasn't providing the funding for anyone's swim, as it happened. Mr. Black's newspaper was funding Catherine, and Trudy was funded by the New York *Daily News* syndicate. Mr. Burgess had asked Catherine on the first day if he might add Lillian to his group and she'd said of course. It had been a bright spot since arriving in France, spending time with Lillian and the dogs. Now Trudy wanted Lillian thrown off the team.

Andrew laughed. "Well, yes, officially you're both representing the WSA. But, you see, Burgess told Trudy he'd coach her and only her. And after last year, Trudy's not willing to share a coach and risk failure again."

"But swimming together makes it easier, not harder," Catherine said. "It's better to have a few of us together."

"Maybe," Andrew said. "But it's not what she wants. I think there's going to be trouble. At least we'll have something to file. SWIMMER SIMMERS!"

Catherine turned sixteen, although no one with her knew it and she didn't tell them—not even Andrew. It upset her to be so alone in the world that she had no one left who remembered the day she was born.

It was nearly a year now since she'd been expelled from Henley. She'd had a letter from Aileen, who was getting more excited about starting college. Catherine wondered what on earth she was doing in this little French village not swimming, and Mr. Black, who she'd hoped to do well for, wasn't even here. And Louisa. It felt as if her aunt had deserted her too.

Late in the morning on the day after her birthday, Catherine was down on the beach watching the water. Every day had been the same, relatively calm on the French side, but the tides were wrong or the sea beyond was wild. It was frustrating.

Andrew came down the sand to join her, stopping first to take off his shoes and roll up his long trousers. "How goes the swimmer?" he asked.

"Oh, you know," Catherine said. "Wishing she could swim."

"Do we know when yet?"

"Mr. Burgess says there are three days coming up he likes. It might even be the day after tomorrow, but I think Trudy gets first pick of the day to try."

"Well, that would at least take her out of contention."

"You don't think she'll succeed?"

"I think you're the only one who has a chance, Catherine."

"You know a lot about swimming?"

He smiled. "You're quite right. I don't. But I know Mr. Black. He is rarely wrong and you're his swimmer."

Catherine nodded but didn't respond.

"Are you all right?"

She looked out toward the water. None of it had been what

she'd expected. "Oh, Andrew, I think of myself here, swimming the Channel, and I don't know if it's what I want."

"Whatever do you mean?" he said. "What are you talking about?"

"Nothing," she said. "Nothing at all." He'd never understand, she thought. No one would.

38

Louisa hadn't seen Catherine when she'd arrived late the night before, so she left a message suggesting they meet for breakfast. Louisa had waited in London to make sure everything would go as planned. She knew she would have to tell Catherine the truth. It wasn't even a choice now. She'd wired Mr. Witherspoon the money and he had made the payment and freed the boys. Thank goodness. How close it had been, Louisa didn't know, but the fact she'd put a boy's life in danger had been enough to convince Louisa she must tell her niece the truth. She'd wired Florence and explained everything. They were coming to London. Nellie would meet them at Southampton. They'd be waiting for Catherine when she arrived home.

⟨───⟩

Catherine came into the dining room. Oh, the change those few weeks had wrought. Louisa was shocked by the sight of her.

Catherine had lost weight when she was supposed to be putting it on. Mr. Burgess had told them she'd need to put by some fat for energy and as insulation against the cold. Louisa remembered what Nellie had said when Catherine had returned from New York. Now she could see it herself. The girl was positively haggard, with dark circles under her eyes. It was almost as if Catherine knew without knowing what was happening in Australia. Louisa imagined having to explain to Catherine what she'd done. She should stick to her guns, Black told her. She'd done right, he said. It wasn't wrong to keep the letters from the girl, and it wasn't Louisa's fault if the boy did something stupid. She never had to tell Catherine. But of course she would have to tell her. She just needed to work up the courage.

She looked at Catherine walking toward her now. Even her gait was less certain. When Louisa thought back to the girl who'd come out of the Thames, the girl who'd left Australia, even the girl who'd been the first to the beach at Sandy Hook, she could see how this girl was different. What I have done? she thought again.

They hugged, Catherine holding on longer than usual. Louisa didn't say anything but the look of concern on her face must have told a story.

"Nothing's wrong," Catherine said, sitting down heavily on the chair opposite Louisa. She smiled, but even her smile was less than it had been.

"Have you been swimming this morning already?" Louisa was upset to see Catherine like this but she was trying not to show it.

"No, just walking with Lillian Cannon. I'll introduce you after."

"I saw Mr. Black in London. He's very pleased that you're here."

Catherine nodded. "Mr. Black," she said, her face brightening a little. "Did you tell him I'm training?"

"Oh, yes, he's very proud," Louisa said, seeing how pleased it made Catherine. "Are you sure you're all right, dear?"

"I just . . . I don't even have a minute when they're not there."

She was close to tears, Louisa saw.

"The newspapermen?"

"They follow my every move. I hate it. Mr. Burgess said yesterday that they come in the boat, that they take the whole trip with us. How am I supposed to swim with all that?"

"They think it's the news."

"Why aren't they interested in swimming, then? Why don't they talk about swimming? They talk about who my boyfriend is, and what I'll wear. But they never talk about kicking or which crawl I'll do."

"Oh, dear girl. I never would have wished this on you . . . I . . ."

"I suppose you'll say you told me so." She looked at Louisa.

"Did I tell you so? I don't think I quite thought it through as well as all that. But I do understand. When my mother was doing medicine, all the newspapers wanted to know was whether she blushed when she saw a man naked. She'd studied anatomy in her nursing training, so she was well past the blushing stage when they were asking. But they persisted. She was like you in that way, Catherine. She didn't like the limelight. She didn't want to be any different from the others."

"What did she do about it?" Catherine said.

"Oh, she put up with it until they stopped. Eventually they did. But she never had to endure anything like what you're facing. It wasn't her body they focused on. Do you still want to do this?"

"The swim isn't what's bothering me. Ever since New York, they've been following everything I do. I can't even eat breakfast without someone writing about it. I have to do the swim. For Mr. Black."

"No, you don't, Catherine," Louisa said firmly. "If you don't want to swim, you shouldn't swim."

Catherine didn't respond.

In the afternoon, Louisa watched the training session with Burgess. The newspapermen were down on the beach. They were taking pictures and calling out their questions. Burgess did nothing to stop them and Louisa approached him afterward and told him that it was bothering Catherine. Now that Trudy Ederle had arrived, the newspapers were making much of the tensions among the swimmers, Louisa noticed. Burgess nodded, said he'd see what he could do.

Louisa had met all the other swimmers during the day. She liked Lillian Cannon, a little blond girl who meant well. But Trudy Ederle was the one who had what it took, Louisa thought. Like Catherine, she was a good swimmer who loved the water. But unlike Catherine, she saw this as a race, and she wanted more than anything to win.

～～～

The next day, Mr. Black arrived. He came along the promontory where Louisa and Catherine had been walking. He kissed

Louisa on the lips, Catherine noticed, and Louisa didn't turn and give him her cheek like Catherine might have expected. He embraced Catherine briefly. She found herself happy to see him. It had been the same when Louisa arrived. She'd been missing them, wanting familiar faces. She still felt lost, though, and couldn't say why.

"Let's go back to the hotel," Mr. Black said. "What a wild place we've brought you to, Catherine."

"Catherine's still worried about the reporters," Louisa said when they were back at the hotel lounge. "They follow everything she does." She turned to Catherine. "Mr. Black and I spoke of this in London. He can help."

"Maybe," he said. "The thing is, it will only get worse once you swim the Channel." He was looking at Catherine and his eyes were kind. "But to be the first woman to do that, Catherine—what an achievement."

"I know, Mr. Black," Catherine said, "but at the moment I don't even want to go swimming because the reporters are watching and taking their pictures."

"Just ignore them," Black said.

"How do I do that?"

"By taking no notice. That's what I do. In England, they call me the mad American. That's what you first heard about me, right? In Baltimore, I own the newspaper, so they tend to write what I want. But in New York, I'm a big bully with shady leanings, according to the *Post*. I'm a friend of Franklin and Eleanor, which makes me corrupt. That's just how they work, Catherine. They need sensation. Truth is, swimming isn't interesting. But swimmers are. That's why they want you. But I'll see what I can do."

It's different for you, Catherine wanted to say. They don't take a picture of you with hardly any clothes on and have the world look at it. She would never have understood how this might feel until it happened to her.

Catherine had a flash of memory then. She was on the island, running down to the sea with Michael. They would have been nine and eleven, she guessed. They got to the beach, hot from the run, and decided on the spur of the moment to swim. They stripped off and ran into the sea.

It was Florence who took Catherine aside afterward. "Where was your swimsuit?" she wanted to know.

"I left it at the house," Catherine said. "We weren't planning to swim."

She still remembered the feel of the water on her body, the freedom it gave her. But she also knew, from Florence's face, that something was wrong.

"You mustn't do that, Catherine," Florence said.

"Why not?"

"You just mustn't. There are bad men . . . You must wear your swimsuit."

Catherine wanted to ignore Florence. It felt so peaceful to have the water flowing over her skin. She tried several times to get Michael to go along with her after that, but he wouldn't. The memory came back now. It was innocent, she knew, but Florence had made her feel guilty. It was the same feeling she had when the reporters followed her around, as if she, and not they, were at fault.

The next day there were squally showers, and it felt as if the weather matched Catherine's mood, changing constantly, restless. She wanted to be doing more than swimming out to the rocks and back. Mr. Burgess sensed her restlessness. Now he was training Catherine separately from Trudy Ederle, so there wouldn't be further trouble. Sometimes Lillian Cannon still swam with Catherine, which Catherine didn't mind, but Trudy wanted to work on her own with her coach.

Catherine was down on the beach waiting for Mr. Burgess when she saw up on the sand a tall blond man in swimming trunks with a sweater over them, a towel around his neck. She thought he must be another Channel likely. But then he waved and called out her name. The accent. She looked again.

"Sam?" she called back. It was Mr. Black's pilot. "What on earth are you doing here?" She ran toward him.

When they met, he embraced her warmly.

"I flew Mr. Black over to come see you and Dr. Quick. I brought trunks; I thought maybe we could swim together."

"You swim?"

"I'm the Lake Louise champion."

"What does that mean?"

"It means this water will be warm as far as I'm concerned." She laughed. "Oh, goodness but it's wonderful to see your face."

"Yeah," he said, grinning. "You look like a real swimmer."

"I'm just waiting for my coach," she said. "We swim to the point and back a few times. It's all about acclimatizing and the right tides. We're lucky this morning. No reporters." She grinned, so happy to see him.

"I read your column in the paper," Sam said.

"I don't write any of it. Andrew writes it for me."

"I wondered. It doesn't really sound like you."

"That's because it's not me. Oh, it's good to see you. So you're still working for Mr. Black?"

"This is my last run with him."

"Why?"

"I'm going home."

"Are you, Sam, to Canada?"

He looked at her. "I just can't stay anymore," he said. "I thought I'd go on and be a pilot, you know, like that fellow Lindbergh. Mr. Black even offered to fund a flight. But I need to be back in the mountains. I'm just not happy anywhere else." He looked sad for a moment, then brightened. "I'm sure I'll be back with him. He's a great boss. But you—it turns out Mr. Black was right. You're a champion."

"I suppose I am. I think it's grand you're going home." Catherine felt tears in her eyes. "Look, now, here's the coach. I'll introduce you and we can swim together."

Sam had asked about her column. She didn't even look at the words he wrote now. Andrew was just like the other reporters. All he cared about was getting a story. Seeing Sam made her remember what it had been like, nearly a year ago now, when she'd started to feel happy again after her father's passing. And it was so very different from how she felt now.

39

Louisa and Catherine had a morning to themselves; the reporters and photographers were gathered down at the other hotel where Trudy Ederle was staying. They mostly camped down there now.

It was time, Louisa decided, to tell the truth. They were in the little lounge at the hotel that overlooked the terrace and the sea. As she'd been getting ready that morning, she'd thought of how oddly things had turned out. She hadn't wanted responsibility for Catherine, hadn't felt ready to take on a child, a young woman. It had been Nellie and Ruth who'd pushed her. She's your blood, they'd said. You can't refuse her. And now, Louisa had never been more committed to anything in her life than she was to Catherine's welfare. And the thought of losing her was terrifying.

Even so, she knew she had to tell Catherine the truth about what she'd done. More than ever, Catherine had a right to know that there was an alternative life for her, the life she'd chosen in the first place, even if it meant Louisa would lose her. And it shouldn't wait until the swim. Louisa must tell her now, she'd decided. Catherine needed to be able to make choices based on the truth.

"Catherine, I did something I shouldn't have done," Louisa said.

Catherine had picked up the newspaper from the table between them. "It says here I'm a greater swimmer than . . . someone, I can't find them now, an Italian fellow, who holds the record. I'm so glad Mr. Black is here, Louisa. Have you noticed the reporters are leaving me alone now? I'm sure he's done something. He's been so good to me . . ." Catherine looked up at her aunt. "What's wrong? You look like you've seen a ghost."

Catherine looked serious suddenly and Louisa felt the weight of what she'd done. She smiled hopefully.

"Did you know Andrew's getting married?" Catherine said.

"Is he? Yes, I think I did know that, dear."

"Yes, to some girl his brother was engaged to. I think he's getting married to make his mother happy. Can you believe that?"

"Oh, I see," Louisa said. "Poor boy. Catherine, you need to listen to me, darling. I've done something I shouldn't have and I have to tell you."

"I mean, I'm not upset about it, Louisa, if that's what's worrying you. I don't even like Andrew anymore. He's become one of those awful reporters. We're very different."

Louisa nodded. "Yes, you are," she said. "But we need to talk."

"Shoot," Catherine said. It was a term the Americans used. Andrew had started her on it.

"Do you remember when you swam the river?"

"The terrible Thames," Catherine said. Her face could break your heart, Louisa thought, so open and trusting.

"The terrible Thames. Well, afterward, do you remember you kept wondering why you weren't getting any letters from the island? You waited every day for news and they didn't write. And you wrote to Michael and he still didn't write."

"No, he didn't," Catherine said, frowning.

"The thing is, I shouldn't have done this, and it was with good intentions, but I think I didn't see quite how much . . . What I mean to say is, I didn't want to do the wrong thing."

"Louisa, what are you talking about?" Catherine said.

"He did write."

"Who?"

"Michael. He wrote. A few times. And I didn't pass on the letters."

"What do you mean? You hid them?" Catherine stared at her in disbelief.

"I hid them."

"Why are you telling me now?"

"I couldn't go on in a lie."

"You took my letters, Louisa? You hid them and lied to me?" Catherine's voice was failing her. She looked so afraid. "Why would a person do that?"

"I thought he'd taken advantage of you."

"What do you mean?"

"I thought he'd . . . I thought he was your lover."

"He's my brother, Louisa. He's been in my life since we were little. How could you think that?"

Louisa was embarrassed. "I read one of his letters to you.

He said you were joined in body. I assumed." She looked at Catherine flatly.

Catherine stared at her. "Joined in body?" She frowned. "It's swimming. It's when you swim the three islands together. You're joined in body. The islands are the body." She was gesturing with her hands. "Oh, it doesn't matter now. You'd never understand. But, Louisa, how could you do that? How could you stay friends with me?"

It was this question that broke Louisa's heart, for it showed not only how young Catherine was but the extent of the breach of trust. Louisa could tell herself she had Catherine's best interests at heart, but it was simply wrong, what she'd done.

"And Nellie? Did she go along with this?"

Louisa looked at her. "No. She told me I should give you the letters, right from the start. I'm sorry, Catherine."

"Where are the letters?"

"At home, in London," Louisa said. "As soon as we get back, I'll give them to you. I should have brought them. Catherine, I did the wrong thing. But I really did believe it was for the best. I know I haven't been very good at this, but I was worried. I thought if I brought you to London, and sent you to a good school, it would open up the world to you; you'd find you could do and be anything as a woman." She was about to tell Catherine that Michael and Florence would be home in London when they returned but something stopped her. It would be too much, she thought.

"And now look at me," Catherine said, her eyes wide with fear, her face set in anger. "I'm not anyone."

She stood and looked at Louisa again, shaking her head slowly. "I just don't understand you," she said. "I never will."

She left the room, leaving Louisa sitting alone, looking out toward the sea.

Louisa would tell her the rest of the story later. Nellie had wired her just that morning. Michael and Florence had arrived safely at Southampton and she'd taken them to the flat in London. They'd be there when Catherine and Louisa came home from France. They'd know what to do. Surely, they'd know what to do.

The next day, the third of August, was Catherine's birthday. Louisa had brought from England a little gold chain with a heart-shaped locket. Catherine came into the dining room, which Louisa and the hotel owners had decorated for lunch. Andrew was there, Lillian Cannon and her husband, the coach Burgess, the young pilot, Sam. Black wasn't there. He'd gone to Paris on the train for a couple of days. They hadn't spoken of Catherine again before he'd left.

Louisa had made Andrew promise that there would be no reporters or reporting, that this would truly be a private party.

Catherine hadn't spoken to her aunt since Louisa had told her about the letters, and now she took a seat with Lillian Cannon and her husband. Louisa felt emptied out. She'd been so foolish, she thought, so foolish.

The night before, she'd dreamed of Elizabeth, fit and well, smiling at her, telling her she'd grown into a good woman. "I'm so proud of you," her mother was saying. Louisa woke and wept.

After lunch, she went over to where Catherine sat. The

Cannons had just left the table. She gave Catherine the gift. "I had it made," she said. "I am sorry, Catherine. I truly am."

Catherine looked at her. "What you did, I just can't believe it. You lied to me. I don't know how you could do that. And Aunt Louisa, you really have no idea who I am. It's not my birthday."

"Yes it is," Louisa said. "Third of August."

"My birthday is the twenty-seventh of July—it was a week ago."

"Your birthday is when?" Louisa said.

"I told you—the twenty-seventh of July."

"But last year . . ."

"Last year, you weren't even home on the twenty-seventh. I was too scared to tell you because you'd gone to all the trouble of planning a celebration for the third of August. So I just let it go."

Louisa looked at her niece. "How do you know?"

"How do I know what?"

"How do you know you were born on the twenty-seventh of July?" The twenty-seventh of July, a date etched in Louisa's consciousness.

"I've always known," Catherine said. "What's the matter, Louisa? You've gone awfully pale."

40

There was a knock on Catherine's door just after midnight. "Come on, out of bed. It's time." It was Mr. Burgess. Trudy Ederle was sick. Mr. Burgess had been down to her hotel in the afternoon and ruled her unfit. Without telling the Ederles, he'd made other plans.

Catherine dressed quickly and came down the stairs. Mr. Burgess had gotten the cook out of bed. There was a plate of stew and potatoes on the table.

"I'm not hungry," she said.

"It's not food, it's fuel, girl," Mr. Burgess said. For the first time since she'd met him, he seemed excited.

Clarabelle Barrett had failed. She set out on August 1st and swam bravely, Mr. Burgess told Catherine, but a fog "so thick she couldn't see her hands" made her give up after twenty-two hours in the water. The Channel had thrown its worst her way and the fog just did her in. Miss Barrett was within shouting distance of the coast. "A sight I know well," Mr. Burgess said.

"Was she all right?" Catherine wanted to know. "Afterward, was she all right?"

"Aye," said the coach. "She knew it beat her, and she won't be back. But that's not your concern. Your concern is getting yourself across."

Lillian Cannon and her dogs were returning to America the next week too. She'd made two attempts herself, Catherine knew, the second shorter than the first. It was just too difficult, she'd said, which had given Catherine pause. If Lillian had found the swim too difficult, if Trudy had failed the year before, and if Clarabelle now hadn't managed it, how would Catherine succeed?

As if he guessed her thoughts, Mr. Burgess said she had to think of one thing and one thing only out in the Channel tonight.

"What's that?" she said.

"The swim. Just think of the swim. No one ever swam a long way by thinking of the opposite shore. You let me worry about Dover, and we'll be fine. You're a bonny swimmer, Catherine." He didn't use people's names very much, and it made her look up. His light eyes shone.

He would be in the pilot boat, he said. They both knew the rules. She could take sustenance, bottles of broth, cake, crackers, tied to a pole extended from the rowboat, so long as her hands never touched the boat or a person.

The newspapermen would follow them in a second boat, Catherine knew, but, Mr. Burgess said, with a twinkle in his eye, that he'd forgotten to alert the boatman. "Let's have the water to ourselves for a while," he said. "You don't like all that other business."

"Thank you," she said.

"You're going to do this swim, girl. You really are," he said. "Now, is there anyone else you want to wake up, that tall young fella that hangs off you like a puppy?" At first she thought he meant Sam, but he was talking about Andrew.

She shook her head, then reconsidered. "Yes, there is," she said.

"Hurry up then," he said.

She took the steps two at a time and knocked softly at the door.

Louisa must have been up because she came to the door quickly, in her nightdress and socks, her hair a mess. "Catherine," she said. "Are you all right?" She looked so tiny standing there.

"I'm going. I'm swimming," Catherine said. "And I wanted to tell you, just in case anything happens. It's all right, Louisa. Not what you did. That was terrible. But . . ." She stopped. "I'll just send the letters and explain what happened as soon as we get home."

"Of course," Louisa managed to say. "Can I come in the boat? I'd like to be there."

"Can you dress quickly?"

"Yes."

"We'll meet you down there."

They made their way by lamplight down to the little beach. Sam was there and Catherine was relieved. He'd said he'd swim with her when she was feeling tired and she was glad that Mr. Burgess had remembered to wake him. Sam would go on the pilot boat with Mr. Burgess. And coming toward them now was Louisa, tiny in her cardigan and woolen skirt.

"Come on, girl," Mr. Burgess said to Catherine. "Let's get you ready."

He and Louisa helped Catherine to slather grease and

lanolin over herself. "Stinks," Catherine said. She was wearing her woolen suit. She knew it would chafe on such a long swim and she'd already decided what to do about that. Through the night, she was going to take off the suit and leave it in the dory until first light and then put it back on. She hadn't told Burgess but knew he'd agree.

"You'll be glad of the grease when you're out there," was all Mr. Burgess said, his eyes bright in the midnight. Then he looked up toward the inn. There were lights bobbing down the hill. "Quick, here come the newspapermen. Pity their boat's not here. Let's row out quiet now. I'm not letting them on with us. Just you and me and the Channel, eh?" They'd moored the pilot boat out in the bay. The boatman had been the one to see Mr. Burgess himself safely across all those years ago.

There was no time for good-byes. Catherine dived into the waves while Mr. Burgess rowed out with Louisa and Sam. They cheered her on quietly, although she'd hardly swum fifty yards. There was a moon rising over the water. She was swimming the Channel, and it had happened just like that. She felt like laughing for no reason she understood.

41

The water hadn't felt cold when she'd set out. That was the strange thing. Perhaps it was the excitement. But now all she was aware of was the cold. The muscles of her arms had cramped an hour ago but now they were past cramping. The weather had been kind so far, although Mr. Burgess said they were far from out of the woods. It had been a bad season, he'd said the week before, too few days that were on a swimmer's side.

Mr. Burgess had rowed with her for a while to keep her spirits up, and he'd given her some broth and chocolate cake. Her hands were numb when they brushed against the woolen suit at her hips. She knew she had to keep moving or her body would begin the process of shutting down. Her body was begging to shut down, in fact. It would be the easiest thing in the world, to curl up here, to sleep.

She suspected this was what had happened to Trudy Ederle the year before. She'd gone to sleep in the water and another swimmer had pulled her out. Later Trudy said she'd been fine, but the other swimmer saw her go under and come up, water flowing out of her mouth, he said. She also said she was sure her coach had fed her whisky with the beef broth. Mr. Burgess would not be feeding Catherine whisky, he'd assured her. "But I won't think twice about pulling you out, girl," he'd said. Catherine knew that Trudy's father had told Burgess he wasn't to take Trudy out of the water without her permission. Mr. Burgess had made Mr. Ederle and Trudy sign a waiver to release him from any legal responsibility. If Catherine was unconscious, she thought, of course she'd want him to pull her out of the water. It was only a swim, for goodness' sake.

Trudy's father wanted his daughter to win. Catherine's father had never been like that. He'd only ever encouraged her. Now she had Louisa, and she'd disappointed Louisa at the start, she knew. She hadn't been the girl Louisa had wanted her to be. They'd both learned along the way, Catherine thought now. But in telling Catherine what she'd done, hiding the letters from Australia, Louisa had been honest, and Catherine had felt, strangely, that while Louisa went the wrong way about showing it, her aunt truly cared about her. She cared enough to intervene to protect Catherine's interests. Louisa was on her side in a way her father had been on her side, Catherine realized; in a way she imagined her mother might have been on her side. Still, Louisa shouldn't have lied.

Catherine had so much wanted to please Mr. Black. She'd thought he was a bit like her father. She couldn't remember when she'd decided she wanted to swim the Channel, to become the first woman to do that. Mr. Black had told her the newspapermen would only become more interested in her once she succeeded. He was ambitious on her behalf, not like Trudy Ederle's father but not that different either, when Catherine thought about it. She didn't think she wanted that for herself. In truth, she'd have liked Clarabelle Barrett to be the first woman. She was the one of them who most needed money.

Mr. Black had come to see Catherine the evening before, after he'd returned from Paris. He'd wished her a happy birthday. She didn't bother explaining that it wasn't her birthday.

"We might be making the attempt tomorrow," she said. "Mr. Burgess says the tides look good."

"Well, that's the best news. If you go in the morning, I'll fly overhead. I'll come down low and wave. Will you wave back?"

"Of course," she said.

"I'm glad you're a swimmer," he said. "I lost my sister and mother to drowning."

"I know, Mr. Black. Louisa told me."

"And I don't have anyone left but you." It was so odd, the way he'd looked at her as he said it.

She was cold now in her bones, nothing left inside to keep them warm. They'd hit a squall and Mr. Burgess had recalculated their route, which would see her swim an extra two miles. She was more than halfway there, he said, but she wasn't, if she knew what he meant, which she didn't, because nothing made much sense to her right then.

She made herself think of the island, the warm sand, so hot in the middle of the day you could burn your feet on it, Michael's smile. If she wrote to him, would he be the same? Would he understand that it hadn't been her fault, that Louisa had stopped the letters? Would anything be the same? She thought of Florence, dear Florence.

The grease and lanolin, designed to stop the worst of the cold and chafing, had worn off now. She wondered why they bothered with it. She never did get her swimsuit off. She'd worried she wouldn't be able to put it back on and the photographers, who would catch up to them soon, would snap the picture of a lifetime. Her suit was hurting at her shoulders and underarms. But pain was a better sensation than the cold, which unnerved her now. There was a darkness in it.

Louisa had asked her once whether when she was swimming, she thought of her mother. Louisa meant her mother drowning. She'd said no, but that was a lie. On a long swim, she always thought of her mother. She thought of the way Julia had given up. Sometimes, like now, she would talk to her. You didn't hold on, she'd say. You had a life preserver and you didn't hold on. Why not? I would have held on, she'd say to her mother. I would have stayed with you, no matter what.

The moon had come up full and round over the sea. Louisa could see Catherine. She didn't take her eyes off the girl.

The twenty-seventh of July. The twenty-seventh of July was Catherine's birthday. And all these years, Louisa had thought her birthday was the third of August. Not because she'd got the date wrong, as Catherine had assumed, as Louisa had pretended after lunch that day, not because she couldn't keep a date in her head, not because she didn't care enough, but because she had been told Catherine was born on the third of August. By her mother, Elizabeth. By her brother Harry. Because if they'd told her the truth, that Catherine was born on the twenty-seventh of July, she'd have known what they were hiding from her.

On the twenty-seventh of July that year, Louisa's own child was born: the child her mother had told her was a boy, a boy who'd died.

Catherine could remain here in the water forever, she thought suddenly, swim on and on. Until what? said a voice she didn't recognize. Until she ran out of energy and life ended, she thought. She looked across at the pilot boat. For hours now it had been nothing but a haze of lights. She'd swum through the night, Sam diving in to swim alongside her when she needed company, and she'd lasted through the morning, the afternoon, and now it was another night. She would finish alone, she knew. It was the end or not, she knew.

The newspapermen were on the boat behind them, the photographers wanting their pictures, reporters wanting their stories. They'd caught up now. They wanted a dream, she thought. Everyone wants that, Mr. Black had said. Everyone wants that. "You're a model of what it means to be a modern woman," he said. "What do you think of that?"

Mr. Black said he wanted to talk to her when she made land. She already knew what he was going to say. He'd sponsor the next swim and the next. He'd been so good to her, and she felt she owed him something. He wanted her to become an American citizen, to swim for the U.S. in the Olympics in 1928.

Her father had told her the story of the selkie, half woman, half seal, who came to live among men and dried out for want of the sea. Someone had stolen the selkie's skin so she couldn't go back. In one version of the story, the selkie left a child, like Catherine's mother left her. In the water the world was quiet but the sound of her breath was loud. What a lovely thought, the quiet of the sea floor and no one to worry about.

She could hear the shouts.

It was Burgess. "Catherine, are you all right?"

She waved. Had she dozed off?

Perhaps she had.

One arm up and over, the other, and this way you go forward.

She could see the shore, barely, the lights, hear Mr. Burgess yelling from the boat. "That's the Forty Lights," he said. "You're there, girl! You're nearly there! Just keep swimming."

She didn't know that it had been less than thirteen hours since she'd left France. She didn't know that once she completed this last mile, she would not only be the youngest person to swim the English Channel. She would not only be the first woman, she would set a record, beating the last swimmer by over three hours. The tides had been kind, the Channel had admitted her, and Catherine had kept swimming.

The journalists called to her. "How are you feeling, Catherine?" "Are you tired?" "Are you nearly there?"

They were like ants, she thought, like nothing. She knew other swimmers had faltered in the last mile, and she understood why. It wasn't fear of failure; it was fear of success. She was beyond any particular emotion, joy or sorrow or pain. That's what swimming was for her, she realized, a way to come to this place in herself. She felt not tired, but beyond tired, beyond cold. And, yet, fully alive.

Mr. Burgess was telling her to turn to the right. She saw she'd come too far over. They were supposed to come in at Deal but he'd decided to make instead for Kingsdown. She could see little lights on the beach now, thousands of them. The word had gotten out while she'd been swimming, Mr. Burgess said. They'd transmitted their stories to their newspapers and had made the late morning editions in London. Crowds on the beach were there to welcome her, Catherine Quick, the first woman to swim the English Channel. She wondered was Nellie among them. Had she seen the newspaper?

Catherine couldn't see anyone on the boat now. She was almost past them, she thought. For a few moments, she became disoriented, couldn't see the boat itself, couldn't see the lights on the shore either now. Had she lost consciousness? She rolled over and thought she could float here forever.

She heard, in the distance, a voice. It was a voice she knew; not Mr. Burgess, although it must have been him.

Again, someone was calling her name. She looked to where she thought the boat was but still couldn't see it. She stopped a moment, lifted up her goggles. Her eyes were stinging with the salt and cold. It was infuriating trying to keep up in the darkness.

The voice again. It was calling her name. Not Catherine— her other name. "Waapi, I can see you in the light! I'm coming. I'll swim you in."

And then, Mr. Burgess was there in the dory. "Who is that?" he said.

"Catherine," Louisa said. "It's all right."

There were lights everywhere around her now, from the pilot boat, and from the shore, even a beam from the light-house trained toward her. She could make out his funny little head bobbing up and down in the water in silhouette.

"Bid!" she yelled. "Over here, you idiot. I'm over here."

"Just tell him not to touch her," Mr. Burgess said. "It will disqualify her."

She heard Louisa cheering. Catherine looked up to Burgess.

Michael came closer. "Waapi," he said. "It's really you."

"It is," she said, swimming to him and throwing her arms around his neck. "It's me. You smell like coconut."

42

London, August 1926

Well, that's good you told her the truth, Louisa. I don't know what possessed you to lie." Nellie was sitting in the kitchen at Wellclose Square, packing up the kitchen things.

"I thought it was best for her," Louisa said. She'd told Nellie everything—well, almost everything.

"But it wasn't best for her," Nellie said.

"Yes, I know that now, but I didn't know it then." She looked at Nellie's dear face. Catherine had disqualified herself from the race. Mr. Burgess was devastated. He thought she was fine, but she must have had a madness come upon her, he said. "A madness," Louisa had said. "A bit of sense, more like."

Catherine was packing to go home to the island. Sister Ursula was moving to another school in two years, and a government school would take over. Catherine would do her training in Brisbane, staying with Sister Ursula's family, so she could be the teacher at the school.

Andrew had returned to America with his bride, after covering Trudy Ederle's successful swim of the Channel, three days after Catherine's aborted attempt. The girl he'd married was from a nice London family. They might even make a go of it, Louisa thought. Catherine, for her part, had had enough of reporters to last a lifetime, although she and Andrew had parted friends.

Sam the pilot was already home in Canada. He'd sent them a telegram promising to visit the island, so long as Catherine came to visit his mountains.

Louisa kept the truth about her own past to herself for now. She knew she'd have to tell Catherine, but not yet. For now, the girl had enough to contend with. For Louisa, Catherine was the good that had grown from something awful. Here was the child born from that violence. Here was the fact that made it bearable. Here was Catherine. Louisa would leave the clinic, of course she would. She would take up the still-vacant post as the doctor on Thursday Island, and remain with Catherine, her daughter.

Florence had been waiting with Nellie on the beach at Kingsdown when Michael and Catherine swam to shore. She looked at Louisa, and Louisa saw only kindness in those eyes. "I know," Louisa said quietly. "Catherine's birthday."

Florence nodded. "I'm sorry. There's a letter. Mr. Witherspoon found a letter in his files. I'm glad you know. I wanted to tell you."

Louisa took the letter from Florence and put it in her bag, watched her brave niece on the shore hugging Michael while the onlookers stared. They thought she must be mad, like Burgess did, devastated to have failed. But Catherine hadn't failed. She had swum the Channel. She just wouldn't have to deal with being a Channel swimmer.

How had Louisa ever assumed Michael and Catherine had been lovers? The girl was perfectly innocent, Louisa should have realized. He *was* like a brother to her. It was Louisa's own experience, she realized. She'd seen everything through a particular lens, of her own experience. Michael was not like Jonathan. Hardly any men were like Jonathan.

"And it's not the only lie I told," Louisa said to Nellie now.

"There are more?" Nellie said.

"Yes, Nellie. I lied to you."

"When?"

"Do you remember when you first came to the clinic, and you were very sick, and your period had stopped?"

Nellie nodded. "And you told me some story about a little procedure, when in fact I was pregnant."

Louisa stared at her. "How did you know?"

"I guessed, but also, Dr. Luxton talked to me. She said I had choices. I wanted to stop the pregnancy. I didn't have any way of caring for a child when I was so sick, and I knew that."

"So why did you never tell me?"

"Dr. Luxton said you'd tell me I was sick and needed a little procedure and that it would help her immensely if I didn't tell you about our little chat. So I didn't. But I knew."

Thank goodness for Ruth Luxton, who had been so happy to learn Louisa's news. Ruth was recruiting new doctors for the clinic. "I'd pack your bags for you if I could, Louisa. You must go with her now."

"So would you rather have known, or not known?" Louisa asked Nellie.

"I'd rather not have had to make that decision. But if the decision had to be made I knew it was me who had to make it."

Nellie was right. One day, Louisa would tell Catherine the truth, she thought. One day she would let her know who she was and where she'd come from. For now, though, what was important was that Catherine knew she was going home.

Dearest Louie,

If you are reading this letter, then I am gone and Catherine is your ward.

Firstly, I want you to know that I am sorry to be the bearer of this news. You have been a good sister, and I have wished many times I'd told you the truth when you came to Australia. My reasons for not telling you have been entirely selfish. At first I didn't want to make you angry with our mother, who did her best. But then I didn't want to lose what I had.

I had hoped you would never need to know, to be honest, for I was so sure that knowing would be more difficult than not.

Louisa, I did not set out to deceive you, and you must believe me that Mama did only what she thought was best.

When Julia and I came through England, Julia was expecting a child, the child you have always believed was Catherine. But Julia lost the baby on the ship. I wrote and told Mama that Julia was expecting. She told you, I think. I also wrote when we lost the baby and my letter must have arrived when you were at Aldeburgh awaiting the birth of your own child. Mama chose not to tell you. Perhaps in her mind she already had plans. Whatever her reasons, it made the next steps easier.

Your blood pressure was high in the labor and you fell into unconsciousness soon after the birth. All of this you know. But

Mama made a decision about the child. She decided that if you knew the child lived, you would spend your days worrying about what you'd done. You might even decide to keep the child, which Mama thought would be wrong for both of you. She told you it was a boy. But the child was Catherine.

The midwife, Mary Breen, had a baby herself, you might recall, a boy of nearly two. She breastfed your baby on the ship to Australia. Mama was particular about that. No cow's milk after Margaret. Mama paid Mary's fare to Australia and back, since Julia couldn't feed a baby. In Cairns we found Florence, who'd lost her own child and could feed ours.

When Julia died, I wondered if I should tell you the truth. I hope I did the right thing. You were so busy with your work, and I thought to know you had a child would be the last thing you'd want. And in truth, I loved Catherine so dearly I couldn't stand the idea that she might be taken from me. She was my only link to Julia, whom I had loved so much.

So Catherine is your child, Louisa. I hope you will love her as much as I do.

Your loving brother,
Harry

Harry. All those years, he had kept the truth from Louisa. Florence too. How could they? How could they not tell her? She supposed he thought Louisa might make some claim on the child, might want to take her. He was right. Louisa would surely have taken Catherine back to England at three, once she knew. She wouldn't have left the child motherless on the island. How could Harry have been so selfish?

But really he was no different from Louisa herself, thinking he knew best. Louisa had kept letters from her niece on the same basis.

"We all do our best," Ruth Luxton said. "You did your best, Louisa. He did his best. And look what you got. You got a daughter." The word still didn't make sense to Louisa, who felt anything but a mother.

Black had come to see Louisa at her office in London before he left for America and she'd told him everything; she saw no reason not to. She thought he'd be angry to lose his swimmer but it was as if a spell had lifted. "C'est la vie," he'd said. "She's doing what she wants."

He paused, regarded Louisa carefully. "We won't see each other again then?" he said.

"Probably not," she said.

"I'll be sad about that."

"I will too," she said. She took the hands he offered her and held them. His were warm and soft. She could see the loss in his eyes. He'd lost so much. What would happen to him now? she wondered.

"Will you go to the island?" he said.

"I will. That's where Catherine wants to be for now. And they haven't replaced Harry."

"So you'll be the doctor."

"I'm guessing I will."

He smiled. "Well, you know me, Louisa. Don't be surprised if I fly over your way to visit some time soon." He became serious then. "Did you expect it to end like this?"

"I'm not quite sure this is the end," she said. "It feels much more like the beginning."

PART X

Thursday Island,
July 1927

43

Y ou don't trust yourself," Catherine said. "That's the biggest problem." They'd been in the water since three that afternoon, or Catherine had. Louisa had mostly skirted the shallows.

Catherine still took the children swimming every afternoon after school and she'd told Louisa that they were easier to teach, "even though they haven't had much of an education yet. That's what you always told me was the key to something. Not to swimming, it seems."

Catherine saw the look of disappointment on Louisa's face and softened. "But I know it's not easy learning something new."

Louisa was wearing the bathing costume they'd bought in Cairns four weeks before, when Catherine came home from university for the July holiday. It was in the new style, with short legs and shoulder straps. Louisa had told Catherine she felt terribly daring. But to Catherine, Louisa looked so small and delicate, and she was so fair compared with everyone else on the island. Like a tiny flightless bird, Catherine had thought, tears in her eyes for no reason she could articulate.

"I'll teach you to swim," Catherine had said. Louisa loved her work at the hospital, Catherine knew. Already she'd raised money for a hostel for women. They were training Islander midwives and nurses, and one day, she said, Islander doctors. But she'd resisted getting in the water. "You can't live on an island and not swim," Florence had said. Louisa had just smiled.

It had taken the entire first lesson to convince Louisa to go in at knee level. She hadn't enjoyed the water, not even the delightful chill on her skin, and now, after four lessons, Catherine was wondering if they should give up. At the very least, you had to be able to float on your back; you could save yourself if you could do that. But every time Louisa tried, she'd panic, fold at her hips and go under the water. She needed to find her buoyancy but couldn't seem to do it.

In the third week, Catherine had tied a rope around her wrist and looped the other end around Louisa's waist. "I can reel you in if you get into trouble," she'd said. But it didn't make any difference. Louisa couldn't trust herself or Catherine.

Today Louisa had managed a full five seconds on her back before she panicked and went under, coming up spluttering as Catherine got there to pull her up out of the water. There was a hint of a smile as she'd started to float and Catherine had been hopeful, but the next try was the worst yet.

"What are we going to do with you?" Catherine said now, and laughed. "I think you hate the water."

"I think the water hates me," Louisa said.

Catherine shook her head. "No, you're a Quick, born to the sea."

We're both Quicks, Catherine thought.

It was a year ago, when they first came back to the island, that Louisa had sat down with Catherine on the front verandah and told her the story. September, already warm, the weather glorious, the island just as it had always been.

Louisa's story reminded Catherine of Harry's story about Julia. Louisa was Catherine's mother. "You're the baby I carried, the baby I truly believed I'd lost," she said at the end, her voice tight with emotion. "I didn't know whether to tell you, but I decided there should be no secrets." She smiled weakly then, and looked across at Catherine. She looked afraid.

Catherine had sat for some minutes without speaking. It was an odd sensation, hearing something so surprising, and yet, unsurprising. Finally, she said, "Is it all right if I keep calling you Louisa?"

"Of course. What else would you call me?" Louisa said. "The thing I want impress on you, and the reason it's taken me this long to tell you, is that I want you to always know that Harry loved you. Of that I am very sure. I wanted to wait until we were here, until you were back in your home so you could take it all in."

Catherine nodded, looked out to the sea which was her home. "I mean, if I don't call you Mother or Mama. Is it all right if you don't feel like my mother? Florence feels more like my mother, and even Florence . . . I've never really had a mother." Catherine didn't feel emotional at the time, although later when she was on her own, she cried. But even then, she couldn't say quite why she was crying. And they weren't unhappy tears, just tears.

"That's probably a good way of looking at it." Louisa had

said. "We shouldn't worry too much about it, I shouldn't think." Catherine couldn't see her aunt's face but she could hear that her voice was still tight.

"The Islanders often give babies to others," Catherine said.

"Yes, I know," Louisa said. "When they come in to the hospital, it's not always easy to know who's who. The important thing is that you know the truth. It's just what it is, Catherine, nothing more." She turned to her and smiled again.

"What I'm trying to say is that it doesn't really matter," Catherine said. "The Islander babies belong to everyone. It's not that different from what happened with us, is it?"

Later that week, Catherine told Florence what Louisa had told her. "You said once that mothers are always sad," Catherine said to Florence. "Is that what you meant?"

"Oh, it's more sad for Louisa. She's your mama, like I'm Michael's mama. But she didn't get to raise you and that's always hard for a mama. That's always sad."

"But the Islander babies go to other mothers."

"That doesn't mean it's easy for the mothers," Florence said now. "Even the ones who give their babies willingly feel that sadness. A mother might know that someone else won't have children unless she gives them a child, so she does it for them, for all of us, but it's not ever an easy thing." Florence looked at Catherine.

"But that's not what happened to you and Louisa," Florence said. "Louisa's mother didn't tell her. That wasn't right."

Catherine looked at her aunt in the water now. Her curly hair, cut short, flopped on to her face. The late-afternoon light softened her features. "Am I very exasperating?" Louisa said.

"You really are," Catherine said. They both laughed. "We'll go home after one more try."

"We couldn't just give up now?" Louisa said. She'd managed to work her way back to the shallows where she could stand up easily.

"You can't live on the island and not be able to swim," Catherine said. She untied the rope from Louisa's waist and took Louisa's arm and led her back out to the deep. The day was ending, the water burnished bronze suddenly in front of them as the sun emerged from under a cloud. They could hear gulls overhead and the voices of the fishermen who were cleaning their catch on the beach. She looked across at Louisa, her eyes ablaze with life. "You are my mother," she said. "Just do it."

And Louisa did. "I'm floating!" she cried out. "Oh my, I'm floating. Catherine, I'm in heaven."

Just then they heard the sputtering buzz of an engine, so unlikely here on the island. Catherine looked up just as Louisa pointed. It was a little aeroplane, two wings, an engine like an annoying insect now, and although they couldn't see, Catherine was sure that she knew the identity of the pilot and his passenger.

Author's Note

I was inspired by the lives of Dr. Louisa Garrett Anderson and Van Lear Black, who never met in real life, as far as I know, and who have only scant biographical details in common with the fictional Dr. Louisa Quick and Manfred Lear Black. In his early twenties, my great-uncle René MacColl was Van Lear Black's confidential secretary, but that, and a subsequent distinguished career in journalism, are all he had in common with the fictional Andrew Mackintosh. René MacColl's memoir *A Flying Start* was also an inspiration. He writes with style and wit.

Gertrude Ederle was the first woman to swim the English Channel. Other swimmers who existed outside these pages include Mercedes Gleitze, who swam the Channel on her eighth attempt in 1927 and went on to a career as a distance swimmer. Lillian Cannon never made it across and neither did Clarabelle Barrett, although both were extraordinary swimmers and people. The fictional Aileen Ryan shares some biographical details in common with Aileen Riggin. Many great women swimmers were lost in the wash of history.

I'm indebted to John Zarrillo, archivist at the Brooklyn Historical Society, who found the Hotel Touraine for me, and to the Women's Swimming Association, New York, which charted a true course for women who wanted to swim.

Writing a novel is a swim of sorts. Thanks to those beside me, or in the pilot boat, readers, writers and dear friends, and some who are all three. Thanks Brisbane neighborhoods, Bar Merlo Paddington. Thanks the Banff Centre and Wild Flour, East Hotel and Silo. Thanks Gurrumul. Thanks *Qweekend*.

I set out with a great Australian team at Curtis Brown and Allen and Unwin of Fiona Inglis, Christa Munns, Ali Lavou, Sarina Rowell, and Nada Backovic. I was carried a good deal of the way by my publisher Annette Barlow. I am also particularly indebted to Daniel Lazar from the Writers' House, who worked incredibly hard to see this book published, and Kathryn Court and Victoria Savanh, who have been immensely generous.

David has always been on my team, and Otis gives me a reason to swim at all.

In Falling Snow

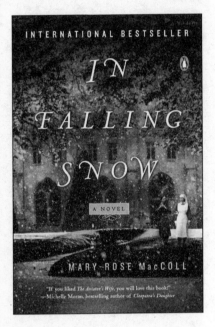

Iris, a young Australian nurse, travels to France during World War I to bring home her fifteen-year-old brother, who ran away to enlist. But in Paris, she is persuaded to help establish a hospital at Royaumont—a decision that will change her life. Interwoven is the story of Grace, Iris's granddaughter, in 1970s Australia. Together their narratives paint a portrait of women in medicine and the powerful legacy of love.

"A tale of selflessness and youthful indiscretion as singular and seductive as one could hope for." –Robin Oliveira, *New York Times* bestselling author of *My Name Is Mary Sutter*

PENGUIN BOOKS   prh.com/nextread